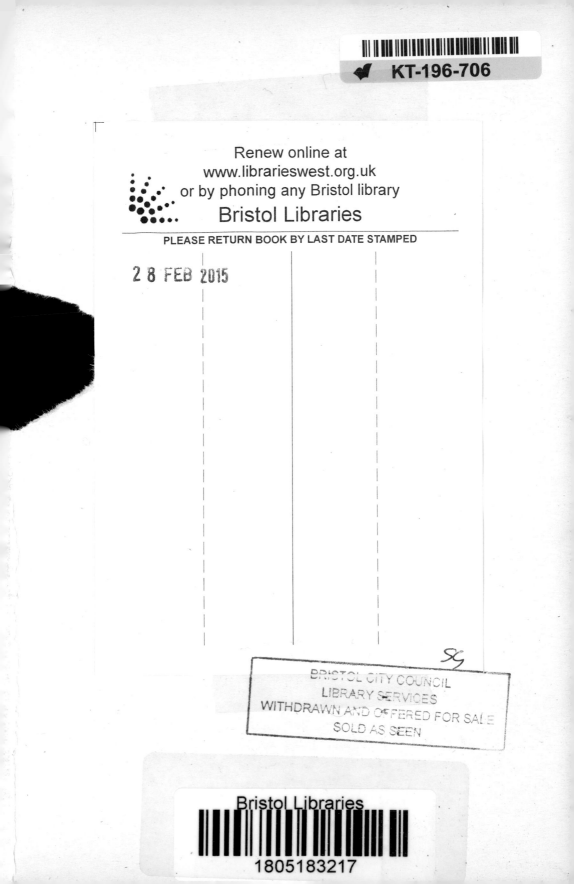

JASON DEAN

THE
HUNTER'S
OATH

headline

First published in 2014 by
HEADLINE PUBLISHING GROUP

1

Cataloguing in Publication Data is available from the British Library

Trade Paperback ISBN 978 1 4722 1260 3

Typeset in Adobe Garamond by Palimpsest Book Production Limited,
Falkirk, Stirlingshire

Printed and bound in Great Britain by
Clays Ltd, St Ives plc

Headline's policy is to use papers that are natural, renewable and recyclable products and
made from wood grown in sustainable forests. The logging and manufacturing processes are
expected to conform to the environmental regulations of the country of origin.

HEADLINE PUBLISHING GROUP
An Hachette UK Company
338 Euston Road
London NW1 3BH

www.headline.co.uk
www.hachette.co.uk

For my mother

ONE

Amanda Philmore looked down at her stainless steel Rolex and saw it was 11.07 p.m. The kids would be in bed, but Gerry would probably still be up. At least she hoped so, because they really needed to talk. And it couldn't wait until morning.

She was still the only pedestrian on Fort George Hill. Hardly any vehicles, either. This late on a weeknight the normally attractive tree-lined street looked intimidating, with few visible reminders that you were actually in Upper Manhattan.

Pulling her coat collar up against the crisp October air, Amanda gave a small sigh and began walking south. Towards Audubon Avenue and home. She could make out the top floors of an apartment block behind the trees on the other side of the street, with a few lit windows to remind her there were still a few people awake.

The thought of home pushed Amanda to walk faster. But then she heard the sound of a vehicle coming from behind and slowed a little and turned. It was a silver Ford sedan. Worse, it was the same one that had gone by a few minutes before. She was sure of it. It contained the same three shadowy shapes, and from within the same indistinguishable dance music thumped away like a giant's heartbeat.

It was all one-way around here, so the driver must have circled round via Fairview, then Broadway, then Hillside. That single thought made Amanda pause. Because this time round the car was moving a lot slower. Almost cruising. She watched it pull into the kerb fifteen yards away and stop.

Amanda stopped, too. *Not good*, she thought.

She heard the engine tick over, then die. The driver's door opened and a man slowly got out. The front and rear passenger doors opened and two more men joined him, at which point Amanda knew she was in trouble. Or would be very soon.

But one thing Amanda didn't do was panic. It just wasn't part of her DNA. Instead, she used what little time was left to quickly think through her options. There weren't many.

The men barred the way north, so that was out. She could keep going south for the junction to Fairview Avenue, and then it was just a couple of blocks to her apartment building. But the interesection was over three hundred yards away. Too far. She kept herself in good shape and knew she could run fast, even in the ankle boots she was wearing, but she was also forty-four years old. And the men looked at least fifteen years younger.

And with a seven-foot-high chain link fence barring access to the trees and residences on the other side of the street, that just left the open wooded area immediately to her right.

So only one option, really.

Without further hesitation, Amanda turned and sprinted into the foliage. Her messenger-style shoulder bag slapped against her back as she ran through the trees and up the shallow hill. She controlled her breathing and kept moving as she heard one of the men shout something, followed by a faint rustling of dead leaves somewhere behind her.

Without looking back, Amanda kept pushing up the hill. A few seconds later she found herself at the top with Highbridge Park surrounding her on all sides. The area ahead was dense with trees, but she knew it was less than two hundred yards to Dyckman Street on the other side. Even at this time of night, there'd be traffic there. And help.

She could hear the men behind her and continued running east. Stray branches snagged her coat as she reached into a pocket and pulled out her stun gun lipstick. She gripped the tube hard in her right hand, thankful she'd recharged it yesterday. It was metallic pink and looked incredibly real, which was the whole point. But it also claimed to deliver a million volts when activated. Still running at full pelt, Amanda reached into another pocket with her free hand and pulled out her keychain alarm. The hard plastic felt good in her hand. Like a shield. But she knew she could only set it off as a last resort.

Then something caught her foot and she tripped and fell to the ground with a grunt.

She shook her head angrily and got to her feet, her heart hammering in her chest. She was about to take off again when she detected a movement at her left. Like a shadow or something. But before she could process it, something large suddenly erupted out of nowhere and cannoned into her right side.

Amanda fell to the ground again. Quickly, she rolled onto her back and saw a human shape above her. She could smell the sickly sweet scent of marijuana. Without thinking, she flipped the top off the lipstick, jammed the end hard against the man's hand and pressed the second button down.

There was a sharp *z-z-z-t* sound and a brief sliver of light. The mugger cried out and fell onto his back. He'd be out for a minute, at least. But she also knew that if he was up here already, the others would be close by.

Amanda got to her feet again. It was now or never. She pressed the keychain alarm and threw it far into the shrubbery to her left. As its shrill, piercing sound echoed through the park, she began running in the same direction as before.

She'd covered twenty yards when another shape thumped into her, knocking her off balance. In an instant, an arm snaked around her neck and dragged her upright.

She smelled hot pizza breath on her cheek and felt a hardness at her back. Which told her these weren't just muggers.

Closing her eyes, Amanda Philmore focused all her thoughts on her children sleeping less than a mile away. As her attacker plucked the stun gun from her grip, she wondered if she'd ever get the chance to see them again.

TWO

Approximately three hundred and fifty miles away, in western Pennsylvania, James Bishop was standing in an old warehouse that had long ago fallen into disrepair. Whole sections of the walls were missing, as well as parts of the roof. The only illumination came from the dipped headlights of an SUV parked at the open entrance a hundred yards away.

There were three other men in the vicinity. Two wore dark off-the-rack suits similar to Bishop's. The first was Seth Willard, a frail-looking blond man with a wispy beard. The second was Hector Doubleday, a stocky Latino with short spiky hair and a three-day growth of stubble. He was standing behind the rusted husk of a sedan that had been left there to rot years before.

The third man was called Darryl Foland. He had longish brown hair and wore a dirty black leather jacket and faded green combats. He was kneeling in front of Bishop with his arms wrapped around his head, scared out of his mind. As well he should be.

'Okay, you, on your feet,' Bishop said, motioning with the Micro-Uzi in his hand. The faint smell of gunsmoke still hung in the air.

Foland pulled his arms away and stood up shakily, his eyes watching the gun. Bishop noticed there was a damp patch in his pants that hadn't been there before. *Good.*

'This is a one-time only deal,' Bishop said, 'so listen very carefully. Forget Ellen Meredith exists. Forget that bank exists. You are never to come within a thousand miles of here, understand? Because if *any*thing happens to disrupt her day-to-day life and affect the long-term case we're building against that bank, we *will* track you down and deal with you. That's a guarantee. Also, if she ever comes to us

4

with the slightest suspicion you've shown a renewed interest in her, same thing applies.'

Foland swallowed and said, 'Swear to God, you'll never see me in this part of the—'

'Shut up,' Bishop said. 'I'm not finished. I need you to understand that we won't be coming to kill you. That if anything happens to that woman, anything at all, even if it looks like an accident, we'll find you and plant enough shit on you to put you away for a lifetime.'

Willard was nodding his head. 'And as treasury agents we got access to evidence rooms all over the country, so we can get hold of the sickest paedo shit imaginable, believe me. And you know what they do to kiddie-fiddlers in the pen.'

'You'll be singing soprano the rest of your life,' Doubleday said. 'If you're lucky.'

Foland's Adam's apple moved up and down like a golf ball as he swallowed again. 'I hear you. Loud and clear. I'm gone, I swear.'

'Then get lost.' Bishop waved the Uzi. 'Before I come to my senses.'

Foland looked at each of them in turn, clearly not quite believing it. Then he turned and simply ran full pelt for the open entrance. They all watched him go. Once he was finally out of sight, Bishop turned to Willard and said, '*Paedo* shit? Was that in the script?'

Willard grinned. 'The idea just came to me. Worked, didn't it?'

Bishop smiled. It had worked, all right. A few minutes earlier, Bishop had been about to 'shoot' Foland in the head when Willard had gripped his wrist and jerked the barrel away. Bishop's finger had contracted on the trigger and Doubleday had immediately dived out of the way as the sound of a dozen rounds suddenly ricocheting off the vehicle carcass echoed throughout the warehouse. It had all looked and sounded perfect, just as Bishop had hoped.

Handing the prop Uzi back to Doubleday, Bishop said, 'Real nice work. Those squibs on the car looked so good you almost had *me* believing it. Great sound effects, too.'

'That's why the studios pay me the big bucks,' Doubleday said as he ejected the magazine and inspected the remaining blanks. 'So we can wrap this up now?'

'Yeah, we're done.'

Which meant they could all go back to their normal lives until the next job, which would be mainly down to Bishop. And he might not even use the same people. That was what he liked about contracting for Equal Aid. The almost complete freedom with which he was allowed to pick and choose. But then, he'd insisted on that right from the start, or forget it.

He liked his clients too, which made a change from his old career. But that wasn't too surprising. After all, Equal Aid was a non-profit organization for domestic abuse victims. Most could escape their predicaments with financial aid alone. But some needed more than just a cash injection, and that's where Bishop came in.

Ellen Meredith, for example, had managed to put a long history of drug abuse and petty thefts behind her to start a new life for herself in Pennsylvania. She'd even gotten herself a job in a bank. But her old boyfriend, Foland, had recently been released from prison and tracked her down, threatening to open up her past if she didn't siphon off some cash for him. Knowing he wouldn't ever stop pushing and that he would only get more demanding and more violent, Ellen had approached Equal Aid and asked for help.

Enter Bishop, who decided to pose as a maverick treasury agent 'investigating' Ellen's bank for drug money laundering, with Ellen as his inside source. The rest was just a matter of details, preparation, and personnel. Doubleday was a movie special effects whizz Bishop had used before. Willard was a newbie recommended to him by Ed Giordano, the supervisor at Equal Aid's Brooklyn Office. The three of them rehearsed everything over and over until they had it all down. Then earlier tonight they'd raided Foland's apartment, knocked him out and brought him here.

Bishop was pleased with his two choices. They'd acted their parts well. To be honest, if it had been up to Bishop he would have used a real gun to threaten Foland with, and real bullets. After eight years in the Marine Corps and another six in the close protection business, he was used to being around live ammunition, but he was aware most people weren't. But Doubleday had definitely come up trumps this time. Bishop's instincts told him Foland wouldn't be back after tonight's performance. And his instincts were rarely wrong.

Rubbing his hands together to counter the chill, Bishop walked over to the SUV and pulled his cell phone from his pocket. He unmuted it and was greeted with a message telling him he had voicemail. He dialled the number and punched in his personal code.

The phone message started. 'Bishop, this is Gerry,' the familiar voice said. There was a pause. 'I thought I should . . . Look, we're at the hospital. It's about Amy . . .'

As he listened to the rest of the message, Bishop's heartbeat quickened. He was staring at the car, but didn't see it. All he saw was his sister's face. *Amy.* The only direct family he had left since the deaths of their parents over twenty-five years before. The main constant in his life. If he was honest, the only one.

As soon as the short message ended, Bishop, still staring straight ahead, pressed the off button and carefully placed the cell back in his pocket. In the space of a minute, everything in his life had been reduced down to one simple objective.

He had to get back to New York immediately.

THREE

When Lisa Philmore saw Bishop come through the door, she got up from her seat and walked over. Above the baggy sweatshirt and jeans, her mouth was set in a straight line and her jaw was clenched. Once again, Bishop was amazed by the physical resemblance to her mother. Same long blond hair. Same perfect bone structure. And those piercing, hazel eyes. Another few years and the boys would be falling at her feet.

Jesus, thirteen already. Where did the time go?

Lisa reached Bishop, placed her hands on her hips, and said, 'So you got here, then.'

'Well, we're family, aren't we? Where else would I be? And what happened to "Hey, James, it's good to see you"?'

'Maybe it isn't good to see you. You ever think of that? Or maybe it's been so long I hardly recognize you any more.'

Bishop saw her father watching them from across the room, with Lisa's eight-year-old brother, Patrick, fast asleep on the chair next to him. Bishop had actually expected them to be in the emergency waiting room, but the receptionist had said Amy had been transferred to Intensive Care an hour before. That could only be promising. He hoped. It was now 07.14. Bishop had made the trip back from Pennsylvania in just under five hours. Most of it over the speed limit. After dropping the SUV back at the rental place on West 83rd, he'd taken the 1 train to the 215th Street stop and walked the rest of the way to Allerdyne Hospital.

And now this welcome. Bishop sighed and said, 'Why the attitude, Lisa? I do something to offend you?'

'More like what you *didn't* do. Yeah, we're family all right, but only when it suits you. I mean, Mom gets attacked last night and where were *you*? Off doing whatever it is you do, I expect, while your own

8

sis needs you here. Well, you're a little late, *James*. We can handle things fine by ourselves now, thanks.'

'Look, Lisa, I was in Pennsylvania, working. I got here as fast as I could when I heard. But even if I was in town I would have had no control over what happened to your mom last night. You must realize that.'

She snorted. 'Sure. If it makes you feel better, why not?' Lisa turned and walked back to her father and brother and sat back down. Simply dismissed him. Just like that.

Bishop only had himself to blame. She was overreacting, sure, but it *had* been too long since his last visit. Amy kept pressuring him to come over, but he always seemed to find excuses not to. And even when he did, it was just a fleeting visit. He wasn't sure why.

He walked over and took the free seat next to the sleeping Patrick. There were plenty of visitors in the waiting room, but Gerry had managed to find a little nook of chairs slightly separate from the others. Bishop noticed dark bags under his brother-in-law's eyes and his thin hair was in disarray. He looked devastated, which was understandable. Bishop and he had never really clicked, but Bishop knew the man was devoted to Amy and the kids. One of the few plus signs against his character.

'Hello, Bishop,' he said. 'So nice of you to make the effort.'

Bishop ignored the veiled jibe and slowly rubbed a palm back and forth over his scalp. One of the many minuses against Gerry's character was his habit of always saying the wrong thing at the wrong time. It seemed he just couldn't help himself. Maybe that's why they didn't get along. In fact, no maybe about it.

'So update me on Amy's condition,' Bishop said.

Gerry gave a sigh. 'She's out of ER, but she's still not out of danger. The doctors have stabilized her as best they can, but it's still touch and go. She'd already lost a lot of blood from the two abdominal stab wounds and there was a lot of internal damage. They had to remove her spleen altogether. Dr Meeker said they only just missed the aorta, which would have been fatal. He also told me they had to do a partial hepatectomy on the left lobe of her liver when it starting haemorrhaging. They've managed to save her left lung, but her breathing's still unsteady. They've got her on a ventilator now.'

Bishop briefly closed his eyes. He hadn't realized Amy's condition was this grave. Gerry hadn't been able to tell him much over the phone. Or maybe he'd simply held back the news out of spite. Bishop wouldn't put it past him.

'But if she's no longer in the ER, that means she's out of immediate danger, right?'

Rubbing his forehead, Gerry said, 'Amy's in a coma, Bishop. The surgeons found plenty of swelling in her skull where they beat her. This Meeker said they relieved some of the pressure, but there are still a lot of complications to deal with. Some of Amy's motor responses are still working – she withdraws from painful stimuli, for instance – but that's all they've gotten from her so far. The doctor warned me she might not . . .'

He stopped and turned away. Lisa was staring at the floor, trying to look brave. Bishop looked down at Patrick's sleeping form and gently ruffled the boy's hair, waiting for Gerry to collect himself.

Bishop knew the man had been having a rough time of it, even before all this. A year before, Gerry had been the account director of a small but rapidly growing advertising agency just off Madison Avenue. According to Amy, he'd been very good at his job, and after years of penny-pinching his boss had finally started paying him a salary that reflected his hard work. The future had looked good. But that all came to an end one night when he was tasked with entertaining the top executives of the agency's largest account, a major dental hygiene company. It seems Gerry got a little too drunk and made an off-colour comment concerning the CEO's wife and the use of Botox injections. The CEO immediately made it clear to Gerry's boss that if Gerry wasn't fired, he'd take his firm's business elsewhere. Naturally, Gerry was handed his cards the next day. And with the exception of a few temp jobs here and there, he'd been effectively unemployed ever since.

After a few moments, Bishop said, 'If she's made it this far, she'll make it the rest of the way. You know Amy as well as I do. You need to believe in her will to survive.'

'That's what *I* said,' Lisa said, looking at the floor. 'Mom's tougher than anybody.'

'Tougher than me,' Bishop said, 'that's for sure. Always has been, and if you ever tell her I said that, I'll deny everything.'

Lisa didn't smile at the weak joke. She just kept staring at the floor.

Bishop turned to Gerry and said, 'Let's you and I get a coffee, huh?'

Gerry shrugged, got up and rubbed some circulation back into his legs. Lisa moved into his seat and put her arm around her brother's shoulders, purposely ignoring Bishop as he led her father outside.

The third-floor corridor was long and wide, with hospital staff coming and going, and the occasional patient wandering about. They headed straight for the two vending machines halfway down that Bishop had noticed on the way in. Bishop reached them first and pulled some change from his pants pocket. 'The coffee any good here?'

'Haven't tried it,' Gerry said. 'Probably not.'

Bishop put money in the slot and got them a lukewarm cup of brown liquid each. He leaned against the wall and said, 'I assume Amy's got medical insurance?'

Gerry nodded. 'Yeah, her and the kids. Her company's pretty good with that.'

'Well, that's something. So tell me, what did you leave out on the phone?'

Gerry took a sip of his drink and looked at the wall. 'From the footprints at the scene, the police figure there were three muggers.'

'Yeah, I figured Amy could have handled one by herself.'

'And they raped her. The bastards raped my Amy. Robbing her and beating the shit out of her wasn't enough for them, Bishop. They had to have their fun, too. Then they stabbed her a few times afterwards for good measure. The sick bastards.'

Bishop slowly relaxed his grip on the plastic cup and frowned at the coffee that had just spilled on his hand. He'd half suspected it, but hoped he was wrong. After all, Amy was a very beautiful woman. Not that that would matter to the kind of pond scum who'd do this. They wouldn't give a damn what their victim looked like. To them, she was just a body. Bishop took a sip of the tasteless coffee and warned himself to stay in control. When it was family it was almost impossible, but allowing his emotions to get the better of him wouldn't solve anything here. If he was going to find whoever did this, he needed to be objective. On the drive over, he'd whittled his anger down until it was a small, cold, hard thing in the pit of his stomach. And he'd have to keep it that way if he wanted to operate free of distractions.

'I'm surprised a cop would give out details like that,' he said. 'Especially to a victim's husband.'

'They didn't. I got it from one of the paramedics after slipping him an extra twenty. Afterwards I wished I hadn't.'

Bishop raised an eyebrow. Getting the information straight from the source was exactly the kind of thing Bishop would have done. He was surprised Gerry had thought of it.

'And what else did this paramedic tell you?'

'What do you mean?'

'I mean, was Amy still conscious at the scene, for example? And if she was, did she say anything in the ambulance? Was she able to identify her attackers?'

Gerry looked down into his cup and said, 'No, nothing like that. Just what I told you.'

'So have the cops interviewed you yet?'

'A couple of hours ago. A Detective Medrano came and filled me in on what they found at the scene, which wasn't much. The marks on the ground that showed three men were involved. He also showed me some crime scene photos so I could identify the missing items from her personal belongings.'

'And what was missing?'

'What difference does it make to you?'

Bishop sighed. It sure didn't take long for the guy to return to form. 'It might make all the difference,' he said. 'And I'm her brother.'

'Yeah, and what a great brother you are, too. When exactly was the last time you came to visit Amy? Nine months ago? A year? And don't get me started on the kids. Pat still gets nervous around you, and Lisa barely knows who you are any more.'

Bishop knew the reason he didn't come visiting too often was standing right in front of him. Sometimes Amy really puzzled him. He knew she had a good head on her shoulders, so what had she ever seen in Gerry? Bishop had tried to figure it out over the years, but he still came up with nothing.

'I didn't come here to discuss my failings with you, Gerry,' he said. 'Now are you gonna tell me what was missing or not?'

Gerry rolled his eyes and said, 'Her wallet was gone, okay? Her Rolex, too. Also her cell phone, a lipstick stun gun, and her keys with one of those keychain alarms attached.'

'An alarm? Did she have time to set it off?'

'That's what got the police involved. This Medrano said somebody reported hearing what sounded like an emergency alarm in the park area and called 911. But mostly he just kept asking me questions, like what was Amy doing out in the park at that time of night, did she have any enemies, and stuff like that. He also said he'd be back to see me later.'

'And what *was* Amy doing there? Doesn't she usually take the subway home?'

'Sure, every day. Usually the 1 train.'

'In which case, the nearest stop to your apartment would be 191st Street, right?'

'That's right.'

'So what was she doing walking along Fort George Hill? That's in the opposite direction.'

'Sometimes she gets off at the Dyckman Street stop. She says that walk uphill keeps her in shape.'

'Really? At that time of night?'

Gerry sighed. 'Look, all I know is Amy called me earlier to say she'd be very late, okay? She said she had a lot of things she wanted to get done at work. I was at home working on a job application. After I'd seen the kids to bed, I kept working and didn't even realize the time until it was too late. Next thing I know the cops are on the phone and telling me to get down to the hospital, pronto. And here I am. And here *you* are.'

'Have they let you go in and see her yet?'

Gerry shook his head. 'They said in a couple hours, once they're sure she's stabilized.'

'So is anybody in there with her now?'

'I don't know. Why?'

Because that's my next stop, Bishop thought.

FOUR

Bishop knew Amy was in room 32 on the east side of the building. The helpful receptionist had told him when she'd made out his visitor's ID badge. Bishop followed the corridor down that part of the building, checking room numbers. He passed a number of beam-mounted plastic seats situated along the corridor at thirty-foot intervals. They looked uncomfortable. All were empty. He noticed a security camera affixed to the ceiling a few yards away, pointing away from him. He calculated room 32 was about twenty feet up ahead on the right.

Bishop slowed his pace as he got closer. There was a northbound corridor further down on the left, about fifty feet away. He could also make out part of a nurses' station down there, but since most of it was hidden from view he had no idea if anybody was on duty. Bishop walked straight over to the door to 32 and looked through the glass panel. Apart from the patient on the bed, he saw nobody else inside. He pushed the door open and went in.

For a brief moment, as he gently clicked the door shut behind him, Bishop thought he had the wrong room. The patient sure didn't look like his sister. But as he moved closer, he began to make out details and saw it really was Amy after all.

She lay on the bed with her arms atop the sheets. A single IV line was attached to each arm. Her face was a map of contusions and swellings. Bandages covered part of her scalp, and her blond hair looked dark, damp and lifeless. She had an oxygen mask affixed to her nose and mouth, through which he could hear the sounds of her breathing. The mask was connected to a complicated-looking ventilator machine next to the bed that emitted a steady electronic beeping sound every two seconds. On the other side of the bed, two more monitors made their own unique electronic sounds.

Bishop found he was unconsciously matching Amy's breathing rhythm and stopped himself. He pulled the room's only chair from against the wall and placed it next to her bed, kissed her on the cheek and sat down. He reached out and clasped her left hand. The skin was warm, but the hand felt like a dead weight.

Bishop gave a long, slow exhalation and looked at his sister's face. He sure didn't feel too good about himself right now. Lisa's barbed comments hadn't helped. And the things she'd said had hit home in a way she couldn't possibly have anticipated. Because Amy had actually tried to contact Bishop a couple of weeks before and he hadn't gotten back to her. She'd left two voicemail messages, asking him to call her when he had a chance. And he hadn't.

Why? Because he'd been too busy with the Foland job. At least, that was the excuse he'd given himself at the time. But, really, how much time would it have taken to make one simple phone call? None at all, that's how much. And now it was too late.

Christ, what an idiot.

Bishop thought back to the last time he'd actually seen Amy in person. Gerry had still been at the ad agency, so it would have been over a year ago. It had been a weekday evening. Possibly a Monday. It had been an impromptu visit while he was in town. Bishop still remembered Amy's look of surprise and delight upon opening the door and seeing her brother standing there. They'd spent the next couple of hours catching up as she prepared the evening meal, and once Gerry came back from work they all sat down to eat. He still remembered what it was: fusilli, with roasted tomatoes and fresh asparagus. Naturally, it had been delicious. But then Amy had always been a great cook.

And he also remembered the evening turning celebratory when Lisa informed everyone she'd won first prize in an art contest at school that very day. Which indicated she'd inherited the creative gene from her mother's side, since Amy had always enjoyed painting as a kid. Amy had never looked prouder of her daughter than that night. She'd even allowed Lisa to have a small glass of wine with her meal.

It had been a happy evening all round. Even Gerry had been bearable for the most part. Amy had started urging Bishop to stay the night in the spare room, but he knew Gerry would start sniping after a few more glasses of wine. So he'd begged off and left early to avoid any unpleasantness. Now he wished he hadn't.

Amy, he thought, squeezing her hand, *why did it have to be you? If anybody deserves violence in their life, it's me. But what did you ever do to anybody?*

His thoughts went back further. Back to when it was just the two of them against the world. Back to the moment twenty-eight years before when they learned of the car accident that had claimed the lives of their folks.

Bishop remembered it as if it was yesterday. He'd been ten at the time. That very day, in fact. Amy had only been sixteen herself. A couple of uniforms from the Staten Island Police Department had shown up at the door to deliver the bad news to her. Once they'd finally gone, Amy had taken Bishop's hand and sat him down at the kitchen table. He knew something was badly wrong when he saw her moist, puffy eyes. He'd never seen Amy cry before and it scared him. But somehow she managed to hold herself together for his sake.

'Where's Mom and Dad?' he asked her. 'Who were those guys at the door? Why are you crying, Amy? What's going on?'

'They were policemen, kiddo,' she said, sniffing. 'And they just gave me some very very bad news. Look, I'm gonna need you to be strong for me, okay?'

He just stared at her. 'It's about Mom and Dad, isn't it?'

She wiped her nose with a tissue and nodded. ''Fraid so. See, there was a pile-up on the New Jersey Turnpike tonight, because of the fog. It was a big one involving lots of vehicles. And Mom and Dad were . . . well, they were right in the middle of it.'

'Were they hurt bad?'

'Very bad, kiddo. They're both . . . well, they won't be coming back.'

'You mean they're dead?'

She just nodded at that point, unable to speak further, and then the torrent of tears came. And that finally made it real for Bishop. His parents really were gone forever. If Amy said it was so, then it was a fact. Bishop didn't remember much else except clutching his sister and crying silently with her for what seemed like hours, although it was probably more like fifteen or twenty minutes. Amy just held him close and comforted him until no more tears would come. He didn't know it at the time, but he'd never cry again. Nor would he celebrate another birthday.

'We'll make it through,' she'd kept whispering into his ear, holding him close. 'You and me. Just the two of us. Looking out for each other. We'll be just fine. You believe me?'

'I believe you, Amy,' he'd whispered back.

And until she'd left for college at eighteen, Amy had stayed true to her word. Dad's folks, Tom and Annabel, had opted to act as guardians to the two of them, but it became clear early on that they were more interested in the house than in their grandchildren. They'd always been aloof, though, even towards their own son. So instead, Amy had done her best to act as surrogate mother to Bishop for the next eighteen months. She'd done a good job, too, forgoing any kind of social life to take care of her little brother. With just themselves to rely on, they both grew up quickly in a very short space of time. Bishop especially.

He stared at Amy's closed eyelids and wondered what was going on in there. Could she hear anything? He knew it was the last sense to go when a person lost consciousness. And he also recalled reading something in *Scientific American* about studies done on patients who'd recovered from comas. Many of them had said that they'd heard and understood many of the conversations around them while in their comatose state. Maybe Amy was in there right now, fully aware that somebody was in the room with her.

So Bishop talked to her.

'Amy, it's Bish,' he said. 'The kids are outside. Gerry, too. They'll be in later, but for now it's just you and me. Like it was back when we were kids, right after Mom and Dad's accident. I don't know if you can hear me, but I'm hoping some part of you can. And I swear to you I'll track down the men responsible for this, Amy. Not a moment goes by when I don't see images of you at the mercy of those bastards. Not one moment. And there's only one way I know of to make those images go away.'

Amy just breathed in, then breathed out again. No other response. No movement but the rise and fall of her chest. Bishop raised his head to the window and studied the clouds outside. 'I'm pretty sure if you could talk you'd tell me to let the cops handle it. But you also know I can't do that. To them you're just another statistic. And even if by some miracle they found the scum who did this, the bastards would only get some smart lawyers and plea-bargain their cases down to nothing. Either that or they'd get off on a technicality. That's how it usually works.'

He squeezed her hand. 'I know we've always looked out for each other, and that won't stop. I'll make sure Pat and Lisa are okay while you're in here. I'll even try and get along with . . .'

He stopped and turned at the sound of the door opening to his left. A young nurse stood there with an armful of towels, her brow furrowed.

'What are you doing in here?' she said.

'Just talking to my sister,' Bishop said. He released Amy's hand, slowly stood, and placed the chair back against the wall.

Her face relaxed a little. 'Well, visitors aren't allowed in here right now. The doctor should have told you.'

'It's okay,' Bishop said, and moved past her. 'I already said what I needed to anyway.'

FIVE

When Bishop re-entered the waiting room, he saw Gerry in a corner talking to a man in a nondescript grey suit. Bishop could always tell a cop, even from a mile away. As usual, Lisa spotted Bishop before anyone else. She had a kind of sixth sense about things like that. She turned away quickly when he met her eye, so he went over and sat next to her.

'Still hate me?' he asked.

Lisa shrugged.

'Because I don't think I could handle it if you did.'

She turned to him with one side of her mouth turned up. 'You mean you actually care what I think?'

'Of course I do. And what you said before really hit home. I'm sorry I haven't come to see you guys more often. I really am. I accept all blame. It's my fault completely.'

She looked at him for a while, then shrugged and turned to look at her dad again.

'That the same policeman as before?' he asked.

Lisa nodded.

He looked down at the still sleeping Pat. 'How's the little guy taking this so far?'

Lisa smoothed Pat's hair, just the way Amy did. He didn't think she was going to answer, but finally she said, 'Don't think it's sunk in yet. He's only eight. He probably thought it was a bad dream or something. But I'm not looking forward to when he wakes up.' She turned back to Bishop, and her expression told him she had a question for him. But she needed a prod.

'Go ahead,' he said. 'Ask.'

She paused. 'What you said before. You really think Mom'll wake up?'

'You already know the answer to that, Lisa. And I wasn't lying when I said she's tougher than me. I even remember a conversation one time where I told her she should have signed up instead of me.'

'What, you mean like in the Marines?'

'Uh huh. Know what she said?'

Lisa shook her head.

'Her exact words were, "Who needs the Marines? Try giving birth. That'll make a man of anyone."'

Lisa's lips parted in a faint smile. 'Yeah, that sounds like Mom all right.'

Bishop smiled too. He still had a way to go before they were friends again, but Lisa's glacial exterior was melting a little. Which was as much progress as he could hope for right now. He turned and saw the cop looking over at him. 'Lisa, can you do me a favour?'

'Depends. What?'

'I'm going over to talk to that policeman. I'll have my back to you, but I'd like you to keep your eyes on me at all times, okay? And if you see me scratch my left shoulder, I want you to call out to your dad. Just say you need to go to the bathroom or something and can he hold Pat for a while. Can you do that?'

Lisa raised one eyebrow. 'I guess. Why?'

'I'll explain later. Thanks.'

He gave her a quick smile and walked towards the two men. The cop was half a head taller than Gerry, Bishop guessed about an inch over six foot, the same height as him, or near enough. But around the same age as Gerry, somewhere in the mid-forties. He was thickset with short curly dark hair, a straight line for a mouth and hooded eyes. But Bishop wasn't fooled. Those kinds of eyes were always watching. Especially on cops.

Once Bishop was close enough, the cop said, 'You're the brother, James Bishop?'

'Right. And you're Medrano?'

'*Detective* Medrano. That's right. I'm currently in charge of the case. I take it Mr Philmore here's updated you so far?'

'He told me Amy was assaulted by three men.'

'That's what we figure at the moment. So can *you* give me any clue as to why Mrs Philmore would be walking around Fort George Hill at that time of night?'

'Can't help you there,' Bishop said. 'I haven't even seen Amy in over a year.' *Apart from that time a few minutes ago.* 'Why, you think that particular location has got something to do with why she was attacked?'

'I don't know yet. We're just gathering information at this point. And you've had no other contact with your sister since that time?'

'No.'

Medrano twisted his lips. 'Okay. Tell me, does the word "sooker" or "zooker" mean anything to either of you?'

Bishop noticed the muscles in Gerry's neck tense as he shook his head, and wondered why that was. 'Well, I remember there was a famous Croatian soccer player called Davor Suker,' he said, turning back to Medrano. 'Nothing else springs to mind. Why?'

The detective shrugged. 'It's just one of the paramedics said Mrs Philmore mumbled something that sounded like it a couple of times before she went into the coma. I thought it might mean something to—'

'Wait a second,' Bishop interrupted. He looked from Gerry to Medrano. 'You're telling me Amy was *conscious* before she came here? I didn't know that.'

'Well, I think *semi*-conscious is probably a better description,' Medrano said. 'The paramedic I talked to said she was in and out for a while there. That she was having real trouble breathing and was coughing and mumbling stuff before she went completely under. "Sooker" was about all he understood, but let's face it, she could have been saying anything. I just thought it might mean something to you.'

'It does now you've given me some context,' Bishop said. '*Suka* is a Russian word. It means bitch.' He was aware of a slight, convulsive movement from his brother-in-law and looked at him quickly, but Gerry's face was expressionless.

Medrano raised an eyebrow. 'Are you sure?'

'Pretty sure. Google it if you don't believe me.'

Lines appeared on Medrano's forehead. 'So it's possible Mrs Philmore could have been replaying the event and just repeating some of what she heard. Which would mean one of her assailants is a Russian speaker. That's interesting.'

Bishop agreed. But he was also thinking of his arrangement with Lisa. He wouldn't get a better chance than right now. 'Who was it who found her?' he asked. 'And when, exactly?'

'Two patrol officers got to the scene first,' Medrano said, still frowning. Bishop knew cops hated answering questions. That was everyone else's job. But he pulled a small, ring-bound notebook from his jacket pocket and flipped through until he found the right page.

'The call went out on the wire at eleven thirty-two,' he said. 'And they found the victim, Mrs Philmore, at, let's see . . . eleven thirty-seven. Why?'

Bishop reached up with his right hand and rubbed his left shoulder. 'Well, it's just that Highbridge Park is a pretty large . . .'

'Dad,' Lisa called out on cue from behind them.

Gerry snapped his head round at the sound of Lisa's voice and began walking back to her and Pat. Bishop turned round to look, and as he did so made sure his arm 'accidentally' knocked against the notebook Medrano was still holding. It fell from the cop's hand and landed face down on the floor.

'Hey, sorry about that,' Bishop said, and quickly crouched down and picked the notebook up. He scanned the writing on the open page for a second and then rose and handed the notebook back to Medrano. 'I've always been clumsy.'

Medrano was still frowning as he put it back in his pocket. 'Yeah? Somehow you don't strike me as the ham-fisted type.'

'Looks can be deceiving,' Bishop said. Gerry was taking his daughter's place with Pat as Lisa walked towards the restrooms. *Good girl.* 'All I was saying was that Highbridge Park is a pretty large area to cover at night, and the patrolmen got there and found Amy in a matter of minutes. That's damn fast. Probably helped save her life. I'd sure appreciate it if you could thank them for me.'

The lines on Medrano's forehead finally smoothed themselves out and he almost smiled. 'I could do that next time I see them, sure.'

'So what do *you* think happened?'

Medrano moved his shoulders. 'Most of it's guesswork at this stage, but I figure the suspects must have either chased Mrs Philmore into the park or dragged her there. From the fresh footprints at the scene, I'd say she was chased. They then beat her, and then . . . the rest happened. At some point she must have had the sense to grab that little alarm of hers and activate it. For a short while, at least. Probably threw it into the trees to give any passer-by a decent chance to hear it. If so, that was some smart thinking on her part. But the alarm could also be what set them off. That would explain the stab wounds.'

Bishop nodded. 'So somebody heard the alarm and called 911. Who was it? Some guy out walking his dog?'

'A local resident. That's all I can say.'

'Fair enough. So what are the chances you'll find the three men?'

'Hard to tell right now. We were able to take DNA samples from the scene, so with luck positive matching against any future suspects won't be a problem. And we'll follow up your suggestion that one of them might have been speaking Russian. But obviously, we're waiting for Mrs Philmore to regain consciousness so she can give us something more concrete to work with. In the meantime you can be sure we're doing everything we can.'

'Right,' Bishop said.

Medrano reached into his back pocket and pulled out a card. 'Here. You can contact me on one of these numbers if you think of anything else.'

'Sure,' Bishop said. The card gave the man's title as *Detective First Grade Joseph Medrano*. It also gave his four-digit badge number and the address of the 34th Precinct along with a bunch of phone numbers, including the one for Medrano's cell. Bishop put it in his pocket and shook hands with the detective, then watched him leave.

Once Medrano had gone, Bishop went over and sat down next to Gerry. 'You reacted twice during that conversation,' he said. 'First when Medrano mentioned the word *suka*. Second when I said it could be Russian. Why is that, Gerry?'

Gerry looked down at his sleeping son and gently rubbed the back of the boy's neck. 'I don't know what you're talking about,' he said. 'If I reacted at all it was because I don't like my wife being referred to as a bitch. That's all.'

Bishop frowned. 'That's possible, I guess. But I'm still confused. You and Medrano clearly spoke to the same paramedic, which means whatever the guy told Medrano he would also have told you. Especially as you were paying him for the information. So why didn't you share it with me at the coffee machine earlier?'

'I guess I didn't think it was that important at the time.'

Bishop stared at him. 'You didn't think Amy regaining partial consciousness before lapsing into a coma was important? Nor that she might have given a possible lead as to the nationality of her attackers? Seriously?'

Gerry puffed out his cheeks, clearly getting agitated. 'Look, the paramedic just told me Amy mumbled some stuff and that she wasn't exactly coherent at the time, okay? That's all. He sure didn't mention this *suka* thing. That's a new one on me. What do you want from me, anyway?'

'The truth would be nice.'

'I've just told you the truth.'

'Have you? Sure you haven't left anything out this time?'

Gerry turned to him with narrowed eyes. 'Just what are you implying, Bishop?'

'I'm not implying anything,' Bishop said, hiding his exasperation behind a smile as he got to his feet. Because this was getting him absolutely nowhere. Gerry clearly knew more than he was saying, but Bishop couldn't force the guy to talk. At least, not without knowing a few more facts. So that was his next task. To get some leads. He could always come back to his brother-in-law later if necessary.

Gerry was watching him. 'So now where are you going?' he asked.

'Out,' Bishop said, and left.

SIX

Bishop took off for Highbridge Park on foot. He could have found a cab, but he wanted to think. And he generally thought better when he walked. Besides, it was only a couple of miles away. Sometimes it was easy to forget how small Manhattan was. That at less than twenty-four square miles in size, just about *every*where was within walking distance. In point of fact, twenty-three point seven square miles, if he remembered correctly. Which he usually did. One of the benefits of possessing an eidetic memory.

He spent most of the walk trying to figure out why Amy would be hanging around the park area when she could have bypassed it completely by going straight home from the 191st Street stop. After all, her apartment was only a few blocks away from the station. Gerry's explanation that she sometimes liked to go one stop further and walk back for the exercise was fine for daylight hours, but not at eleven at night. Amy was too smart for that. Manhattan's crime rate wasn't anywhere near as bad as it used to be, but muggings still occurred with regularity. Last year they'd averaged out at slightly less than ten a day. And rapes in the borough were a tenth of that. Assuming the official police statistics were correct, of course; Bishop had his doubts.

So what was Amy doing there?

Maybe the 'working late' story was just that. A story. Maybe she'd come back from meeting somebody nearby. Like a boyfriend, perhaps. With Gerry as a husband, Bishop wouldn't have blamed her at all. But hard as he tried to imagine it, it just didn't mesh with what he knew of Amy's character. She was the loyal type; always had been. On top of which, she'd never really had much interest in men, despite her stunning looks. Or maybe because of them.

He remembered her coming out to Parris Island to see him graduate

Basic Training, and how almost his entire platoon had begged him for her phone number. After the final ceremony, Bishop had bought them both a late lunch at the food court and told her just how popular she was. She'd simply chuckled as she took a bite of her burrito.

'Not impressed, huh?' he'd asked.

Amy shrugged. 'By blind infatuation from a bunch of horny alpha males? Well, it's kind of flattering, I guess, but it doesn't really mean anything, does it?'

'Well, it means you can have pretty much any man you want. Not too many women can say that.'

She smiled at him in a maternal way as she patted his hand. 'Sweetheart, in time you'll learn that having more choices than the next person just means you got more ways to screw up. Especially when it comes to prospective partners.'

'Sounds like you're speaking from experience.'

'I've made my share of screw-ups, bro. Believe me.'

'You mean with boyfriends?'

'Sure. But that's life, isn't it? You learn from your mistakes and move on. It's what separates us from the fishes.'

'And what have you learned, Amy?'

'To figure out what it is you really want and then settle for nothing less. I now know exactly the kind of man I want, Bish. I just haven't met him yet. But I will. See, that's one quality we both share: tunnel vision. Mom had it, I've got it, and so do you. Once we make a decision, nothing on this earth can divert us from our goal. When you made your choice to enlist, I bet your friends tried to talk you out of it, right?'

He nodded. 'Most of them tried, yeah.'

'Yet you ignored them all and did what you set out to do. I totally understand because I would have done exactly the same.' She gave him a gleaming smile and said, 'I'm proud as hell of you, Bish. I really am. You're so damn handsome, it's like the uniform was made for you. But that doesn't mean I'm about to date any of your buddies, so put that idea out your mind right now.'

And he had. Like him, she was comfortable with her own company. She didn't need another half. She was already a complete person. Until Gerry came along and swept her off her feet a few years later. Bishop still couldn't figure out how he'd done it when so many others had failed.

But you couldn't ever really know a person's thoughts. To Bishop, Amy had always seemed perfectly happy with Gerry, but maybe there had been something missing in their marriage. Something that caused her to look elsewhere.

It was possible. Unlikely, but possible.

Halfway along Nagle Avenue, Bishop paused at the major intersection from which Dyckman Street, Hillside Avenue and Fort George Hill all led off. Above, his eyes followed the elevated tracks he'd been walking alongside as they disappeared into the Dyckman Street Station on the south corner.

He knew this station only served the 1 train. Did Amy get off here rather than at the previous stop? After which she might have then walked up Fort George Hill just up ahead in order to get home. Again, possible. No way of knowing for sure. Not yet.

Bishop crossed the intersection and began walking up the hill.

On any other day it could have been a pleasant walk, but not today. Bishop focused on the surroundings. Traffic was minimal on the one-way street, and there were already plenty of south-facing vehicles parked along the sides. Considering it was still rush hour, there weren't many pedestrians. Just a few smartly dressed men and women making for the station down below. Trees lined both sides of the street, getting heavier and thicker the further he went. There was a high chain link fence that continued all along the right-hand side, and a low guard rail on the left. About halfway along, the guardrail came to an end, allowing free access into the park above. On the right, a single twenty-storey apartment block was set back behind the trees. But no entrance from this side.

He kept walking. After a couple of hundred yards, he could see he was nearing the intersection that marked the end of the street. Apartment blocks on both sides quickly replaced the greenery. So Bishop turned back and stopped at the street's midway point. He looked over to his left at the apartment block on its own. Only the uppermost floors were visible behind the trees, but the building wasn't set too far back. Maybe twenty or thirty yards.

'A local resident', Medrano had said. And this was the only

apartment block along Fort George Hill that directly overlooked the park. It would be interesting to know the name of the building to see if it matched the one he'd seen written down in Medrano's notebook. The cop's handwriting had been pretty bad, but legible. Maybe it was the witness, or maybe somebody totally unrelated to the case. Either way, he'd go and check for himself shortly.

First, though, there was the matter of Amy's alarm to consider. Bishop had tested a wide range of personal alarms in his old career, so he knew most were able to emit around a hundred and twenty decibels. That was equal to an ambulance siren, or a small jet taking off. Which meant a tenant on an upper floor could easily have heard it from the park.

But there was also a time discrepancy there, wasn't there?

Bishop studied the trees leading up to the park above and thought it all through. All kinds of scenarios were running through his mind, but the clearest one was of Amy on this street. Possibly alone. Since Fort George Hill was pretty quiet at this time of day, he had to assume it was even more so at night. And then she notices the three men.

Medrano had to be right about that part. Amy wasn't dragged to the park. She ran there herself. If the suspects were in a car, or even if they weren't, she'd have known she couldn't outrun all of them. She would have considered the chain link fence over there and discounted it almost immediately, figuring one of them would catch her before she got to the top. Which just left the trees leading into the woods right here.

And if he knew his sister, she wouldn't have thought about it for long. Like him, Amy thought fast, then acted. So she would have run into the trees and up the slope while she still had some lead time. Hoping to get to Dyckman Street on the other side of the park.

And then they overtake her. Or one of them does. Could be she doesn't even get the chance to use the stun gun, but that keychain alarm's another matter. As soon as she felt cornered she'd use it. As Medrano had said, the best thing would be to throw it into some bushes and play for time. Then maybe just keep running until they caught up with her.

But one of them would surely have found it and turned it off. Or destroyed it. And then they'd be free to have their fun. Beating Amy. Playing with her. After which they'd really get down to business. But that would all take time, wouldn't it? At the very least, Bishop figured between fifteen or twenty minutes.

So why the long delay between the sound of the alarm and the call to the police?

SEVEN

Bishop walked along Hillside Avenue, the road that ran parallel to Fort George Hill, and slowed when he came to the apartment building he'd seen behind the trees. It was the only twenty-storey building in this area. It was probably a co-op, like most of the apartment blocks in Upper Manhattan. There was a long, narrow grassy area just in front of it. The main entrance was a square block protruding from the centre of the building, with access via a set of glass double doors. Bishop got closer and gave a thin smile when he saw a plaque with the words *Ellwood Terrace* on it affixed to the wall next to the doors.

Exactly what he'd seen written in Medrano's notebook. *Ellwood Terrace*. Along with a name, *Charles Everson*. And a number. *1607*. There'd also been another number which Bishop assumed was a phone number, but he hadn't had time to memorize it. It didn't matter. He was here now.

Bishop briefly checked himself over. His black sports jacket, black pants and grey shirt were all looking a little worse for wear. Which was probably a good thing. If a person kind of squinted, they might mistake him for a cop. Possibly.

He walked up to the building entrance, pulled open the left-hand door and went inside. He strode along the entrance hall, passing a wall of mailboxes, and stopped at a second set of doors. There was an intercom to the side, with about two hundred numbered buzzers arranged in three columns. No names. Bishop pressed the one marked *1607* and waited, hoping there was somebody home during the day. If not, he'd just have to come back this evening.

Thirty seconds passed with no response. He pressed the buzzer again, and almost immediately an out-of-breath female voice said, 'Hello? Who is it?'

Bishop pressed the talkback button. 'Mrs Everson?'

'That's right. Who is this?'

'Police, ma'am. I've just come by with a few follow-up questions for Mr Everson about last night's incident in the park.'

'Oh, you again. Well, Chuck's at work now. You'll need to go and talk to him there, unless you want to come back later tonight.'

'Now would be better,' Bishop said. 'Can you give me his work address? I don't think I've got it written down here.'

'Sure. You'll find him at the end of East 3rd Street, number 322B. Runhome Couriers. He's got one of the big offices upstairs. There's a sign on the door.'

'Got it. Maybe you can call him and tell him I'm on my way? That way I won't miss him if he goes out for lunch.'

'Well, he usually takes his lunch with him, but I'll call him anyway.'

'Appreciate it. Thanks.'

Bishop released the button and walked back to the double doors. He pushed one open, stepped outside and stopped.

Gerry Philmore was standing there on the sidewalk, looking straight at him. He was wearing a dark raincoat over the same dishevelled shirt as before, and looked as surprised as Bishop.

Bishop walked over and said, 'What are you doing here? Shouldn't you be with Lisa and Pat?'

'My folks arrived an hour ago,' Gerry said, 'so they're looking after them for the moment. I just needed to come out here. To see . . . To see if I could . . .' He shrugged and shook his head. 'Christ, I don't know what I thought. I just felt I had to come.'

'How'd you find me?'

'By chance. I was standing at the south corner back there when I felt sure I saw you walking into this building so I came over to check. I was just about to leave when you came back out. What were you doing in there?'

'Just tracking down somebody.'

'Who?'

'The witness who heard the alarm.'

'And did you find him? Or her?'

'I found out where he works.' Bishop paused and looked at Gerry.

The guy looked totally worn out. Bishop actually felt sorry for him, which was a first. 'When was the last time you ate?'

'I don't know. Yesterday evening, I guess. I'm not all that hungry anyway.'

'Well, I am.' Bishop looked at his watch. It was just after eleven. 'I'm gonna walk back to the intersection and see if I can find somewhere. Come along if you want.'

Gerry shrugged and said nothing. But he walked with Bishop.

At the intersection, they crossed to the other side of Dyckman and Bishop entered the first deli he saw. It was pretty cramped inside, but not too busy yet. He spotted a counter at the rear with a couple of small tables and chairs set against the opposite wall. A row of customers already sat at the counter, eating and talking, but one of the tables was still free. Bishop told Gerry to sit down, then went to the counter and ordered a couple of ready-made hero sandwiches and Cokes.

Two minutes later, he came back with the orders and placed them on the table. He took the chair across from Gerry and said, 'Salami, pastrami and turkey. They looked the freshest out of all the choices.'

'Okay.' Gerry peeled off the cellophane, picked up half and took an uninterested bite. Bishop dug into his and both men chewed in silence for a while. Despite what he'd said, Bishop wasn't particularly hungry either. But he hadn't slept in a while and he knew he needed to eat something if he was going to keep going.

After a long drink of his Coke, Gerry said, 'Wherever you're going next, I want to come along.'

'That so?'

Gerry put down the sandwich. 'Look, Bishop, I need this.'

'Need what, exactly?'

'Look, the only woman I've ever loved is in a hospital room, a hair's breadth away from . . .' He closed his eyes and took a breath. Opened them again. 'And I couldn't protect her. Don't you get it? Those bastards used her like a piece of meat while I was sitting at home less than a mile away. How do you think that makes me feel? You were hundreds of miles away, like you usually are, yet you're here now and actually doing something about finding them. I know you are.'

'I'm just making sure all the boxes are checked, that's all. Cops have heavy workloads. They can miss things. I've trained myself not to. It's just the way I am.'

'Yeah, Amy once said you took after your dad in that. She said he was very methodical, too.'

Bishop frowned. She was probably right. He wouldn't know. At six years his senior, Amy had gotten to know Mom and Dad a lot better than Bishop ever could. He took another bite of his food and chewed in silence.

'Just let me help,' Gerry said. 'So I can feel I'm doing something useful.'

'You're the father of two great kids. If you think being there for them at a time like this isn't important, then you're not thinking clearly.'

'My folks can take care of Pat and Lisa for a few hours,' Gerry said, 'and they won't let us see Amy for a while yet anyway. Just let me come with you now to see this witness. See what he's got to say. Then take it from there.'

Bishop polished off the last piece of his sandwich and sat back in the chair, studying Gerry. He tried to put himself in the other man's shoes. Not being a family man, it was difficult. But he knew he'd feel pretty much the same way if the roles were reversed, and not just because of the way he was made. He appraised Gerry's physical appearance. It looked as if he'd slept in that shirt. If he'd slept at all, that was. And his tired, haggard expression couldn't be ignored either. Gerry was a major pain in the ass, but having him along right now might actually work in Bishop's favour. But only temporarily.

He took a swallow of his Coke and said, 'Okay, Gerry. I usually work better alone, but it just so happens that right now you could probably pass for a cop better than I could. So just say as little as possible and act the way you feel, tired and short-tempered.'

'I can do that,' Gerry said, and took another bite of his sandwich.

EIGHT

322B East 3rd Street was actually a grey door, sandwiched between a Korean laundromat and a Spanish grocery store. Attached to the door were three signs, one for a photographic studio, one for a fitness equipment supplier, and one for Runhome Couriers.

Bishop said, 'Remember, say nothing. I'll do all the talking.'

Gerry nodded. 'You won't even know I'm here.'

Bishop pulled the door open and went in first. The interior was just a narrow hallway ending in a steep stairway straight ahead. Bishop led the way up the stairs to the second-floor landing. On the wall ahead were signs giving directions. Runhome was to the right, the other two businesses to the left. Bishop and Gerry turned right. At the end of the corridor was a closed door through which Bishop could hear the sounds of female voices and people moving around. He opened it and stepped inside.

Runhome Couriers was an open-plan area with two sets of windows at the far end and a number of computer-laden desks in the centre. Bishop counted four middle-aged women there with headsets, talking to either customers or couriers. A fifth was frowning at her monitor. In the far corner was a glass-partitioned office. Inside, Bishop saw a black guy in shirt and tie, talking on the phone.

The woman who wasn't talking looked up at the visitors with a question in her eyes. Bishop simply nodded at the office and walked towards it, Gerry at his side. As they got closer, Bishop saw the legend *C. Everson, Supervisor* on the wooden door. He knocked once, then opened it and entered.

Everson looked up at them both without pausing in his conversation. Something about compensation for a package Everson insisted had been delivered on time. Bishop tuned it out and looked around the office. There wasn't much. Just Everson behind his busy desk, a visitor's chair in front of it, and two more lined up against a wall. There was a metal filing cabinet in the corner. The wall behind Everson was covered with various charts and notices.

Bishop sat in the chair and watched Gerry go over and lean against a wall with his hands in his pockets. Perfect. Exactly how a cop would act. Bishop turned back and studied Everson, who he guessed was in his early to mid-fifties. He had short greying hair cut close to the skull, a heavily lined forehead and a moustache that was too black to be true.

'Listen, Ramon,' he said, 'we can keep going over this until I die of malnutrition, but I've got a copy of the signed receipt right in front of me so I know for a fact you're trying to pull one over on me. I've told you I'll give you a discount next time to prove I'm a nice guy, but if that ain't good enough I'll give you the number of my lawyer right now. What's it gonna be?' He paused for a moment, listening, then said, 'Fine. You do that.'

He replaced the phone and sighed at his guests. 'And what can I do for you?'

Bishop said, 'Didn't your wife tell you we were coming?'

'Oh, yeah. Police, right? Look, I don't know what more I can tell you guys. I already told you what I saw. Or rather, what I heard.'

'It's just routine, Mr Everson. Just making sure we got all the facts straight.'

So far, so good, Bishop thought, pulling a small notebook and pen from his inside pocket. This wasn't the first time he'd pretended to be something he wasn't in order to get the answers he needed. He'd learned a while back that as long as you looked and sounded the part, people generally believed you were who you claimed to be. You just had to stay in character, that's all. And getting Everson's wife to call ahead had also legitimized them to a certain extent. If the guy hadn't asked for identification by now, chances were good he wasn't going to. Opening the notebook, he clicked the pen and said, 'Okay, so you called 911 when, exactly?'

Everson pinched the skin between his eyes. 'Just after eleven thirty, like I said. Sheila was in bed. I was on the balcony finishing my cigar and about to go in to watch Letterman. Then I heard that alarm go off. Sounded like it was coming from the park. Sheila's got one of those personal alarm things too, so I had a pretty good idea of what it was. It went on for about a minute and then stopped. So I called 911 and reported what I heard. End of story.'

Bishop stopped doodling and said, 'Then what did you do? Watch Letterman?'

Everson swallowed. 'Yeah. Why?'

'Just asking. See, I'm a little confused here. You said you heard that alarm go off at eleven thirty?'

Everson looked at Gerry behind him. Then at Bishop again. 'Give or take a minute.'

Bishop closed the notebook. 'Well, here's the thing, Mr Everson. We found somebody nearby who said she heard an emergency alarm going off about fifteen or twenty minutes earlier than that. She didn't know the direction it came from, so she didn't bother reporting it. But one thing she's absolutely sure about is she didn't hear any alarm at eleven thirty. And she lives near the park, too. So you see the problem we got here? Now, are you sure you didn't hear that thing go off some time earlier than when you claimed?'

'What are you talking about? Why would I wait twenty minutes before calling you?'

'I don't know,' Bishop said, scratching his cheek. 'Could be you weren't entirely convinced what you'd heard was a personal security alarm. So you brushed it aside and kept smoking your cigar. And then around eleven thirty, you see something, or some*one*, that causes you to think you might have made a mistake. That there might be a person in real trouble over there. So this time you do call 911, but you feel guilty about waiting so long. So you say you're calling because of the alarm and nothing else. That sound possible?'

'I don't know what you're talking about,' Everson said, shifting in his seat. 'I heard that alarm go off at eleven thirty. That's what I reported and that's what happened.'

'Look, Mr Everson,' Bishop said, 'I'm not here to bust your balls, okay? Any citizen who reports a crime is already aces in my book, so I know you're one of the good guys. All I want is the truth. Because if that alarm did go off earlier, it pushes this case in a whole different direction, know what I mean? Believe me, something like this, it's important.'

Everson said nothing for a few seconds. Then he cleared his throat. 'Look, if I *was* slightly wrong about the exact time, just saying *if*, you sure it won't come back to me later?'

'Tell us how it really went down and you won't hear from me again. I guarantee it.' Since Bishop had no authority here at all, he felt this was a promise he could safely keep.

Everson closed his eyes for a moment. Then he opened them and said, 'This other witness said it was about eleven ten when she heard it?'

'Give or take,' Bishop said. 'But definitely somewhere around that area.'

Everson tapped his fingernails on the desk. 'Well, that's about when I heard it, too.'

'Go*dammi*t,' Gerry said. 'You mean to tell us—'

'What did I tell you before?' Bishop snapped, glaring hard at Gerry. The first rule in these situations was to always stay in character, no matter what. He knew the slightest mistake from Gerry and the guy would sense something was off. He might even ask for ID. 'This is *my* case,' he said. 'You're just along for the ride. Got it?'

Gerry clenched his jaw, but he stood down and didn't say anything else.

Bishop turned back to Everson. 'Sorry about that. He's kind of excitable. So what made you finally make that call?'

Everson paused, frowning at Gerry. Then he said, 'Well, I saw these three guys coming out of the woods on this side, and it got me thinking.'

'Three men. Okay. And what were they doing?'

'Well, they looked pleased with themselves, you know? Two of them were high-fiving each other like they'd just scored a touchdown. There were a few cars still parked at the kerb, and they all got in one and just drove off.'

The image of the rapists casually high-fiving each other almost caused Bishop to lose it. He could feel the rage threatening to take over. He gripped his pen until he could feel it about to snap in two.

Almost immediately he relaxed his hold. *Stay in control, man. Don't let your emotions ride you. Not now. Stay objective.*

He saw Everson hadn't even noticed his brief loss of control. The manager showed Bishop his palms and said, 'You see something like that on a normal day and it don't mean a thing, but I was thinking about that alarm from earlier and figured there was a chance they might have been the cause of it. I couldn't be sure, though, so I didn't bother mentioning it.'

'Right. So did you get a good look at the men? Or the make of vehicle?'

'Hey, come on. You know how far away I was? I'm up on the sixteenth floor *and* it was almost midnight. Not too many streetlamps along that stretch, either. At least, not working ones. I'm pretty sure they were guys, but I couldn't even swear to that.'

'What about the car?'

Everson shrugged. 'A modern-looking sedan. Could have been a Ford something, I guess. And it looked kind of grey, but then everything does in the dark.'

Bishop rubbed his forehead with a thumb. He'd managed to bring the guy this far, but he'd been hoping for something a little more than vague shapes in the night. 'Nothing else that sticks in your mind at all? Take a moment and think, Mr Everson.'

Everson sat back and stared at the ceiling. After a few moments he straightened up again. 'Nothing, except I noticed the car was kind of juddery as they took off.'

Bishop raised his eyebrows. 'Juddery? What do you mean?'

'Well, I don't know if they had a stick shift or what, but it looked like the driver maybe put it in too high a gear? You know, like sometimes when you accidentally put it into third or fourth instead of first and the whole car starts shaking before stalling? It looked like that. Then it smoothed out some and they just drove off. So there it is, that's everything.'

'And they took off at eleven thirty, after which you immediately called 911?'

'That's it. I went straight in and made the call on my cell. I figured I'd wasted enough time already, you know?'

Bishop nodded and started tapping his thumbnail against his lip. It was something, all right. Not much, but enough to keep them going forward. Because he was pretty certain the shaking had nothing to do with being in the wrong gear.

Bishop stood up to go. 'Okay, Mr Everson. Thanks. You've been a help.'

Everson smiled. 'Good to know I did *some*thing right today.'

NINE

Once they were outside again, Bishop began heading west, back to the station on Second Avenue and East Houston. As they walked, Gerry said, 'You were pretty convincing in there. For a few moments I actually thought you *were* a detective.'

'Acting a part's easy,' Bishop said. 'A monkey can do it.'

'So were you lying to Everson? Because I don't see how he was any help at all.'

'Then you weren't listening. For a start, how many cars do you think there are in Manhattan with manual stick shifts?'

Gerry frowned. 'Okay, not many, I guess. I don't drive, but I take it automatic transmissions are the norm?'

'Exactly. With the constant traffic jams and red lights, it wouldn't be long before you got a permanent cramp in your left leg from all the clutch movements.'

'Okay, I get it. So if those three were driving a car with manual transmission, it'll be a hell of a lot easier to track down than a standard automatic, right?'

'No, I'm saying they weren't driving a manual at all.'

'Huh? What are you talking about?'

'That juddering Everson mentioned didn't sound like the driver chose the wrong gear to me. That's the act of somebody in a panic, or flustered. But these three were kidding around with each other, Everson said. They were in control and relaxed.'

Gerry looked at the ground. Clearly, he hadn't wanted to hear that part again.

Bishop continued, 'It could possibly be a fault in the engine, but what that sounded like to me was a vehicle running on empty. Or close to it. Could be they hadn't realized how low they were getting until that point. See, if you pull out and the fuel injection system's unable to deliver enough gasoline into the engine block, the vehicle starts shuddering. For a few seconds, at least.'

He thought for a moment as he walked. 'It could also be low fuel pressure caused by a faulty fuel pump, but I don't think so. You get the same shuddering effect, but it doesn't just go away like it did here.'

'You know your cars.'

Bishop shrugged. 'Back in my old career I had to be prepared for all contingencies. Troubleshooting basic engine problems was one of them.'

'Okay. So assuming they *were* low on gas, that means their obvious next stop would had to have been a filling station.'

Bishop nodded. 'And what I need to do now is find out which one.'

TEN

They didn't take the A train all the way back to Dyckman Street, but got off two stops earlier, at 181st Street and Fort Washington Avenue. Once they'd made their way up the escalators to the south exit on 181st, Bishop paused on the sidewalk outside and checked his watch. He was glad to see it was still only 12.33. He still had most of the day ahead of him.

'Let me see that map again,' he said.

Gerry pulled his Samsung Galaxy from his coat pocket and played his fingers expertly across the screen, looking for the same site as before.

Bishop thought these smart touch-phones were great. He didn't have one himself, or even want one. As far as he was concerned the ability to make and receive calls was all he needed from a cell phone. The simpler, the better. In all things. But he could see why people would be attracted to these gadgets. He imagined it could all get pretty addictive in no time at all. Your whole life, available at a single touch.

'Here,' Gerry said, and passed the phone over.

Bishop took it and studied the onscreen map. Gerry had found the website earlier, just before they'd descended to the subway. Every gas station in New York was listed, with a map marking each one's location. There weren't that many. One of the consequences of Manhattan's steady gentrification was the gradual reduction of places to buy gas on the island. Bishop knew most filling stations simply weren't profitable enough when balanced against their site's real estate value. But there were still a few left, mostly on the east and west sides. More important, there were also half a dozen in the Upper Manhattan area.

For instance, there was one along Broadway, south of the crime site. Then there was a place north of it. Both were about the same distance from the park. And there was a third option if those two came up blank, a 'gaseteria' on Nagle Avenue.

It also depended on where the attackers' next destination had been. If they'd been heading for the Bronx, then the last two would have been the best choices. Heading back to Jersey or Queens, the Broadway option would have been the most attractive. He picked out the Broadway station to check first.

They headed east along 181st and turned left when they reached the Broadway intersection. About ten minutes later, Bishop saw the tall green sign up ahead with its familiar star-shaped logo. He looked at the green roof above the pumps and spotted at least two internet protocol cameras up there. Further back was a one-storey building that doubled as a convenience store. The place looked busy.

'What now?' Gerry asked.

'Same as before. Follow my lead and let me do all the talking.'

'What if they ask for ID this time?'

'Let me worry about that.' Bishop led the way across the forecourt until they reached the store, then pushed open the glass entrance door and entered. Inside, he saw two cashiers, one male, one female. The man was serving a customer with three more waiting in line behind him. The woman's till was closed. She was leaning on the counter, writing something in a ledger.

Bishop walked over to her and said, 'Can you call your manager and ask him to come out? I'm Detective Hurley.' He pointed a thumb at Gerry behind him. 'This is Detective Adams. Tell him we'd like to talk to him about last night's customers.'

The cashier took the request in her stride. She shrugged and picked up a phone next to the cash till. Then she paused and said, 'Wait a second. What time last night?'

'Primarily between eleven thirty and midnight,' Bishop said. 'Why?'

She replaced the phone. 'Well, I can call Mr Motta if you want, but from about ten thirty onwards the only fuel we had here was diesel, and we ran out of that half an hour later. We put up a sign outside to warn people. And the fuel supply trucks didn't get here until about two a.m. We still had a few people buying stuff here in the store, but no gas customers. Or did you mean everybody?'

'No, just gas customers,' Bishop said. 'But thanks anyway.'

'You're welcome,' she said automatically, and went back to her ledger.

Outside, Gerry said, 'So that's one down, then.'

Bishop nodded. But how many more to go? He was thinking back to the map. If the suspects *had* been heading south, then the next filling station in that direction was in the Hamilton Heights area. Miles away. Too far for a vehicle running on empty when it would have been simpler to hang a U on Broadway and head north. Which meant checking on the other two he'd already marked in his mind. But there were still far too many variables for his liking. What if they hadn't been low on gas at all? What if it *had* been an engine fault that caused the shudder? Or a faulty fuel pump. Then what?

He mentally shook himself out of that kind of thinking. It was pointless and got him nowhere. He was tired, but that was no excuse. Logically, all he could do for now was explore all the possibilities to hand. And if he got nothing out of it, he'd have to try something else. Simple as that.

'Okay,' he said, 'on to the next.'

ELEVEN

When the cab came to a stop just before the Dyckman Street intersection, Bishop gave the driver a five and they got out. He and Gerry continued north-east along Dyckman, passing a small residential park area before stopping on the corner of Seaman Avenue.

On the opposite corner was another open forecourt with another steel canopy, this one overlooking three pump dispensers. There was a small shop further back. Next to that were three open garage areas with signs promoting auto repair and wheel alignment services. He could see a few mechanics working on vehicles, but the filling station itself only had one customer pumping gas into his station wagon. The whole area was almost entirely overlooked by apartment blocks, which made Bishop think this particular site could soon be the next victim of the all-consuming gentrification god.

The two men crossed the street, walked across the forecourt and entered the shop.

Straight away, Bishop could see the same approach wouldn't work here. The shop wasn't much bigger than a shoebox, with just the one guy working the cash till. If Bishop had to guess he'd say he was looking at the proprietor. He looked in his fifties, with neat, greased-back grey hair and the kind of lined, lived-in face that told the world he was nobody's fool. He watched his two customers with a careful scrutiny. One thing Bishop knew for sure was that if he came on as a plainclothes detective this guy would want to see a badge. In which case it looked as though it was time for plan B.

Bishop stepped over to the counter. The man said, 'Help you?'

'Possibly,' Bishop said. 'You're the owner here?'

'Uh huh.'

'Were you on duty last night?'

45

He shook his head. 'We got a night boy for that. Why?'

'But you've got security cameras covering the forecourt, right?'

The man shrugged. 'That a trick question or something? What's it to you, anyway?'

'Well, I'd like to check out last night's footage. Specifically from eleven thirty onwards.'

The man chuckled. 'Sure thing,' he said. 'Want me to stick a floor mop up my ass so I can clean the floor as I leave?'

Bishop shrugged. 'If you really feel it's necessary.'

The man suddenly lost his good humour. 'Who the hell are you? You're not cops.'

'I didn't say we were.'

'So why am I even talking to you?'

'I don't know. Maybe because you think there's possibly something in it for you.'

The man looked at Bishop. Then at Gerry standing by the window. 'Maybe that's exactly what I'm thinking,' he said.

Bishop nodded and reached into his jacket pocket and pulled out his billfold. He extracted three fifties and fanned them out on the counter.

The man looked at the notes. 'Know what my pet peeve is?' he said. 'Odd numbers. Call me weird, but I can't stand the sight of them.'

Bishop added another fifty to the fan.

'Now we're talking.' The man picked them up and placed them in his shirt pocket. He turned to the wall phone behind him, put it to his ear and pressed 2. A few seconds later, he said, 'Harry, you wanna come and look after the store while I take care of something? . . . Yeah, right now . . . Okay.' He replaced the phone and said, 'Be a minute.'

'Sure,' Bishop said and looked out the window. The guy outside had already finished filling his tank. Bishop watched as the station wagon slowly pulled out of the forecourt.

The owner said, 'So what you looking for that's worth two hundred bucks?'

'Last night,' Bishop said, 'somebody close to us was attacked by three men over in Highbridge Park. A witness gave us information that indicates they might have been seriously low on gas when they took off. And you're one of the filling stations closest to the crime scene.' As he spoke, Bishop's eyes followed a shaven-headed young guy in mechanic's overalls walking past the window.

He appeared at the door. 'What's up, Tony?'

'Just need to show these two gentlemen something out back. This way, guys.' Tony lifted up a hinged part of the counter, then opened a door at the side of the shop and stepped through. Gerry, then Bishop, followed him inside.

Bishop closed the door behind him and saw they were in a small, windowless storeroom-cum-office. Various boxes were stacked up against two walls. Three TVs in various states of disrepair were lined up against a third. In the centre of the room was a chair and a desk. On the desk was an old PC and keyboard, a printer, two full filing trays and various components that looked like hard drives, or modems. Or perhaps both.

Tony sat down and switched on the computer. 'We only got the one camera right above our heads. It's aimed at the pumps, but it's pretty old. Don't know how useful it'll be.'

Gerry stood over his shoulder and tapped a small black box next to the computer. 'And everything gets automatically saved onto this hard drive?'

'Right,' Tony said, moving the mouse around. 'My brother set it all up for me. I wipe it every fortnight and then start over, but that's not for another couple of days yet.' He cleared his throat. 'Okay, let's see what we got here.'

Bishop came and stood next to Gerry as Tony opened up a folder. He moved the cursor down a short list of files and finally clicked on the third one from the end. The Windows Media Player opened and soon the screen was filled with a monochrome shot of the forecourt at night. There was no sound. The resolution wasn't exactly high-definition quality, but it still looked pretty good to Bishop.

The time code in the corner gave yesterday's date. The time was 21.32.28.

'We want from about eleven thirty p.m. onwards,' Bishop said.

'Gotcha.' Tony dragged the playhead across until it was close to the end and let it play. The time on the screen now read 23.27.09. The forecourt was empty. 'Don't get too much business this time of night except at weekends,' Tony said. 'Want me to fast forward?'

'Sure,' Bishop said.

Tony pressed the fast-forward button and Bishop watched the time code speed up. Minutes began to pass. Taillights and headlights whizzed by on the street outside. The occasional light blinked out in a distant apartment block. Then a vehicle suddenly zipped into the forecourt and jerked to a stop next to the first pump.

'Well, hello,' Tony said, and immediately pressed rewind until the car reversed out. He pressed play and then sat back.

Bishop looked at the time in the corner. 23.32.07. Three seconds later, the car pulled into the forecourt again and stopped. Bishop saw it was a light-coloured Ford. Possibly grey or silver. It looked like an older model Taurus. Late nineties, maybe. Pre-2001, anyway, since the licence plate was made up of three letters followed by three numbers. After 2001, New York began issuing plates with a three letter, four number format.

Except the last number wasn't too clear. It looked like an eight or a nine, but a splash of something dark obscured the lower part. Probably mud. He watched as a stocky man in a hooded sweatshirt got out the driver's side and went over to the dispenser. For a brief second, Bishop saw a thin goatee, but no other facial features. The hood kept them mostly hidden in shadow. The man pulled some bills from his pocket, fed them into the payment slot at the dispenser and pulled the pump out. He unlocked the fuel cap and inserted the pump, keeping his head turned towards the dispenser as he filled the tank.

Bishop turned his attention to the car. With the forecourt lights reflecting off the windshield, it was that much harder to see inside, but he could just about make out another figure in the passenger seat, plus a third sitting in the back. The car was also swaying slightly from side to side, as though the passengers were rocking along to something playing on the stereo.

Then the man pulled the pump out and replaced it on the dispenser.

He locked the fuel cap, then walked around to the driver's side and got in and shut the door. The headlights came back on. The car started moving and soon the vehicle went out of shot. It was 23.35.49.

'So what do you think?' Tony asked.

'It was them all right,' Gerry said, his voice loud in the small room. 'You could see the other two partying like it was a regular night on the town. And after what they'd just done. Bastards.'

'It's a little too soon to jump to conclusions,' Bishop said. 'Play it to the end, will you, Tony? I want to be sure nobody else comes along who fits the bill.'

Tony did as asked. But the only other customers were a businessman in a black SUV at 23.46, and a female driver in a new Mustang who came in just before midnight.

Bishop said, 'You able to burn DVDs on this thing? I'd like a copy of this.'

'Uh uh,' Tony said. 'I can burn CDs, but that'll only give you about a minute's worth, and I don't know how to split up the footage. *And* I got no blank CDs either.'

'Wait a minute,' Gerry said, and reached into his pants pocket and pulled out his keys. He went through them, then peeled a specific one off the ring and handed it to Bishop.

Bishop looked down at it. It almost looked like a key. It had the same metal finish. But there were no teeth, and the blade ended in a USB connector. Bishop slowly shook his head, amazed at what you could fit on a key ring these days. After spending three years behind bars for another man's crime he sometimes felt technology had left him behind. Which was only natural, he guessed. Nowadays everything was getting faster and smaller and he either had to accept it or go live in the mountains. He'd always been old-school when it came to his personal equipment, though. On his own key ring, for example, he kept a miniature Swiss Army multi-tool. It was flightsafe, which meant no blade or scissors, but it had still come in useful more times than he could remember.

'How much space is on this?' Bishop asked.

'Sixteen gigs. There's nothing else on there right now except maybe a few old Word documents.'

'That should be enough,' Bishop said. 'You mind, Tony?'

'Sure,' he said, and got off the chair. Bishop took his place and inserted the flash drive into the back of the black box. He dragged the movie file and dropped it onto the external hard drive icon. A progress bar told him the transfer would be done in less than a minute.

'Did I see a coffee machine out there by the entrance door?' Bishop asked.

'Yeah,' Tony said. 'It's pretty good, too. And only a dollar a cup.'

'Gerry, get me some, will you? And make it strong and black. I need something to keep me from passing out. I'll be with you once this is finished.'

Gerry shrugged, said, 'Okay,' and left, closing the door behind him.

Bishop looked up at Tony. 'You said you empty this drive every fortnight?'

'That's right. Planning to do it the day after tomorrow.'

'How would you feel about bringing it forward a couple of days?'

Tony brought his brows together. 'What, wipe it now? And what if the cops show up later wanting to see it?'

'They're not likely to, but if they do just tell them the truth. That you wipe the drive clean on a regular basis and they're too late.'

'Yeah, but why?'

The progress bar disappeared. Bishop pulled the flash drive from the slot and got to his feet. 'I've just given you two hundred reasons why.'

Tony snorted and said, 'Can't argue with that kind of logic, can I?'

Then he sat down and began deleting the files.

TWELVE

Bishop took a sip of the hot coffee and sat on one end of the park bench. Gerry sat at the other and drank some of his. They were the only visitors in the small triangular-shaped residential park area they'd passed earlier. Trees concealed them from the streets on all three sides and even filtered out some of the noise.

The coffee wasn't likely to win any awards, but it wasn't bad. And it was strong. Which was exactly what Bishop needed right now. It was almost half past one and he realized he hadn't slept in over thirty hours. And probably wouldn't for a long while yet. But the caffeine would help keep him going for now. That and constant forward motion.

But mostly it was the knowledge that he was getting closer to finding these animals. And when he did find them, he had definite plans for all three. He'd been thinking about it all morning. About how he wasn't going to kill them. That would be too easy. No, Willard's little speech to Foland last night had given him the idea. He knew from personal experience that prison life was almost a hell on earth, and he wanted these three to get the full effect. A lifetime's worth. But even if he managed to link them to Amy's rape and mugging, they'd still only end up serving a few years inside. And that wasn't nearly enough. Which meant he'd have to set them up for something worse. Either individually or as a group, it didn't matter. But the thought of framing them for a crime that would guarantee they'd never see daylight again was something that really appealed to Bishop. Especially as the same thing had happened to him a while back.

What goes around comes around.

Gerry said, 'So will you be able to track down that licence plate?'

Bishop emerged from his thoughts. 'Maybe.'

He pulled out his cell and began scrolling through his contact list until he got to Raymond Massingham. Bishop had met him some months ago in Saracen, Arizona. The guy had a computer repair shop there. He was also able to access information generally unavailable to the public, often through unauthorized back doors passed on to him by like-minded friends.

Bishop pressed the call button. A few seconds later a voice said, 'Yeah?'

'This is Bishop. You remember me?'

Raymond made a low chuckling sound. 'You kidding me? How could I forget? Five months after the fact and people are still talking about what went down here. So how's things back east?'

'Things could be better. Look, I need a small favour.'

'Ha. Never were one for chewing the fat, were you, Bishop? How small?'

'I've got most of a licence plate and I'd like a name and address to go with it. And I seem to recall you had a special relationship with the dedicated servers at the DMV.'

'Yeah, well, you know what they say, "Servers don't change, only people." I can sure give it a try. Hit me.'

Bishop gave him the first five digits and said, 'The last number was partly obscured, but it's either an eight or a nine. And the sooner the better.'

'Yeah, I kind of guessed that. Okay, let me work and I'll call you back in three.'

Bishop ended the call and placed the cell phone between them on the bench. He smoothed out the heavy creases in his pants, took another sip of coffee and said, 'Okay, I think now would be a good time for us to part ways.'

Gerry turned to him. 'Hey, wait a minute, back at that deli you said I could come along.'

'And you did. Now you need to go back to the hospital.'

'Hey, don't shut me out yet, Bishop. Come on.'

Bishop stared up at the sky. Back at the deli he'd felt sorry for the guy, but he was already regretting bringing Gerry along. Even part of the way. It had been a mistake. Especially as he looked to be getting close to locating his quarry.

He turned to his brother-in-law. 'What do you think's going to happen when I finally catch up with these men?'

'You'll . . .' Gerry frowned at the grass. 'Well, you'll deal with them.'

'Deal with them. Okay. And how am I going to deal with them?'

Gerry made an impatient rotating gesture with his free hand. 'You'll . . . Are you going to make me say it?'

'Yes.'

'Okay. You'll kill them.'

'What, like Charles Bronson, you mean?'

Gerry winced. 'No, I don't mean that. But you're not—'

'Even assuming that's the case,' Bishop interrupted, 'how do you think Amy would react if she ever found out I took you along? She's already accepted me as a lost cause, but you're the father of her children and I assume the love of her life. You think she'd ever forgive me for involving you in a personal vendetta? Because if you do, you don't know her as well as I thought.'

'Believe me,' Gerry said, 'I know full well how Amy would react, but right now she's somewhere I can't even reach her. And the men who caused it are treating the whole thing like it was just another night on the town. They're animals, Bishop. You know they are. I just need to know that at least we're on the right track and getting somewhere. Just for my own peace of mind. After that I'll let you get on with it and leave you alone. I swear.'

Bishop drank down the rest of the coffee. This was getting them nowhere. And no amount of arguing could change the fact. Gerry wasn't coming. It was that simple.

The cell phone started ringing. Gerry reached it first and put it on speaker. Bishop shrugged and said, 'Any luck?'

Raymond said, 'Hey, luck's for the other guys, right? Okay, we've got two results. Both Fords. The one with the eight at the end is for a Discovery, first registered back in . . .'

'That's not it,' Bishop said. 'The other one. Is it a Taurus, by any chance?'

'Ker-ching. You notice how I don't even ask how you knew that? Don't suppose you wanna take a guess at the owner's zip code, too?'

Bishop already had a pretty good idea. According to the time code, the car had pulled into the filling station at 23.32, only two minutes after Everson had spotted them leaving the scene. Which made it a good bet that Tony's place had been the first place they'd tried. So if they were heading in a northerly direction that meant only one destination.

'The Bronx.'

Ray let out a bark of laughter. 'You ever wanna play the tables in Vegas, just let me know, huh? Yeah, Co-op City, to be exact. Vehicle is registered to a Pablo Whelan, whose abode is apartment 1902 in building 30A, Section 5. How's that for service?'

'Pretty good. I appreciate it, Raymond.'

'Sure. So if I were to ask what's the hell's going on, would I be wasting my breath?'

'Yeah, but you already knew that. Thanks. We'll talk again.'

'When you need another favour, I expect. Be good.'

Bishop ended the call and pocketed the cell phone. He turned to Gerry and said, 'Well, that's it.'

'Right,' Gerry said, 'let's go find a cab.'

Bishop stood up with his eyes narrowed. 'Forget it. This is where we part, remember?'

Gerry shook his head. 'Sorry, Bishop, but I need to see one of them in the flesh first. Just to be able to look into his eyes. That's all. I'm sure you understand.'

'I said forget it. You're not coming.'

'In that case, I have to make a call.' Gerry reached into his jacket pocket and pulled out a card along with his Samsung. Bishop could see the card was a duplicate of the one Medrano had given him. Gerry began pressing numbers on the phone.

'What are you doing?'

'Updating Detective Medrano on what we've found out so far, including this Whelan's address. I'll also tell him about Tony, so he can view the same footage we saw.'

Bishop didn't need this. Not now. 'Trying to call my bluff, Gerry? Is that it?'

'No bluff, Bishop. If I don't go, then we leave everything in the hands of the police.' He keyed in two more numbers.

'That phone looks expensive. Don't force me to break it.'

'If you do, I'll just use a pay phone.'

Gerry pressed another three numbers, then Bishop heard a ringing tone. Soon a familiar voice said, 'Detective Medrano. Who's this?'

'Hello, detective. It's Gerry Philmore.'

'Oh, right. Yeah. So what can I do for you, Mr Philmore?'

Gerry looked up at Bishop without expression. Waiting.

'Mr Philmore?' Medrano repeated. 'You there?'

Bishop knew he'd already lost. The stupid bastard would do it. He'd give the cops everything if he didn't get what he wanted. He was that self-centred. And Bishop could do nothing to stop him. Except one thing. Bishop sighed, then gave a small nod of his head.

Gerry nodded back and said, 'Just wanted to see if you'd progressed any since this morning, detective.'

'Look, Mr Philmore,' Medrano said, with a hint of impatience. 'I told you we'd keep you updated, but I also got a full caseload to deal with, so I can't be giving you reports on an hourly basis. That's not why I gave you my card. Now, when your wife regains consciousness, you give me a call. But until then I need you to let me do my job, okay?'

'Sure, I understand, detective. Sorry to bother you.' Gerry closed the connection and pocketed the phone. 'Sorry, Bishop, but I really need this.'

'You don't know *what* you need right now,' Bishop said. 'But no more games, understand? You get one look at this Whelan and then you go home. Because if you try pushing me into a corner again, you'll lose. That much I can guarantee. Do you believe me?'

'I believe you. So now we get a cab?'

'Not just yet,' Bishop said. 'I need to buy a few things first.'

THIRTEEN

Situated west of the Hutchinson River at the north-eastern tip of the Bronx, Co-op City wasn't exactly a place you visited unless you had to. But Bishop guessed it wasn't supposed to be. It was a public housing development, after all. One of the largest in the world, with its own public safety department, its own power plant, and two weekly newspapers. And more besides.

They were heading south along Hutchinson River Parkway East when the Indian cab driver pointed at the vast, chevron-style building to their left. 'Building 30, guys,' he said.

'Anywhere along here,' Bishop said.

The driver pulled in and Bishop and Gerry got out. The driver had agreed to keep the meter running rather than look around for another fare to carry back to Manhattan. Gerry wouldn't be staying long. If Whelan was here, he'd get his one look at the man and then go home, like he'd promised. And if Whelan wasn't home, the deal still stood.

Bishop looked up at the 26-storey high-rise. This one was almost as wide as it was tall, covering almost half a block. It wasn't pretty. But that was sixties architecture for you. He turned to Gerry. 'Remember what we agreed?'

'I remember. Don't worry, I'll keep my promise.'

Bishop wasn't sure he believed him. But they crossed the quiet street and walked down the concrete path onto the property without another word. Bishop looked through the concrete pillars that took up much of the ground floor, saw a set of double doors to the left and went that way. He spotted half a dozen bored teenage males standing around and smoking up ahead. They stopped talking and stared at Bishop and Gerry as they approached.

'Need somethin' to take the edge off, m'man?' one of them called over. 'Smokes? Candy? 'Cause if we ain't got it, we can get it.'

'We're good, thanks,' Bishop said without slowing. *Unless you got some coffee.*

He opened one of the doors and stepped into a plain windowless lobby area. There was an elevator bank straight ahead and a door leading to the fire stairs on the right. The concrete walls were painted in uneven hues of grey, probably in an effort to cover up old graffiti. The floor was grimy with dirt.

'What's that smell?' Gerry asked from beside him.

'I don't want to know,' Bishop said, and stepped over to the elevators. He pressed the up button and waited. A minute later the doors slid open and they stepped inside. It smelled even worse in the confined space. Bishop breathed though his mouth as he pressed the button for 19, and a minute later the doors opened again.

Directional signs on the wall ahead advised them to turn left for rooms 1901 to 1910. As they walked down the bare, dimly lit corridor, Bishop could hear loud music and equally loud televisions coming from apartments on both sides. When he reached 1902 at the end, he looked at Gerry and raised a finger to his lips while pointing to the left. As Gerry moved out of the way, Bishop pressed his ear against the door just below the glass peephole. He heard no sounds coming from inside.

He pressed the buzzer and waited thirty seconds. There was no response. He tried again and waited a little longer. Same result.

Bishop reached into his pocket, pulled out the pair of cheap cotton gloves he'd bought in the store on Seaman Avenue and put them on. Gerry did the same. Now wasn't the time to get start getting careless. Bishop knelt down and checked the lock. It was a deadbolt, which was about what he'd expected. From another pocket he took out the EZ Snap lockpick gun he'd brought back with him from Pennsylvania.

He usually took it with him on jobs. It was amazing how often it came in handy. And it wasn't even illegal. Yet. Bishop had ordered this one from Amazon. He also had a few more lying around his house on Staten Island, just in case they ever decided to ban them. From the same pocket he also took a double-ended tension wrench, which he worked into the keyhole. He inserted the needle of the gun just above it and pressed the trigger a few times, using his thumb to apply torque pressure to the wrench. When he felt the pins jump into the hole casing, he pocketed the tools and quietly opened the door.

'Wait here,' he whispered. Gerry nodded and Bishop went inside.

There was a long, narrow hallway leading off to his left, with three open doorways on the right hand side. The hallway ended in another open doorway that looked as if it might lead to the bedroom. There was a fifth doorway directly in front of him, but the door was closed. Bishop used the knuckle of his index finger to push it open.

It was a large living area. Bishop took a few steps inside and saw magazines and old pizza boxes scattered over the hardwood floor. Against one wall was a fairly large flat-screen Sony TV. Underneath that, a Blu-Ray player with numerous discarded DVD cases. Items of clothing were strewn about. No female clothing. The room's sole east-facing window overlooked more high-rises in the distance. The only furniture was a ratty-looking couch, two matching chairs and an uneven coffee table, one leg supported by a coverless paperback. On the table were more magazines. Lying amongst them were a small, clear plastic bag containing a few crumbs of off-white powder, a Zippo lighter and a discoloured spoon.

A Latino man with a thin goatee was lying on the couch with his eyes closed. He looked to be in his mid-twenties. Bishop couldn't be sure, but he looked like the driver from the footage. He was stocky and wore the same hooded sweatshirt. One arm was looped over the side of the couch with the hand touching the floor. Next to the hand was an empty hypodermic syringe.

Even from here, Bishop could see he wasn't breathing.

FOURTEEN

'Christ,' Gerry said from behind him. 'Is he dead?'

'I told you to wait outside,' Bishop said, and crossed the room. He removed his left glove, knelt down and felt the carotid artery under the man's ear. No pulse. But the skin was still warm. This had happened recently. He dipped a finger into the bag on the table, then tapped it against his tongue. He was no expert, but the intensely bitter taste suggested heroin. Bishop replaced the glove and said, 'Dead, all right. Looks like an overdose.'

'Shit. Really?' Gerry paused, then said, 'The son of a bitch got off easy.'

'The end result's still the same,' Bishop said, despite agreeing with the sentiment. He *had* got off easy. 'But it makes things difficult.'

'What do you mean?'

'He can't exactly tell me who his friends are now, can he? I just hope he left some names lying around.' He turned to Gerry, who was standing at the doorway and staring at the body with large eyes. His thin hair was in complete disarray and hanging off his forehead in coils, while his skin had an unhealthy pallor. Not surprising if this was the first time he'd seen a dead body. 'And what you need to do is leave, like you said you would. I'll handle things from here on.'

'Yeah. Okay.' Gerry took a deep breath and said, 'But look, it'll go a lot quicker if we both search. And the cab's still waiting outside. If you find an address or a lead, I can let you out on the way and then head on back alone.'

Bishop rubbed a hand over his scalp, thinking. He didn't like Gerry hanging around any longer than necessary, but on the other hand he couldn't really find a hole in his logic. Especially as he hadn't seen too many cabs patrolling this particular neighbourhood on the way in.

Finally, he said, 'Okay, start with the room at the end while I check in here. I want notebooks, paperwork, or even better a cell phone. Anything with a name on it. And keep your gloves on at all times.'

'You don't have to remind me,' Gerry said, and left.

Bishop took in the room again. He'd already seen enough to know something wasn't right here. Apart from the obvious, of course. He inspected Whelan's arms. The right had a few old gang tats, but nothing else. On the left, buried amongst more tats, was a single needle mark. And it was fresh. So Whelan had just this day decided to start mainlining pure heroin. Which didn't seem too likely. He might have snorted the stuff up till now, but Bishop doubted it. The guy was in too good a shape. The last thing on an addict's mind is his physical fitness. And then there was the TV and the Blu-Ray player over there. And all the DVDs. Anyone with a serious habit would have traded them in for junk long before now.

All of which suggested there'd been somebody else in this apartment recently. Helping Whelan on his way. But why?

He searched the man's clothes and paused when he felt something in the rear pants pocket. He reached in and pulled out a stainless steel butterfly knife. Or *balisong*, as it was known in its native Philippines. An intricately designed folding knife made up of two handles that counter-rotated around the tang. Loved by gang members everywhere and illegal in most states. Bishop had once trained up on them in the Corps and knew all too well how deadly they were. Holding it by the safe handle, Bishop flicked his thumb under the catch, performed a double twirl of the wrist and watched the knife flip open in a rapid blur of motion.

Good, smooth action. Somebody had kept it regularly oiled. Bishop flipped it closed in a single movement and stuck it in his own pocket. Never knew when something like this might come in useful, and it was no good to Whelan any more. Assuming it ever had been.

He finished his search of the clothes, but didn't find a cell phone. Just a cheap, faux-leather wallet with the usual stuff inside. Driver's licence. Social Security card. A few other pieces of ID. No cash. He placed the wallet on the table and flipped through the magazines. *Guns & Ammo. Black Booty. Tactical Knives. Teenage Nymphs.* More variations along the same general theme. But no paperwork hidden between them.

Bishop suddenly heard the muffled sound of a ringing phone coming from somewhere in the apartment. He walked over to the discarded clothes and the sound became more pronounced. He picked up a pile of T-shirts and saw it was coming from an AT&T console and answering machine on the floor. The cordless phone was still in its charging base. The ringing stopped and an automated voice asked the caller to leave a message after the tone.

'Pab,' a man's voice said, 'it's Carlos. Where you at, man? You ain't been answering your cell. I tried Yuri's, but it keeps going to voicemail. Look, we need to talk. I think our black boy's following me around. Wherever I go, I keep seeing flashes of a dude looks just like him. I'm telling you, man, that guy freaks me out and you know I don't scare easy. And I don't like Yuri switching off his cell either. I'm getting the feeling our employer's tying up loose ends, and we're at the shit end of the stick. Look, you get this message then you come meet me by the pool tables at the back of Angelo's, okay? I'll wait here another hour or two. And if you can get hold of Yuri, bring him along. We need to talk about what to do. Okay, man? Later.'

Carlos hung up and a beep sounded from the answering machine. Bishop just stood there and looked at it, trying to make sense of what he'd just heard. Yuri was a Russian name. Meaning he could well be the one who'd referred to Amy last night as a *suka*. But more important, it sounded to Bishop as though these three, Whelan, Carlos and Yuri, had been *paid* to assault Amy. Maybe even kill her. Which made no sense at all. And who was the black guy? Was he the one who'd hired them? Because if this Carlos was right about him tying up loose ends, it would answer the questions hanging over Whelan's death. It also explained the missing cell phone. *Cleaning up loose ends.*

And although it didn't explain why Amy was at the park at all, it implied they'd known she'd be at that particular place at that particular time. The attack hadn't been random at all. It had been *planned* that way.

Which put a whole new perspective on things.

First things first, though. Bishop needed to find out more about

Angelo's. He was reaching down for the cordless when he noticed Gerry standing in the doorway, holding a rolled-up magazine.

'What was he talking about, Bishop?' Gerry asked. 'Is he saying somebody told them to go after Amy *on purpose?*'

'Hey, I just got here, same as you. Did you find anything in the other rooms? A cell phone, maybe?'

'No phone. And the only paperwork I found was a rental agreement for this place.'

'What's that in your hand?'

'Just an old gun magazine he had lying around.'

'Let me see.'

Gerry paused for a beat, then brought it over and said, 'Check the mailing label.'

Bishop took the magazine and saw it was a year-old copy of *Soldier of Fortune*. And in the bottom right-hand corner was a subscriber's address label. It was made out to a Mr Y. Vasilyev. The address was Apt. 1907, Building 23, Benchley Place. Looked like Pablo and Yuri might have made a habit of borrowing magazines from each other. Which simplified things.

He looked up at Gerry. 'Planning on keeping this from me too, were you?'

'No, of course not. I was coming to show you when I heard that message.'

Bishop wasn't sure Gerry was telling the whole truth, but he said nothing. It was a good lead, but it could wait. He picked up the cordless and dialled 411 for information.

Right now he needed to find out where the hell this Angelo's was located.

FIFTEEN

Both men were silent as the cab driver took them down Westchester Avenue. Mid-afternoon and the elevated IRT lines above shrouded everything in shadows, making the day seem older than it was. Bishop just stared out of the window and watched the passing street signs.

The local operator had told him there was only one Angelo's in the 718 area code. Located on St Paul's Avenue in the Pelham Bay area. Right around here, in fact. He'd kept the exact address from Gerry, though. He didn't want him getting any more ideas. He just wanted him gone.

Bishop suddenly spotted the sign he wanted on the right. He let the driver carry on for another block and said, 'Pull over here.'

As soon as the driver came to a stop, Bishop turned to Gerry and said, 'You're going straight back to the hospital, right? Because Lisa and Pat need you there. Amy, too.'

Gerry gave a single nod. 'You kept your promise,' he said. 'I'll keep mine.'

'Good.' Bishop got out. He shut the door and watched the cab as it slowly pulled out into the traffic. Once it disappeared from sight, he turned and began walking in the opposite direction.

It was a noisy street. There were no traffic lights and large delivery vans constantly zoomed by in both directions. Bishop narrowly avoided colliding with a kid on a bike and then turned left onto St Paul's Avenue. On the left-hand side was a fenced-off parking area. On the right, a one-storey building which extended all the way back for about fifty yards. About two-thirds of the way down was a tinted glass door with a sign above that read *Angelo's – Bar & Pool Hall*.

Bishop crossed over and walked towards it. Two men stood near the door, smoking and not talking to each other. Bishop ignored them, opened the door and went inside.

The place was dimly lit, with no windows. There was a bar running along the opposite wall. Half a dozen men of various ages sat on barstools, drinking, and a wide-shouldered, pony-tailed bartender was wiping glasses behind the bar. He looked up at Bishop without interest, then went back to cleaning.

There were some tables and chairs to the left. All empty. Signs for the restrooms pointed to a hallway in the corner. Some kind of rap music was coming from the right. Not too loud in volume, but heavy on the bass. Underneath that, the familiar sound of cue sticks smashing hard resin balls across felt. Bishop saw six pool tables in a single row, all in use. It looked pretty busy down there. Especially in comparison to this side.

Bishop walked over to the bartender, paid for a bottle of Corona and took it over to the pool section. He found a space against one wall and stood there, sipping at his beer and getting a sense of the room. Looked like everybody was playing regular eightball. Mostly one-on-one, although on the third table a pair of girls were playing two boys. There were a few customers standing around and watching as they drank, like Bishop. Others carried on conversations with friends who were playing. Bishop saw a fair few Latino guys in their twenties amongst them, but that didn't necessarily mean anything. Apart from the two girls, any one of these people could be Carlos. Assuming Carlos was in here at all.

Well, there was an easy way to find out.

Bishop pulled out his cell, accessed his settings and turned off his caller ID. He'd already dialled *69 at Whelan's place and gotten the number for the last received call. Now he keyed it in and held his thumb over the call button. He checked to see who was already using their cells. Just one of the girls, texting. Nobody else that he could see.

He pressed the call button.

His eyes darted in all directions, trying to watch everybody at the same time. Seeing who'd reach for their phone. Then he noticed a movement to his right. Between the fourth and fifth table, a guy with his back to Bishop was reaching into his pocket as he watched the game. He pulled out a cell phone and brought it to his ear. Bishop disconnected the call and kept watching. After a few moments, the man took the phone from his ear and peered down at the screen. Then he turned around.

Bishop kept his eyes on the game in front of him. In his peripheral vision, he could see the man slowly moving his head as he searched the room. Carlos must have already figured somebody was trying to draw him out. But then he'd sounded pretty paranoid in that message. His gaze finally came to rest on Bishop and his head stopped moving.

Bishop had the bottle to his lips and took a sip, trying to look as bored as possible. But his instincts were telling him he'd already been made. For all he knew, he was the only non-regular in here, standing out like a T-bone in a vegan restaurant.

Carlos casually crossed to the opposite side and began walking towards the long bar. Purposely not paying attention to anyone. He was about five-nine, wearing tracksuit pants and sweatshirt. His long dark hair was held in place with a headband. Bishop watched as he continued down past the bar and kept going. When he entered the hallway in the corner, Bishop placed his bottle on the nearest empty table and followed.

He hadn't given too much thought to what he was going to do next, except that he wanted the man alive. Thanks to an enigmatic message left on an answering machine, what had at first seemed like a random assault and rape had turned into something more. And he needed to know what. But it couldn't hurt to be prepared for the worst. Carlos had to know he'd be getting company soon. As he entered the hallway leading to the restrooms, Bishop pulled the butterfly knife from his pocket and held it at his side.

The corridor was about twenty feet long with a sharp right turn at the end. There were two doors on the right. Men's and women's. Bishop placed a hand on the door to the men's room. He was about to push it open when he heard the sound of a metal door being slammed further down.

Bishop ran to the end and turned right. The fire exit door was in front of him. He ran out into a small rear yard, and saw a wooden gate on the left hanging open. He ran through and looked right. Nothing. He turned left and saw Carlos about thirty feet away, sprinting along the sidewalk towards Westchester Avenue. Bishop set off after him.

If he lost the creep now, he'd never find him again.

Up ahead, Carlos had almost reached the corner. He glanced behind him, saw Bishop going full out and faced front again. A gap presented itself and he ran into the street. A car sped by, narrowly missing him and honking its horn as it passed. Carlos reached the centre line and stopped, traffic still whizzing by on either side. He took another quick glance behind him. Bishop was only twenty feet from Westchester. Ten feet.

He'd just reached the corner when he saw Carlos suddenly backing into the lane he'd just crossed without checking the traffic behind him. *What the hell?*

Bishop was about to shout when a loud horn erupted from his left. There was a savage screeching of brakes. Then he watched as a large box truck slammed right into Carlos at forty miles an hour. The man twisted through the air like a rag doll in slow motion and landed on the asphalt in a broken heap. The truck came to a halt inches from his body. Vehicles in the other lane slowed. Within seconds all the traffic on the street had come to a standstill.

From the unnatural angle of Carlos's neck, Bishop could immediately tell he was dead. Probably killed on impact. But what had got him so scared? Bishop scanned the sidewalk on the other side and saw numerous pedestrians glancing over. They were talking amongst themselves, clearly curious about what the commotion was. But Bishop's attention was drawn to a large black man standing on his own. He had his hands in his overcoat pockets and didn't look curious at all. Bishop couldn't make out too many details at this distance, but he seemed to be looking directly at Bishop. Then a group of people ran into the street, blocking his view, and Bishop lost sight of him.

He dashed into the street, reached the centre line and looked in both directions, trying to get a glimpse of the man again.

But there was no sign. The guy was gone.

SIXTEEN

Bishop gave the cab driver an extra twenty and got out. The journey had taken less than ten minutes, and he'd spent most of it wondering what the hell Amy had gotten herself into. He still found it inconceivable that she could have done anything that warranted the kind of treatment she'd received. And now two of his suspects were dead. Yuri Vasilyev was his last chance to get some answers. Assuming the black guy hadn't gotten to him already.

As the cab pulled away, Bishop studied the street. Benchley Place was a short cul-de-sac off the Bellamy Loop, with three imposing, cross-shaped towers looming over it. Bishop moved towards the entrance for Building 23 on the right and went inside. He walked down a long hallway and eventually found himself in another lobby. It was cleaner than the last place, but no less bleak. A young Latino woman with a sleeping kid in a stroller was waiting in front of the elevator bank. Bishop stood next to her. It was another minute before the next car arrived. They entered and the woman pressed 12. Bishop pressed 19. The elevator rose.

When the doors opened the second time, Bishop stepped out onto the landing. He saw a floor plan stuck to one of the walls and went over for a look. Seen from above, the building was shaped like a fat plus sign, with the elevators taking up the central axis and all the apartments running off from the four branches. Bishop saw he wanted the corridor to his immediate right. He walked in that direction and stopped outside the door to 1907.

There was no spyhole in this door, but Bishop stood just to the side anyway. He put on the gloves again, then rapped twice on the door.

About five seconds later, a muffled low-pitched voice said, 'Yeah?'

'It's Carlos,' Bishop said in his best imitation of the voice he'd heard on the answering machine.

'Oh, okay.'

Bishop heard the sounds of latches being drawn back. He got himself ready. As soon as the door began to open, Bishop slammed his body hard against it and bulldozed his way in, shoving the door back as far as it would go. There was the sound of something thumping against the wall, and then Bishop was inside. He quickly shut the door and looked down at the figure on the floor.

'Oh, great,' he said, shaking his head. 'Just wonderful.'

The low-pitched voice had belonged to a scrawny, petite, long-haired brunette dressed in vest and panties. Bishop guessed she was no older than twenty. Possibly younger. Must have smoked a hell of a lot of cigarettes to get a voice like that. She was also unconscious. That sound he'd heard would have been her head colliding with the wall.

He looked around and saw they were in a small foyer with four doors leading off from it. Straight ahead was the living room. To the left were the kitchen and the bathroom. To the right, the bedroom area. He listened for other signs of life in the apartment, but heard only silence. He checked anyway, and discovered the place was empty.

He came back, reached down and picked up the girl. She weighed practically nothing. He carried her into the bedroom and laid her out on the unmade double bed. She was out of it for now, but for how long? He'd prefer not to be identified if he could help it. He checked the bedroom door and saw a keyhole, but no key. Not a problem. From his pocket, he pulled out his own set of keys and found the one with all the grooves filed down to their minimum settings. This was his bump key. Same principle as the gun, but for simpler mechanisms. It could also lock them, too. You just had to do everything in reverse.

Once the girl was locked inside, Bishop made his way into the living room. It had a similar layout to Whelan's, but this one boasted a floor-to-ceiling window with a small balcony outside. A couch and some chairs were arranged around an old TV. There was an old mountain bike resting against one wall, and next to that a bookcase filled with piles of magazines. Bishop could guess the subject matter. At the bottom of the bookcase was a set of long drawers.

Bishop knelt down and pulled open the first drawer. Inside were piles of what looked like old bills, with pens and pencils scattered around. There was also a half-used roll of ¾-inch electrical tape at the back. That would come in useful. He put it in his pocket. He was about to close the drawer when he heard the sound of rattling keys in the hallway outside.

Bishop jumped to his feet and ran into the bathroom, closing the door until all that was left was a thin sliver. The bathroom was pretty cramped, with a large sink and a john against one wall. Opposite was a combo bath and shower, with an empty towel rack affixed to the wall further along. Light came from a long, thin, frosted window at head height. Bishop watched the foyer through the crack. He pulled the *balisong* from his pocket and did his rapid hand flick thing, and the blade popped out. Then he heard the sound of a key being inserted into the front door lock.

The door opened and a Caucasian man stepped inside. He was about Bishop's height, but stockier. He wore an army jacket and baggy chinos. His hair was cut close to his head and Bishop could make out a tattoo crawling up his neck like a snake.

'Jeannie, you stupid little bitch,' he called out, 'you forgot to lock door again. How many times I have to tell you? You want me to teach you another lesson?' The accent behind the words was unmistakably Russian, but Bishop thought his English was pretty good. He closed the front door with his foot and said, 'Where are you? Jeannie?'

Bishop edged back from the bathroom door and coughed softly.

He got himself ready. The bastard wouldn't know what hit him.

Two seconds later, the door exploded inwards and a freight train smashed into Bishop. He lost his grip on the knife and heard it clatter across a surface as something hard connected with his chin. Then he was down on the floor with the heavier Russian on top of him. Bishop quickly reduced the man's options by wrapping his arms around him in a bear hold, but the Russian used what little space he had left and started pummelling Bishop's guts and kidneys with both fists.

One-two-three-four. The blows came in quick succession. Each hit forced more breath from Bishop's body, but he held on as if his life depended on it. Which it did.

He kept kicking out with his right knee, but the Russian was too close and he couldn't get any traction. He also knew he couldn't take much of this. If he didn't get on top of the situation fast, he was a goner.

The bathroom was too small. No room to move. But he'd been in close-quarters skirmishes before. You just had to adapt and use what you had. Bishop glanced around quickly but couldn't see the knife anywhere. So no weapons except his hands and feet. Fine. Bishop calculated the possibilities and in less than a second decided a well-aimed frog punch would work best for this situation. He took another hit to the gut. Then he grunted in response to another one in the ribs.

Ignoring the damage being done, he clenched his left hand into a fist, extending the second knuckle of his middle finger outward to form a point. He had to be careful here. He'd seen a man die from one of these delivered to the temple, and that was the last thing he wanted. But he needed to get control of the situation and this was the best he had.

He took another punch to the kidneys, then released the Russian from the bear hold and aimed a left hook about an inch below the man's left temple. He felt the middle knuckle connect with the soft area at side of the man's skull and the Russian cried out in pain and rolled off Bishop with one hand clasping his head.

Bishop went with him, then flexed his right arm and rammed the tip of his elbow into the man's stomach with all his weight. The Russian let loose a hoarse grunt and Bishop delivered another elbow punch to the same place. And with the same amount of force. The Russian cried out something and doubled over.

Bishop had raised his arm for another shot when the Russian spun round and swiped at him with a backhand punch. Bishop moved his head back to avoid the blow and felt it connect with the sink behind him. Ignoring the sudden pain, he reached up and grabbed hold of the porcelain with one hand to steady himself and quickly clambered to his feet.

The Russian was on his back now and had one hand pressed to the floor as though about to rise. Bishop didn't let him get any further than the thought. He pulled his left foot back and kicked the Russian in the balls with everything he had.

While the man writhed, Bishop took a deep breath and shook his head to get rid of the cobwebs, then looked around until he saw the knife he'd dropped. It had fallen into the bathtub. He bent over and picked it up.

The Russian was still doubled over in agony and Bishop crouched down and leaned in close. He pressed the point of the *balisong* blade against the man's Adam's apple and said, 'You want to die, Yuri?'

'No,' Vasilyev hissed. His eyes were shut and his hands were pressed against his groin. 'I don't wanna die. Shit. Who are you?'

'Shut up,' Bishop said. He quickly patted the guy down with his free hand, but Yuri wasn't carrying. 'Okay, on your stomach. Hands behind your back. Now.'

Yuri grunted and slowly straightened himself out until he was face down on the linoleum floor. He pulled his arms around until both hands were resting against his butt. Bishop pulled the electrical tape from his pocket and jammed a knee in Yuri's back to keep him in place. He tucked the knife in his waistband, found the end of the tape and used most of it to bind the man's wrists together. It wasn't as good as duct tape, but it would do. Once he was satisfied, Bishop got to his feet and said, 'Okay. Get up.'

'Where to?'

'Next door. Move.'

Yuri tried to bring his knees up, but the linoleum was slippery. He quickly slid back onto his stomach. 'I can't get up. Help me, yeah?'

Bishop grabbed the neck of his jacket and hauled him upright, then pushed him through the doorway and into the living room. 'Sit on the floor against the couch,' he said. 'Legs crossed.'

Yuri stopped just before the couch and gingerly lowered himself to the floor. 'Oh, my balls,' he said. He carefully crossed both legs until he was in the lotus position and looked down at the floor. 'So what now?'

Bishop crouched down in front of him. 'Now we're gonna have us a little talk.'

SEVENTEEN

Bishop was in no rush. He let the man get his breath back first. And his own too, if he was entirely honest. The bastard had really put up a fight in there. Bishop would be all aches and bruises for the next twenty-four hours. But then, nothing in life came easy.

He studied the man's neck tattoo. It showed a snake coiled round a thin stiletto, not too dissimilar to those worn by the old Russian mafia. Another gangster wannabe, no doubt. After about a minute, Yuri finally looked up from the floor and said, 'I do something to you? Because if I did, I don't remember it.'

'What about last night? You remember back that far?'

Yuri blinked. 'Last night?'

'Yeah. You and your two pals, Pablo and Carlos, went for a walk in the park. Along with a lady named Amanda Philmore. Except only three of you came back out again. Is it coming back to you yet?'

'Park?' Yuri said. Bishop noticed a slight twitch beneath the man's right eye. 'What park? Hey, Jeannie let you in, yeah? What you do with her?'

Bishop pulled the butterfly knife from his waistband. Time to get this one focused on the subject at hand. He flipped it open with an exaggerated flourish and said, 'You don't want to know. But she won't be disturbing us. Trust me on that.'

'Oh, shit.'

'That's right, Yuri. Oh, shit. You recognize this knife?'

Yuri shook his head.

'I got it off your pal Pablo. He's dead in his apartment, by the way. Overdose, if you can believe that. Carlos, too. His death will go down as a road traffic accident, but I can assure you there's more to it than that.'

Yuri's eyes grew wide. 'You kill them both? Why? Who are you?'

'I'm the brother of the lady you and your pals raped and left for

72

dead last night. You all have yourselves a fine old time out there, or what?'

Yuri's shoulders slumped. He stared down at the floor again. 'You kill me too.'

'Well, that kind of depends on whether I get answers or not. Pablo and Carlos thought they could play me. They were wrong. They were also very stupid. I just hope you're a little smarter, Yuri, or this is going to be a very brief conversation.'

Yuri looked up. 'I'm smart. I learned English from book. What you want to know?'

'Everything. From the beginning. I want to know who hired you, and I want to know why.'

Yuri breathed out. 'I knew this was all wrong from the start. I just *knew* this.' He shook his head. 'Okay, look, this big black guy, yeah? Two days ago, he comes into this place we go to called Angelo's and gets talking to Carlos and me. I don't know where he gets our names from, but he knew we were available for work, yeah? He was a scary bastard, too. No sense of humour.'

'His name.'

Yuri snorted. 'You think he give us his name? It don't work that way.'

Bishop shrugged. It had been a long shot, but he'd had to ask. 'Go on.'

'Okay, so this guy, yeah? He says he wants us to get another guy and make sure we ready to move on his say-so. He says there's somebody causing problem in the city needs to be dealt with. But he isn't sure when yet. Or who. He'd pay good money for us to be on call, though. Like on standby. What's this word he used?'

'Retainer.'

Vasilyev nodded. 'Retainer. Yeah, yeah, that's it. We were retainers.'

Bishop didn't bother correcting him. 'He tell you why she'd been marked?'

'No, and I don't ask. All I care about was being paid, yeah? He said he'd call me soon on the public phone at Angelo's and wanted us all to be ready at a minute's notice. So me, Carlos and Pablo were there that night and last night, just playing pool and waiting for the call. Shit, you really kill Pablo and Carlos? And Jeannie, too?'

'Focus, Yuri. What time did the call come yesterday?'

'Uh, about fifteen after ten.'

'The same guy or somebody different?'

'Same guy. He had this weird accent, too, yeah? Like almost English, but not.'

'You mean mid-Atlantic?'

Yuri brought his brows together. 'Mid-Atlantic?'

'Half English, half American.'

He nodded. 'Yeah, yeah. Mid-Atlantic. Anyway, he said it would be a woman, and she'd be waiting halfway down Fort George Hill at eleven exactly. He gave us description of what she's wearing and told us to get moving. Pablo drove. We got there just before eleven and she was standing there just like he said.'

'What were your instructions?'

Yuri looked down again. 'We chase her into the park, yeah? We beat her up and make the whole thing look like a mugging, and then . . .' He fell silent.

'Then kill her.'

Yuri said nothing, just glanced out the window at his right.

Bishop was finding it very hard to stay in control of his emotions. Every part of him wanted to slowly slit Yuri's throat from ear to ear and watch him bleed out like the pig he was. Just listening to him talk about Amy was enough to make him go crazy. But he couldn't afford to lose it. Not now.

He showed Yuri the knife again. 'Who used this on my sister? You?'

Yuri turned back. 'Hey, not me, guy. I don't carry knives. It's Pablo who liked using the blade. Plus he was still pissed at her for using a taser thing on him. She was a real tough bi—'

Bishop had the knife at Yuri's throat before the Russian even knew what was happening. Yuri pulled his head away and Bishop stayed with him, pressing the knife point until it punctured the skin. A tiny stream of blood trickled down Yuri's neck. The Russian whimpered. Just an extra pound of pressure. That's all it would take. Bishop wanted to. He really wanted to. But he pulled back and said, 'What was that, Yuri?'

The Russian swallowed. 'Lady. That's what I was gonna say. She was a real tough lady. She don't go down easy.'

'No, she wouldn't have. The three of you sure taught her a lesson though, right?'

'Four.'

Bishop's eyes narrowed. 'What?'

'Four. *He* was there, too. The black guy. He must be waiting there in the park already. I don't know. But I noticed him first. He was standing under one of the trees, watching. Maybe he wanted to make sure job got done right. I don't know. He just let us work on her. Later he came over and took something from her bag and put it in his pocket.'

'What did he take?'

'Hey, I don't know. It was dark, yeah? But something small. That's all I can tell you.'

'Then what did he do?'

'He, uh, he warns us not to get carried away and make sure we finish the job like we agreed. Then he went away.'

'Uh huh. So the rape was like a bonus to you guys. Who went first on her, Yuri? You?' Bishop flipped the knife closed, one-handed. Then he flipped it open. The image of Amy's battered face was at the forefront of his mind. He could feel the rage taking over. Things were starting to turn grey around the edges. Part of him welcomed it, but the logical part told him to keep his anger at a slow boil. He wasn't done with this idiot yet. He wanted to make absolutely sure he'd extracted every last piece of information from him first. Then he'd place him in cold storage somewhere until he figured out what kind of hell he was going to send him to.

Yuri was watching the knife's progress with wide eyes. 'Hey, guy, I tell you the truth, I swear. It was just a job, yeah?'

Bishop gave Yuri a smile completely devoid of humour and said, 'Sure, Yuri, I understand. Now let's go through it all again. Only this time we're gonna go into a lot more detail, okay?'

'Sure,' he said, nodding, 'okay. But I tell you one thing I—'

Then Bishop heard a sharp crack and a hole suddenly appeared in Yuri's left cheek.

EIGHTEEN

Bishop instantly dived to the left and rolled his body along the floor away from the couch. Behind him he heard more popping sounds in quick succession. When he felt he'd covered enough space, he rose on one knee and turned at the hip until he was facing the doorway. His left hand was already drawn back, and he prepared to throw the knife . . .

And saw his brother-in-law standing there, with a revolver still aimed at Yuri, the hammer clicking on a now empty chamber.

'Gerry?' Bishop said, and slowly lowered his arm. He pocketed the knife and glanced over at Yuri to his left. The man's head lay back against the couch, his eyes staring sightlessly up at the ceiling. In addition to the cheek wound, Bishop saw two small holes in his forehead and one in his left temple. Blood leaked slowly from each wound and dripped onto the couch. If he wasn't dead now, it was only a matter of seconds.

Gerry just kept pulling the trigger as though in some kind of trance.

'Hey, Gerry?' Bishop said quietly. 'How we doing over there?'

He stopped firing then. He pulled his finger from the trigger guard and slowly lowered the gun. It looked to Bishop like an old .22 Colt Trooper. Which explained the muted sounds of the shots. In an enclosed space, a .22 usually sounded more like a firecracker going off than actual gunfire. That was something. Bishop was also glad to see Gerry was still wearing the gloves.

Gerry turned to Bishop. His eyes were orbs. 'When I heard him . . .' he mumbled. 'When I heard . . .' He shook his head, then dropped the gun on the carpet.

Bishop said, 'Where'd you get the gun?'

'Huh?'

'The gun. Is it yours?'

Gerry shook his head. 'No. No, it's not mine. I . . . I found it in that other apartment. In one of the bedroom drawers.'

Bishop nodded to himself. Gerry was a fool, but he was also a cunning one. He must have had this in mind all along. Earlier, when he'd said he'd keep his promise, he'd clearly been talking about the one he made to himself. To act out his Charles Bronson fantasy. Since he already had the address from the magazine cover, he must have gotten himself over here after Yuri arrived, then slipped in quietly through the front door and listened to the whole thing. Or most of it. Before he just lost it and started shooting. Complicating everything in the process, which is what idiots usually did. Well, the how and why didn't matter at the moment. Now it was simply a case of getting them both out of here, leaving as few traces as possible.

Gerry was staring at Yuri's body with a blank expression on his face. Bishop said, 'Have you taken those gloves off at any point this afternoon?'

Gerry slowly looked down at his hands and shook his head. 'No.'

'You sure? It's important.'

'No, I haven't take them off at all.'

'Okay. Good. Just leave the gun there on the floor. We're going now.'

Bishop grabbed Gerry by the arm and led him into the foyer. Pulling the front door open, he looked left and right. The outside hallway was empty. But it wouldn't stay that way for long. He glanced briefly at the locked bedroom door. The girl had to still be unconscious in there or they would have heard something. Bishop didn't feel comfortable with the thought of her waking and finding the body, but there was no other choice. They had to leave. Once they were out of the area, he'd call the cops. Hopefully, they'd get here before she awoke. They might even have the foresight to cover the body before letting her out.

'Come on,' he said, and pulled Gerry into the hallway. He silently pulled the door to 1907 shut, then began leading his brother-in-law towards the elevators at the end.

'Where are we going?' Gerry asked as they walked. He still sounded dazed.

'Away from here. Don't talk now.'

They carried on down the hallway and reached the centre of the building without seeing anybody. Luck appeared to be with them. Not that Bishop believed in luck, particularly. He was more a believer in will, determination and opportunity. Ignoring the elevators, he kept moving until he found the doorway to the fire stairs. He pushed it open, took himself and Gerry down one level and opened the door to the eighteenth-floor landing. He dragged Gerry over to the elevator bank and pressed the down button. Hidden machinery began to whirr.

Gerry looked around and said, 'What are we doing on this floor?'

'I think it's better all round if we call the elevator from somewhere other than the nineteenth, don't you? You clear-headed yet?'

Gerry brought a hand to his forehead. 'Christ, Bishop, I just killed that guy.'

Yes, you did, Bishop thought, *and I've a feeling he still had plenty more to tell me.* But he said, 'It's done now, so try and forget it.'

'*Forget* it? I'm not like you, Bishop. It's not that easy.'

'You're right. You're not like me. And nothing in life ever comes easy. But you'll get over it. A month from now and this'll all seem like a bad dream.'

Gerry just looked at Bishop as though he'd just told him the moon was square. The elevator arrived. The doors slid apart, revealing an old black couple standing there, looking back at them. The man nodded at Bishop and said, 'Going down?'

Bishop pushed Gerry inside and said, 'All the way.'

NINETEEN

Bishop pushed open the door to the hospital waiting room and let Gerry enter first. A balding, grey-haired, rugged-looking man in his late sixties sat next to Pat, showing him something on his phone. In the next seat, a handsome, smartly dressed woman of the same age sat with her arm round a sleeping Lisa.

Gerry's parents. Bishop had never actually seen them in the flesh until now. He would have met them at Amy and Gerry's wedding fifteen years before had he not been posted overseas at the time. One of the drawbacks of military life was that sometimes you had to miss out on important family events.

The woman noticed them first. She carefully disentangled her arm from around Lisa's neck without waking her and got up. Gerry reached her and she gave him a long hug. The father and Pat got off the chairs and also came over.

'Where have you been?' the father said. 'We were getting worried when you didn't answer your phone.'

'Sorry about that, Dad,' Gerry said, and reached down to ruffle Pat's hair. 'I found out I had it on mute for some reason. Have they let you in to see Amy yet?'

'Not yet,' his mother said. 'But definitely within the hour. One of the doctors said she's still in the coma, but her condition's a lot more stable. We wanted to tell you.'

'Oh, thank God,' Gerry said, closing his eyes. Bishop also allowed himself a small smile. At least things seemed to improving here.

'Hi, Uncle James,' Pat said.

Bishop smiled down at his nephew. It always amused him when Pat and Lisa used his first name. They were about the only ones who

79

did. The boy's eyes were still red-rimmed, but he managed to smile back. 'Hey, Pat,' Bishop said. 'How you doing?'

Pat shrugged his small shoulders. ''Kay, I guess. I wanna see Mom, though.'

'And you will. Won't be long now. Just be patient.'

Gerry turned to him and said, 'You haven't met my folks, have you, Bishop? This here's my dad, Arnie, and this is Janice.'

Bishop shook their hands. 'Hello. Glad to meet you both.'

'It's just a shame it has to be under these circumstances,' Janice said. 'Poor dear Amy. The whole thing's just terrible. What's wrong with people these days?'

'The world's going to hell is what's wrong,' Arnie said. 'I just pray the police catch the bastards responsible and send them down forever. Do you think they will, Bishop?'

'The detective in charge seems capable enough,' he said.

After a moment's silence, Janice asked her son something about the kids' school situation. Bishop tuned out and just watched Gerry. He'd been watching him in the back of the cab, as well. It seemed whatever remorse he'd initially felt over the shooting had quickly dissipated. Either that or he was one of those people with the ability to compartmentalize their actions and move on without a backward thought. Gerry seemed the type. Or was it something else? Bishop still couldn't rid himself of the feeling that Gerry was hiding something from him. But what? And why?

He excused himself and left the room. He needed another coffee, but he also needed a few moments alone to think. He went to the same vending machine as before, got himself a cup and sipped at the warm liquid, gazing blankly at the hospital staff passing in front of him and mulling over his next step.

Because this wasn't finished yet. Not for him. Not by a long shot. The worker ants had been dealt with, but the one who'd given the order was still out there. And Bishop needed to find him. Or her. And not for any romantic notions of revenge, either. That might have been his overriding motive before, but not now. As far as the people behind this were concerned, Amy was unfinished business. She'd been marked for death, but the three morons they'd hired had bungled the job. Which meant as long as she was still breathing she was in danger. And it was up to Bishop to erase that danger.

He took a moment to reflect on the few facts he'd gleaned so far.

First, there was the black guy who'd recruited the three dead men. The one he'd caught a glimpse of outside Angelo's. Bishop couldn't quite see him as the man in charge, though. He was too much the professional. Bishop marked him down as a point man for his boss. The one who got things done. The one who'd been tasked to tie up the loose ends, and had almost succeeded before Bishop entered the picture.

But his presence at the park during Amy's assault was a crucial factor, too. The item he'd taken from her bag might have been the reason she'd been targeted in the first place. Possibly a data CD, or a memory stick, containing information that was vital to somebody. And the fact that Amy had been privy to that same information appeared to be reason enough to have her killed. These people clearly weren't taking any chances.

So the question was, from where had Amy acquired the information? Well, her workplace seemed the obvious bet. Amy had been a researcher with a company called Artemis International for almost a year now. Ever since Gerry had lost his job. Bishop knew they had offices out in Sunnyside, in Queens. Apparently, it was a small outfit that often worked alongside foreign governments to track down war criminals and bring them to justice. Real righteous stuff. Amy had been pretty jazzed about it at the time. Except what if it wasn't quite so righteous? What if it was also involved in some less-than-legal sideline that Amy found out about? Or she'd simply discovered something about one of her clients that they wanted to keep secret at any cost? Or what if one of the people they were hunting thought Amy was getting a little too close to their whereabouts and decided enough was enough?

It could even be a simple case of Amy's selling sensitive information on to somebody for profit. But Bishop didn't believe it. Not Amy. She'd always been the moral one. Always. She wouldn't suddenly change character now.

But there were any number of reasons why somebody might want

Amy dead. He just didn't know. He was still working in the dark at the moment. But he had to start somewhere, and her workplace seemed the obvious choice.

Bishop ran a palm over his head as he thought through one of the possibilities. Amy discovers something she can't ignore and decides to approach somebody about it. An outsider. Maybe a journalist. And this somebody urges her to gather evidence and physically smuggle it out, since lots of companies nowadays monitor email traffic. She stays late one night, waits until she's alone and then gets down to it. She arranges to hand the information over to the third party, at a pre-arranged spot at a pre-arranged time. That's why she's standing on Fort George Hill at 23.00.

Bishop frowned as he took another sip of the coffee. The bad guys must have suspected something was up, because they ordered the black guy to recruit some cheap thugs and keep them close by, just in case. And they had to have found out about Amy's meeting just beforehand, because Yuri had said he'd only been given forty-five minutes' notice. But it also raised the question of what happened to the third party. Why didn't he make the meeting? Had he been killed as well?

And then there was Gerry. Back at the start he'd withheld information from Bishop. He'd tried to explain it away, but Bishop wasn't completely convinced. Was there really something in it, or was it just Bishop's natural distrust of the man coming through? It was hard to tell. But he couldn't ignore it. All leads had to be checked, without exception. He just didn't know how yet.

Still too many questions, and too few answers. He needed to start reversing that ratio.

Then something else occurred to Bishop. Something that immediately made his blood run cold. Amy had tried to get hold of him two weeks ago. Could this have been the reason why? Had she been concerned enough about her situation to approach her kid brother for help? Was it possible? And by not getting back to her, was he to blame for her current condition? He knew it was more than possible. It was actually probable.

'Oh, Jesus Christ,' he whispered. 'No. Amy.'

He leaned back against the wall and closed his eyes. If that were the case, it meant *he* was the reason his sister was in a coma. Nobody else. Him alone. If he'd gotten involved earlier, Amy would still be up and walking about. He was sure of it.

Suddenly, for the first time in his life, Bishop wished he were dead. Then the pain he was experiencing would go away. It was like a knife in his ribcage. He couldn't believe he'd been so thoughtless. Why hadn't he called her back? How much effort would it have taken?

None. That's how much. None at all.

He opened his eyes and stared up at the ceiling. He took a long deep breath. And another. This was no good. Thinking this way served no purpose other than to cripple him. And right now, he was the only person who could prevent further harm from coming to Amy. Much as he hated the thought of leaving her, he wasn't going to get the answers he needed by hanging round the hospital. But he wasn't about to leave her unguarded, either.

Bishop pulled his cell phone out and keyed in a number from memory. After a few rings, a male voice said, 'Hello?'

'Willard, it's Bishop. Where are you?'

'Home.' Bishop knew home meant an apartment in Jamaica, Queens. 'Just got back a couple of hours ago and my girlfriend's already giving me shit. Why?'

'I need your help with something. It's a personal matter.'

'Personal, huh? Okay, shoot. I'm all ears.'

Bishop described what had happened to Amy and explained his concern for her continued safety. 'Which means I need someone to stand guard over her when I'm not here. It would only be temporary until I can find a permanent guy, but I really need somebody right this minute. I can pay for your time.'

'Not necessary,' Willard said. 'I'll get a cab now and I should be with you in about thirty, depending on traffic. Good enough?'

Bishop checked his watch. It was 15.21. 'Perfect. I'll be waiting in Intensive Care for you. You'll want room 32.'

He ended the call and keyed in another number. His contact at Equal Aid, Ed Giordano, picked up after two rings and said, 'So how's your sister? She okay?'

Bishop had already spoken to Giordano on the drive back from

Pennsylvania, advising him that although the Ellen Meredith situation was all wrapped up, it might be a while before Bishop could update her in person. Once Giordano knew the reason why, he'd said that anything he could do to help, all Bishop had to do was call.

'Not really,' Bishop said. 'But she's breathing. For now, anyway. But what I really need is a professional to keep Amy company around the clock until I get to the bottom of things. I was hoping you could recommend someone for the job.'

'Well, I can think of a number of people off the top of my head. It all depends what kind of qualifications you're—'

'Put it this way,' Bishop cut in. 'If Amy was your sister, who would *you* call?'

'Scott Muro,' Giordano said.

'Okay. And what is he?'

'He's a private investigator works out of Brooklyn. Just a few blocks away from our offices, in fact. I've used him a few times for various assignments and he's always come through. He's ex-army, and he's also licensed to carry a firearm, which is a rarity in New York. He'd definitely be my first choice, but I don't know how busy he is. Want me to get you his number?'

'If you've got it handy.'

'Hold on.' Bishop waited. A short while later, Giordano came back and reeled off a phone number. 'And if he can't help you, call me back and we'll find somebody else, okay?'

'Thanks,' Bishop said and hung up. Then he keyed in the number he'd been given.

It was picked up after a few rings. A man's voice said, 'Muro Investigations.'

'That Scott Muro?'

'The same. And who am I talking to?'

'My name's Bishop. It seems we've both done work for Ed Giordano in recent months. He passed along your name as somebody he trusts.'

'Good old Ed.' There was a short pause. 'Bishop . . . Bishop . . . Yeah, I seem to recall your name coming up in conversation once or twice. So you have a need of my services?'

'For the next few days, at least. How busy are you right now?'

'Right now? Very. I won't be free until tomorrow morning at the earliest. You still interested?'

'Yes,' Bishop said, and quickly explained the situation and what he wanted. 'And I'd want you to take care of this personally. No assigning it to one of your operatives. Just you. Is that acceptable?'

'Sure, but I gotta warn you, my time doesn't come cheap.'

'That's fine. I'll pay whatever it costs.'

'Okay, then. I don't see any problem. At least it makes a change from the usual divorce cases. I'll contact you early in the morning to let you know when I'm coming.'

'Good. Bring a contract with you and we'll make everything legal.'

Bishop ended the call, satisfied that at least Amy wouldn't be left alone at any point. He would be free to focus his efforts on finding those responsible for putting her in here.

He threw the empty coffee cup in the trash and walked in the direction of room 32 to wait for Willard.

TWENTY

Bishop and Seth Willard were sitting on two of the beam-mounted chairs in Amy's corridor. The seats were as uncomfortable as they looked. It was no wonder they weren't used much. But their location more than compensated. From here, both men could clearly see the door to room 32 on their right, less than twenty feet away.

'I've hired a private detective to take over from you,' Bishop said, 'but he won't get here until tomorrow morning. Can you stay awake that long?'

Willard finished clipping the temporary overnight visitor's pass Bishop had given him to the lapel of his jacket. It had taken all of Bishop's diplomatic skills to get a doctor to issue it to him. They were like gold dust around here.

'Don't worry,' Willard said, 'I won't get bored. I already got a bunch of new movies on my iPod I haven't seen yet. Plus I'm not sure it's possible to sleep in these chairs.'

'Yeah, they are pretty bad.'

Willard used a hand to brush his hair away from his forehead and looked over at Amy's door. 'But, like, wouldn't it be easier if I was in the room with Amy, rather than out here?'

'It would be, but they told me it's something to do with insurance. It's probably bullshit, but you can see everything okay from here. Anything else you need from me?'

Willard pulled a pair of earbuds from his pocket and said, 'Can't think of anything.'

'Okay, then,' Bishop said, standing up. 'I appreciate this.'

Willard smiled. 'No problemo.' He pulled his iPod from his jacket pocket and began scrolling through his playlists.

Bishop left him to it and headed back in the direction of the waiting room. When he got there, he pushed open the door and saw everybody seated at the far end, as before. Lisa was awake now, and in conversation with her grandmother. Good. Bishop just stood there in the doorway for a few moments, waiting. Sure enough, Lisa's sixth sense kicked in, and when she looked over Bishop beckoned with a finger before slipping back out into the hallway.

Lisa pushed through the doorway a few seconds later and came over to him with raised eyebrows. 'What?'

'So you still angry with me?'

She shrugged. 'Nothing's changed. Maybe I was too hard on you before, but you still should have been around more.'

'You're absolutely right, and that'll change in future. I guarantee it. But for now, do you mind if I ask you a few questions?'

'Depends. What kind of questions?'

'Like how have things been at home recently?'

The girl gave a sigh. 'Well, Dad hasn't been a whole lot of fun since he lost his job at the agency, although things picked up a few months back when he got himself a job as night watchman at some warehouse in Brooklyn. But they laid him off again a few weeks ago and that was the end of that.'

'What about your mom? Has she been acting any different recently?'

'Different?'

'Preoccupied, or stressed out, like she had something on her mind.'

Lisa made a face. 'Mom *always* looks like she's got something on her mind.' Then the girl slowly brought her eyebrows together. She even frowned like her mother. 'But she *has* been a lot pricklier than usual the last few weeks. Like if I did something wrong like not cleaning my room in time, she would totally bite my head off. Which she *never* used to do. Then she'd quickly say she was sorry and that'd be that.'

'And did she ever talk to you about anything that was bothering her? Like at work, for example?'

'What's work got to do with anything?'

'I don't know yet.' He paused. 'Did she ever take you out to see her office?'

'No. Why would she?'

'Some parents do. So you wouldn't know if she's got any personal items on her work desk. Like photos, or trinkets, anything like that.'

Lisa shrugged. 'Well, I guess she's got photos of me and Pat there. But I don't . . .' She stopped and looked off into the distance.

'What?'

Lisa turned to him. 'Mom'll have her special little Japanese tree at work. She loves that thing.'

'Japanese tree? You mean a bonsai?'

'Yeah. Mom said she got it just after I was born. Whenever she gets a new job that thing goes with her. She told us it always makes her feel calm and relaxed.'

'I didn't know that,' Bishop said. 'Maybe I'll go get it for her.'

TWENTY-ONE

Bishop took the 7 train to 33rd Street in Sunnyside, and from there it was just a short walk to 32nd Place. It was 16.09 already. The beginning of rush hour in the big city. Pedestrians everywhere were already starting to make their way home. He just hoped Artemis was still working to standard office hours.

This part of Queens, especially west of 37th Street, was essentially a huge industrial area. 32nd Place was atypical. It was four blocks long, and lined with large commercial buildings that got smaller in size the further south you went. As Bishop crossed 48th Avenue he passed a mailbox on the corner, then a long brick building on the left claiming to be the headquarters for the Steamfitters Association. A small, overgrown plot of land separated the latter from its immediate neighbour, a two-storey tan adobe building with windows all along the second floor, but on the first just a large, shuttered garage door to the right and a tinted glass door to the left. *Artemis International* was pasted across the front in tasteful bronze lettering, with a simple crescent moon logo at the end.

Bishop went over to the glass door, pulled it open and stepped into a large, well-lit reception area containing a number of soft chairs arranged around wooden tables bearing magazines and newspapers. There was nobody waiting. Bishop saw a concrete stairwell at the far end of the room, with a large desk set against the wall to the left. A young, heavily made-up woman in a white blouse sat behind the desk, working on her computer.

Bishop walked over to her. The receptionist saw him coming and gave him a professional smile. She had short brown hair and wore a wedding ring on her left hand. Bishop guessed she was fairly good-looking, though it was hard to tell under all the make-up.

'Good afternoon,' she said. 'Can I help you?'

'Amanda Philmore,' Bishop said. 'She works here, right?'

The girl brought her eyebrows together. 'Yes, but Amy's not in today, I'm afraid.'

'Yeah, I know. I've just come from the hospital. I'm her brother.'

Her eyes instantly softened. 'Oh, I'm so sorry. Isn't it just terrible? The police came this morning and told us what happened. None of us here can believe it. Why would anybody do something like that? Will she be all right?'

'It's a little too early to tell. Look, is her boss around? I'd like to see him.'

'Graham? Of course. I can take you up to his office right now. Just follow me.' She clicked on something with her mouse, then got up, came around the desk and walked over to the stairwell. As Bishop followed her up the steps, she half turned and said, 'I arranged for a large bouquet to be sent to the hospital earlier this afternoon. From all of us. It seemed the least we could do. Do you know if it arrived okay?'

'No, but thanks anyway,' Bishop said. 'So this Graham, he won't mind me just turning up without warning?'

'No, we're all pretty informal here.'

When they reached the top of the stairs, Bishop paused and looked around. This part of the building was mostly open-plan, with a dozen work desks arranged in four groups of three. On one of the vacant ones, he spotted a small bonsai juniper tree. There were five men and three women working quietly at the other desks. All of the men were Caucasian. At the back of the room was a large, glassed-in office. Through the window, Bishop saw a blond, bearded man sifting through some paperwork on his desk. To the right of the office was a hallway going back towards the rear of the building.

'This way,' the receptionist said, walking towards the office. Bishop followed. A couple of the women looked up from their work as they passed. When they reached the office, the receptionist opened the door, leaned in and said, 'Graham, I've got Amy's brother here. He said he'd like to talk to you.'

Graham saw Bishop and said, 'Sure.' He rose from his seat and walked round his desk. 'Come in, come in.'

Bishop stepped inside. The woman gave him a brief smile, closed the door and left them. Graham came over with his hand outstretched. Bishop noticed the fingers were very long. He wore a shirt and tie and was about five-ten, with narrow shoulders and the beginnings of a pot belly.

As Bishop shook the hand, the man said, 'Sit down. Please.'

Bishop took the chair in front of the desk while the blond man resumed his place behind it. 'I'm Graham Bryson, the office manager,' he said, moving some of the papers to the side. 'And you're Amy's brother . . . ?'

'Bishop.'

'Bishop. So tell me, how is Amy? All we know is what the police told us this morning. That she was mugged and assaulted in one of the parks late last night. Is she all right? Has she been able to identify her attackers yet?'

'She hasn't been able to do anything yet,' Bishop said. 'She's in a coma.'

Bryson's eyes widened. 'Oh, sweet Jesus. I didn't realize. A coma? That's serious. Is there anything I can do?'

Bishop was watching him carefully, but couldn't detect any false notes. The man seemed genuinely affected by the news. But affected in what way? 'Not really,' he said. 'It's just a waiting game for now. But I wouldn't expect her back at work any time soon.'

'No. Of course not. God.'

'So the police came to see you this morning?'

'A detective, yes. Asking if anybody here knew when Amy left the office last night.'

'And did they?'

Bryson shook his head and rubbed a palm against his beard. 'Most people had gone by six thirty, which is when we officially finish for the day. When I left at six fifty, Amy was still working. I knew she was planning to stay late and finish up some stuff, so she could have left any time after that.'

'She's got a key to this place, then?'

Bryson shook his head. 'No. There's a rear exit staff can use if any of them want to work late. You don't need a key to leave, only to get back in. Or rather the correct keypad combination. It locks itself automatically, you see.' He pursed his lips, then looked at his watch. 'Um, look, I don't know if—'

The door behind Bishop burst open and a grey-haired man came

into the room, saying, 'Graham, I need that Castor file as soon as—'
He stopped when he saw Bishop, then turned back to Bryson with a
quizzical look.

'Roger, this is Bishop, Amy's brother. Bishop, this is Roger Klyce,
our CEO.'

Bishop got up and turned to face the newcomer. Klyce was wearing
a dark sports jacket, dark pants and a pale shirt, but no tie. He was in
his mid to late fifties. About Bishop's height and fairly chunky with it,
but otherwise in good shape for his age. He had a plain face with deep-
set eyes, a large nose and a thin mouth that curved downwards.

'Bishop?' he said, narrowing his eyes. He offered his hand and
Bishop shook it. The man's grip was strong. 'We only heard about
the assault this morning. How is Amy? Is she okay?'

'She's in a coma, Roger,' Bryson said.

Klyce raised his eyebrows. 'A coma? You're not serious? But I got
the impression from that detective it was a simple mugging.'

'We all thought that,' Bryson said. 'But it looks as if it's a lot worse
than we thought.'

Bishop was watching Klyce's face. Trying to sense any hint of arti-
ficiality. Bryson still seemed genuinely disturbed by the news, but
there was something about Klyce that got Bishop's radar pinging. He
wasn't sure what, exactly. Certainly nothing concrete. Just a feeling
the CEO might be holding something back.

'That's terrible,' Klyce said, turning to Bishop. 'I don't know what
to say. Amy's a very popular figure around here. It's hard to believe
anybody would want to do her harm. But listen, you didn't have to
come all this way . . .'

The desk phone started ringing. Bryson picked it up and began
talking in hushed tones. Klyce said, 'Maybe we should go to my office?
It's quieter. Fewer interruptions.'

'Sure,' Bishop said. 'After you.'

Klyce took him into the hallway he'd spotted before, which ended
in a sharp right turn. There were three doors along the left-hand side.
The first one was open. Bishop looked in as he passed and saw a large
conference table, but no people. The second door was closed. Klyce
opened the third door and stepped inside. Bishop followed him into

a large office with a single window overlooking the rear of the building. There were a few abstract art prints on the wall, along with some framed photos and certificates. One corner of the room was taken up by a large, polished oak desk bearing a computer and the usual peripherals, along with three neatly stacked piles of folders. Against another wall were an antique-looking oak bookcase and three art deco oak filing cabinets.

'Take a seat,' Klyce said, and gestured at the two director's chairs in front of the desk. Bishop chose one while Klyce fell into his own leather chair behind the desk. 'I was just saying there was no need for you to come all this way, Bishop. A simple phone call to explain the situation would have been fine. We'd understand.'

'I had another reason,' Bishop said. 'Amy's daughter thinks putting her favourite bonsai tree next to her bed might help. I came to pick it up.'

'Ah, I see. Well, I'm sure we can find something for you to transport it in.' Klyce smoothed a palm across the surface of his desk. 'You know, I find it odd that Amy's never really mentioned you before.'

Bishop shrugged. 'Not so odd. Amy's family probably takes up most of her thoughts these days. I'm just a part of her past who comes to visit every now and then.'

'I see. And what is it you do, if you don't mind me asking?'

'Well, you could say I'm in the problem-solving business.'

'A problem-solver.' Klyce smiled. 'That's a definition that could cover a lot of ground.'

Bishop smiled back. 'You're right. It could.' He passed his eyes over the office and said, 'So has Amy helped you catch any international fugitives recently?'

'Well, we don't actually "catch" them, you know. We're not equipped for that kind of work. We're solely an intelligence-gathering service. Tell me, are you familiar with the Olympian legend of Artemis at all?'

'Sure. Greek goddess of the hunt, wasn't she? And daughter of Zeus.'

Klyce nodded. 'And twin sister of Apollo. You know your classics. Well, we've made our own hunting ground that of paper trails and computer databases. That's where we're most at home. See, we have a whole network of contacts across the globe now, as well as a solid reputation that's growing exponentially. Based on our past record, foreign governments and agencies now come to us first to help track down war criminals they've judged in absentia, or those guilty of crimes against humanity. We assign researchers to each case, and when we get a break we pass the relevant information on to the clients, who then do the groundwork necessary to bring those in question to justice.'

'Meaning the client sends in an extraction team to snatch the fugitive and bring him back.'

Klyce waved a hand. 'What the client does with the information isn't any of our concern. We just supply the data.'

'Plausible deniability,' Bishop said. 'I get it. And you charge for this service, right?'

'Expenses only. We're a non-profit association, although we do receive hefty donations from satisfied clients on occasion. Enough to tide us over when we go through the inevitable slow patches. And to answer your question, yes, Amy's certainly helped bring a number of fugitives to light. She's a very capable researcher.'

'Uh huh. What's she been working on recently?'

Klyce shifted in his seat. 'Well, I can't go into too much detail about open cases, but let's just say it involved tracking down some leftovers from the Bosnian war.' He shook his head and said, 'And now this random mugging. The poor woman.'

'I'm not convinced it was random.'

Klyce's brow became furrowed. 'Not random? I don't understand.'

'Nor do I,' Bishop said. 'Not yet. But I've discovered a few things today that tell me there's more to this than Amy simply being in the wrong place at the wrong time.' He stood up. 'Anyway, thanks for your time, Mr Klyce. It's been interesting.'

Klyce stood too. He was still frowning. 'No problem. I'll ask one of the girls to find you a box for that tree. And if you have any more news about Amy, please let us know.'

'I'll come to you first,' Bishop promised.

TWENTY-TWO

Bishop was approaching one of the side entrances to Allerdyne Hospital when he saw Gerry puffing on a cigarette about thirty feet from the entrance doors. Which was a first. Three other people, a female nurse and two men, were also smoking near a pedestal ashtray.

Gerry looked up and his lips parted when he saw Bishop coming towards him. He looked like a kid caught by teacher.

'Didn't know you smoked,' Bishop said.

Gerry's smile looked strained. He jammed the lit end of the cigarette into the sand and said, 'I quit in high school. Now I know why.' He jutted his chin at the small box Bishop was carrying. 'What's that?'

'Amy's bonsai tree. I got it from her work. Apparently, it's her favourite. Maybe you could place it next to her bed for her.'

'Can't hurt, I guess,' Gerry said, taking the box from Bishop.

As gracious as ever, Bishop thought. He briefly considered mentioning Willard's presence on the ward, but decided against it. Gerry didn't need to know the details. Instead, he said, 'So have they let you in to see Amy yet?'

'About half an hour ago. Seeing her face all beat up like that was something I don't think I'll ever forget. Those scummy bastards really did a job on her, didn't they?'

Bishop said nothing. He had a feeling the question was rhetorical anyway.

'Look, Bishop, about, uh . . . what happened earlier. You were right. It's done now. I think we should just forget it and move on, like you said. My family's all that matters now.'

'That's good.' *Just a shame you didn't feel that way earlier.*

'Yeah, well,' Gerry said, puffing out his cheeks. 'You gonna look in on Amy while you're here?'

Bishop checked his watch. 17.13. It would start to get dark pretty soon. And he still had things to do. 'I don't think so,' he said. 'Maybe later.'

'I get it,' Gerry said. 'Got more important stuff to do than check in with your own family, huh?'

'Look, save it for another day, Gerry. I don't have the patience right now. Are Pat and Lisa still upstairs?'

Gerry shook his head. 'No, my folks saw how beat they looked and took them back to the apartment. They're probably there already.'

'Okay. I'll go check in with them now.'

Without another word, Bishop turned and made his way back to Broadway. Once again he wondered how his sister had ended up with such a dickhead for a husband. Knowing Amy as he did, the guy had to have *some* virtues or he would never have gotten past the starting gate. But if so, they were very well hidden.

He considered walking the mile to Amy's, but decided to take a cab instead. As he stood on the sidewalk and waited for one to come along, he thought about Artemis again.

That Roger Klyce interested him greatly. Bishop couldn't put his finger on it, but there was definitely something shady about the guy. For instance, while Bishop was no expert on antiques, that oak furniture in his office had looked as though it could fetch a fair few bucks. Not the kind of stuff you generally saw in places financed by donations. Not if the threadbare offices of Equal Aid were any kind of benchmark. And with an information network stretching across the globe, there seemed to be a lot of scope for using that information for personal gain. He'd definitely like to know a little more about Artemis and Roger Klyce. It was just a matter of where to start.

But first he wanted to check Amy's home office. He knew his sister better than anybody else on this planet, and one thing he could guarantee was that she never did anything without having some kind of back-up in place. They were similar in that way. So his next task was to take a good look around her PC and see if he was right.

Bishop saw an on-duty cab approaching and flagged it down. When it stopped, he gave the driver Amy's address and got in. Four minutes later, the driver pulled into Audubon Avenue. When they reached

Amy's building, Bishop signalled for him to stop. It was a six-storey walk-up tenement like most of them on this street, with its entrance set back from the sidewalk. Bishop walked down the short path, entered the building and took the stairs up to the fourth-floor landing. He walked to the end of the hallway and knocked on the door to apartment 23. He had a key, but he preferred not to use it unless absolutely necessary. A few seconds later, he heard the deadbolt being released from the bolt casing and Arnie Philmore appeared in the doorway.

'Oh, hello again, Bishop,' he said. 'I wasn't expecting you. Come in.'

'Thanks.'

Bishop followed Arnie down the hallway, past the kitchen and diner on the left, and into the large living room at the end. The three-bedroom apartment hadn't been much to look at originally. That all changed once Amy and Gerry refurbished it. Now it was all polished wood flooring, exposed brick walls and modern furniture. It had cost, but in Bishop's opinion it was well worth it. The place felt like a family home. All that was missing was Amy's warming presence.

Bishop saw the TV was tuned to a football game. There was nobody else in the living room. 'Where is everybody?' he asked.

'Janice went out for some groceries and Pat begged to go along. Lisa's in her room.'

'Okay, I'll go and say hello. I need to talk to her about something, anyway.' He looked at the TV and said, 'Who's playing?'

Arnie walked back to the easy chair. 'No idea. I was just taking forty.'

'Well, I'll let you get back to it then,' Bishop said, and moved to the entranceway on the left. It was another hallway, containing two doors on each side. He rapped a knuckle against the second one on the right. There was no response. He tried again and said, 'Lisa?'

Still nothing. Bishop opened the door and saw his niece sitting cross-legged on her bed, listening to her iPod. She was marking a page in a large book as she made notes on a pad. Then she looked up, saw Bishop and removed her earbuds.

'Don't you ever knock first?' she asked.

'I did,' Bishop said. 'Twice.'

'Oh.' She glanced at her iPod. 'Okay.'

'What's that? Homework?'

Lisa closed the school book. 'English Lit. Helps keeps my mind off Mom.'

'Sure, I understand.'

She gazed levelly at him. 'So did you want something?'

'Yes. I'm hoping you can help me out.'

'What, like you helped out Mom, you mean?'

Bishop winced. 'That again? Want me to get a knife from the kitchen so I can commit ritual suicide in front of you? Think that would help my case at all?'

'I dunno. I guess it would prove you're good for something.'

'Look, I really hate arguing with you, Lisa. I much preferred it when we were friends.'

Lisa swept a hand through her long hair. 'So did I. But Mom always told me real friends look out for each other. Know what I mean?'

'And that's what I'm trying to do now. I just need your help to do it.'

'What are you talking about?'

'Come next door and I'll show you.'

TWENTY-THREE

Lisa opened up the Internet Explorer browser, clicked on the Hotmail link in the Bookmarks folder and waited for the page to load.

Bishop sat next to her. Computers had never been his strong suit and he generally preferred to let others do the work. He also took forever to type. They were in a corner of Gerry and Amy's bedroom that had been set aside for use as a home office. It consisted of a large, L-shaped wooden desk bearing a PC, a printer and a scanner. Underneath was a cabinet with three drawers, and a wastepaper basket. On the wall in front of them were numerous photos of Pat and Lisa at various ages.

There was also a framed colour shot of Bishop's parents up there. One he hadn't seen in a long time. It was of the two of them on a park bench somewhere, laughing at the camera. They looked young – early thirties, maybe – and full of life. The shot was at a low angle and at a slight tilt, which made Bishop think they'd gotten Amy to take it. That was probably why they were laughing. She would only have been a toddler then. Bishop would have been nothing more than a glint in his father's eye.

But looking at the photo now, he was surprised to see how much he took after his old man. He'd never really noticed before, or maybe he'd simply grown into it. But they had the same dark hair, the same light blue eyes, the same strong jawline. And his mother was just as beautiful as he remembered, too, with her long brown hair and dazzling smile.

Bishop felt himself strangely affected by the photo, which was unlike him. He wasn't the sentimental type, never had been. No doubt it was brought on by Amy's current condition. But that was no excuse. He had work to do, and needed to stay objective. He mentally shook himself out of it and came back to the here and now.

'How many personal email accounts does your mom have?' he asked.

'Two I know about,' Lisa said. 'Although there could be more, I guess. Look, you wanna tell me why I'm doing this at all?'

Bishop thought about what to say. He had to be careful. Telling his niece too much would only worry her even more. Best to keep things as simple as possible.

He said, 'I think it's possible what happened to your mom might have had something to do with her work.'

Lisa gaped at him. 'Her work? Are you serious?'

'I said it's *possible*. I could be on the wrong track altogether, but I have to know for sure. That's why I'm here now. To see if she left anything that tells me one way or the other.'

She frowned at him for a couple more seconds, then turned back to the screen. The page had loaded and Bishop watched her quickly key Amy's email address into the space. Then she filled in the password slot.

'PATLISA?' he asked.

Lisa shrugged. 'Yeah. Pretty lame, huh?'

Bishop said nothing. It seemed doubtful Amy would send sensitive information to an account with such an easily decipherable password. The inbox appeared and Bishop saw seven new messages today. They came from a wide variety of sources. Amazon, eBay, Mastercard, plus a few others that looked personal.

'So what are we looking for?' Lisa asked.

'I'm not sure,' Bishop said. 'Possibly a file that your mom sent to herself for safekeeping. Can you check each message for me?'

'Sure,' Lisa said, and started going through each one. Bishop could tell she was becoming absorbed with the problem at hand despite her ambivalent feelings towards him. As he'd hoped. But a few minutes of searching was enough to tell them there was nothing of interest there. Lisa then navigated to another email site. She typed in a new address and the same password and pressed enter.

Bishop saw only one new message in this one, from a Pauline. Sent yesterday. Lisa opened it up and Bishop saw it was merely a message from a friend. Nothing more.

'They're the only two I know of,' Lisa said. 'Course, Mom might have sent this file to an online storage service. Let me check her bookmarks and history.' She scrolled through them both and clicked on several sites that looked like possibles, but each one came up empty. She finally slumped back in her seat. 'Nothing.'

Bishop rubbed his palm over his scalp. Something was tingling at the back of his neck. Something to do with his visit to Artemis earlier. But what was it?

Lisa leaned forward again and started looking through the Applications folder. Bishop watched her highlight the Firefox icon and smile to herself. 'Thought so. Mom downloaded another browser.'

'She uses more than one,' Bishop said. 'Now why didn't I think of that?'

'Because you're *old*,' Lisa said, and opened it up. She clicked on the drop-down Bookmarks menu and produced a long list of sites.

'To you, *every*one's old,' Bishop said. 'That Hushmail link. Try that.'

Lisa clicked on it. The home page appeared and Bishop was pleased to see the first field was already filled out. *Amy745*, followed by the Hushmail address. But the password field remained blank. 'I don't think your mom would have used PATLISA for this one,' he said.

Lisa tried it anyway, and got an 'incorrect password' message in return. She tried variations, adding or subtracting various letters, all with the same result.

'Ideas?' Lisa asked.

'Let me think,' Bishop said. He looked down at the cabinet at his feet and then slowly pulled open the top drawer. It contained various items of stationery. Lying on top was a small package from Amazon. Opened, from the looks of it. He pulled it out and opened the flap. Inside was an obscure Sinatra CD he'd never heard of before. That was something else Amy had inherited from Mom. 'Still into Frank, I see.'

Lisa nodded. 'Yeah, still buys everything. I tell her she can get it all off iTunes, but you know how old school Mom is. She likes having the actual CD in her hand.'

Bishop could sympathize, but then he was of the same generation. But seeing the CD, it occurred to him that while he loved his sister unconditionally, it was this younger version of her that always came to mind. The version before the husband and the kids. He'd seen so little of the person she'd grown into. Did he really know her as she was now? Or was he just transposing his own feelings onto her? He didn't know. But he did know now probably wasn't the best time to start analysing it too deeply. Maybe once this was all over.

He looked at the CD again. He could still remember Amy's favourite album of Sinatra's. It was the bossa nova one he did back in the sixties with that Brazilian guy, Jobim. Amy had made him listen to it enough times. Bishop had never particularly liked the genre, but he had to admit it was a pretty good album, with Frank's voice at its silkiest. And he also recalled Amy's favourite song on the album. Which would logically put it into contention for being her favourite song of all time.

Why the hell not? 'Try DINDI,' he said, and spelt it.

Lisa keyed it in and pressed enter.

'Incorrect password.' Lisa sat back in the chair and looked at him.

Well, it had been worth a shot. Then he remembered something else. About how Amy had almost been angry at the song's spelling on the cover. 'Frank sings it as Jinji,' she'd said to him once, 'so why can't they just spell it right?'

'Try J-I-N-J-I,' Bishop said.

Lisa typed it in and pressed enter. And then a new page suddenly came up. 'Hey, cool,' Lisa said. 'I'm in.'

Bishop smiled, then caught sight of the inbox notification and groaned. There were no new emails listed at all. Another dead end. 'We're gonna have to think of something else.'

He looked down at the packaging he held in his hand. And then it suddenly came to him. The mailbox he'd seen when he visited Klyce, right there on the 32nd Place and 48th Avenue intersection. Just a few steps away from the Artemis building. And Amy with her old school mentality. To a person like that, what could be more natural than making a copy of whatever she'd taken and dropping it in the mailbox, addressed to herself? Perhaps with an additional touch of subtlety to ward off any suspicion.

'Lisa,' he said, 'has any mail arrived for your mom today?'

'Uh, I think there was some stuff next to the phone in the living room. Want me to go get it?'

'If you could.'

She got up, left the room, and returned a few seconds later carrying two envelopes and another small package similar to the one he'd just opened. She came over and handed it all over to Bishop.

He checked the unopened envelopes. One was an advertising mailer from a credit card company. The other was from the WSPA, Amy's favourite animal charity. He put them down and looked at the package. Another one from Amazon. The company name was printed in big type across the middle of the packaging. Above it was a row of stamps. Underneath was a printed label with a barcode and Amy's name and address.

'That's interesting,' he said.

'What?' Lisa asked.

'Well, big companies like Amazon use pre-paid address labels. Yet this one's got a whole row of stamps on it.'

He raised an eyebrow at Lisa, then carefully opened the package. There was another CD case inside. He pulled it out and saw it was the album he'd just been thinking about: *Francis Albert Sinatra & Antonio Carlos Jobim*. The cover photo was a moody shot of Frank in the studio, smoking as he consulted his music sheets.

So after all these years, Amy had only just gotten round to buying her favourite album on CD? Bishop didn't believe it.

Opening the jewel case, he saw the disc was the correct factory pressing. And the booklet was just an eight-page thing with nothing else hidden inside. He pulled the disc out and turned it round. And then he looked down at the jewel case and frowned. The weight was all wrong. It felt too heavy for what should have been an empty case. Carefully, he pulled the black plastic tray away from its housing.

'Hey, look at *that*,' Lisa said, wide-eyed.

There was a second disc hidden underneath. A recordable Sony CD-R.

TWENTY-FOUR

Bishop handed the CD to Lisa. Without a word, she opened the disc tray on the hard drive and inserted the CD. After she double clicked on the disc icon a dialog box instantly appeared, asking for a password.

She turned to him and said, 'JINJI again?'

'Try it,' Bishop said, and watched her key in the five letters. She pressed enter and the dialog box immediately disappeared. Another folder opened up, containing a single file.

'Excellent,' Lisa said. 'Looks like we're in.'

The file was merely called *Untitled*. From the avatar, even Bishop could tell it was some kind of Word document. Lisa double-clicked on it and the program started up. Within seconds the screen was filled with a page showing what looked to be a basic audio surveillance log.

'This what you meant?' Lisa asked.

'I'm not sure,' Bishop said, leaning in closer to look.

It was a two-page document listing calls made from a New York phone number to a 202 number, and gave the date, the time, and the exact length of each call down to the second. They started on September 29 of this year and ended on October 16, two weeks ago. Bishop counted thirty-seven separate calls in total, all originating from the New York number. There were no outgoing calls from the DC number. Or if there were, they were on another list. The shortest call was twenty-three seconds long. The longest was just over six minutes.

'So what's it all mean?' Lisa asked.

'I have no idea,' he said. 'I guess there's only one way to find out.'

He pulled his cell phone from his pocket, and was about to key in the New York number when he heard Gerry's voice outside. He put the phone back in his pocket and said, 'Sounds like your dad's back from the hospital.'

'You not gonna call the number?' Lisa asked.

'It can wait for now.'

Gerry's voice became steadily louder until the bedroom door opened and he stepped through. He was speaking to somebody on his cell, and when he saw Bishop and Lisa he said, 'Um, look, I'll call you back,' and hung up. He looked from Lisa to Bishop. 'What are you two doing in here?'

'Chill, Dad,' Lisa said. 'We're just checking Mom's files. Hey, can I borrow your cell for a sec?'

Gerry furrowed his brow as he absently handed the phone to his daughter. 'But what are you checking for?'

Bishop watched helplessly as Lisa keyed in the New York number. He would have preferred to do it without Gerry present. He said, 'To see if Amy left any clues as to why she was attacked.'

'And what makes you think she left anything at all? I mean, do you honestly believe she expected to be attacked last night?'

Lisa turned and handed Bishop the cell phone. 'It's ringing,' she said.

Bishop glanced at the screen and was wondering why the number wasn't displayed when he heard somebody pick up. He brought the phone to his ear and a familiar voice said, 'Roger Klyce.'

Bishop quickly disconnected the call. So that was Klyce's direct work line at the office. Interesting. Gerry plucked the phone from his hand. 'Who are you calling?' He looked at the display and frowned. He wiped a finger across it and said, 'Well?'

'That was her boss,' Bishop said. 'And Amy sent herself a CD that—'

He stopped talking as Gerry's cell phone started ringing. Gerry answered and said, 'Hello? Oh, right. Yeah, I know. Look, wait a second . . .' He quickly left the bedroom and closed the door after him.

Lisa stared after him with raised eyebrows.

'Busy man,' Bishop said, and pulled out his own phone. He keyed in the DC number and waited. After six rings, a recorded message came on. An accented female voice said, 'Sorry, we are closed. Embassy offices hours are between nine a.m. and five p.m., Monday to Friday. If you would like to leave a message, please speak after the tone, giving your name, your contact number, and the name of the person to whom you wished to speak. Thank you.'

Bishop hung up and said, 'Lisa, can you type the 202 number into Google for me?'

'Sure,' she said. Her fingers played across the keyboard and within seconds a new Google page opened up with a list of links. Right at the top was a link to the embassy of the People's Republic of Konamba website. Which was part of East Africa, if Bishop remembered correctly.

Again, interesting. But it didn't really tell him much. By his own admission, Klyce was in constant contact with representatives from numerous countries, so what was so special about this one? And why had Amy saved these particular calls onto a CD and then sent it to herself in such a clandestine manner? The information had to be of great importance to somebody. But who?

'And the other number was Mom's boss?' Lisa asked.

Bishop nodded. 'His direct work line.'

'Okay. So why would Mom send this to herself?'

'You got me,' Bishop said. 'Is that all that's on the CD? Just that one file?'

'That's all I can see.'

'Can you print it out for me?'

Lisa reached over and switched on the printer. As she printed off the document, she said, 'So what are you gonna do now?'

'Only one thing I *can* do. Delve deeper till I get answers.'

'How?'

'By going to see her boss again and asking him about this.'

'Why didn't you do that on the phone?'

Bishop ejected the CD from the disc drive and placed it back in the jewel case under the Sinatra CD. He put the case in Amy's drawer and said, 'I find person to person works best in these kinds of situations. But thanks for helping with this. It would have taken me hours without you.'

Lisa actually smiled at him then, making him feel good for the first time that day. She said, 'Yeah, well, you're old. Like I said before.'

'That I am,' he said, smiling back. 'Pray it never happens to you. So are we friends again?'

'I guess.'

'Good. That makes my job a lot easier.' Getting to his feet, Bishop took the two sheets of paper from the printer tray, folded them and stuck them in his jacket pocket. 'I'd better get going then.'

Lisa looked up at him. 'Hey, look, sorry if I was rough on you before. I didn't really mean it.'

'Yes, you did.' He smiled at his niece as he went over and opened the bedroom door. 'And I deserved it, too. But we'll talk again later, okay?'

'Okay.'

Exiting the bedroom, he heard the muffled sound of Gerry in conversation in another room. Bishop left the apartment without saying goodbye.

TWENTY-FIVE

It was 18.21 by the time Bishop returned to the Artemis offices in Queens. The office manager, Graham Bryson, had said they closed at six thirty. Bishop hoped he'd been accurate.

The front door was still unlocked, though, which was a good omen. He pulled it open and went inside. The same receptionist as before was still at her desk. When Bishop walked over to her, she looked up from her screen. 'Oh, hello again. Is there any more news about Amy?'

'Not yet,' Bishop said. 'Look, is it okay if I go talk to Roger Klyce about something? He said I could come by any time.'

'Oh, I'm sorry, Roger left about an hour ago. I think Graham's still up there, though.'

'No, it's Roger I needed to speak to. It's kind of urgent. Have you got his home or cell number?'

She smiled at him. 'Oh, we can't give out personal numbers, I'm afraid. Besides, he said he'd be away from the office until Monday, and when Roger's gone that long it usually means he's out of the country on business, so it wouldn't do any good anyway.'

'He tell you where he's gone?'

'No, but he rarely does. He *is* the boss, after all.'

Bishop sighed. *Wonderful. Another wasted trip.* Thanking the receptionist, he turned and left the building and began strolling north.

All it meant was with Klyce unavailable for questioning, he'd have to come at the problem from a different angle. There was always a way. As he walked past the mailbox on the corner, he wondered again why Amy had gone to such lengths to send that CD to herself. Obviously as back-up, but why? All that was on there was a surveillance log of calls from Klyce to somebody in the Konamban embassy. But Amy must have sent it to herself for a reason. Just as she did everything for a reason. Bishop just had to figure out the 'why'. After all, it was still the only lead he had. So maybe that was the approach to take. If Bishop couldn't get to Klyce directly, he'd simply have to find out who his contact in the embassy was. And what he represented.

He'd almost reached the 47th Avenue intersection when he began to feel a faint itch at the back of his neck. He'd always trusted that itch. It was an early warning system that had helped him out of some serious scrapes over the years. It usually meant somebody was taking an interest in him. Bishop resisted the urge to look behind and turned left at the intersection. There was a large sandwich bar on the corner up ahead. The first one he'd seen in this section of Sunnyside. He couldn't fault the location. It probably made a fortune from all the blue- and white-collar workers in the neighbourhood. When the traffic thinned, he crossed over and walked towards the low building.

When he reached it, he saw one of the windows had a photocopied menu stuck to it. He went over and looked at it while checking the reflection in the glass. There was nobody following him that he could see. Just the occasional vehicle passing by. And he couldn't see anyone in his peripheral vision. But *some*thing had activated his radar. He stayed where he was and waited, pretending to study the sandwich choices.

Bishop had counted to twenty when in the reflection he saw a dark stretch limousine double park on the opposite side of the street. The driver of the car behind it beeped his horn a few times, then swerved round it angrily and carried on. Bishop turned from the window and looked at the limo. It looked like a Lincoln. Maybe ten years old. After a few seconds, a guy in a suit got out the front passenger side and crossed the street towards Bishop. He had dark, close-cropped hair and an athlete's build. Bishop also noticed a discreet bulge under his left armpit.

He stopped in front of Bishop and looked him up and down. 'My boss is over there in the car. He wants to talk to you.'

'That old line,' Bishop said. 'Forget it. I prefer girls.'

The man's expression remained impassive. 'Just get in the car, huh?'

'Or what? You gonna shoot me?'

The man sighed. 'Look, I'm just the messenger here. Get in or don't. It's up to you. But I imagine you'll get something out of it if you do.'

Bishop couldn't fault that kind of logic. He said, 'Okay, let's go.'

They waited for a car to pass and crossed to the limo. The windows were tinted so all you saw was your own reflection looking back at you. Bishop had used his fair share of them back in his close-protection days. Usually bullet-proofed to hell and gone. He wondered if this one was similarly armoured. His escort reached it first and pulled the single rear door open.

Bishop peered in and saw a bespectacled man in a dark suit sitting inside, looking through some papers. The interior lights made everything garish. The man looked to be in his late forties, with a high forehead and a stern but otherwise unremarkable face. His salt and pepper hair had been brushed forward in an effort to conceal his receding hairline. Bishop looked around and saw the car interior was all polished wood and white leather, with the requisite mini-bar and TV concealed tastefully within the sides.

The man looked up from his papers, blinked at Bishop and said, 'It's all right, I won't bite.' He turned and gave a single nod to Bishop's escort. 'Okay, Nowlan.'

Bishop lowered his head and entered the vehicle, taking the seat across from the man. He watched as the man called Nowlan shut the door and got in the front passenger seat. Bishop turned his head, but the dividing glass was also heavily tinted. Their driver was just a silhouette. He turned back to his host, who was still engrossed in his paperwork. 'So you gonna tell me who you are, or am I supposed to throw twenty questions at you?'

The man looked up again before reaching into his jacket pocket. He pulled out a small black leather wallet and passed it over. Bishop took it and opened the flap.

There was a gold badge inside. And behind the clear plastic window directly above it was a card identifying the owner as a senior special agent of the FBI.

TWENTY-SIX

Bishop raised an eyebrow as he looked it over. Bishop had seen a few federal IDs over the years; this one looked to be the genuine article. The signature on the card gave the owner's name as Dermot Arquette, while the photo pretty much matched the face in front of him. Although Arquette had had a little more hair when it was taken.

'Nice,' Bishop said and passed it back. 'Where can I get one?'

Arquette pocketed the wallet and set the papers down on the seat. 'Sorry, but there's a strict vetting process. Applicants with criminal records need not apply.'

'My conviction was overturned. I even got an apology from the mayor.'

'Yes, I know. In fact, I know all about you, Bishop.'

'That's comforting.' The vehicle began to move. Bishop said, 'Where are we going?'

'Nowhere in particular. I just figured this was probably as good a place as any to have us a talk.'

'Uh huh. So it's now standard practice for the FBI to supply its agents with stretch limos?'

Arquette flashed a smile. 'I'm just borrowing this one from our special lot in Jersey. Stretch limos are so common here in the city that it works better than any natural camouflage. Which, as it happens, is perfect for the case I'm currently involved with.' He leaned forward. 'But let's talk about your sister. Has she regained consciousness yet?'

Bishop kept his face expressionless, although he'd already figured this had to be about Amy somehow. 'What do you care?'

'Believe it or not, I care very much what happens to Amanda Philmore. Has she come out of her coma yet or not? A simple yes or no will do.'

Bishop just stared at the agent. His first instinct when confronted with law was to clam up, but he realized that might be self-defeating in this case. Especially as they both had questions that needed answering. 'The answer's no,' he said. 'Your turn. What's your interest in Amy?'

Arquette sat back, lifted his glasses and began rubbing his eyes. 'Before this morning, I actually had very little interest in Mrs Philmore. It was when I happened to see a police report of the attack in the park last night, and noticed the name of the victim, that my antennae immediately shot up.'

Bishop thought about that for a moment. 'You recognized her name from Artemis International's list of employees.'

One side of Arquette's mouth turned up. 'That's exactly right. How did you know?'

'If it's not Amy you're interested in, then that only leaves her employer. Which means you don't believe it was a simple mugging, either.'

'No, I don't. I think it was possibly planned well ahead of time.'

Bishop pondered that for a second. The obvious next question was *By whom?* But he had a feeling Arquette was building up to that, and he could afford to be patient. To a point. 'So is the company currently under some kind of federal investigation?'

'No. Well, not officially, anyway. This is something I'm following up on my own. You see, I'm pretty sure there's something going on over there that warrants further attention, but I don't have enough to take it upstairs and get the official wheels rolling. At least, not yet.' He sighed and said, 'How much do you know about Artemis?'

Bishop looked out the window at the warehouses and office buildings passing by. 'Not much. I know they're a non-profit group that helps track down war criminals. According to Roger Klyce, they're pretty good at it, too.'

Arquette adjusted his glasses. 'You've spoken to Klyce? When?'

'A couple of hours ago. In his office.'

'And what else did he say?'

'Just that he hoped Amy would get well soon. Oh, yeah, we discussed Greek mythology, too. Look, Arquette, this is starting to be one-way traffic here. Why don't you just tell me what your involvement is in all this?'

'I guess that's only fair,' Arquette said, reaching over and opening the mini refrigerator. Bishop saw a variety of canned soft drinks lined up in rows inside. Arquette pulled out a Sprite and cracked open the top. 'Go ahead, help yourself,' he said.

Bishop grabbed a Coke, opened it and took a slug of the cold drink. 'I'm listening.'

Arquette took a sip, then said, 'Okay, have you ever heard of a temporary organization called the Coalition for International Justice, or the CIJ?'

'Wasn't it involved with the war crimes tribunals in The Hague a few years back?'

'That's right. It was established in the mid-nineties to aid the international tribunals for Rwanda, Sierra Leone, Cambodia, and the former Yugoslavia. As well as a few others. They'd help build cases, supply legal and technical assistance, gather evidence, that kind of thing. They were pretty successful as far as it went, and finally closed operations in 2006.'

'Good call. As far as I know, atrocities are still being committed on a fairly regular basis in most parts of the globe.'

'Yes, and I imagine the same thought occurred to our friend Roger Klyce. Artemis International was set up a year later in 2007 as a private, non-profit enterprise. Ostensibly with similar objectives to the CIJ, but taking it one step further by actually helping to track these people down. And Klyce already had a vast network of contacts and informants to help him do it. Are you aware he used to be a fairly large cog in the Lewis, Cartwright & Taylor machine? Or LCT, as they're more commonly known? I'm sure you've heard of them.'

Bishop assumed it was a rhetorical question. LCT was the second largest security contractor in the States. His old employer, RoyseCorp, was still the nation's number one choice, but it was a close run thing. He knew any government contracts RoyseCorp turned down generally ended up on the desk of LCT's chairman.

Arquette continued, 'One day Klyce just resigned from his senior post at LCT and decided to get into the humanitarian business. He started up Artemis International with a skeleton staff, and over the next several months used his contacts to track down several suspected war criminals who had eluded capture up until that point. Then Klyce simply offered the information to the relevant governments, free of charge. The resultant trials ended up as big news in their respective countries. Of course, Artemis's reputation was made from then on.

'Now the company's the go to choice for those countries looking to rid themselves of their bloody past and elevate their standing in the international community. Especially those with a history of ethnic cleansing or wholesale civilian massacres. These countries' governing bodies pass down names of those they deem directly responsible, then request that Artemis help track them down. Then once they're in custody, they arrange public trials to show the world their willingness to own up to their past. After that, you'd be surprised how quickly offers of financial aid start coming in to help them get back on their feet. Then their sovereign credit rating gets upgraded, which lures in the major foreign investors. And it's not long after that that the real money starts rolling in. It's big business.'

Bishop took another long gulp of cola and said, 'I take it you don't think Klyce is doing it all for purely humanitarian reasons.'

Arquette smiled. 'Well, I guess I became suspicious when I learned Artemis isn't actually Klyce's baby at all. The company is in fact a subsidiary of LCT. A very well hidden subsidiary, I might add. I lost count of how many overseas shell companies I had to discard before I got to the real owners. And even then there's still some room for doubt. But I'm about as sure as I can be that Klyce is still working for his old employers.'

'So it's a tax write-off.'

'Oh, I'm sure that's part of it.'

'And the rest?'

'I believe LCT are also using the company as a cover for illegal arms trafficking.'

TWENTY-SEVEN

Bishop stared at Arquette. 'That's quite a jump. How'd you arrive at that conclusion?'

'With the help of a disgruntled ex-employee of Artemis named Cesar Hernandez. He was a researcher who was fired about a year ago as a result of a sexual harassment charge. He approached me not long after, claiming it was all a frame-up to discredit him. He said it was because his bosses had found out he'd been looking in places he shouldn't and discovered the real reason for Artemis's existence.'

'International arms trafficking.'

'Think about it, Bishop. Most security firms would jump at the chance to be associated with a humanitarian enterprise like Artemis, wouldn't they? So if LCT are keeping their involvement totally hidden, then that says something about what must be really going on behind the scenes.'

'I guess,' Bishop said. 'I'm just trying to figure out why Hernandez approached you. Unless the law's changed since I last looked, the FBI only deals with crimes committed within US borders.'

Arquette shrugged. 'That's right, but Hernandez said he'd been given my name by a friend of his who'd met me during a RICO case I headed up. To be honest, I got the impression he just wanted to talk to somebody senior in law enforcement and get advice on what to do next. But I soon found myself very interested in what he had to say and tried looking for reasons to involve the agency. Even if we only ended up a small part of a joint investigation with another agency like Alcohol, Tobacco & Firearms.'

Bishop frowned as he fiddled with the pull tab on his Coke can. Something about that didn't add up. But he let it go for now. 'I'm also trying to figure out why you're telling me all this. Care to enlighten me?'

'Why don't you just listen to what I have to say first?'

Bishop shrugged. He'd learned long ago some people had to be allowed to explain things their own sweet way. Sometimes just as a way to show off their knowledge. And that trying to speed things along would often just slow them down. He decided to remain patient.

'Now this trafficking scheme of theirs is really very simple,' Arquette said. 'See, LCT are often contracted by overseas buyers of US weaponry to have trained men guard the shipments and make sure everything arrives safely. They're also contracted to accompany certain large arms shipments to US troops stationed in war zones.'

'And I guess some of these shipments don't actually make it to their final destinations.'

'Most do, of course, or they'd soon go out of business. But a few shipments might get unexpectedly waylaid along the way and diverted to other destinations. Specifically, to countries on the arms blacklist. Three years ago, LCT were responsible for guarding a shipment of new automatic weapons being sent over to the remaining ground troops in Iraq. Turns out none of the fourteen crates arrived. It was like they just vanished into thin air. Yet nobody kicked up a stink about it other than a few pissed off commanders on the ground. And it wasn't long before they became very quiet about the whole thing, too.'

'Somebody high up in Washington was paid to hush things up.'

Arquette nodded again. 'And that's just one example. But you can see where the FBI would come in. High-level corruption is something we take very seriously.'

'So where do Artemis fit in?'

'Hernandez said they, and Klyce in particular, act as a middleman between LCT and the buyers. They deal personally with the buyers, arrange the contracts, take receipt of the fees, falsify the end-user certificates, and handle the payoffs to the various export-control authorities in the region. And probably a lot more besides.'

Bishop finished his Coke and took a new one from the fridge. 'Got anything to back that up?'

'I've got bits and pieces, that's all. Hernandez handed me printouts of email communications between Klyce and several of their customers for shipments ranging from small arms to the latest surface-to-air missiles. All coded, of course, but easy enough to decipher. And the recipient email addresses were all from blacklisted countries.'

Bishop opened the new can of soda and jutted his chin at the papers beside Arquette. 'Is that them?'

Arquette leafed through the papers, pulled out several and passed them across.

Bishop scanned them quickly. As Arquette said, they were all written in code. And not a very complex one, either. In one, a representative from a manufacturing company in Belarus wanted certain guarantees regarding delivery dates for his aeroplane parts. And he also wanted to renegotiate the prices for some items. Except the prices he was being quoted far exceeded what those particular parts would be worth on the open market. The second email came from a buyer in the Ivory Coast. Another blacklisted country. It contained more of the same. The third was from a representative in Myanmar.

He handed them back to Arquette. 'Pretty thin. And emails can be faked.'

'Agreed. But these were just supposed to be a taster. Basically what Hernandez had been able to take with him before being fired. But he said that if I were to personally back him up, he'd be willing to go back in there and get more. Enough to enable me to set the official machinery in motion and initiate a full scale investigation into the company. I was hesitant at first, because I knew he could only do it by breaking and entering, but I eventually agreed.'

'And did he go back?'

Arquette's expression looked strained. 'I can only assume so. Because that turned out to be the last I ever heard from him. After that, Hernandez simply disappeared off the face of the earth. No trace whatsoever. Just gone. And believe me, I've searched. He also left a wife and a young boy, and neither of them have heard from him in a year.'

Bishop frowned. 'Doesn't bode well, does it?'

'No, it doesn't. And while I'm pretty sure he was killed by Klyce or one of his men, there's no possible way I can prove it. Not without a body.'

Bishop took a sip of his drink and thought about how all this might connect with his particular problem. Which was all he really cared about. 'You think Amy found out what was going on, too, then? And that she arranged to meet somebody and hand over the evidence you've been hoping to obtain?'

'That's what I think, yes. But if you're going to ask me who she was planning to pass it to, then the answer is I simply don't know. Yet.'

'And your involvement in all is still unofficial?'

'Right. I try to keep up with Klyce's movements as much as I can, but I can only do it outside my normal duties, and I don't have any additional manpower to fall back on.'

Bishop motioned behind him. 'What about these two?'

'They occasionally help me out with surveillance, but mostly they have their own assignments to keep them busy.'

Bishop shook his head. 'I don't get it.'

'Don't get what?'

'This obsession you've got with Roger Klyce.'

'Obsession?' Arquette lowered his eyebrows. 'It's hardly that. A decent man trusted me to help him find justice and he was killed for his trouble. I want the man responsible.'

Bishop set the second empty can on the floor of the car. 'That's not what I meant. How come you even entertained Hernandez's story in the first place? Other than the vague possibility that a state official is taking backhanders, this kind of case has nothing to do with the FBI. But you listened and you stayed on board. And the only reason you'd do that would be if you had a personal stake in bringing Klyce down.'

Arquette turned his face to the window. Bishop figured he'd either answer or he wouldn't. He didn't really care either way. Outside, he saw they were now moving west on Queens Boulevard, heading for the 59th Street Bridge into Manhattan. The traffic was still thick and the going slow. But since they weren't really going anywhere, what did it matter?

Finally, Arquette turned back and said, 'Okay. If you must know, Klyce was instrumental in destroying the career of my partner, Larry Ratner. I can't go into specifics, but there was a big money laundering case we were helping the NYPD with. LCT was one of the companies who came under suspicion, if only peripherally. One of the LCT employees Larry interviewed was Klyce, and he was usually pretty heavy-handed with suspects. LCT was cleared of any wrongdoing fairly early on, but Klyce must have taken exception to how he was treated. He accused Larry of trying to extort money from him, and got a couple of his underlings to back him up. Didn't matter that my partner's rep was spotless up until that point. The agency chose to dismiss him rather than risk a public backlash. He lost everything, his wife sued for divorce, and his life quickly went downhill. A few years later he died of alcoholic poisoning.'

'Okay, that would explain it,' Bishop said. 'But I've got another question for you.'

Arquette gave a ghost of a smile. 'I thought you might have.'

'Was it Klyce who was behind Amy's assault?'

'This will surprise you, but I don't think so.'

'No? Who, then?'

Arquette reached down for his paperwork again and flipped through until he found three large photo prints. He passed them over and said, 'I think it was the man in these pictures.'

Bishop studied the top photo. It was in black and white and clearly taken from long-distance, but the details were still pretty sharp. It was a daylight shot of three men as they talked outside a nondescript warehouse. It could have been anywhere. But the time code in the corner gave the date as October 11, just under three weeks ago.

One of the men was Roger Klyce, wearing an expensive overcoat and carrying a thin black briefcase in his right hand. The other two men were both black. Both wore dark, functional suits. Using Klyce as a gauge, Bishop estimated the first man to be about six-two or six-three, and weighing about two hundred and thirty pounds. None of it fat. His face was indistinct in this particular shot. The other man was about six foot and probably about two hundred pounds. His profile showed deep-set eyes and a straight nose.

Bishop turned to the next shot. It must have been taken just a few seconds later. All three participants were in similar positions, except the larger man's face was now turned towards the camera.

Bishop studied that face. It had a lot of hard edges, as though somebody had sculpted it out of granite. The small eyes were hidden under the man's prominent brow. Bishop couldn't be sure. Not really sure. The distance had been too great. But it looked like the same man he'd seen outside Angelo's Pool Hall this afternoon.

TWENTY-EIGHT

'Who is he?' Bishop asked.

'His name's Rapulana Bekele,' Arquette said. 'Currently chief security officer at the embassy for the People's Republic of Konamba, in Washington, DC.'

Bishop kept his face a mask, but it seemed his patience with Arquette had been rewarded. Finally, the Konamban connection he'd been seeking. He briefly considered mentioning the surveillance log he'd found on the CD, but the impulse passed quickly. He'd never been in the habit of sharing information with the law, and he wasn't planning to start now.

'Go on,' he said.

'He's ex-army, with a reputation for extreme ruthlessness. I don't know the other guy's name, but it's likely he's a member of his security team. Possibly his deputy.'

'How did you make him?'

'Their car was parked nearby. I traced the diplomatic plates back to the Konamban embassy and got a contact over at the State Department to send me photos of their senior staff. My contact also informed me that Bekele very rarely sets foot outside the embassy grounds, which makes this meeting all the more remarkable. Apparently, he even sleeps on site. Probably in one of the rooms down in the basement.'

'Who took these shots?'

'I did. I had a couple of free days and spent most of them parked outside the Artemis building in the hope that Klyce'd finally give something away. On this particular Sunday morning, I got lucky. He drove to an industrial park a few blocks south of the offices for this meeting. It was pretty deserted out there, but I found a good vantage point.'

Bishop turned to the last shot and immediately realized he'd gotten them out of order. This one showed Bekele handing the black briefcase to Klyce.

'I remember reading about Konamba,' Bishop said, frowning at the large man's profile. 'They gained their independence from Ethiopia in the late eighties, right? I seem to recall the maniac who took charge made a pretty good attempt at slaughtering as many of his countrymen as he could before he was finally overthrown.'

'Self-proclaimed president-for-life, Erasto 'The Scythe' Badat,' Arquette said, nodding. 'They say almost half a million innocent civilians lost their lives thanks to him and his militia. It's been almost fifteen years since he disappeared, but Konamba is still on most countries' blacklists, ours included, because of him. The current coalition government are steadily trying to rebuild their image, but they're finding it a long hard road, especially with all the civil unrest back home. They've made it clear to the world media that to bring any kind of lasting peace to the region they need up-to-date weaponry, and I guess if they can't get it legitimately . . .' He waved a hand at the photo.

Bishop tapped a finger against the top one and said, 'What makes you think they're buying arms here? For all you know that briefcase contains Klyce's lunch.'

Arquette smiled. 'Like I say, I can't prove anything. But I do know that three days after these photos were taken, another arms consignment failed to turn up at its final destination. Afghanistan, this time. And once again, the shipment was overseen by a large team of heavily armed LCT bodyguards.'

Bishop handed the photos back to Arquette and sat back in the seat. He was well aware this kind of thing went on all the time, and would most likely continue to do so for years to come. If LCT and Artemis were involved, and he wasn't convinced they were yet, then they were merely a drop in the ocean. But if Amy *had* found out about it, Bishop was fairly sure she wouldn't have been able to sit back and just forget it. Not Amy. It wasn't in her nature. Out of the pair of them, she'd always been the one with the high ethical standards and sense of duty. But he still had a few more questions.

'Why would this Bekele want Amy out of the way?' he said. 'What would he gain?'

Arquette shrugged. 'For a deal like this to go through, there'd have to be heavy involvement from high-ranking Konamban government officials. And that would undoubtedly include some senior people stationed at the embassy. If your sister found out somebody high up was involved over there, then that could be reason enough to want her gone. These people may be blacklisted, but they still maintain a diplomatic presence here as they try to claw their way up to respectability. To have diplomats expelled from the US as undesirables would set them back years. They couldn't risk the chance of that happening.'

'But how would they even know Amy was aware of what's going on?'

Arquette reached down for his paperwork again and leafed through until he found a specific sheet. He passed it across to Bishop, who saw it was another itemized telephone bill. It was for a 202 number, but a different one from that listed on Amy's CD. The page covered incoming and outgoing calls for October 18. There were a lot of them. Bishop quickly scanned the list of numbers and stopped halfway down when he recognized the number for Amy's cell phone. She'd called the 202 number at 13.23. The conversation had lasted for thirteen minutes. Then, at 14.17, the Washington number called Amy back. That conversation only lasted four minutes. After that the list continued with more numbers that meant nothing to Bishop.

He said, 'I take it this number belongs to somebody in the embassy?'

'Not just anybody. That's the office number for the ambassador himself, Mwenye Byakagaba. I think it's entirely possible that your sister found out some of what was going on between Bekele and Artemis, and decided to take her suspicions to their top man over here. Maybe they talked it over on the phone, or maybe Amy arranged to meet Byakagaba and discuss it in person the next day. After all, DC's only a short train ride away.'

Bishop pursed his lips. 'Why go to him? Why not take what she had to the law?'

'Well, that depends on what she'd discovered, doesn't it? Maybe she only had a few pieces of the jigsaw at that point. I really don't know.

Only your sister can say for sure, and she's not talking right now. But I'm pretty sure she discovered the rest at some point, then found somebody with influence who was willing to take it further with enough proof. At which point, Bekele decided to act.'

'So you're suggesting the Konamban ambassador's in on this, too?'

Arquette shook his head. 'Not necessarily. It might be that he simply talked over Amy's accusations with his head of security, who then decided to deal with the problem himself. He probably kept a close watch on her until he figured out a game plan. I do know it wouldn't be that hard to find three men capable of making her death look like a mugging, though. Especially if the money was right.'

Arquette was closer to the truth than he knew, but Bishop saw no reason to enlighten him. 'You could be totally wrong about all this, you know. It could simply be Klyce seeing history about to repeat itself, and deciding to take care of business like before.'

'I'd really like to believe that, but the MO's all wrong. If Klyce wanted her dead he'd simply make her disappear, like he did with Hernandez. No muss, no fuss.'

'That's assuming he was the one who got rid of Hernandez in the first place. There are a lot of ifs and maybes in your theory.'

Arquette showed his palms. 'That's why it's just a theory at this stage. All I can do is work with the facts that are available.'

'So here comes the big question. Why you telling me all this?'

'I've been keeping track of you today, Bishop. Or trying to. There are a lot of blank spaces. See, after reading up on your history, I suspected you might investigate Amy's assault on your own and so far you've proved me right. I'd probably know a lot more if we hadn't lost you at that dollar store in Seaman Avenue this afternoon. I presume you and your brother-in-law both left by the rear exit?'

Bishop said nothing. At the time, he hadn't been quite sure why he'd chosen that way to leave. Just that it had felt right at the time. One more tick for his instincts.

'Don't suppose you want to tell me where you went next?'

Bishop just looked at him.

'Didn't think so. Anyway, my point is I think we both have similar aims. I want Klyce. You want the person who ordered your sister killed. I think Bekele's the key to both. I can't touch him for a variety of reasons, one of them being that as a senior official in the embassy he has diplomatic immunity. But as a free agent, you can go where I can't.'

'So that's what all this is about. You want me to do your dirty work for you. Okay, you can let me out here, thanks.'

'Come on, Bishop. You're not about to ignore the information I've given you. I could hear the wheels turning when you looked at those photos. I know you plan to have a very serious talk with Bekele. And all I ask is that whatever information you discover you share with me. No obligation. Just a simple request, nothing more.'

Bishop said nothing. This subtle approach was a new one on him. He'd generally found cops got in your face at the smallest opportunity. Arquette had obviously learned a few things over the years. But Bishop wasn't about to commit to anything just yet. The less anybody knew of his actions, the better. Especially the Feds.

Which reminded him. Bishop pulled his cell phone from his pocket and said, 'You operate out of the New York field office? The one on Federal Plaza?'

'That's right,' Arquette said. 'Why?'

'What's the number for the switchboard there?'

Arquette brought his brows together, then slowly reeled off a ten-digit number. Bishop keyed the figures into the phone and brought it to his ear.

It was picked up almost immediately. A clipped female voice with a heavy Bronx lilt said, 'Federal Bureau of Investigation, New York Office. What's the nature of your call, please?'

'I need to speak to Special Agent Dermot Arquette. My name's Alan Carraway. He's expecting my call and I lost the cell phone number he gave me. It's kind of urgent.'

'One moment, please,' the woman said, and put Bishop on hold.

Arquette was still frowning as he took his own cell phone from his inside jacket pocket and placed it on his knee. Seven seconds later, it began to ring. He picked it up and took the call. 'This is Arquette,' he said. After a pause, he said, 'Fine, put him through.'

Bishop watched as Arquette said, 'Happy now?'

Bishop heard the words in stereo. 'Just checking,' he said, and hung up.

Arquette smiled. 'So now what?'

'Now you let me out of here, like I asked.'

After a few moments of silence, Arquette sighed and pressed a button set into his armrest. 'Pull over, will you, Wescott?' he said. 'Our guest wants to leave.'

The driver slowed and pulled up next to a fire hydrant. Bishop looked out the window and saw they were on East 59th Street. He checked his watch and saw it was 19.08. The caffeine in the sodas had kept him going a little longer, but he still felt beat. His body needed rest. He'd catch the 4 or 5 train to the end of the line, then the ferry over to Staten Island, then the bus to his house in Great Kills. With any luck, he'd be asleep in his own bed within the hour. Ninety minutes at most.

Arquette pulled a card from his pocket and held it out. 'Well?'

Bishop took the card, memorized the phone numbers on it and handed it back. 'Let me sleep on it,' he said. Then he opened the door and stepped out into the night.

TWENTY-NINE

Bishop woke up at 05.30 the next morning. It was still dark, but the early start was necessary. He didn't know what time Muro would be at the hospital, and he wanted to be there when the guy arrived.

Once he'd showered and shaved, Bishop went downstairs to the kitchen, carrying a knapsack full of items he might need if he was going to check out Arquette's story. Which obviously meant a trip to DC. The thought of being away from Amy for any length of time made him edgy, but he couldn't stay at the hospital, either. That was what he'd hired Muro for. Bishop needed to go where the leads took him if he was going to protect Amy from possible further harm.

He poured some tap water into a pot and switched on the stove. Whenever he was home he always began the day with tea if he could. He generally avoided set routines, but he figured a mug of the hot stuff in the morning was a pretty harmless one. If it was good enough for the ancient Chinese it was good enough for him.

As he waited for the water to heat up, his thoughts turned to the house around him, and what it signified. Bishop generally didn't think about it much. To him it was just a base where he could lay down his head whenever he was in town. He'd never been the nostalgic type. But he and Amy had both spent their formative years here. He guessed that had to count for something.

Dad had left the place to both of them in his will, the deeds held in trust until they reached twenty-one, but after their grandparents died it had remained unoccupied for a long time. After leaving the Corps, Bishop had rarely been in one place for too long so he'd never used it. And Amy had no emotional attachment to the place at all, thanks to those couple of years she'd spent under the care of Dad's parents.

Tom and Annabel. They'd been a cold pair of oddballs, without a doubt. They weren't bad people, exactly. They just had no empathy for anybody else. Not even their own blood. Bishop sometimes wondered how his dad had turned out so different from them. Strength of character, probably. But after Mom and Dad died, it was a simple fact that the only affection Bishop ever received came from Amy. And she'd never let him down. Not once. Not even when she'd had to leave him alone with them.

It was inevitable she would, of course. Bishop knew it, even at twelve. That was the year she departed for university in Bridgeport, Connecticut. Amy's last day at the house had been one to remember, though, because it was on that day that Bishop witnessed a ruthless side to his sister he'd never seen before. It left him tremendously impressed.

It had been a bright September morning and the four family members, Tom, Annabel, Amy and Bishop, had been standing in a loose circle by the front door while out front the cab driver waited to take Amy to the Staten Island Ferry. Annabel was trying to hide her joy that this last threat to her authority was about to leave, and not doing a very good job.

Bishop allowed Amy to hug him for about the twentieth time in as many minutes, and when she finally released him she said, 'Remember, kiddo, I'm only a phone call away. Call me any time, even it's once or twice a day. And for any reason whatsoever, even if it's just to hear my voice. And if I'm in class, leave a message and I promise to get back to you as soon as I can. Okay?'

Before Bishop could answer in the positive, Annabel cut in with, 'That might not be possible, Amy.'

Amy turned and looked at her grandmother with narrowed eyes. 'Why not?'

Annabel gave a thin smile, which was probably the worst thing she could have done. 'Well, Amy, we're not a rich household as you well know, and we'll have to start being a lot more careful with our finances from now on. Neither Tom nor I are working and I can't really justify unnecessary long-distance calls every day. I'm sorry, but I just can't.'

Amy raised an eyebrow. '*You* can't justify it. Is that what you just said?'

'Well, as head of the household, I think I have the right to—'

'Listen to me carefully, Annabel,' Amy interrupted. 'You're both here because you are my brother's legal guardians until he reaches eighteen, but don't ever think that gives you any rights as far as this house is concerned.'

Tom said, 'Now wait a minute—'

Amy stopped him with a raised hand. 'And I also know for a fact neither of you are suffering financially, either, so let's not go there.'

'I have absolutely no idea what you're talking about,' Annabel said.

Amy smiled then. 'Annabel, I know the exact amount you got after selling your Brooklyn apartment two years ago, so let's not pretend any more, okay? You're both sitting pretty with money in the bank and free boarding in your beloved house in the suburbs. But don't forget that in three years the property deeds for this place come to me, after which I'll have total authority over who stays here and who doesn't.'

Annabel's mouth dropped. 'You'd actually be willing to throw your own grandparents onto the street? I don't believe it. Who'd look after James?'

'I would. I'm his sister, after all. And I'm a hell of a lot closer to him than you are.'

Tom said, 'You'd really do that? To *us*?'

Amy shrugged. 'I'd prefer not to, but when you start throwing your weight around I lose my temper, and when that happens I make regrettable decisions. So my advice to you is to not make me lose my temper. And that means letting Bish here call me any time he feels like it. And for as long as he wants. Is that clear?'

Annabel just glared at her and said nothing.

'Please don't make me ask twice,' Amy said. 'I might lose my temper again.'

Finally, Annabel said, 'Of course James can call you whenever he wants. I was just putting forward a suggestion, that's all.'

Amy had smiled at that point and said, 'Wonderful. So we're all friends again.'

And that had been the end of it, but the steel in his sister's voice that day was something Bishop would never forget.

Amy always came back during vacations too. She always made time for him, no matter what. After all, they only had each other. Naturally, things had changed for her over time, what with her family and all. But for him, Amy was still the one true constant in his life. Always had been. And if she got through this, she probably always would be.

But her continued survival was down to him now. That much was clear.

The water started bubbling. Bishop picked up the pot and poured some of it into his plain black mug. He was just placing a bag of Earl Grey in there when his cell phone started ringing. He picked it up and immediately recognized the number as Willard's.

He took the call and said, 'What's wrong?'

'Better get over here as fast as you can,' Willard said. 'Somebody tried to kill Amy again.'

THIRTY

When the elevator reached the third floor Bishop exited and marched down the corridor towards Amy's room, trying to keep his anger in check. It wasn't easy. After suffering the ferry ride to Lower Manhattan, he'd taken a cab straight to the hospital. He'd spent most of the 45-minute drive fuming. He wasn't used to feeling so powerless and hated every second of it.

Willard had been full of apologies when he'd explained what had happened on the phone. He'd also accepted all the blame. He'd said that at 05.45, a nurse had come over and said that there was a call for him at the nurses' station. When Willard took the phone, somebody who sounded exactly like Bishop had said to meet him down in the hospital cafeteria ASAP. Willard had taken the elevator down to the second floor and, when he saw no sign of Bishop anywhere, realized he'd been had. He then raced back up to see an army of emergency staff running in and out of Amy's room.

Somebody had gone in and removed the ventilator tube from her throat, and it was only thanks to the quick thinking of a doctor who'd looked in by chance that she was alive at all. They calculated she'd stopped breathing for between ninety seconds and two minutes, and that any longer could have resulted in permanent brain damage. Willard said she was still in the coma, but at least her condition was no worse.

Bishop took a right turn and saw Willard sitting in the same seat that Bishop had left him in, staring expressionless at Amy's door. Further back, Gerry was at the nurses' station talking to two men. One was a thin guy in a raincoat, with olive skin, centre-parted black hair and a neat goatee beard. The other one was older and stockier. He had perfectly groomed grey hair and wore a dark grey suit that

131

looked as though it had been moulded onto him. Since there was also a uniformed cop standing close by, Bishop assumed one of them was a detective. He carried on towards Amy's room. Willard saw him coming and got up to meet him.

'I'm real sorry, man,' he said, 'I was only away from my seat for a few—'

'How's Amy?' Bishop cut in.

Willard shrugged. 'Same as before. Still unresponsive, but she's alive.'

'Okay, fine. And who called the cops? You?'

'Yeah, I thought it best. That guy in the raincoat back there is Detective DuBay. I already told him what I know, and that somebody must have come and cut off Amy's oxygen while I was away from my post, but he didn't sound too convinced. Why, did I do wrong?'

'I don't know yet. When did Gerry get here?'

'Maybe ten minutes after the alarm went out. It wasn't long. I guess he must have already been on his way here or something.'

Bishop had more questions, but first he needed to see Amy with his own eyes. He left his knapsack with Willard and went over to her room. He stepped inside and approached his sister. She was lying in the same position as before, arms still atop the sheets. There were three IV lines attached to her now. Her steady breathing echoed throughout the room. The ventilator was still making its electronic beeping sounds, although it looked to be a different model from the one he remembered.

Just hang in there, Amy, he thought, and went over to her. He leaned down and kissed her cheek. *We'll get there. I'll make sure of it.*

He watched her breathing for another minute and then stepped back out. He looked down the hallway to his left and noticed the ceiling security camera he'd passed before. He turned the other way and saw Gerry and the detective walking towards him. Willard also came over, with Bishop's bag over his shoulder.

Gerry spoke first. 'This is Bishop, detective. My wife's brother I told you about.'

DuBay nodded at him. 'Mr Willard here said you were on your way. I'm Detective DuBay.'

'I know,' Bishop said. 'So what's your take on this? Seems clear to me that this was a deliberate attempt on my sister's life.'

DuBay scratched his goatee with a long index finger and said, 'I don't agree. And neither does Mr Philmore here. As far as I can make out from interviewing the staff, it appears Mrs Philmore had a violent convulsion and dislodged the ventilator tube herself. They said she's already suffered a number of minor spasms since being brought in, and it seems this was a big one.'

'It happens, Bishop,' Gerry said. 'I wish to God it hadn't, but I don't see anything suspicious about it.'

Bishop looked at him, then at DuBay. 'That's interesting. So how do you explain the phone call when somebody told Willard to leave his post at exactly the same time as the incident took place? Doesn't that raise any kind of flag at all?'

'It's an anomaly, I gotta admit,' DuBay said, and turned to Willard. 'And this caller didn't actually identify himself to you by name?'

'No,' Willard said, 'but he sounded just like Bish—'

'Because I spoke to the nurse who called you over,' DuBay continued, 'and he didn't identify himself to her either. Nor did he ask for you by name. He just asked her to go get the guy in the chair. That's all.'

Willard frowned. 'So?'

'So it's possible it was a wrong number. Or maybe he got the wrong floor. This is a big hospital, after all. Maybe he thought he was talking to somebody else. Lots of people sitting around on chairs. And no offence, Bishop, but I can think of a dozen colleagues of mine who sound just like you.'

'None taken,' Bishop said. 'Putting aside your theory for a second, have you at least checked with the hospital's phone carrier to see where the call originated from?'

'I did. It came from an unlisted cell phone. Completely untraceable.'

'Convenient.'

DuBay shrugged. 'If you say so. And there's also the fact that we're missing a motive. I don't know why anybody would want to kill your sister, unless there's something you're not telling me?'

Gerry looked down at the floor and said nothing. Bishop looked DuBay right in the eyes and said, 'I'm not keeping anything from you, detective. But what about security safeguards? Surely there would have been an alarm if the respirator malfunctioned?'

'There was. But whoever set the machine up accidentally set the alarm at a much lower volume than usual. It activated, but nobody heard it. It's just lucky a doctor checked on her and was able to perform emergency CPR when he saw she wasn't breathing.'

'That's something we can agree on.' Bishop turned and pointed at the security camera in the ceiling twenty feet away. 'As for what caused it, I take it you've checked the security footage from that camera over there?'

'Of course.'

'And?'

'And nobody entered Mrs Philmore's room immediately prior to the incident.'

'Not that I doubt you,' Bishop said, 'but is there any chance I could see for myself?'

DuBay's brow wrinkled as he studied him. Bishop thought he'd refuse, but he must have seen something in Bishop's expression because he just sighed and said, 'Okay, follow me, then.'

THIRTY-ONE

The security room was located on the first floor, in the east wing. There were no markings on the door. Just a spyhole at head height, and a square steel plate with a keycard slot at the top in place of a door handle.

Bishop stood to the side as DuBay knocked on the door. A few seconds later there was a brief buzzing sound and the door opened inwards. A wide-shouldered, blond-haired security guard stood there looking at them both.

'Me again, John,' DuBay said. 'We'd like to see that footage again.'

'Sure,' the guard said and stood to one side so they could enter. 'Come on in.'

The surveillance room was about thirty feet by thirty. No windows. Against one wall, a counter ran the length of the room with a couple of chairs underneath. Above that were two long rows of LCD monitors showing real-time colour footage of the hospital interior. Bishop counted twenty-four screens. Two of them were switched off. An older second guard was sitting at a large circular work desk in the centre of the room with a laptop in front of him. On the other side of the table was another open laptop.

The second guard watched as Bishop and DuBay followed John to the wall of security monitors. John took a seat and switched on one of the blank monitors. Then he turned to a large console on the counter and pressed some more buttons. Bishop saw three sets of red LED numerical figures light up at the top of the device. The first line read 018. Underneath that was an active clock readout showing the current time of 08.19.37. Another readout underneath read 05.44.02. This one was static, though. Under that were rows of switches and buttons, as well as a miniature joystick.

Bishop watched as a still shot of a familiar hallway appeared on the monitor. He could make out the small figure of Willard sitting in his seat. He had his legs stretched out as he watched something on his iPod. He was the only person in sight. The corridor was fairly well lit. Much further down on the left, Bishop could just about make out part of the nurses' station. The time code in the corner of the screen matched that of the third readout. 05.44.02.

'You know to work it all, right?' John said, standing up.

'Thanks, John,' DuBay said and took his seat. Bishop watched the guard return to whatever he'd been doing on the open laptop.

Bishop turned to the monitor. DuBay pressed the play button and the footage began. The time code and the matching readout on the console both progressed simultaneously. The only evidence that this was actual footage was when Willard momentarily shifted in his seat at 05.44.37. At 05.45.08, the figure of a nurse appeared in the distance. She was standing about where the nurses' station was. She seemed to be calling to Willard, because he turned his head in her direction, and then got to his feet and walked over to her. At 05.45.24, both figures turned into the next corridor and disappeared from view.

DuBay said, 'Nothing else happens until five forty-eight.'

'That's when the doctor decided to check on room 32?' Bishop asked.

'Right.' DuBay found the fast forward button and pressed it. 'X2' appeared in the corner of the screen and the footage began moving faster.

Bishop watched in silence. The corridor remained empty of people. Nobody went into Amy's room. At 05.47.31, Dubay took his finger off the button and let it play out at normal speed. At 05.48.17, Bishop saw a man in a white coat emerge from the bottom of the screen and enter Amy's room. At 05.48.27, the door opened again and the doctor leaned out and yelled something in the direction of the nurses' station. A male and a female nurse quickly appeared and ran over to the room. A few seconds later, another doctor appeared from the bottom of the screen and joined them inside.

But Bishop had already seen what he came for. He wasn't entirely sure, though. He'd need to double check. But not with DuBay present. 'Okay,' he said. 'You can stop it now.'

DuBay grunted and paused the footage.

'I guess you were right, after all,' Bishop said. 'No sign of foul play.'

'That's what I been telling you. Sometimes these things just happen.'

Bishop said nothing to that.

The younger guard let them out and locked the door behind them. Bishop and DuBay began walking towards the front of the building where the elevators were. They were almost at the end of the corridor when Bishop saw the universal male and female signs a few yards ahead.

'I need to make a stop here,' Bishop said. 'You go on without me.'

DuBay shrugged and carried on walking towards the elevators.

Bishop went into the restroom and spent a minute washing his hands. When he came out again, DuBay was gone. He was walking back to the security room when his cell phone began ringing. He brought it out and took the call. 'Bishop.'

'This is Scott Muro,' the familiar voice said. 'I'm on my way to the hospital now. Where do I go once I get there?'

'Intensive Care. Room 32. And just so you know, somebody made a second attempt on Amy's life this morning.'

'No shit? Christ. Is she okay?'

'Yeah, the doctor got to her in time. I'll tell you all about it when you arrive. If I'm not there, wait for me. I'm following a lead right now.'

'Ten-four,' Muro said, and hung up.

Bishop kept on walking. He reached the door to Security and knocked twice.

After a few seconds, John opened the door and smiled at him. 'Maybe we should start selling tickets,' he said.

Bishop smiled back. 'Maybe you should. My partner had to go back upstairs to do some more interviews, but I wanna take a second look at that footage. I think I saw something before, but I can't be sure.'

'Sure, why not?' He led Bishop to the counter and said, 'Want me to set things up the same as before?'

137

'If you could,' Bishop said. 'But do it at normal speed this time.'

'No problem.' John sat down and played with the console controls again. He began the footage at 05.43.13.

'And pay particular attention to the time code,' Bishop said.

The guard nodded and they both watched the screen. Seconds turned into minutes. At 05.45.56, Bishop said, 'Right around here.'

The corridor on the screen was still empty of people at this point. The time code advanced to 05.45.58 . . . 05.45.59 . . . 05.46.00. Then it stayed on 05.46.00 for an extra beat before continuing to 05.46.01, then 05.46.52 . . .

'Hey,' John said, 'did you see that?'

'I did,' Bishop said. 'I assume it's easy enough to pause a camera while it's recording, right?'

John shrugged. 'Ain't nothing easier. Select a camera number, press pause and that camera stops recording. Press it again and it continues without a break.'

While he'd been talking, the other guard had come over to listen. He was standing behind John, watching the monitor. Now he said, 'But the time readout would still carry on as normal. Like, if you started up again thirty seconds later, there'd still be thirty seconds missing in the time code when you viewed the footage.'

'Right,' Bishop said. 'Unless there was a way I could also reset the current time readout before continuing. Like taking it back thirty seconds, say. Then it would carry on recording as if I hadn't paused at all. Or close to it. Is that possible?'

'Well, it could be done,' John said, 'but the corridor would have to be empty both times or it wouldn't match up. And doing it that way would mean Camera 18's time code would now be running out of sync with all the other cameras. Check for me, will you, Phil?'

The other guard walked over and checked one of the screens near the end. 'Uh uh,' he said. 'Eighteen's showing the same time as all the others.'

Bang went that theory then. Or maybe not. Bishop leaned against the desk. He rubbed his palm over his scalp, trying to come up with an answer that would cover all the variables. A few moments later he had one. And it was simple, too, as the best solutions usually are. He turned to the guards and said, 'You were both here at the time, right?'

'Right,' Phil said. 'We relieved the two night guys at five a.m., like we usually do. Our shift starts an hour before the nurses' changeover, so we don't miss anything.'

'And who else was in this room during the next hour?'

'Well, the cleaner.' John stared up at Bishop. 'It's usually a guy called Mike, but today it was some guy we hadn't seen before. He told us Mike was off sick.'

'This new guy, was he light or dark-skinned?'

'Dude was white.'

'And what time did you let him in?'

'About twenty to six, wasn't it?' Phil said. 'Something like that.'

John was nodding his head. 'Sounds about right. He was here until six, or just before. And come to think of it, he was spending a lot of time on the carpet in this part of the room.'

'And you were over there working on your laptops the whole time?'

Phil looked sheepish. 'I guess we were. We both take evening courses, and . . .'

'Sure, sure,' Bishop said. He was thinking it could work, but only if the cleaner was in constant contact with his partner on the third floor. 'Was he wearing earphones?'

'Yeah,' John said. 'Most of the cleaners listen to music while they work.'

'This guy was also wearing a surgical mask,' Phil said. 'And a base-ball cap.'

Bishop grunted. A surgical mask in a hospital. What could be more natural? He took a moment to go through everything, step by step, to see if it had legs.

'So the cleaner's watching the monitor for Camera 18 while he works,' Bishop said quietly to himself. 'At the same time he'd have to be in constant communication with his partner, probably via the hands-free on his cell phone. At five forty-five or thereabouts, he phones the duty nurse and asks her to bring the guard to the phone. He then makes out he's . . . somebody the guard recognizes and calls him away from that floor. Meanwhile, the second guy's close by and makes his way to that same corridor and waits just outside the camera's range. Soon as the corridor's empty, the cleaner presses the pause button on the console at exactly five forty-six and tells his partner to proceed to room 32. He goes in, resets the volume on the alarm and removes the respirator tube. As soon as the patient starts experiencing breathing problems he exits, and his partner up here resets the clock back to 05.46.00 and continues recording.' Bishop nodded to himself. 'Very nice. It was planned right to the second.'

'Okay,' John said, 'but that still don't explain how Camera 18's time readout is still in sync with the others, does it?'

Bishop turned to him. 'Right. Which means the cleaner would need to stick around here for a short while, then do the same thing again. Except when he paused the recording the second time, he'd need to set the clock *forward* to bring it back into sync with the others.'

They all stared at the monitor. It was 05.52.45. There was a lot of motion in the corridor now. People walking back and forth. Others running.

'Fast forward if you want,' Bishop said. 'I have a feeling the join will be a little more obvious this time round. Our boy would have figured nobody would bother watching the footage for too much longer after the incident.'

John found the fast-forward button without taking his eyes from the screen. The footage began to speed up and they all watched in silence.

Bishop was right. When the moment came it couldn't have been more obvious.

At 05.57.04, a man and a nurse were standing by the row of chairs, discussing something. In the next frame they had both simply disappeared. Just vanished. And the time had jumped forward to 05.57.51. Forty-seven seconds. That must have been the amount of time the killer was in Amy's room.

Bishop turned to John and said, 'Okay, next step is to see where our guy went next.'

THIRTY-TWO

'I take it there's a camera in the hallway outside?' Bishop asked.

'You know it,' John said, and pressed a switch on the console. The monitor above them went blank. The 018 number at the top of the console was immediately replaced by 009. He used the keyboard for a few seconds, and said, 'I'll start it at five fifty-seven a.m.'

Bishop watched as the screen filled with an image of another corridor running off into the distance. The time was 05.57.18. Bishop spotted the distinctive keycard panel on the third door up on the left. The security room. This corridor was busier than the one upstairs, with people walking back and forth, going in and out of doorways.

The door to Security opened at 05.59.02. A man wearing a black baseball cap and a surgical mask exited, pulling a well-stocked cleaning cart. The man was dressed in dark blue overalls that looked a size too small. He also looked to be wearing gloves. He kept his head down as he left the room. Bishop couldn't make out any features. He turned and walked away from the camera, pushing the cleaning cart ahead of him. He continued down the hallway at a casual stroll. Just before he reached the end, he positioned the cart next to the right-hand wall and entered a passageway on the left. He was too far away to be anything but a silhouette.

'Is that the men's room he's heading for?' Bishop asked.

Phil frowned. 'Hard to make out at that distance, but it looks like it, yeah.'

'Any more cameras down that end of the building?'

'Once you turn the corner at the end,' John said, 'you're in the main reception area. Cameras 6 and 7 cover that part of the building. Seven points the other way, but 6 might help us.'

John switched on the second unused monitor and pressed some

more buttons on the console. Bishop kept his attention on the first screen. He watched a thin, long-haired girl enter the corridor from the reception end and turn into the same passageway as the cleaner.

Then the other monitor came online. The static image showed the main reception desk on the left of the screen and the entrance to their corridor on the right. There were about six people in shot. Three at the desk, two sitting behind it, and another in the foreground about to exit stage left. The time code in the corner read 05.58.45.

'Keep that one paused for the moment,' Bishop said. On the first monitor the long-haired girl exited the passageway at 06.01.32 and walked towards the reception area. At 06.01.54, a male figure in a baseball cap appeared, then moved off in the same direction.

'Okay,' Bishop said, 'let's see Camera 6 now. Take it to just before the girl came out of the restroom.'

John turned to the other screen and fast-forwarded until he reached 06.01.28. Then he let it play at normal speed.

At 06.01.36, the long-haired girl exited the corridor at a brisk pace. She wore loose-fitting pants and a T-shirt. She continued past the reception desk and soon went out of shot.

At 06.01.59, the man in the baseball cap also exited the corridor, wearing dark glasses. No surgical mask. He was also wearing tan pants, a dark blue sweatshirt and a faded black denim jacket. Bishop knew it was the same man, just from the way he moved. He had the same casual walk as the cleaner. With his head angled down, he walked towards the camera and immediately disappeared at the bottom of the screen.

'I assume he just left via the front entrance,' Bishop said.

'That's right,' Phil said.

Bishop sighed and shook his head. 'It was worth a shot, but he clearly knew where all the cameras were. Can one of you check the trash in the men's room?'

'I'll go,' Phil said, and left the room.

John said, 'Don't you think it's worth tracking the second guy, too?'

Bishop shook his head. 'We don't know what he looks like, or even from which direction he came. And he probably did an even better job of avoiding the cameras than this one.' He thought for a moment and said, 'Do you keep the contact details for hospital employees here? Specifically, your cleaner Mike?'

'Sure do,' John said, and went over to a filing cabinet set against the wall. He unlocked it and started going through the drawers. A short while later, the door opened and Phil came in holding what looked like a set of dark overalls.

'Found these,' he said. 'Also this.' He reached into a pocket, pulled out a hospital ID card and passed it to Bishop.

The card listed the owner as *Michael Esteban*. The photo showed a Latino guy in his forties with a wide neck and slicked-back hair. 'This is his genuine ID card?' Bishop asked.

Phil nodded. 'It's genuine.'

John was turning pages of a ring-bound folder. 'Okay, Darwood . . . Easton . . . Here we go, Esteban, Michael. Got a phone number and an address out in the Bronx.'

'Good,' Bishop said. 'You wanna give him a call?'

John went over and picked up one of the phones on the desk. After consulting the folder, he dialled a number, put it on speakerphone and replaced the handset. They all listened to the ringing tone. A minute passed. Two. John was about to hang up when there was a loud click on the line. Then a hoarse male voice said, 'Yeah?'

'Mike?' John asked.

The sound of a phlegmy cough echoed through the room. Then, 'Yeah. Whosis?'

'John over at hospital security. Look, I got a detective here who wants to talk to you.'

Bishop stepped closer to the speaker and said, 'How you feeling there, Mr Esteban?'

'Shitty.' He coughed again. 'Look, what's this about? I done nothin' wrong.'

'I know you haven't. Tell me what happened to you.'

'You really wanna know?'

'I do.'

'Went out to my local last night, didn't I? Some guy kept buyin' rounds for the house so I stayed longer than I should've. But I musta drunk or eaten somethin' that didn't agree with me or somethin'. I don't remember too much, to be honest. I been pukin' and shittin' all night, and my brain feels like it's gonna explode.'

Bishop didn't doubt it. Wouldn't have been hard to slip something into his drink and wait for the drug to take effect. 'How'd you get home, Mr Esteban?'

'No idea. Somebody musta taken pity on me, though, 'cause I woke up in my own bed. So you gonna tell me what this is about?'

'Somebody was pretending to be you this morning, Mr Esteban. He had your ID and your overalls. This guy buying everybody drinks. Can you describe him?'

There was a pause. 'Pretendin' to be me? Shit, why would anybody wanna do that? Most days, even *I* don't wanna be me.'

Bishop sighed. 'Focus, Mr Esteban. The man in the bar. What did he look like?'

'Oh, uh, well, he was a big black fella. Tall and wide, you know? Wore a suit and a nice overcoat. That's about all I can tell you. We maybe swapped a few words, but I can't remember what we talked about. All I know is he just came in, told everybody he'd just got a promotion and wanted everybody in the place to get drunk with him. Since he was buyin', most of us were happy to oblige. I'm sure payin' for it now, though. Hey, you think somebody in there slipped me a mickey?'

'Sounds like it, Mr Esteban,' Bishop said. 'Go back to bed and get some rest.' He made a cutting motion to John, who reached over and ended the call.

It definitely sounded like the same man he'd seen the day before. Maybe the same guy as the one in Arquette's photos. That was something Bishop needed to find out.

'Well, that's that,' he said, and got to his feet. 'Thanks for your help, fellas.'

John walked him to the door and said, 'Hey, any time. Things ain't been this exciting for months.'

THIRTY-THREE

Back on the third floor, Bishop saw no sign of DuBay or the uniformed cop. Willard was sitting in the same seat as before, looking uncomfortable. Gerry was also there. He was standing outside Amy's room, talking to the grey-haired man Bishop had seen before. As Bishop went over, the man turned and held out his hand. He had a triangular face that ended in a pointed chin. His grey eyes studied Bishop with casual interest.

'You're Mrs Philmore's brother, yes?'

Bishop shook the hand. 'That's right. And you are?'

'Hospital administrator and Dean of Medicine, Grant Fisher. I was just explaining to Mr Philmore how regrettable this whole incident was, and that you can rest assured that nothing like this will happen again. In fact, I've already ordered another ventilator to be brought up, purely as back-up.'

'Good thinking,' Bishop said. 'And just so you know, I've also arranged for somebody to stay with Amy in her room on a twenty-four-hour basis. I'll feel better knowing she's got somebody watching over her when I'm not here.'

Fisher gave him a politician's smile. 'Oh, I'm sorry, but that would be entirely impossible. We can't allow visitors in patients' rooms outside normal hours. Hospital policy, you understand.'

Bishop smiled back. 'Well, it's either that or you're facing a lawsuit.'

'Lawsuit?' Fisher's face slowly fell, like wax melting.

'I'd call what happened here this morning a clear case of negligence, wouldn't you? I mean, somebody should have double-checked the alarm on that machine in there. My sister could have died. At the very least, I think there's a good case for medical malpractice.'

'You can't be—'

'Now look, Fisher,' Bishop interrupted, 'it's clear one of two things happened here. One, whoever set up the machine in the room screwed up by setting the alarm volume too low. Or two, somebody with malicious intent sabotaged it before removing Amy's ventilator tube. Now between you and me, I'm inclined to go with option two. In which case, you'll understand why I want somebody close by so there's no chance of it happening again.'

Fisher opened his mouth, then closed it again.

'It's up to you,' Bishop said. 'But as a major metropolitan hospital, you must already be up to your neck in civil lawsuits. You can't want another one. Especially when it could be avoided so easily.'

Fisher paused. 'Well . . .' he said finally, 'I suppose an exception could be made in this instance.'

'Excellent. Oh, and I'll want it in writing, of course. And signed by you. You know, just in case anybody tries to go back on it. The man's name is Scott Muro.' He smiled again. 'And I'd like it right now, please.'

'Very well. I'll have my secretary work something up immediately.'

'Appreciate it,' Bishop said, and watched him walk over to the nurses' station and pick up a phone.

Gerry blocked his view. 'Who's this Scott Muro? You never discussed this with me.'

'He's a private investigator who was recommended to me yesterday. And I don't need your permission, Gerry. Why, you got any objections?'

Gerry glared at him for a moment, then said, 'No, of course not. I want Amy safe, same as you. But I don't—'

'Good,' Bishop said, and turned and left him. He walked over to Willard and sat in the next seat along.

Willard made a face. 'I don't know what to say, Bishop. This is all my fault.'

Bishop wasn't about to argue the point. Instead, he said, 'Amy's still alive. It could have been worse.'

'Yeah. No thanks to me.'

'I probably should have been more explicit with my instructions.

Anyway, it's done now. I came over to tell you that the private investigator's on his way, so you can take off if you want.'

Willard smiled as he handed Bishop his knapsack and got to his feet. 'I get the message. My services are no longer required. So I guess this is the last time we'll see each other, right?'

'Nobody can see into the future, Willard.'

'Well, I can. Adios, Bishop.' Willard shook his head, then walked off in the direction of the elevators.

Bishop watched him until he pushed through the double doors and went out of sight. He hadn't been lying to the guy. Willard had made a mistake in leaving his post, but he'd clearly been tired when he showed up, so Bishop couldn't entirely lay the blame at his door. But he thought it might be a while before he decided to use him again.

He was still watching the double doors when an Asian-American man pushed through, looking at the numbers of each door he passed. Bishop had a hunch this was the guy he'd hired. In which case, the odd surname now made sense. The man looked in his mid-thirties with close-cropped black hair, and wore a dark sports jacket over a white polo shirt and black jeans. Bishop stood up and walked over to Amy's room. The man saw Bishop and raised an eyebrow. As he got closer, Bishop saw his eyes were dark blue, which suggested one of his parents was of western descent.

The man stopped when he reached Bishop, looked at the number on Amy's door and said, 'Hello. I'm Muro.'

'And I'm Bishop. Glad you made it.' Bishop quickly looked the guy over. About five-ten. Average weight. Average looks. Smooth facial features. Good build. If first impressions were anything to go by, he certainly looked capable enough.

'Let's go inside,' Bishop said. He opened the door to Amy's room and motioned for Muro to go first. As he shut the door, Muro glanced at Amy in the bed.

'Maybe you better fill me in,' he said.

Bishop nodded and told him as concisely as possibly everything that had happened since the initial attack on Amy. It took about two minutes. Muro didn't interrupt, which Bishop appreciated. When he finished, Muro blew out his cheeks and said, 'Now I'm glad I brought my piece with me.'

'So am I. That's one of the reasons I hired you. New York gun permits are hard to come by.'

Muro smiled. 'Tell me about it. This one cost me a month's worth of favours. So what's the deal here? Are the staff gonna give me grief about staying in Amy's room like this?'

'Don't worry about it. I'm arranging signed authorization for you right now from the hospital director himself. You'll have it before I leave.'

'Music to my ears.' Muro reached into his jacket pocket and pulled out two folded documents. He unfolded each one and said, 'Okay, this one's our standard contract and this is a copy. All I need is your John Hancock on the dotted lines and we're good to go.' He handed Bishop a pen and his ID wallet.

Bishop scanned the licensed private investigator's ID, then checked the form. Muro's daily rates were high, but Bishop didn't care. Equal Aid generally paid him well for his services and he was glad to put part of the money to good use. He signed his name on the last page, dated it, and did the same with the copy. He handed everything back to Muro, who countersigned both documents and gave the copy back to Bishop. 'This is yours.'

Bishop placed the papers in his knapsack and said, 'You got a card for me?'

Muro pulled a business card from his billfold and handed it over. It was very simple. Just the words *Muro Investigations* in a classy engraved font, then Muro's name, an address in Brooklyn, and a bunch of telephone numbers. 'You need to contact me directly,' Muro said, 'call the cell phone number.'

'Right.' Bishop pocketed the card. 'So is there anything else you need from me?'

'Just your professional opinion. Should I be expecting more trouble?'

'I think so, yeah. The people behind this have made two attempts on her life already. I don't know to what lengths they'll go to finish the job, but in those kinds of situations I generally prepare for the worst. All I can say is don't trust anybody. Except for me, that is.'

'Fair enough. In that case, I'll settle in and let you get on with whatever you're getting on with.' Muro then pulled the room's only chair away from the wall and positioned it next to the window. He sat down, pulled a smart phone from his jacket pocket and wiped an index finger across the screen.

Bishop gave a thin smile. The man wasted neither words nor motion. He liked that. His instincts told him he'd made the right choice in hiring him. Which made him feel a little better about leaving Amy to go to Washington. After a final look at his unconscious sister, Bishop left the room and looked around for Fisher.

First, the authorization papers. Then on to the airport.

THIRTY-FOUR

At 11.48, Bishop was sitting in the back of a cab as it slowly made its way down New Hampshire Avenue NW. It was a pleasant sunny day for late October. He was playing the visitor from out of town, here to take in the sights. He even had the camera to prove it.

At LaGuardia he'd caught the 09.40 Delta shuttle to DC, landing at Ronald Reagan Airport a few minutes after eleven. After making his way through the trials of passport control, he'd picked up his checked knapsack from the carousel and then it had been a short cab ride to Embassy Row. Although most of the larger embassies were located on Massachusetts Avenue NW, Bishop was only really interested in the smaller examples found on New Hampshire Avenue. Especially one of the newer ones.

He aimed his high-speed compact digital camera at the townhouses to his right, specifically the narrow four-storey building standing alone, and clicked off close to a dozen shots in three seconds. He'd taken plenty of photos already as cover, but it was this building he was interested in most. The one with the two poles on the second-storey balcony, displaying a pair of identical flags made up of three horizontal bars of black, red and green. Then he turned to his left and took a few shots of the buildings directly opposite.

Bishop kept taking photos as the cabbie made his way towards Dupont Circle four blocks down. Just before they reached it, Bishop said, 'Okay, let me out here.'

'You got it,' the driver said, and pulled in close to the kerb, near the corner.

Bishop paid the fare and added a decent tip. Then he slung his knapsack over his shoulder and got out. He was directly outside the Hotel Dupont, which took up almost half the block on this side.

Bishop stood by the steps leading to the entrance and looked around, as though deciding where to go next. Once the cab had pulled off and entered the traffic circle, he turned and began walking back along New Hampshire.

There was a ten-storey apartment complex on the other side of the street, then it was embassy after embassy on both sides for the next couple of blocks. Bishop walked quickly past, but when he reached the next block along he slowed his pace to a leisurely amble. Along this stretch it was mainly apartment buildings and large townhouses, most of which had long since been converted into apartments themselves.

But on the left, among a number of normal-sized townhouses in a row, was the narrow, tan stucco building with the two flags outside. Bishop took another look at it, noting everything. He still had the photos he'd taken as back-up, but nothing beat on-the-spot recon. Behind the second-floor balcony were two sets of double floor-to-ceiling windows, behind which probably lay the ambassador's office. Then two more rows of windows on the floors above, and two windows on the ground floor along with a dark wood entrance door. Bishop spotted the large plaque next to the door informing visitors they were about to enter *The Embassy Of The People's Rebublic of Konamba*.

The townhouse was separated from its neighbours on both sides. On the far side, Bishop remembered, was a gated entrance to what seemed to be an underground garage. A six-foot-high concrete wall closed the gap between the embassy and its nearer neighbour. A glance at Google Earth last night had shown him that it was just empty space behind there, although that might have changed since the satellite photo had been taken. It went quite a ways back, and as he approached he noticed more windows running along the side of the townhouse, as well as some steel fire escapes near the rear.

Bishop turned and was about to cross the street when he saw a police cruiser coming from the left, heading towards Dupont Circle. Bishop averted his face, opened a zip on his bag and pulled out a tourist map he'd picked up at the airport. He opened it up and waited for the cruiser to vanish. He already knew this area had a heavy police presence. He'd just have to work around it, that was all.

Once the cruiser was gone, he replaced the map and crossed the street. The building directly opposite the embassy looked promising. It was a fairly large six-storey apartment complex. On the ground floor was a set of tinted glass double doors under a tasteful portico with columns on either side.

Bishop walked up the short path, opened the door and stepped through into a simple foyer. There were twenty-five buzzers in a single row beside the inner door. He checked the typed names on the buzzers and nodded to himself when he saw the last one. Next, he studied the inner door. Instead of a normal deadbolt, it had one of those entry systems where you had to swipe a keycard to gain admittance. He was pretty good with most locks, but these systems were well beyond him. He'd have to find another way.

He turned and exited the building.

Outside, Bishop remembered seeing a coffee shop at Dupont Circle and began walking back in that direction. Ten minutes later, he was sitting in a booth next to a window overlooking the traffic circle. He stared past the large espresso on the table in front of him as he thought it all through. What he'd seen this morning. What Arquette had told him in the back of the car yesterday. And how much of it was open to question. Most of it, Bishop decided. Regardless, he knew he'd have to keep a watch on the Konamban embassy for a while and make sure Arquette was right about Bekele rarely leaving the grounds. Because if it were true, it meant Bishop had to find a way inside. He needed to get his hands on the guy and force some answers out of him. Which meant finding out what security systems they had in there and then bypassing them.

Sure. Nothing simpler.

Except the germ of an idea was already forming itself in his mind. It was a start. He'd just have to figure out the rest somehow. He wasn't about to give up now. But he was also aware he wouldn't be able to do it alone.

He picked up the coffee cup and took a sip of the lukewarm liquid. Then he reached into his bag and pulled out his cell phone.

THIRTY-FIVE

Charlie Monahan was just sitting back to enjoy *The A-Tag Team* for the third time in as many days when he heard the door buzzer go.

Cursing under his breath, Charlie stopped the DVD player and got up off the couch. He adjusted his tracksuit pants and waddled over to open the front door. The hallway outside was empty. The buzzer went off again. Which meant it was coming from outside. Sighing, Charlie grabbed his large keychain from the hook on the wall and walked over to the front entrance. Looking through the spyhole, he saw a young skinny bearded guy in the foyer, chewing gum. He was wearing a grey cap and grey work overalls, and had a clipboard in his hand. Frowning, Charlie unlocked and opened the door.

The workman smiled up at Charlie. 'Hey, there. How you doin'?' He checked the paperwork on his clipboard and said, 'You're the super here, right? Charles Monahan?'

'That's right,' Charlie said. 'What's up?'

'What's up? The reported leak is what's up. Didn't the gas company call and tell you I was on my way?'

'Gas leak? What are you talking about?'

The workman sighed. 'Unbelievable. One simple thing is all I ask. "You'll phone ahead and tell 'em I'm coming, right?" I say. "Sure, Sy, don't worry about it," they say. And what happens? Nothing is what happens.' The man who called himself Sy reached down and picked up the large metal toolbox at his feet. 'One of your tenants called head office yesterday morning, complaining about a gas smell in the building. So here I am. We're backed up to doomsday right now and this was the earliest one of us could get out here.'

Charlie was still frowning. This didn't make any sense. 'Who called it in?'

'Hey, we're not allowed to give out those kinds of details, man. Now are you gonna let me in or not? I got three more calls to fit in this afternoon and it's almost two already.'

Charlie moved aside. 'Okay, but maybe I should call the management company first. Nobody mentioned any of this to me.'

Sy stepped inside. 'Hey, it's your dime,' he said. 'But if you want my advice, I'd hold off till we see if there's a problem or not. Lot a times these kinds of calls are false alarms, but we have to check anyway. It's up to you.'

Charlie bit his lip. It was good advice. He liked a trouble-free existence and so did the management company. Better all round if he were to call them only if it became absolutely necessary. 'Okay, I'll wait,' he said. 'Where do you want to check first?'

'Where's your utility room?' Sy asked. 'In the basement?'

'Right.'

'Then we go there first. You wanna lead the way?'

'Sure.' Charlie turned and began walking down the hallway towards the door at the end. He heard Sy follow him. He came to a stop outside the basement door and was searching for the right key when he decided he *could* smell something. Very faint, but it had that hint of sulphur in there, like rotten eggs. *Oh, Christ. Just what I need.*

'You smell that too, huh?' Sy asked as he rooted around in his toolbox for something. 'Might not be anything to worry about, but let's see.'

Charlie unlocked the door, turned on the lights and led the way down the stairs. It was dank and musty in the utility room. Sy went over to look at the pressure gauges on the wall. He checked something on his clipboard, then tapped the second gauge from the left a few times with his finger. Then he checked the various gas meters, writing the figures down on his clipboard.

As he worked, he said, 'How many of the apartments are vacant at the moment?'

'Vacant? Well, none of them. We're always at full occupancy.'

'Nah, that's not what I meant. I mean like if any of the tenants go on holiday for extended periods or something, they'll tell you, right?'

'Sure, they usually keep me informed. Why?'

'Maybe the gas smell's coming from inside one of those apartments, you follow? Maybe we'll need to get inside and check. I don't know yet. Which ones are empty right now?'

Charlie thought for a few moments. 'Well, 3B are in Costa Rica for a week; 4A and 4C are both away for at least another month or more. And, um . . . oh yeah, 6D. He won't be back until Christmas. They're the only ones I know of.'

Sy nodded and kept writing. After a while, he came back and said, 'All seems to be okay at this end. Could be a false alarm, but we'll still need to check each floor. Maybe it's a localized problem. Okay if I leave my toolbox here for now? The thing's a bitch to carry.'

'Sure,' Charlie said.

'Okay, we'll take the stairs and do a floor-by-floor search. You take the first while I take the second. Then you do the third, and so on until we get to the top. You follow? And if you smell gas anywhere you come and let me know.'

'Right.' Charlie pointed Sy to the stairs halfway down the next corridor, then began his inspection of the first floor. He checked every inch of the hallways, but there was no gas smell anywhere. Even the faint odour from before had vanished.

He then took the stairs to the third floor and repeated the procedure, breathing deeply through his nose at every step and wondering who it was who'd made the call to the gas company. Probably Ms Egleton in 6C. She was always the first to complain about the heating not working properly, or some other penny ante problem she wanted him to fix.

The third floor was okay, too, though. No gas. Same with the fifth floor. Charlie figured about ten minutes had elapsed in total by the time he made it to the sixth floor. Sy was pacing up and down the corridors with his nose in the air. He noticed Charlie and said, 'Anything?'

'All clear on the odd-numbered floors. You?'

'Not a whiff anywhere. I think we can chalk this one up to another false alarm, but better safe than sorry, I say.'

'I hear you,' Charlie said and smiled as he led the way back to the stairs. He was a happy man now that a possible disaster had been averted with the minimum of fuss. Everything was roses again. And the sooner he could see this guy off to his next job, the sooner he could get back to his movie.

THIRTY-SIX

Crouching on the fourth-floor fire escape, Bishop pushed open the window Willard had unlocked during his floor 'inspection' and leaned his head in. The hallway was empty. All was quiet. He slid his body the rest of the way in until his feet touched the floor, then closed and latched the window behind him.

Eager to rectify his earlier mistake, Willard had jumped at the opportunity to lend a hand when Bishop had called earlier. Bishop could have played the part of the gas engineer himself, but didn't want to risk the possibility of being recognized by the super at any point. Not that he planned to show his face during his short stay, but you never knew. He liked to be prepared for all eventualities.

He'd picked Willard up at the airport at 14.15 in a rented panel van that also contained the work overalls and the brand new toolbox he'd need for his role. Along the way, they'd stopped off at a Home Depot store and picked up a can of sulphur pesticide spray, as the odour it gave off was almost exactly the same as that of natural gas. Bishop also picked up a couple of other items that might come in useful if this didn't work out. Home Depot really did have everything a guy could want.

Bishop walked down the hallway. Willard had said that the A and B apartments were the front-facing ones, and that he had the choice of 3B or 4A. Bishop had decided to take 4A. The occupants were away for a longer period, so there was less chance of them coming back early and finding a gatecrasher in their home. That was the theory, anyway.

He turned the corner and entered another hallway with two doorways near the end: 4A and 4B. He studied the lock for 4A, then took the lockpick gun and tension wrench from his pants pocket and had the door open in seconds.

Closing it behind him, Bishop found himself in a spacious foyer that led off into five other rooms. He quickly checked each one. A pair of bedrooms on the left, living room straight ahead, and bathroom and kitchen to the right. The walls in each room had been painted white and the floor was hardwood throughout. The furniture was tasteful and conservative. The air in the place was a little stale, indicating the place had been empty for a while.

Bishop took a chair from the kitchen and carried it into the living room along with his knapsack. He placed both items next to the window and sat down. From here, the view of the front of the embassy was everything he could have wished for. He could see everybody who entered and exited, either by the front door or by the garage entrance at the side.

He opened the bag and pulled out the Zeiss spotting scope and tripod he'd purchased at an outdoor gear store near the airport. He spent a minute or two setting it up and getting it all focused, then he pulled out his cell phone and called Willard.

'I'm in,' he said when the younger man answered. 'How about you?'

'Yeah, I'm in the back of the van right now, catching some daytime TV on the portable you got me. This crap boggles the mind, it really does. But it's kind of addictive, too. Hey, you know how much they're charging me for all-day parking here?'

'Charging *me*, you mean,' Bishop said. They'd agreed that in the event Bishop saw Bekele exit the embassy, Willard needed to be stationed somewhere close by so he could follow at a moment's notice. Since street parking around here was both impossible to come by *and* limited to two hours, he was currently in the underground Central Parking garage a couple of blocks down the street. Far from ideal, but it would just have to do.

Bishop wished Willard happy viewing, then hung up and got himself comfortable. A few moments later, he saw the front door of the embassy open. A man and a woman stepped outside and began walking down the path, talking to each other. Bishop pressed his eye to the scope, glad he'd forked out the extra money for a name brand. The magnification on this thing was wonderful. He could even make out a shaving cut on the guy's chin. He was looking through his American passport and pointing at something as he spoke. Probably the new visa he'd just gotten.

Bishop sat up again. This was all well and good, but if Bekele didn't show soon he'd have to try something else. And he already had a good idea what. But first, another call.

He dialled the number from memory. Shortly, a male voice said, 'Hello?'

'Hello, Arquette. It's your guest from last night. I need you to do something for me.'

'Oh, really? What's that?' He sounded amused.

'I want you to get in touch with your friend at the State Department again. Tell him to send you photos and personal details of all the embassy staff. And I mean *every*body. From the lowest paid all the way up.'

'Why?'

'I have my reasons. Can you do it or not?'

There was a momentary pause. 'Assuming I can, where would I send the info?'

Bishop had already seen a desktop PC and a laptop in one of the bedrooms, so he gave Arquette the address of an email account he rarely used and said, 'How long?'

'Within the hour, I imagine. So can I assume you're on the job?'

'You can assume whatever you like,' Bishop said, and hung up. Then he lowered his eye to the scope as the front door of the embassy opened again.

THIRTY-SEVEN

Arquette actually missed his own deadline by fifteen minutes. Which was still better than Bishop had expected. After discovering the laptop in the bedroom had wireless capabilities, he had carried it into the living room and accessed his email from there.

The PDF file listed a total of thirty-three employees, including the service staff. Each page had a passport-type photo, along with a DC address and a few lines of basic biographical information. All of which made for some interesting reading. As expected, the address for Bekele was the same as the embassy's. Same with the other man who'd been with him during that confab with Klyce. His name was Teferi Kidanu, age thirty-four, while his job description was simply 'Security Officer'. He looked as tough as Bekele. Both were single, and both were listed as having once served in the Konamban armed forces, Bekele as a colonel, Kidanu as a major. There were also two more security officers who lived inside the embassy.

The rest of the day Bishop spent looking through the scope, watching people come and go. Once he'd memorized the photos he was able to differentiate clearly between embassy staff and visitors. It went slowly. Occasionally he dipped into his bag for a store-bought sandwich or some bottled water. There was stuff to eat in the kitchen, but while Bishop was many things he wasn't a thief. He hadn't quite sunk that low yet. Besides, it was better all round if he left as little sign of his occupancy as possible.

The man he knew as David Mbassu left by the front door at six on the dot, as Bishop had expected he would. He was an accountant with a ten-year history at this particular embassy. Which meant he had a routine he'd fine-tuned over the years. He looked like his photo. He wore glasses and had an average-looking face. Not handsome, not ugly. Just normal, like most people. He also wore a tight-fitting dark suit, which didn't flatter his slim frame. As he began heading in the direction of Dupont Circle, Bishop followed him until he was gone from sight. More people Bishop recognized from the photos began leaving the embassy then. The worker bees generally left by foot, the higher-ups by car. Bishop took note of them all. But he didn't see Bekele come out. Or Kidanu.

At 23.15, Willard knocked on the apartment door and Bishop let him in. No reason for Willard to sleep in the van when there was a perfectly good couch. Willard took his shoes off, spent a few minutes complaining about the state of TV these days, and passed out. At midnight, Bishop stretched out on the floor and did the same.

Willard had already returned to his post by the time Bishop woke at 05.30 the next morning. Bishop washed and then it was more of the same. The embassy's immigration attaché was the first to arrive at 07.14. Then more employees arrived in dribs and drabs. Mbassu arrived at 08.53, wearing the same suit as before. For the rest of the day, Bishop alternated between standing and sitting, but it was still tedious work. David Mbassu left at 18.00 again. Bishop gave it another hour, watching the rest of the staff as they headed on home, but there was still no sign of Bekele.

He was all too aware that this could go on forever. And he didn't have forever. He was getting itchy and impatient. Even with Muro on guard, Amy was at risk right now. He needed to get proactive.

At 19.04, his cell phone went. Bishop saw it was Willard's number. Perfect timing. 'What's up?' he said.

'Hey, I'm not trying to rush you or anything, but how long do you think we're gonna have to keep at this? I mean, there's only so much daytime TV a man can take.'

'I've been having similar thoughts,' Bishop said. 'I think it's time we switched to Plan B. Pay the ticket and meet me outside in five.'

THIRTY-EIGHT

The five-mile journey to the Anacostia district took them almost an hour, but that included a stop-off at a stationer's along the way. Once Willard found the street they wanted, Bishop kept a lookout until he saw a three-storey apartment building that carried on for the length of a whole block. He pointed a finger in that direction and Willard found a space on the street near the entrance and pulled in.

Bishop studied the surrounding area. Lots of clapboard houses with barren-looking front yards. No pedestrians in sight. Barking dogs could be heard in all directions. Bishop was aware Anacostia wasn't one of the capital's better neighbourhoods. They'd already had to pass through several ghetto areas to get to this point. In the last one Willard swore he heard the sound of a gunshot. Bishop had argued it was just as likely a car backfiring, but he knew better.

Willard turned off the engine. 'You sure about this, Bishop?'

'About what?'

'Well, this guy isn't like that asshat Darryl. That moron deserved everything he got, but this is a whole different ballgame.'

'I know,' Bishop said, turning in his seat. He reached into the back and retrieved the cap and clipboard Willard had used before. He also picked up the large thick manila envelope he'd bought and prepared on the drive here. 'But sometimes we have to do things we'd prefer not to. Look, you're under no obligation to stay. You've done your part, so you can go back to New York any time you want with no hard feelings. But I need to know right now if you're in or out. What's it gonna be?'

Willard paused, then gave a smile. 'What do you want me to do?'

'Just wait for my call. Depending on whether the apartment's front-facing or not, I might ask you to wave, but I don't know yet.'

Willard blinked at him. 'Wave.'

'Wave,' Bishop said. 'You can do that, can't you?' Placing the cap on his head, he picked up the clipboard and package, then opened the door and got out.

He walked up the path to the awning-covered entrance, then pulled the glass doors open and stepped inside. He was in another entrance hall. One that hadn't been cleaned in a long while. There were empty torn envelopes scattered over the floor. Bishop stepped over to the next set of doors and checked the buzzers. Some had names and numbers. Others just had numbers. He searched the labels until he found *D. Mbassu*. Apartment 216. He pressed the buzzer twice.

After a few seconds, a male voice burst forth from the intercom. 'Hello?'

'FedEx package delivery,' Bishop said.

'For me? You are sure you have the right address?' The cultivated, English-sounding voice enunciated each word with care.

'You're David Mbassu, right?'

'Yes.'

'Then I got the right address.'

'Very well. Please come in.'

There was a brief buzzing sound and Bishop heard the lock disengage. He pushed the inner door open and walked along the main hallway until he found the stairwell. He climbed to the second floor and looked both ways. It was a very long hallway. He turned left and stopped outside 216, halfway down.

Wearing a long-sleeved black polo shirt and dark pants, Bishop figured he looked the part of a courier. He knew most of these companies also issued their delivery people with power pads, but he'd just have to fake it with the clipboard and hope for the best.

He looked both ways. The hallway was still empty. He undid the top of the envelope and pulled out the ski mask he'd brought along. He took off his cap, pulled the mask over his head until it almost reached his eyebrows, then put the cap back on. Then from the envelope he took out the butterfly knife he'd also brought with him from New York. It had meant checking in the overnight bag on the flight, but the hassle was worth it. He sighed to himself. Willard was right.

He wasn't particularly looking forward to this, either. But he'd given it a lot of thought and couldn't see too many alternatives. None, really.

Bishop rapped his knuckles on the door.

After a few moments, he saw a shadow pass in front of the spyhole. Then a voice said, 'Yes?'

Bishop raised the envelope and said, 'Federal Express delivery.'

'Ah, yes. Wait, please.'

He heard the latch being drawn. Bishop quickly pulled the ski mask down until it reached his neck. He waited. The moment the door began to open, he shouldered his way in. Mbassu, his eyes wide, made a soft cry as he stepped back from the doorway, both hands raised before him.

Bishop grabbed the frightened man by the shirt, flipped the knife open and pressed the blade against his throat. 'Okay, Dave,' he said, 'let's just stay calm, shall we?'

THIRTY-NINE

'Hands behind your back, no sudden movements,' Bishop said, and turned Mbassu so he was facing the wall. The accountant was still wearing his work uniform. White shirt and black pants, but no tie. With the knife pressed lightly against the back of the man's neck, Bishop tied Mbassu's wrists together using the Scotch duct tape he'd bought at the stationer's. It wasn't easy using just one hand, but he managed.

He turned Mbassu round again and said, 'You live alone, right?'

Mbassu just stared back at him through the eyeglasses and said nothing. He was breathing heavily through his nose and looked plenty scared, but Bishop had to give him credit. Most people faced with an armed man in a ski mask would have crumbled by now. That was the main reason he'd worn the mask in the first place. For the psychological effect. But Mbassu was steelier than he looked. Which could be problematic. Bishop really didn't want to have to hurt the guy to get what he wanted. To be honest, he wasn't sure he could.

'Let's go see, huh?' He grabbed Mbassu by the elbow and they both checked the rest of the apartment. It didn't take long. There was just one bedroom, one living room, a kitchen/diner and a bathroom. It was all very neatly laid out, with few decorations and simple furnishings. But no sign of a second occupant, which confirmed Bishop's initial guess. Mbassu was the confirmed bachelor type.

He sat Mbassu down on the living room couch and took a look around. A large bookshelf took up most of one wall. It was full. Several framed examples of abstract African art took up the other walls. The TV in the corner was currently tuned to one of the 24-hour news channels with the sound on low. Bishop walked round the coffee table to the window and parted the drapes a little. He looked out and saw the van parked on the street about two hundred feet away to the left. He nodded to himself. This just might work.

He came back and sat down on the coffee table, facing Mbassu. He didn't say anything. If Mbassu wanted to play the silent card, Bishop was willing to wait. He knew who'd break first. It was always better if they spoke of their own accord.

It only took another forty-three seconds for Mbassu to cave. 'Who are you?' he said.

Bishop shook his head. 'All this time to think, and that's your question?'

Mbassu swallowed. 'What do you want?'

'Better. What I want is certain information about your embassy. Mostly to do with the layout of the building, what security measures you've got, that kind of thing.'

'Why?'

'To get inside, of course.'

'You are a terrorist, then.'

'What, you mean because of the ski mask? No, I'm just a guy with a small problem. One you're going to help me solve.'

'I will not help you. I am a patriot. I will do nothing to bring harm to my country.'

Bishop smiled. 'That's real righteous of you, Dave. Except I couldn't care less about your country. But I do care about your chief security officer, Bekele. He's a man I plan to have a serious talk with, and since he rarely leaves the embassy that leaves only one option.'

'Bekele? What has he done to you?'

'That's not your concern.'

Mbassu was looking at Bishop's knife. 'And if I do not talk, you plan to torture me?'

Bishop did the thing with his wrist and the knife flipped closed. Then he swung it open again in a single movement. 'I'm hoping it won't come to that,' he said.

Mbassu almost smiled. 'Yes, I knew this when I looked in your eyes. I'm sorry, but I will not tell you anything.'

'That's a pity,' Bishop said with a sigh. 'Stand up, Dave.'

Mbassu frowned, then carefully got up off the couch without losing his balance. Bishop led him over to the window and pulled the drapes back. He unlatched the window and slid it all the way open. The sounds of distant traffic became discernible. A small breeze ruffled the thin material of the drapes.

'You see that panel van down there on your left?'

Mbassu poked his head out and said, 'Yes, I see it.'

'Keep your eyes on it.' Bishop took his cell from his pocket and speed-dialled Willard's number. The younger man picked up immediately. 'It's me. Look up towards the second floor. I got our friend here with me. I think he might be a problem. You wanna give him a wave?'

Willard chuckled. 'Sure. Later, you'll tell me what all this means. Wait a second.' There was the sound of a vehicle door opening. Then, 'I'm waving.'

Bishop said, 'You see my partner down there, Dave?'

'Yes, I see him.'

Into the phone, Bishop said, 'Now show him your special box of tools.'

Willard said, 'Ah ha. I think I'm beginning to get the picture. Hold on.' More sounds of scuffling, then, 'Okay, I'm holding it up now.'

To Mbassu, Bishop said, 'You see the toolbox?'

Mbassu brought his head back in and looked at Bishop. He didn't look so sure of himself any more. 'Yes, I saw it.'

'Want me to get him up here so he can show you what kind of tools he keeps in there? Because I'd advise against it. That thing's like Pandora's Box. Once it gets opened, my partner finds it difficult to close. Thing is, he can get a little carried away sometimes and lose sight of what's in our best interests, so I'd prefer not to bring him up here if I can help it. Now you *are* gonna answer my questions, but I figure it's better for everyone if you do it while you've still got all your body parts intact. Look at me. Am I telling the truth now?'

Mbassu stared into his eyes for a few seconds and took a long, deep breath. 'Yes, I think you are,' he said. 'I will tell you what you need to know.'

'Good.' Into the phone, Bishop said, 'Don't think I'll need you just yet. But stick around in case Dave here gets second thoughts.' He hung up and pocketed the phone.

Once they were both seated again, Bishop said, 'Now I already know you've got four security officers who live on the embassy grounds. Where exactly are their sleeping quarters?'

'They all sleep in the basement,' Mbassu said. 'Three rooms at the rear of the building are reserved for their use. One for Bekele, one for his deputy . . .'

'Teferi Kidanu?'

'Yes, that is right.' Mbassu gave a deep frown. 'And the larger room is for the other two men. You seem to know much already.'

'Enough to know if you're lying or not, so be very careful with your answers. Are their doors locked when they're asleep?'

Mbassu shook his head. 'Bekele disabled the locks years ago when he first became security chief. He said he wanted easy access to all rooms in case of emergencies.'

'And how many on duty at night? One or two?'

'One.'

'But not Bekele.'

'No, he only ever works days.'

'This Kidanu guy, then?'

'Sometimes.'

'And what are the night guard's duties?'

'I have never been there at night so I cannot say. Probably he spends much of the night in the surveillance room on the first floor, watching the cameras.'

Bishop nodded. With regular walkabouts to break it up. But how regular? Every hour? Every half-hour? Again, that kind of information would be well outside Mbassu's purview. Instead, he said, 'You've been stationed here for almost a decade now, so you'll be familiar with all the security measures used to keep people like me out. Tell me about them.'

Mbassu rolled his shoulders and said, 'Well . . . there are sophisticated electronic alarms connected to the front and rear doors that are activated at night. I know that. Also the entrance on the roof. We also have security cameras in the central hallways. One on every floor except the basement. There are no cameras on that floor.'

'What about the windows?'

'Yes. On the inside, there are motion sensors all around the frames that set off the alarm if anybody attempts to enter that way.'

'Uh huh. Tell me about the weak spots.'

Mbassu furrowed his brow. 'Weak spots? Why do you think—'

Bishop cut him off. 'This isn't my first time at trying to get into a well-protected facility, and one thing I know from experience is there's always a weak spot somewhere. When was the last time somebody broke into your embassy?'

Mbassu looked personally offended. 'Broke in? Never in my ten years here.'

'Exactly. Which means over time, complacency will have set in. It's inevitable where humans are involved. Now there has to be a weak spot somewhere, and it's in your best interest to tell me where I might find it.'

Mbassu opened his mouth, then closed it. Bishop watched his eyes as they rose to the ceiling. Then they narrowed for a second. Just a split second, but it was enough.

'What?' Bishop said.

'I am not sure.'

'Tell me anyway.'

Mbassu shifted in his seat. 'Well, we had some men come in to do renovations on the third floor three weeks ago. The large office space at the rear used to be the office for our Head of Administration. But it was decided to split the office into three like the other floors. It was a big job and the construction workers and decorators only finished three days ago.'

'So?'

'So when it was just one office, there was just one big window at the rear. But when it became three offices, they reduced the size of that window and added two more at the sides of the building. One for each of these new outer offices.'

'So are you saying they haven't gotten around to hooking up the sensors on those windows yet?' Bishop was remembering those steel fire escapes he'd spotted on the side of the building. They'd been located close to the rear.

'Possibly,' Mbassu said. 'I could be wrong, but my secretary told me they are still waiting for the electrician to finish things up. Apparently, he is in high demand. But he would be the one to make sure the alarm system is connected properly, would he not?'

Bishop scratched under his ear. The thick cotton of the mask was itchy. 'Depends how complex the system is. It might need an alarm specialist to connect it all up.'

'Then I do not know. But if there are any weak spots, that is where they will be.'

Bishop stood up. 'We'll see. But first, tell me where you keep your pens and paper. You and I are going to draw up a complete layout of the building.'

FORTY

At 03.03, Bishop climbed over the six-foot-high concrete wall to the left of the embassy building and dropped down on the other side. With only the streetlights for illumination, he scanned the long, narrow space that separated the building from its immediate neighbour. There was very little back there. Just three heavy-duty wheeled trash cans and a steel fire door set into the concrete wall at the other end. And the exterior fire escapes above.

Willard was parked on the street outside, just in case. Bishop had left Mbassu bound and gagged in his bedroom half an hour earlier, with a warning that Willard would stay on guard in the living room. He felt confident Mbassu wouldn't dare try anything for a while. Bishop had left the ski mask in the van, though. Mbassu's earlier comment was still on his mind, and if the worst happened he'd prefer not be shot on sight as a suspected terrorist.

Bishop opened the trash can lids until he found one that was full. He rolled that one along until it was right under the fire escape ladder. The lowest rung was about twelve feet off the ground. He climbed onto the trash can, jumped up and grabbed hold of it. He climbed the rest of the way until he reached the second-floor latticework landing, then continued up the next set of stairs to the third floor. There were two windows at each end of the narrow landing, but the one he wanted was about four feet to the left. Well out of reach.

Fortunately, he'd come prepared.

He carried on up the next ladder until he reached the roof. The only things up there were a satellite dish located near the front of the building, and at the back a small brick outbuilding with a door set into it. The roof entrance. Bishop walked over and circled the structure. He stopped when he noticed a cast iron plumbing vent sticking out of the roof a few feet away. There was about a foot of pipe showing. He knelt down, gripped the pipe and tried to budge it. It felt rock solid. Good enough.

Bishop lifted his shirt and uncoiled the length of rope around his waist. It was thin, but strong enough. Mountaineers used it. He himself had used it before in a situation not too dissimilar to this one. After tying one end securely to the pipe, he carried the rest of the rope until he was above the window he wanted, then dropped it over the side. He looked down and saw it carried on past the window for about another fifteen feet.

He pulled the rope back up and used the butterfly knife to cut off ten feet. Then he made a loop big enough for his foot and tied it off with a double knot, then a triple knot. He'd learned his lesson after the last time, when the stirrup had come loose and almost scuppered everything from the start. Bishop threw the rope over again, then grabbed hold of it with both hands. He was about to edge over the side when he felt the cell phone in his pocket vibrate.

He pulled the phone out and saw Willard's number displayed. He took the call.

'Police prowler about to pass by,' Willard said.

Keeping the phone pressed to his ear, Bishop looked over the side towards the front. Twelve seconds later, headlights appeared, soon followed by a black and white. Bishop watched it pass from view and waited. It was another forty seconds before Willard said, 'Okay, he's gone.'

'Copy that,' Bishop said, and hung up.

He gripped the rope again and carefully lowered himself over the side, then descended the rope until he was level with the third-floor window. He inserted his right foot into the stirrup and gradually let it take his weight.

Swinging gently, Bishop saw the small room beyond was totally bare. Clearly, they hadn't gotten around to assigning this office to anyone yet. The window itself, although new, was one of the double-hung sash types, in keeping with the windows in the rest of the building. Bishop reached into a pocket of his black combats and pulled out the small, ultra thin metal pry bar he'd purchased at Home Depot along with the bug spray. Some small part of him must have known he'd end up needing it. He carefully inserted the tool in the tight space between the frame and the bottom sash. After several minutes of patient manoeuvring up and down and side to side, he felt the short screws that connected the sash lock to the frame come free. He pocketed the pry bar and got his fingers under the sash.

His cell phone began vibrating again.

Cursing softly, Bishop pulled the phone from his pocket and saw it was Willard again. As soon as he answered, Willard said, 'Cops are coming back. Can't tell if it's the same one or not.'

Bishop put the phone in his shirt pocket, turned his face to the left and pressed himself against the side of the building, trying to make himself as flat as possible. He held his breath and watched the street. At least there was some cloud cover tonight. He could only hope that if the cops happened to look over, they might not see a guy hanging over the side of the building. All he could do was wait.

It took fifteen seconds before he saw headlights approaching from the left. Then the black and white cruised past at about ten miles an hour. It didn't slow. When it was gone, Bishop breathed out again. Staying as still as possible, he pulled out his cell phone and brought it to his ear.

Thirty seconds later, Willard said, 'Okay, he's gone.'

'Right,' Bishop said, and hung up.

He inserted his fingers under the sash again. Now came the risky part.

Bishop slowly raised the bottom half of the window until it remained in the open position. He breathed in deeply. Pointless pussyfooting about. The motion sensors around the frame had either been connected up to the alarm system, or they hadn't. Thereby causing the alarm to go off, or not. There was only one way to find out. If it went off, he could probably swing over to the fire escape railing four feet away, run down the stairs and be in the van in seconds. But it would mean starting again from scratch. With two days lost and Amy still in danger. And Bekele would be even more on guard than before.

Well, Bishop thought, *fortune favours the foolish*. Then he poked his left arm through the open window.

Nothing.

No alarm sounds. He moved his arm around in wide circles. Still nothing. He reached in with his other arm and did the same. Still no alarm. Bishop allowed himself a thin smile of relief. Looked like Mbassu had come up trumps, after all.

Bishop hauled himself up and climbed through the window.

FORTY-ONE

Once he was in, Bishop closed the window and made his way over to the door. There was no light coming from underneath. The whole building was in darkness, as Mbassu had said it would be. Bishop paused, visualizing in his mind the building layout Mbassu had drawn up.

Each floor followed the same basic pattern. Seen from above, two hallways joined to form a T shape. The longer hallway, running from the front of the building and stopping before the last row of offices at the rear, formed the vertical part of the T. The other hallway ran horizontally between these rear offices and the rest of the floor. Bishop was currently in the left-most office in the horizontal hallway. Halfway down the vertical hallway was the central stairwell. Almost directly opposite was the small elevator, which Mbassu had said was very old and very noisy. The security camera was apparently located in the ceiling between the rear hallway and the stairs.

Bishop reached into one of his side pockets and pulled out two pieces of kit. One was a Medit industrial fibre-optic scope he'd used for something else a while back. The other was an MMS ultra-sensitive wall microphone unit. He held on to the scope, put the mic back in his pocket and quietly opened the door.

The hallway was partly illuminated by ambient light coming from the windows at each end. Good enough to see by. The building was totally silent. Bishop closed the door behind him, edged along the hallway and stopped just before the junction with the vertical part of the T. He brought the scope to his eye and aimed the insertion tube around the corner. The view was distorted but he could clearly make out the open stairway about fifty feet down on the right. Before that, about thirty feet away, Bishop saw the fixed camera in the ceiling.

Mbassu had said it was one of those that gave a panoramic view of its surroundings. And panoramic usually meant no blind spots, despite what the movies claimed.

Taking out his cell phone again, Bishop found the number he'd gotten from Mbassu and pressed the green button. It was the extension for the office right next to the surveillance room. Bishop just let it ring and waited. One minute passed. Two minutes. Three.

Then the phone was picked up. A gruff-sounding voice said, *'Selam?'*

'Oh, hi there,' Bishop said. He entered the central hallway and with his head lowered marched quickly towards the stairway. 'Is that Artie's Pizza? You still open over there?'

There was a moment's silence. Then the guard hung up the phone.

But Bishop had already reached the stairway. If the guard was in the office answering the call, he couldn't very well be watching the security footage too. There'd still be an unidentified figure on tape walking down the hallway, but by the time anybody saw the footage it would be too late.

He descended the stairs and stopped just before he reached the first floor. The security surveillance room was two doors down on the left. He listened for the sound of movement from that direction, or of keys jangling, but heard nothing, and continued on down the stairs until he reached the bottom.

It was like entering a catacomb. No windows meant no light, other than the very faint residue coming from above. Otherwise, the basement was in total darkness.

Bishop had a Maglite, but didn't want to risk using it and losing his night vision just yet. But he still needed to see what lay ahead of him. He held three fingers over his cell phone's display screen, aimed it ahead of him and turned it on. The muted light was enough to make out the elevator door almost directly opposite. Exactly the same as above. Bishop stepped out and aimed the display to his left. Same corridor with doors on either side and the T junction at the end, but this time there was no security camera in the ceiling.

He turned the other way and saw the hallway just ended in a concrete wall about fifty feet away. He turned back and began walking towards the junction, his rubber soles silent on the smooth concrete floor. He passed two steel doors on the left and two more on the right. Mbassu had told him there were cells behind some of these doors, but that he had no idea what they were used for. Probably nothing good, though. Hence the lack of cameras down here.

Bishop stopped at the junction. He was facing three wooden doors, same as upstairs. These would be the security officers' sleeping quarters. Mbassu had said the one in the middle, being the largest, was for the two junior officers. Bishop stepped over to that door and pulled the listening device from his pocket.

The manufacturers claimed it could detect the sound of a pin dropping in the next room. Bishop doubted that, but it still picked up most sounds you could imagine. And some you couldn't. The unit consisted of a matchbox-sized amplifier, a pair of earbuds, and the wall contact microphone, which resembled the chest piece on a stethoscope. He inserted both earpieces, switched on the unit and gently pressed the contact mic against the middle door.

Nothing. No sounds at all. Bishop found the volume switch on the top of the amplifier and slowly turned it clockwise.

Now he could hear nasal breathing. Steady, deep and regular. Which indicated a non-REM sleep cycle. And there was something else, too. Bishop frowned and kept increasing the volume until it became clearer. It was a gargling sound, as though somebody was breathing through the upper part of the throat. So there were two sleepers in the room. Which meant that voice on the phone must have belonged to Kidanu.

Bishop touched the mic to the door on the left. Nothing. He adjusted the volume to its maximum setting. Still nothing. The room was empty. So Bekele had to be in the rightmost room. He walked over and placed the mic against the last door. From inside, he could hear more nasal breathing. Steady and regular, but not quite as deep as the others.

Bekele. Had to be.

He removed the earbuds and put everything back in his pocket. Without ambient light, the fibre-optic scope was useless. So he'd be going in blind, something he always avoided whenever possible. But he had no choice. The only thing he knew for sure was that as the door was right next to the right-hand wall, Bekele would be somewhere on his left. It wasn't much, but right now Bishop would take whatever he could get.

He pulled out his Maglite and butterfly knife. He stuck the light between his teeth and silently opened the butterfly knife and gripped it in his left hand. With his right, he reached down until his fingers touched the door handle. He could only hope they kept the hinges regularly oiled or he'd be in real trouble.

Slowly, slowly, Bishop gripped the steel door handle and lowered it. Breathing evenly through his mouth, he began to push the door open, waiting for the sound of a creak. But the hinges made no noise at all. When he felt he had a wide enough gap, he stepped inside and pushed the door back until it was almost closed again.

He pressed his back against the right-hand wall and listened. The rhythm of the man's breathing hadn't changed at all. It was still steady and regular. It was also coming from the other end of the room, on Bishop's right. Possibly in the far corner. If the room matched the one upstairs, it was about fifteen feet by fifteen. At a run, he could cover it in a second. Except he didn't know what obstacles might lie between him and the bed.

Taking the Maglite from his mouth with his free hand, Bishop took one step forward. Then another. And another. Waiting for his shin to come into contact with something, but there was nothing. Only the sound of the man's breathing as each step brought Bishop closer.

When he figured he'd covered ten feet, he snapped on the Maglite and the room lit up. The large black man he'd seen in the photos was less than two feet from him. He was wearing boxers and lying on a single bed set against the wall, head turned to the side. He had fast reflexes. His eyes immediately snapped open at the sudden light and he started to bring his right hand up towards the pillow.

Bishop was on him in less than a second. He clamped his right elbow against Bekele's mouth and with the other hand pressed the knife edge against his throat. The Maglite in his right hand was pointing directly in the man's face.

'Make a wrong move,' he said, 'or a wrong sound, and it'll go badly for you. Understand?'

Bekele nodded his head.

'Good. The gun. Bring it out slowly. By the barrel, and using your left hand.'

Keeping his eyes averted from the harsh light, Bekele slowly reached under the pillow with his left. He pulled out a black Sig Sauer 9mm P250 automatic by the barrel. Bishop took his right elbow away and transferred the Maglite to between his teeth again. With the knife still pressed against Bekele's neck, Bishop picked up the gun by the handle with his free hand. He could tell from the weight it was fully loaded.

'What do you want?' Bekele said.

Bishop slowly took the knife away and started to move back from the bed. Away from Bekele's reach. Aiming the gun at the man's chest, Bishop removed the Maglite from his mouth and said, 'I want some answers. We've got a lot to talk about, and you're going to—'

Bishop stopped mid-sentence. He also stopped moving backwards. Something cold and hard was being pressed against the back of his neck.

Then the same gruff voice from before said, 'Drop the weapons.'

FORTY-TWO

Bishop hadn't heard a thing. Not even a rustle of fabric behind him. The man was good. Bishop thought fast. He could throw the Maglite under the bed. Give himself a couple of seconds of confusion in which to move. Except for two things. One, if Bekele's deputy was skilled enough to creep up on him like that, it was a sure bet he knew exactly what he was thinking right now. He'd pull the trigger at the first twitch.

And two, where could he go?

Kidanu pressed the barrel harder into his neck. 'I will not ask a second time,' he said.

Bishop made stars of his hands. The knife, pistol and Maglite clattered to the floor. He watched Bekele reach under the bed and pull out a large flashlight and switch it on.

'Don't move,' the security chief said, aiming the light at Bishop. Bishop stayed perfectly still. The barrel was still against his neck. Bekele came forward, picked both weapons up off the floor and moved back a little. The knife he threw on the bed. The gun he pointed at Bishop. The pressure against Bishop's neck vanished. A second later he heard a click and the room was bathed in light, courtesy of a frosted glass downlight in the middle of the ceiling.

Bekele switched off the flashlight and said, 'Search him.'

Bishop felt himself being expertly patted down from head to toe. His pry bar was removed from one pocket, the wall mic unit from another. He heard them hit the floor. Then the fibre-optic scope. Then his keys and phone. Everything.

Once Bishop had been cleaned out, Bekele said, 'Sit on the floor, legs crossed.'

Bishop did as he was told, looking around the room as he lowered himself. Bekele lived simply. There was the bed, a large chest of drawers, and a work desk set against one wall with a chair underneath. Bishop saw a laptop and some files and box folders on the desk surface. There was also a large stand fan at the foot of the bed. That was it.

He felt a gun barrel press itself against the back of his skull.

'Patience, Teferi,' Bekele said, smiling. The smile didn't reach his eyes, though.

'You are on Konamban territory,' Teferi Kidanu said from behind him. His voice was a lot deeper than Bekele's. 'You understand it is well within our rights to shoot you right now? Nobody would know. And even if somebody suspected, they could do nothing.'

Keeping his eyes on Bekele, Bishop said, 'Is that how you usually deal with problems in your country? Shoot first, ask questions later?'

Bekele lost the smile. 'Do you think we are savages? The major here is simply making a point. That you are no longer on American soil, so do not expect help to come.'

Bishop already knew that. He was paying more attention to the timbre of Bekele's voice. He heard the same careful enunciation as Mbassu. The accent wasn't mid-Atlantic, but he could see how somebody might think that on hearing it for the first time. Especially somebody like Yuri Vasilyev, who'd had enough trouble with his adopted home tongue.

'Who are you?' Bekele said.

'How about asking Kidanu here to take the gun from my head first? There's such a thing as overkill, you know.'

Bekele gestured with a finger. The barrel was removed. 'Your name,' he demanded.

'Bishop, comma, James.'

'And who do you work for, Mr Bishop?'

'Nobody. I'm just a private citizen, here on personal business.'

Bekele tilted his head as he looked Bishop over. 'Personal? To do with me? I don't think so. I have never seen you before, and I am usually very good with faces.'

'Even at a distance? Like from across a busy street, for example?'

Bekele's frown made his face appear even more threatening. 'What busy street?'

'Westchester Avenue in the Bronx, New York. Wednesday afternoon.'

'Three days ago, you mean?' When Bishop nodded, Bekele said, 'And what time in the afternoon was I there?'

'Between four and five.'

'And what was I doing?'

'If I'm right, tying up loose ends. A man named Carlos was one of them. Unfortunately, a speeding truck splashed his brains over the sidewalk before I could get to him. I looked around and noticed a man who looked very much like you across the street, taking note of everything and then walking away as calm as you like.'

'I see.' Bekele paused, then said, 'Major, please face our guest.'

Bishop turned to his left as Kidanu stepped into view. He still held the gun in his hand. Another Sig P250, from the looks of it. He was dressed the same as in the photos. A dark suit over a white shirt, open at the collar. He also wore black canvas shoes with the laces tucked in. The eyes looking down at him were much larger than the photos had suggested. And much more intense. Bishop was sure they missed very little.

Bekele said, 'Please update Mr Bishop here on where I was on Wednesday afternoon, and much of Wednesday evening.'

'Yes, sir,' he said, looking down at Bishop with a barely concealed sneer. 'At eleven thirty a.m., Colonel Bekele accompanied Ambassador Byakagaba and his wife to the American Vice President's residence at Number One Observatory Circle for an official diplomatic lunch and reception. For the remainder of the afternoon, the colonel waited inside the residence while the embassy driver waited in the limousine. At four fifteen p.m., the colonel accompanied the ambassador and his wife back. They returned to the embassy at approximately five p.m.'

Bishop turned back to Bekele. The security chief was smiling again. And with good reason. It was the kind of alibi that could be checked easily enough. There must have been witnesses all around. Bekele was probably on the security footage, too. More to the point, why would he even bother to lie? He was the one in control here. Not Bishop.

Which meant unless Bekele had found a way to be in two places at once, he wasn't the man Bishop was after. A total of two whole days wasted on a bad lead.

Bishop sighed. 'So what happens now?'

'Now?' Bekele raised the gun and pointed it at Bishop's head. 'Now, you will explain to me why I shouldn't kill you this very second.'

FORTY-THREE

Bishop stared into the barrel. 'Why kill me if you're not the man I'm after?'

'One very good reason. The security of this embassy is my responsibility, yet you found a way in somehow. That makes me look very bad. And while I trust Kidanu to keep this incident to himself, I cannot say the same for you. I am thinking it would be more convenient for me to erase you from existence entirely.'

'So you're not curious about why I broke in?'

Something that almost resembled a smile ran across Bekele's lips. 'There is that, of course. But first you will tell me how.'

Bishop saw no reason to bring up Mbassu's name. Instead, he said, 'I had a talk with one of the men who worked on your renovations on the third floor. He mentioned that they were still waiting for the electrician to come in and finish things up. I figured that probably included the sensors on the new windows. Turned out I was right.' He looked up at Kidanu. 'Speaking of which, what gave me away? I trip an alarm I didn't know about?'

Kidanu looked down at him and said nothing.

'That is an oversight I will rectify first thing in the morning,' Bekele said, also ignoring the question. 'Now you will tell me *why* you came here.'

'Short version?' Bishop said. 'Somebody hired three men to kill my sister on Tuesday night, and to make it look like a mugging gone wrong. I'm working my way up the food chain until I reach the man who gave the order. For a number of reasons, I thought you were a link in that chain, but I wasn't sure. And since you rarely leave this embassy, I decided the only way I'd ever find out was by paying you a visit and talking to you myself.'

Bekele shook his head. 'Fascinating. And this sister of yours. What was her name?'

'Amanda Philmore. Present tense. The men hired for the job screwed it up. She's still breathing, but only just. She's in a coma. They also tried again yesterday morning. And failed again.'

The colonel narrowed his eyes at his subordinate. 'Philmore. That name is familiar to me. Where do I know it from?'

'The researcher from Artemis,' Kidanu said. 'You remember, sir? She came to the embassy a fortnight ago, wanting to look at some files in our library.'

'Yes, yes. Now I remember,' Bekele said.

So Arquette had been correct. Amy *had* come here. But purely for research purposes, or for something more? 'What files was she interested in?' Bishop asked.

Bekele ignored him. He sat on the edge of the bed and said, 'I have many questions, Bishop, but I think it would be easier if you were to give us the long version. We have time.' He gestured towards his work desk, and Kidanu went over, pulled out the chair and took a seat. 'You will begin,' he said.

Bishop didn't see many alternatives. He clearly wasn't going to get anything from these two until he explained his real reasons for coming here. To be honest, he'd be the same in their position. Besides, what did he have to lose by talking, except maybe his life? And he'd long ago come to terms with that inevitability.

So he gave them the long version.

He began with the assault on Amy on Tuesday night, and his tracking down of the three culprits the following day, including his sighting of the man at the scene of Carlos's death. He told them about Yuri's 'confession', including the description of his immediate employer and how he took something from Amy's bag before the assault. Something that could only have come from her workplace. He brought up his encounter with an FBI agent who had his own reasons for investigating Artemis, and mentioned the man's long-term belief that Artemis and its parent company, LCT, were heavily involved in the illicit arms trafficking business. He also spoke of the photos he'd seen of Bekele and Kidanu meeting with Klyce, and how Arquette had traced the diplomatic plates on their car.

His two captors looked at each other meaningfully for a moment.

Bishop continued, theorizing that Amy could have found out somehow and decided to do something about it, and possibly approached an outsider to help. Possibly a reporter at one of the big papers, or at least somebody with a little influence who could take it further with enough proof. But somebody had put a stop to it by silencing Amy and taking the proof. And possibly eliminating the person she was about to meet, too.

'And you came to believe that that somebody was me?' Bekele said.

'"Believe" is maybe too strong a word,' Bishop said. 'But you were definitely a suspect as far as I was concerned. Especially after I saw somebody very similar in looks and build to you at that crime scene. You were simply the best lead I had, that's all.'

'So my motive for trying to kill your sister was that she discovered some alleged underhanded dealings between her employer and myself? That is not much of a motive.'

Bishop shrugged. 'Well, if you *were* buying arms, it's obvious you were doing it with the full knowledge of high-ranking officials in your government. Possibly even high-ranking embassy personnel too. If something like that got out, it wouldn't be too good for the international reputation you people are trying to build. Especially if the US State Department ended up expelling some of your diplomats as a result. What's one life against that? What's two? And I've heard you can be pretty ruthless when the situation demands it.'

Bekele just stared at him for a few seconds without speaking. After a while, he said, 'So who do you now suspect was behind your sister's attack, if not me?'

'Right now, Roger Klyce is the only other person I can think of with a motive. If I get out of here alive, he's the man I'll focus on. Speaking of which, you *were* arranging to buy illicit arms at that meeting, right? What was in the briefcase? The final payment?'

'Even if we were doing as you suggest,' Kidanu said, 'what difference would it make to you?'

'Might make all the difference. See, at my sister's place I found a hidden CD. On it was a document listing times and dates of calls from Klyce to somebody in this building. I've got the printout with me. Okay if I reach into my jacket pocket for it?'

Bekele nodded. 'But slowly.'

Bishop made no sudden movements as he pulled the two folded sheets from his inner pocket. He slid them across the floor to Bekele.

Bekele picked the sheets up, unfolded them and quickly scanned the contents. After a while he looked up and said, 'This 202 number is my office number. The other number is Klyce's. These times and dates look correct. I see nothing mysterious about this. He and I have spoken many times recently.'

'But not about guns. Is that what you're telling me?'

Bekele looked over at Kidanu and spoke rapidly in a language Bishop couldn't begin to understand. Kidanu shrugged and said a few words in response. Bekele nodded and turned back to Bishop.

'I admit nothing,' he said. 'Those conversations were private and will remain so. But I will concede that what you have told me so far has given me much food for thought. For instance, it might surprise you to know that we also are very interested in Klyce. Especially the legitimate side of his business. If you can call it that.'

'Meaning what?'

'I mean that the People's Republic of Konamba have employed Artemis's services to track . . . Have I said something amusing?'

Bishop hadn't realized he was smiling. 'I was just thinking Badat missed a trick by not inserting a "Democratic" in there somewhere. Isn't that usually how it works when despots get to name their country?'

'I see nothing amusing about Badat's reign,' Kidanu said, his eyes turning to slits. 'Nothing whatsoever. Anyway, we are a democracy now.'

'Uh huh.' Bishop turned back to Bekele. 'So you were saying?'

'I was saying that almost one year ago, it was decided to step up the search for those responsible for the ten-year reign of terror that decimated our country. As you may know, many of the perpetrators, including The Scythe himself, fled before they could be captured or killed by the rebels. Although not before siphoning off a large percentage of the country's wealth and hiding it in various offshore accounts. So far we had found no sign of any of them. So I was tasked with approaching Artemis to help us find them. You see, we are not above asking for help from foreigners. And Artemis International has had a very good record at this kind of thing. Or so it would appear at first glance.'

'Something caused you to change your opinion.'

'Nothing concrete,' Bekele said. 'And Artemis have successfully led us to several men on our list over the past year. Thanks to them, we found one in a South American jungle. Two more in Ottawa, Canada. But they all played minor roles in the atrocities, while the more important figures always remain just out of our reach. Artemis would sometimes give us a lead that looked promising, but when specialist teams were sent in to extract the target they'd discover he'd vacated the area days previously. Sometimes even hours before.'

'We even came close to acquiring Badat himself,' Kidanu said. 'In Peru, nine months ago. Artemis supplied us with precise co-ordinates. I was chosen to be part of the extraction team on that occasion. When we arrived, locals told us he'd left the area two days before.'

'So you think Artemis are warning the big guns ahead of time in return for payoffs?'

'I've actually met Klyce twice,' Bekele said, 'and he strikes me as a totally amoral man. This kind of behaviour would be in keeping with his character. Regardless, I believe there is more to Artemis than meets the eye and I would very much like to know what. I also believe that if Klyce warned these people ahead of time, then he'd probably have a very good idea of where they went next. And I want that information.'

'I can see why you would,' Bishop said. 'So why are you telling me?'

Bekele gave him that almost smile again. 'Because I very much want you to continue your investigation into Roger Klyce's affairs. I will be most interested in what you discover.'

Bishop raised an eyebrow. First Arquette. Now Bekele. It seemed everybody was interested in Roger Klyce, but nobody wanted to do the dirty work themselves. He blinked at the gun Bekele was still pointing in his general direction.

'So you plan to let me go,' he said, 'and trust me to keep you updated.'

'Not at all. The major will perform that task. You will find him a very capable partner.'

There it was. Bishop had known there'd be a catch somewhere. He looked at Kidanu. If Bekele's suggestion had caught him off-guard, he didn't show it. He just stared back at Bishop with the same indifferent expression as before.

'I don't doubt he's capable,' Bishop said, 'but I prefer to work alone.'

'You say that as though it might mean something to me,' Bekele said. 'You have a very simple choice here, Bishop. Either the major here goes with you, or you do not leave this basement alive. And please don't make the mistake of thinking I'm bluffing.'

Bishop looked into his eyes. He knew the man wasn't bluffing. He also knew there were many methods of making a person disappear. He wondered if they had a furnace down here. Maybe in one of those cell-like rooms he'd passed. Besides, what did it matter? Once he was out of here, he could lose Kidanu easily enough if he needed to. But not before he answered a few questions Bishop had regarding Amy. In fact, maybe having him tag along wouldn't be such a bad idea after all. At least part of the way.

'Okay,' he said, 'but understand my sole purpose is to find the people who want my sister dead. If the trail leads to Klyce's knowledge of some fugitives' whereabouts, then great. If not, don't blame me. And also don't blame me if Kidanu here gets lost along the way. I can't be looking over my shoulder the whole time.'

'Do not worry yourself,' Kidanu said, smiling at Bishop. 'I believe I will be able to keep up with you easily enough.'

Bishop looked at the man and said nothing. The thing was, he believed it too.

FORTY-FOUR

Bishop left by the front door this time. They'd also given him back all his gear. Even the knife. Kidanu was right behind him. Since leaving Bekele to his morning workout in the basement gym, neither man had said much to the other.

Bishop stood outside and waited while Kidanu keyed in the code to enable the alarm again, then clicked the front door shut. It was coming up to six o'clock and still dark. About an hour and a half till sunrise. The air was brisk. He watched as a couple of joggers ran past, heading in the direction of Dupont Circle.

'How long did the cab company say?'

Kidanu joined him. 'Ten minutes.'

'Fine. I need to talk to my associate first, anyway.'

'Associate? What associate is this?'

'This way,' Bishop said. He walked down the short path and crossed the street. Kidanu walked alongside. The panel van was parked thirty feet away on the right. There was enough light from the streetlamps to show both front seats were empty. When Bishop reached the vehicle, he rapped a knuckle against the side of the van and said, 'It's me. Bishop.'

He heard movement inside and then saw a tired-looking Willard rubbing his eyes as he clambered into the driver's seat. He rolled down the window and looked at Bishop. Then he noticed Kidanu and said, 'Uh . . . everything okay?'

'Kind of,' Bishop said. 'The lead didn't pan out, but we've come to an understanding of sorts.' He turned to Kidanu. 'Look, I need to talk to him for a moment about something private. You mind?'

Kidanu shrugged and took a few steps back. Willard said in an undertone, 'Who's he? Your watchdog or something? What went on in there?'

'It's a long story. I'll fill you in at a later date. We're heading back to New York now, so I need you to return the van to the rental place. But before you do that, can you let yourself back into Mbassu's apartment and make sure he hasn't throttled himself trying to escape? Tell him I didn't mention his name, so he's in the clear. And that if he wants to remain that way he should just go back to work as usual and act like nothing happened.'

'Sure, I can do that.'

'Good. And keep your receipts.'

Willard grinned. 'Always do. You need a lift to the airport?'

'No, my new pal called a cab for us.' Bishop pulled the driver's door open and said, 'You wanna hand me my stuff?'

Willard nodded and disappeared for a few moments. He came back, handed Bishop his bag and shut the door again. He gave a brief salute, then started the engine and pulled out. Once the van was gone from sight, Bishop walked over to Kidanu and said, 'So how long have you been working here at the embassy?'

'That is none of your business.'

So that's how it's going to be, Bishop thought. *Well, it could be worse.*

A few seconds later, Bishop saw the taxi approaching and stepped out into the street. The vehicle slowed to a stop, and after the driver confirmed they were the right fares the two men got in the back and the driver took off for the airport.

After a minute or so of silence, Kidanu said, 'Show me that printout again.'

'Well, since you asked so nicely.' Bishop reached into his pocket and handed him the folded sheets.

Kidanu scanned the data quickly and handed it back. He said, 'The colonel was correct. There is nothing mysterious about this information. It makes no sense.'

'What doesn't?'

'You say your sister hid this.'

Bishop nodded. 'Right. She sent it to herself, hidden under a legitimate music CD.'

'And it contained only this data?'

'Just that one file.'

Kidanu shook his head. 'There has to be more on there. I want to see this CD.'

Bishop sat back in the seat. 'Okay. Once we get back to the city I'll—' He stopped at the sound of his cell phone going off. He'd unmuted it back at the embassy. Pulling it from his pocket, he checked the display and took the call. 'Yes?'

'Bishop?' Arquette said. 'I only just heard about the second attempt on your sister's life. Why didn't you tell me?'

'I guess it slipped my mind. I've been busy. Is there something you want?'

Arquette sighed. 'How about a progress report? If it's not too much trouble, that is.'

'I don't report to you, Arquette. I thought I made that clear at our last meeting.'

'You did. That's why I asked nicely.'

Bishop almost smiled at that. But he preferred not to talk over the phone. Plus he wanted to look in on Amy again before doing anything else. 'Okay,' he said. 'I'm heading back to New York now, so how about we meet in the hospital cafeteria at around eight thirty? We can talk over breakfast.'

'Fine, I'll be there,' Arquette said, and hung up.

FORTY-FIVE

It was 08.23 when Bishop and Kidanu entered the second-floor cafeteria. Bishop had already looked in on Amy upstairs, where Muro had
assured him all was quiet. He hadn't even seen Gerry. Bishop had
asked the PI if he wanted anything to eat, but Muro said a friendly
nurse was already taking care of all his nutritional needs without his
having to leave the room.

The hospital cafeteria was very large. There was a long serving line
along one side, and about fifty tables and booths took up the rest of the
floor space. The place looked about three-quarters full already. The buzz
of conversation filled the room, along with the strong aroma of coffee.

Bishop and Kidanu moved along the serving line, filling their trays
with various items. Kidanu's was mostly fruit and vegetables. Bishop
paid at the cashier's till, then led the way to an empty booth set against
the wall and sat down. Kidanu took the seat opposite. Bishop was
shaking some salt and pepper over his double-smoked ham, hash browns
and scrambled eggs when he saw Arquette and the one called Nowlan
enter the room. Arquette looked around until he spotted Bishop. He
gave a single nod, then took a tray and moved along the line.

The two men reached Bishop's booth a few minutes later. Arquette
placed his tray on the table and sat next to Bishop, while Nowlan
took his coffee to a nearby empty table.

Arquette was frowning at Kidanu. It was obvious he recognized
him from the photos.

'Teferi Kidanu, meet Agent Arquette,' Bishop said and took a bite
of his toast. The men nodded at each other.

'How did you hear about the second attempt on Amy's life?' Bishop
asked.

Arquette started buttering his own toast. 'We're currently monitoring the local police frequencies as part of my official assignment. Last night one of my men brought me the transcripts from the last forty-eight hours, and an incident report from a Detective DuBay caught my eye. Amanda Philmore's name wasn't mentioned, but I figured it had to be her. A single official call to the hospital confirmed it. Is she stable?'

'For now.'

'Good. They could try again, you know. I can't assign an active agent to guard her, but I know plenty of retired agents who'd welcome the chance to strap on the holster one more time. Although I imagine they'd want some kind of reimbursement for their trouble.'

Bishop sipped at his coffee. 'I've already got that covered, thanks.'

'Fair enough.' Arquette glanced briefly at Kidanu and said, 'So are you going to fill me in on what happened in Washington?'

'I don't believe the Konambans are behind it,' Bishop said.

'I gathered that much,' Arquette said with a smile. 'Care to expand a little?'

'Colonel Bekele and Major Kidanu and I had an extensive discussion last night. It turns out Bekele has a pretty good alibi for Wednesday when I thought I spotted him in the Bronx. I'll double check it myself to make sure, but my gut instincts say he's telling the truth. He also told me he doesn't particularly trust your man Roger Klyce, either.'

Arquette turned to Kidanu. 'No? So what were you both doing with Klyce outside that warehouse three weeks ago?'

Kidanu picked up an apple and began polishing it with a napkin. 'I do not believe that is any of your concern, Agent Arquette.'

'You get used to the lack of contractions after a while,' Bishop said. 'And I got pretty much the same answer when I asked.' He turned at a movement to his left, but it was just Nowlan getting up from his seat. Bishop watched him stroll over to the serving line with his mug for a refill. Once he'd reached the serving counter, Bishop turned back and said, 'See, the Konambans have their own reasons for wanting to learn more about Klyce. It turns out even the legitimate side of Artemis's business might not be so legitimate, after all.'

'What are you talking about?'

Bishop turned to Kidanu. 'You want to tell him?'

Kidanu took a bite of his apple, chewed for a while, then said,

'Artemis International are currently assisting the People's Republic of Konamba in tracking down certain fugitives we wish to bring to trial. Yet while they have helped us catch some of the little fish, the larger fish always seem to get advance notice before we arrive on the scene. We cannot prove anything, but we believe Klyce tracks them down, notifies us, then warns the target in return for substantial payoffs. And that being the case, it would seem logical that he has a very good idea where these fugitives go to next. And that information belongs to us. We have paid for it. In more ways than one.'

And what does that mean? Bishop thought. But he kept quiet.

Arquette sat back in his seat. 'And you can't do anything directly since it would affect the other business your country has with him?'

Kidanu didn't answer. He just took another bite of the apple and chewed.

Bishop said, 'And as for those phone calls Amy made to the ambassador, it seems they were related to her research in tracking down these bad boys.'

'That is correct,' Kidanu said. 'She wanted to spend time in our embassy library. We hold detailed files on Badat and the senior members of his military junta, but for security reasons cannot allow them to leave the building. Colonel Bekele simply arranged a suitable time for her to come and make her notes. Under supervision, of course.'

'Of course,' Arquette said. 'So you and Bishop are working together on this now?'

He shrugged. 'I merely follow Colonel Bekele's instructions, Agent Arquette. He believes my presence will come in useful.'

Bishop watched as Nowlan returned with his refill and sat down at the same table as before. 'So there you have it, Arquette,' he said. 'Looks like you were right about some things, but off the mark about a few others. But more to the point, Klyce has just moved himself up a notch on my very short list of suspects.'

'Hmm.' Arquette tapped his fingers against the tabletop. He reached for his own coffee cup and took a sip, made a face and put it down again. Bishop wondered what he was thinking. Finally, he said, 'So what's your next step?'

'I don't know yet.' Bishop gulped down the last of his coffee and stood up. So did Kidanu. As Arquette rose to let him out, Bishop said, 'But I'll be sure to let you know ahead of time.'

Arquette smiled at that. 'Just make sure you understand one thing, Bishop. If you do find out Klyce was responsible for your sister's assault, that in no way entitles you to take the law into your own hands. Do I make myself clear?'

Bishop raised an eyebrow. 'The thought never entered my mind,' he said.

FORTY-SIX

Bishop decided to walk to Amy's this time. Kidanu gave no argument, and they made the ten-minute journey in silence. One good thing about the guy, at least he knew when to keep quiet. Most people didn't. That was one point in his favour.

They were turning into Audubon Avenue from West 193rd Street when Kidanu finally said, 'You lied to Agent Arquette.'

'Did I?' Bishop asked.

'Yes. When he asked you what you planned to do next.'

'What makes you think so?'

'I am not a fool, Bishop. Our journey so far has mostly been spent in silence. I cannot believe you wasted that time by not thinking ahead.'

'Well, you're right. And the reason I didn't tell Arquette is because of a deep-rooted psychological defect of mine.'

'Really? And what is that?'

'With a few rare exceptions, I don't like law. Of any kind. If it wasn't for the fact that Arquette can provide me with intel I can't get anywhere else, I wouldn't tell him dick. Which means I'd tell him nothing, by the way.'

'Yes, I know.' Kidanu stepped around a deliveryman pushing a hand trolley full of boxes. 'And you have a reason for feeling this way?'

'We've all got reasons for behaving the way we do,' Bishop said, and left it at that. He wasn't in the mood to explain how the three years he'd spent behind bars for another man's crime had been mostly down to the ineptitude of the various detectives assigned to the case. Wrapping everything up as quickly as possible had been the name of the game with those morons. A more meticulous team of investigators might have questioned why all the circumstantial evidence against

Bishop had been found with such ease, and begun to suspect somebody was constructing a neat frame-up. But clearly that had been too much to hope for.

Naturally, that wasn't the only reason. His enmity towards the police had started a lot further back than that, but the wasted years spent in prison had only intensified his feelings. There were exceptions to every rule, of course, and he had met some decent cops here and there. But not many. And he saw no reason to think Arquette was any different from the rest. At least not without further evidence.

They came to the entry gate for Amy's building. It was locked today, so Bishop keyed in the correct code on the keypad and both men stepped through and proceeded down the short path. Once they were up on the building's fourth floor, Bishop once again knocked on the door to apartment 23. This time it was Lisa who opened it. She was wearing a baseball shirt and loose black jeans, and she'd pulled her blond hair back into a half-ponytail, making her look even more like her mother.

'Oh, hi,' she said. And she was smiling faintly this time, which Bishop took as a sign he was still in her good books. She turned to Kidanu with her patented frown.

'Lisa,' Bishop said, 'this is Kidanu. He works at the Konamban embassy. Okay if we come in?'

'Sure, come on in.' She opened the door wide. Both men stepped inside and she raised an eyebrow at Bishop as he passed. 'Konamba, huh?'

'The very same,' Bishop said, and led Kidanu down the hallway into the living room.

Janice Philmore, wearing a cardigan and loose slacks, was sitting in one of the easy chairs. Pat, still in PJs, was sitting on the floor with two open books in front of him. To Bishop, it looked like schoolwork. They both looked up as the new arrivals entered the room.

'Hello again, Janice,' Bishop said. 'Apologies for not calling ahead.'

'Oh, that's fine,' she said, getting up. 'Would you like—'

'Wow, you're really black,' Pat interrupted, staring at Kidanu with wide eyes.

'*Patrick*,' Janice said, her brows lowered. 'You apologize right now.'

But Kidanu grinned and said, 'It is perfectly all right. He only says what he sees. He means nothing by it, do you, Patrick?'

'Uh uh.'

'You see? No harm has been done.'

Kidanu was still smiling. Bishop was stunned by the sudden change in the man's manner. He sure was a different character around kids.

'Hope you don't mind,' Bishop said to Janice, 'but we just came over to check something of Amy's. We shouldn't be too long.'

'*I* don't mind, James,' Pat said.

'That's good,' Bishop said to his nephew. 'As long as it's cool with you.'

Pat nodded and said, 'It is. It's cool as a *fool.*'

'Or as cool as a mule,' Kidanu said.

Grinning, Pat said, 'Or cool as a . . . *pool.*'

Kidanu nodded. 'That is correct. Or a zool.'

'Hey, zool's not a word!'

Kidanu frowned. 'No? Are you sure?'

'*Course* I'm sure. I know *all* kinds of words, don't I, Grandma?'

'You surely do,' Janice said, 'and right now you should be using some of them to finish your English homework.'

'Oh, all *right.*' Pat gave one of those long-suffering sighs that only boys of a certain age can do and went back to his book.

Janice turned back to them and asked, 'Can I get you anything? Coffee, maybe?'

'No, we're fine, thanks,' Bishop said. He and Kidanu then left the living room and followed Lisa down the hallway towards Amy's bedroom.

Lisa halted just outside and said, 'Do you need me for anything, James?'

'Not this time.'

'Good. I've got plenty of homework of my own to finish before going back to school.'

'When're you going back?'

'Monday. I asked to go. I hate sitting round here all the time. All I do is think about Mom.'

Bishop nodded. 'I know what you mean. Where's your dad?'

'Probably at the hospital. I haven't seen him since last night.'

'Okay,' Bishop said. 'Well, I'll see you later, then.'

Lisa smiled at both men, then entered her own room and shut the door. Bishop showed Kidanu into Amy's room opposite. After going over and switching on the PC and modem on the work desk, he pulled the Frank Sinatra CD from the drawer and extracted the CD-R.

'This is it,' he said, handing Kidanu the disc.

Without a word, Kidanu took a seat and opened the disc tray on the hard drive. After inserting the CD, he double clicked on the disc icon and a dialog box appeared, asking for the password.

Bishop leaned over and keyed in JINJI. The dialog box disappeared. Kidanu opened the Word document and saw the same information Bishop had already shown him.

'Like I told you,' Bishop said. 'That's all there is.'

'Not necessarily.' Kidanu moved the mouse around until the cursor was on the Folder Options tab, then right-clicked. The folder options menu appeared, with General, View, File Types and Offline Files tabs at the top. 'There is a simple method for hiding files,' he said. 'Any PC owner can do it, but most are not even aware the option exists. It may lead to nothing, but I believe it is worth checking in this case.'

Kidanu pressed View and got a whole list of choices under the Advanced Settings folder. Halfway down was something called Hidden Files and Folders. Then two choices: *Do not show hidden files and folders*, and *Show hidden files and folders*. The first one was checked.

'You see?' Kidanu checked the second option, then returned to the CD directory. Where it became immediately obvious things had changed.

Bishop stared at the screen and said, 'Well, how about that.'

Where there had only been one file before, now there were twenty-seven.

FORTY-SEVEN

'I knew there had to be more,' Kidanu said. He was almost smiling. 'Your sister would not have taken such care to send herself only one file. And an innocuous one at that.'

'It puzzled me, too,' Bishop said. 'I'm glad I insisted you come along now.'

He took the other chair and leaned in closer to the screen. The first thing he noticed was that none of the documents had names. Just numbers. Ranging from 001 to 058. There were twenty-six in total, so naturally there were gaps. There was no 003, for instance. Or 012. Or 014. Along with numerous others. No way of knowing why, unless Amy herself had initially numbered the files she was interested in, then decided to discard the ones she felt were irrelevant before saving them to disc.

'Let's try the first one first,' he said.

Kidanu clicked on 001.

A jpeg of an official looking email opened up. It was at a slight tilt, which indicated Amy had scanned it from a paper copy. It was from the 'FPT Bank & Trust Company Limited' in the Cayman Islands, and addressed to 'The Director of Xerxes Holdings, Inc.' Underneath that was an account number. It was dated January 12 of last year.

The letter was brief, and read, *Dear Sir, Herewith we, the FPT Bank & Trust Company Limited, as represented by the bank officers listed below, do confirm that the amount of USD 3,000,000 (Three Million USD) has now been deposited into the above account from account number . . .* And then it gave the depositor's number.

Bishop said, 'You ever hear of this Xerxes Holdings before?'

'Never.'

'Hmm. I wonder if Klyce is the unnamed director. Okay, let's try door number two.'

Kidanu clicked on the next one. Another jpeg opened up. This one was an invoice addressed to Xerxes Holdings from Continental Surveying, Inc. in Ottawa, Canada, for unspecified services amounting to $87,000. The date was July 17, 2010.

'What about Continental Surveying, Inc.?' Bishop asked. 'Ever hear of them?'

'No.'

'I guess all your unofficial dealings with Klyce were strictly under the table, huh?'

He turned to look at Bishop. 'We are back to this again?'

'I'm the curious type. So was it black market arms you were buying?'

'You had already guessed as much before our initial meeting at the embassy.'

'Yeah, but it's always nice to have guesses confirmed.'

'I confirm nothing,' Kidanu said, turning back to the screen. 'However, you must be aware of the major civil uprisings currently going on in our country.'

'I've seen the headlines. Looks like the usual craziness. A bunch of fanatic militants want to overthrow the current government for some reason.'

'The current *elected* government, I should add. That is a very important detail. But yes, they are fanatics, and they do not care who they kill in the process. Women. Children. Anybody. And why? The leaders have actually stated on record that they want to revert to the kind of dictatorship we had before. Can you believe there are people who *want* another Badat in power? Or another Idi Amin? Or worse?'

Bishop shrugged. 'I can believe almost anything where humans are involved.'

'And these animals never seem to have any problems arming themselves either. Have you noticed that? Yet the Konamban government are forbidden from doing the same. We are a blacklisted country, as you know. So what would you do in such a situation, Bishop? Bearing in mind that all your ports and entry points are under constant watch by UN security forces.'

'Theoretically, I guess I might search around for a black market supplier who wasn't afraid to take a few risks to find a way through.'

Kidanu nodded. 'So there is your answer. Theoretically. Shall we continue?'

He highlighted the next dozen documents and opened them up in one go. As he slowly scrolled through, Bishop saw they were essentially more of the same. A few more notifications from the Caymans bank, regarding large money deposits in the seven-figure range. Some going back six years or more. And more invoices from the Continental Surveying company, some running into the low six-figure territory. But again, never actually specifying what this Xerxes was getting in return for its money.

Bishop shook his head in frustration. Amy probably had a good idea what all these payments signified, but he was still scrabbling around in the dark. So far, he was unable to see why this information was worth a person's life. 'Keep going,' he said.

Bishop watched as Kidanu continued to move his way down the list, opening each one as he went. There were more bank notification letters. More invoices. More . . .

'Wait,' Bishop said. 'Go back one.'

Kidanu moved back to the previous jpeg. Bishop had almost missed it. It was another invoice. This one was for $103,000, dated from December the previous year. But in contrast to the others, it listed *Medical Services* as the reason for the bill. And it wasn't from Continental Surveying, but a company called EMC-Med Associates. No address, either.

'Medical services,' Kidanu said. 'I wonder what kind? And for whom?'

'Could be anything. Let's carry on.'

Kidanu moved on to the next jpeg. This one was also different. It was a scan from another printout. But this one had obviously been taken directly from the FPT Bank & Trust Company website. It was a simple summary statement for the Xerxes account number. There were no dates and no names. The balance of the account was $82,132,550.

'Whoa,' Bishop said softly.

'That is a large amount of money,' Kidanu said.

Bishop nodded. 'The kind of money people will do almost anything to protect. This pretty much tells me I'm on the right track. If in doubt, follow the money. Let's see what else there is.'

Kidanu moved on to the next file. Another invoice from Continental for unspecified services. And another one. Then more bank notifications. They'd almost reached the end of the CD when Bishop said, 'Hello.'

Document 056 was a scanned, handwritten list of two dozen names and numbers. Bishop recognized the handwriting as Amy's. He read the first few entries:

ALLEN, JOHN – 11–04–11 C (213)–457–8355.
BLACK, ANDREW – 02–09–07 C (323)–564–9002.
FOSTER, JAMES – 07–28–08 N (414)–447–1522.
GARCIA, MARTIN – 11–22–09 L (727)–835–8889.
GRANT, ROBERT – 03–21–11 C (213)–954–2265.
JONES, ROBERT – 07–18–11 N (212)–006–3663.

He skimmed over the rest and said, 'First names like John, James and Robert, combined with surnames like Jones, Smith, Miller, Taylor. It's like a list of the most common names in the English-speaking world. All except the last one.'

The last name was separate from the rest. It read, S. BAINBRIDGE? Unlike the others, there were no numbers alongside. Almost as if Amy had added it as an afterthought.

'The numbers next to the other names,' Kidanu said. 'The first part appears to be a date.'

'Yeah, and the last part's probably a phone number. 212 is a New York area code. 323 is for Los Angeles. 414's for Wisconsin, I think. Or Minnesota. No idea about the letters N, C and L, though.' He rubbed his palm back and forth across his scalp as he tried to come up with something that fit, but nothing came to mind. After a while, he said, 'Can you print that page out for me?'

Kidanu reached over and switched on the printer. As he gave the print command, Bishop pulled his cell phone from his pocket. Time for the direct approach.

FORTY-EIGHT

As the printer went into action, Bishop keyed in the John Allen number. Almost immediately, an automated voice said, 'The number you are trying to reach is no longer in service. Please check the number and try again. Thank you.'

Bishop frowned and hung up. He didn't need to try again. He already knew he'd keyed the number in correctly. The printer went silent and Kidanu handed him the sheet.

'Nothing?' he asked.

'Out of service.' He tried the Andrew Black number next. This time there was no automated voice. No ringing tone, either. Just a repetitive beeping sound that meant only one thing. 'And that one doesn't exist at all. Let's see if the third one's the charm.'

He tried James Foster's number next. This time he actually got a ringing tone. After the twelfth ring, the phone was picked up and a female voice said, 'Hello?'

'Hello,' Bishop said. 'Can I speak to James Foster?'

'Who?'

'James Foster.'

'Nobody by that name here, mister. I think you got the wrong number.'

'Oh. That *is* Wisconsin, right?'

'That's right.'

'Can I ask how long you've been at this number, then? Maybe Foster was the owner or tenant before you.'

There was a single bark of laughter at the other end. 'I kinda doubt it, mister. My husband and I built this place over twenty years ago, and before that it was nothing but an empty plot. Wasn't nobody here before us except a stray dog or two, and that's a fact.'

'Well, I guess I got the wrong number then.'

'Yeah, I guess you did at that,' the woman said, and hung up.

Bishop put the phone down on the desk. 'Strike three,' he said. 'I'll try the rest later, but I think I'll get similar results.'

'So they are not phone numbers?'

'Doesn't look like it. But they're made up of ten digits and they've got area codes. I don't know what else they could be. And Googling a name that common won't help either.' He paused. 'Maybe if we tried a name and date together?'

Kidanu turned back to the screen, navigated to Google and keyed in James Foster and the 2008 date. He pressed enter and the screen filled with results.

Bishop saw the top link was for a genealogy forum. The two-line snippet mentioned an Edward *James Foster* from the seventeenth century. July 28 only got a mention because one of the forum posters sent their message on that day.

But his eyes were drawn to the second link down. It was part of an obituary from the *South Dakota Gazette* website. The snippet included the words *James N. Foster, 49, died of heart failure on 07/28/2008, at his home near Wessington Springs . . .*

Kidanu clicked on that link and they were taken to an obituary archives page on the newspaper website. It was the sixth of nine pages listing surnames beginning with F. Kidanu scrolled down until he reached the Fosters. There were lots of them, but only four Jameses. Kidanu clicked on James N. Foster and was taken to another page.

The listing for the guy didn't provide a whole lot more information than the Google snippet. Just three lines in total. *James N. Foster, 49, died of heart failure on 07/28/2008, at his home near Wessington Springs, South Dakota. A graveside service will be held at 2:30 pm on 08/04/08 at Laurel Cemetery in Huron.* More a notification of death than an obit. Bishop guessed you could probably access the complete thing by paying a subscription fee.

'Possibly the same man,' Kidanu said.

'Could be,' Bishop agreed. South Dakota was nowhere near Wisconsin, though. Although if those numbers weren't phone numbers, that wouldn't matter anyway. 'Try Googling the John Allen and Andrew Black names and dates.'

Kidanu tried John Allen first. The first page of results gave them plenty of John Allens, but none with that specific date. The next two pages were the same. Kidanu then tried Andrew Black. No sites listed an Andrew Black with that date. But Bishop still had a feeling they were onto something. 'Try Martin Garcia now.'

Kidanu keyed in the name. The first result was a snippet of another death notice. This time from the *Omaha Courier*. Kidanu clicked on it and was taken to another page. One that gave a slightly more comprehensive history of the late Martin Garcia.

Martin Garcia, 54, died from head injuries caused by an industrial accident on Sunday, November 22, 2009, at Cobre Valley Medical Center in Globe, Arizona. Visitation will be held at Maranatha Community Church from 4:30-6:00 pm on Saturday, November 28. A graveside service will be held at 2:30 pm Sunday at Ruiz Canyon Cemetery.

Bishop skimmed through the rest quickly. The gist of it was that Garcia had never married or had kids, generally kept himself to himself, and spent most of his working life on the shop floor of a large printing works on the outskirts of town. His parents and brother had died some years before, and he had no surviving relatives.

Bishop sat back in the seat, staring at the ceiling as he rubbed a thumb across his lip. 'Interesting. We've got two deaths in two states, sixteen months apart. One heart attack and one industrial accident. If you believe the obits.'

'You think the deaths could have been arranged?'

'I don't know what to think yet. I need more intel.' After a few moments, he sat up and said, 'See if you can get the number for the Wessington Springs Police Department in South Dakota. Or the sheriff's office. Whatever they've got over there.'

Kidanu went straight to Google and began a search.

Meanwhile, Bishop sat back and thought about his sister again. And the whole crazy situation. He was still amazed that it had been she who'd gotten involved with all this rather than him. Of the two of them, it was always Amy who'd wanted the safe mainstream life. And she'd gotten it, too. Marriage, two great kids, nice apartment in the city. The works.

Until she'd stumbled across something in her work she couldn't just forget and brush under the carpet. Something that forced her into action. And naturally, she would have wanted to talk to her brother about it, since she knew Bishop had had experience with this kind of thing before.

Except he hadn't taken the call. Nor had he gotten back to her. He'd just assumed his sister wanted to invite him to dinner again or something. So much for his great instincts.

Jesus, what an asshole, he thought. *I'm so sorry, Amy. Whatever I have to do to make it up to you, I'll do. Once we've gotten through this, things will be different. I guarantee it.*

'Here,' Kidanu said.

Bishop came back and looked at the contact details on the screen. He picked up his cell phone and keyed in the phone number listed.

After two rings, a guttural female voice said, 'Wessington Springs PD.'

'Like to talk to the senior detective, please.'

'Wait one,' she said, and put Bishop on hold.

Less than ten seconds passed before a male voice came on the line. 'Detective Tom Elledge. Who am I talking to?'

'Oh, hey, Tom,' Bishop said. 'This is Detective Joe Medrano, out of the 34th Precinct in Manhattan.' He quoted Medrano's badge number and said, 'Look, I'm hoping you can help me out with some information in regard to one of the hundreds of cases cluttering up my desk here. At least I think there's a desk under all this crap.'

Elledge chuckled. 'Sure, detective, if I can. What do you need?'

'Call me Joe. Well, I don't think it'll come to anything, but I have to check every lead, you know? Think is, we got a possible crackpot down here who's been bragging about all the people he's killed for fun. Most of the names he's handed us have led to nothing, but there is one name that actually exists. A James Foster of Wessington, South Dakota. So I did some checking and discovered a James Foster died around the same time our suspect claimed he offed him. Not at Wessington, but at Wessington Springs, which is your neck of the woods. You familiar with this Foster at all?'

'Jim Foster? Sure, I knew him. Well, by sight, anyways. He was an electrical engineer lived outside of town a ways. And this perp of yours claims he murdered him?'

'That's what he says. Was there was anything suspicious about the cause of death?'

Elledge snorted. 'Not unless you think a heart attack's suspicious. Our medical examiner made a thorough examination of the body and came to the conclusion it was simple death by heart failure.'

'Was Foster overweight, then? Or did he have a history of heart problems?'

'No, he was in pretty good shape. Didn't drink, didn't smoke. Ran every day. No sign of drugs in his body. Not even aspirin. But you and I both know that sometimes it just happens that way. And to the unlikeliest of people.'

'Sure. And what about his family? Were they satisfied?'

'Well, Jim didn't really have much in the way of family. No family at all, now I think about it. And he never married. One of those that are happy in their own company, I guess.'

Another loner with no family ties. That was interesting. 'Well, I guess it proves my suspect really is pulling my chain, after all.'

'Some people'll do anything for the attention, I guess.'

'Yeah, just watch reality TV some time. Okay, well, thanks for your help, Tom.'

'Any time.'

Bishop ended the call. Kidanu said, 'You were very convincing, Bishop.'

'I can be when I want to be.'

'So this Foster died of a heart attack?'

Bishop nodded. 'Sure looked like it. I remember reading about some banned diabetes drugs that can induce heart failure in certain people. Rosiglitazone was one, I think. But the ME found no signs of drugs in Foster's body.'

'Would that not depend on how closely he looked?'

'I guess it would.' Bishop picked up the cell again and said, 'But before we start jumping to conclusions, let's see what the Globe PD have got say about Martin Garcia.'

FORTY-NINE

Half an hour later, Bishop sat back in the chair and slowly exhaled. If anything, he was even more confused.

A sergeant of the Globe PD had said that Martin Garcia had gotten himself trapped in one of his firm's industrial presses and had later died from the injuries. There were plenty of witnesses. Kidanu had found two more obits that matched the dates on the printout. One for Michael Taylor, 52, of Pine Bluff, Arkansas, and another for William Miller, 56, of Rushville, Illinois. Taylor died from injuries sustained from a traffic accident in which two others also perished. Miller died from a brain aneurysm diagnosed years before.

'So all seem to be accidental deaths,' Kidanu said, 'or deaths from natural causes.'

'It's starting to look that way,' Bishop said, rubbing his fingers across his forehead. 'We've got a list of twenty-three seemingly unconnected men who, from 2007 onwards, died in circumstances that appear to be above suspicion. Other than the fact they were born with some of the most common names in the country, what's so special about them? And who's S. Bainbridge? We've also got numbers that are disguised to look like phone numbers, but clearly aren't. So what are they? And why disguise them in the first place? And then those letters, N, C and L.' He turned to Kidanu. 'You know, I got a hunch once I figure out what they signify, I'll really start to get a good handle on what's going on.'

'There is another connection between the four men you enquired about, though.'

'Yeah,' Bishop said. 'All were loners, with little or no surviving family. Which means they won't really be missed by anybody except a few friends and acquaintances. And the first deaths took place in

2007, the same year Klyce set up Artemis International. Then there's all this money going into that numbered account in the Caymans. And what kind of services are being provided by Continental Surveying, Inc. in Ottawa? Or those vague "medical services" from EMC-Med Associates? It seems the more I find out, the more questions arise.'

'There are still two more files to check,' Kidanu said.

'You're right.' Bishop had almost forgotten about them. 'Let's take a look.'

Kidanu opened the 057 file first, but it was just another bank notification. He tried 058 next, but unlike the others this one was a Word file. A single page suddenly filled the screen.

'It is blank,' Kidanu said.

Kidanu was right. The page was totally blank. Except Bishop was thinking like Amy, and remembering how sneaky she could be when she wanted to be.

'Try selecting all,' he said.

Kidanu pressed Command-A. The middle of the page was immediately highlighted in light blue. 'There *is* some text on there,' he said. 'Your sister must have set the colour to white.' He moved the cursor up to the font colour tab and changed it to black.

Bishop smiled. Two small lines of text were now visible in the centre of the page. The first line was a name: *Janine Hernandez*. The second line was an address in Harrisburg, Pennsylvania. There was no phone number.

He narrowed his eyes at the screen. 'Arquette told me the guy who first approached him about Artemis was named Hernandez, and that he suspects Klyce had him killed for discovering too much. He also mentioned Hernandez had a wife. Maybe this is her. Amy obviously found out about this Hernandez somehow, so maybe she was planning to talk to her at a later date, but didn't want anybody to know about it. Or even that she knew of the woman's existence. There has to be a good reason why Amy wrote her address down.'

'But why risk saving this woman's details at all?' Kidanu said. 'Whoever took the copy from your sister's bag can do what we have done and they will see the hidden files.'

'You're assuming she saved this particular document to both copies, which I very much doubt. Or the other files, for that matter. No, this looks like a simple reminder she made for her own use. Knowing Amy, I can't believe she'd purposely double the risk of it falling into the wrong hands if things didn't go to plan.'

Kidanu didn't look convinced, but he didn't argue the point. Instead, he asked, 'What do you plan to do now?'

Bishop thought for a moment, then picked up his cell and dialled the operator. When she came on, he repeated the name and address on the screen and asked for a phone number. A few seconds later, he hung up and said, 'No number listed under that name or address.'

Which was no real surprise. If this Hernandez woman had a phone, Amy would have written it down with the address.

'Then the only way to talk to her is face to face,' Kidanu said.

'Hmm.' Bishop sat back and thought about it.

Harrisburg was a three-hour drive. A trip there and back would keep him away from Amy for most of the day. That made him uncomfortable, even though it was stupid to feel that way. After all, he had Muro there on 24-hour guard duty. He knew he was over-compensating for not being there when it had counted, but he couldn't help how he felt. Not where Amy was involved.

He needed to be moving forward, though. He knew that much about himself. He needed to be making some kind of headway because then he felt in control. He felt moored. Anchored. However distanced and objective he tried to keep himself through all this, he was aware that he was far too emotionally attached to the case. With Amy's safety on the line, it was inevitable. Too much was at stake. So he couldn't afford to stop. He was like a shark. He had to keep moving. Keep following the leads. Get to the source.

And right now the only lead was a three-hour drive away. It was all very simple, really.

Bishop picked up his phone. Keyed in a number. Waited.

After a few seconds, a voice said, 'Muro.'

'It's Bishop. Checking in again. How are things over there?'

'I think I'm putting on weight. That nurse who likes me won't stop bringing me food. Other than that, no change. Which is kind of good and bad, if you get me.'

'I know what you mean,' Bishop said. 'So nobody showing a special interest in Amy at all?'

'Other than the medical staff, no. And I've been sniffing the air for anything that smells wrong. So far, nothing.'

'Good. Has Amy's husband been in to see her today?'

'Haven't seen him.'

'Really? Okay, well, I'll keep in touch.' Bishop ended the call, frowning to himself.

'No change?' Kidanu asked.

'To Amy? No.' But where was Gerry? Something was going on with that guy, but what? He found Gerry's number on his contacts list and called it. He listened to it ring and ring, but there was no answer. It didn't even go to voicemail. He hung up.

'So do we go to Harrisburg and talk to this woman?' Kidanu asked.

'Yes,' Bishop said. He put Gerry out of his mind and scrolled through the contacts list until he found the number he wanted. 'Let me see about getting us some wheels.'

FIFTY

Once they came out of the Holland Tunnel on the New Jersey side, Bishop kept them on I-78 West. Later on it would merge with I-81 South and take them right into Harrisburg itself. The traffic was light. He calculated they should reach their destination by fifteen hundred hours or thereabouts.

He'd used the same car rental place as before. The one on West 83rd. He had an account there so it was easier all round. This time they'd given him a three-year-old silver Infiniti sedan. That was all they had left. No satnav, but that was okay.

Much of the journey was spent in silence. Kidanu watched the scenery go by for the first half-hour, then took that day's *Times* off the back seat and began to read. Bishop spent the time going through everything he'd found out so far, trying to come up with workable hypotheses that fitted all the facts at hand. The problem was, none of them did. He either had too little information or too much. Often one was as bad as the other. Plus he hadn't slept in a while, which wasn't ideal for clear thinking.

For instance, those twenty-three dead men kept causing him problems. For the life of him, he couldn't figure out what they might signify. Were they murdered, or were the deaths exactly as they seemed? And did they even play a major role in all of this? Clearly the commonness of the names themselves held some importance, but what? And those goddamn letters. N, C and L. What the hell were they?

And then there was the matter of Gerry. Where was he if not at the hospital? There was definitely something going on with that guy, but Bishop couldn't put his finger on what. As if he didn't have enough to deal with. He definitely needed a talk with his brother-in-law when he got back from this trip, though. One way or another, he was going to get some answers from him.

He was still brooding on it when Kidanu spoke for the first time in an hour. 'There is an interesting story in this newspaper.'

'There usually is,' Bishop said, grateful for the interruption. 'What's this one about?'

Kidanu carefully folded the paper in half, then into a quarter. 'There was a traffic accident on the New Jersey Turnpike at six twenty-three on Wednesday morning. Apparently, the driver of an SUV lost control of his car just before the toll booths and slammed into the back of another vehicle. The SUV driver survived with some broken bones, but the driver and passenger in the car in front both died on impact. It says here that one of them, Christopher Buckler, was actually a crime reporter for the *New York Times*. A police source said they found a genuine fault in the SUV's steering and that it was not a case of vehicular manslaughter.'

He turned to Bishop. 'You mentioned that Amy could have been working with a reporter on this. What if this Buckler was the man she was supposed to meet on Tuesday night? If Klyce did not know how much Buckler knew, it is possible he arranged the accident to make sure anything he *did* know died with him.'

Bishop made a face. 'That's one hell of a long shot, Kidanu. All because of some small item you've read in the paper. And even if he was the guy, he was clearly still breathing on Wednesday morning. So why didn't he show up at the park the night before?'

'Perhaps he was warned to drop the story. After all, Klyce has a lot of influence. Or there could be any number of other reasons for missing the meeting. For instance, once Klyce found out about the planned rendezvous, he could have pretended to be Amy and sent this Buckler an SMS, postponing the meeting for another day.' Kidanu nodded to himself. 'Yes, now that I think about it, that would be much easier.'

Bishop shrugged. 'I don't see how. Assuming it *was* Buckler she was meeting, and that's one hell of an assumption I might add, then he'd see the message wasn't coming from Amy's number.'

'With the right equipment there is nothing simpler. I know this for a fact.'

'Okay, I believe you. About that part, anyway. The rest? I don't know. I guess anything's possible, so I can't totally rule it out. But Amy's phone was taken along with her valuables, so the only way to verify it would be by checking the messages on Buckler's cell phone. Which wouldn't be easy, even if I knew where it was. But let's see if we get what we want from this trip first.'

'Very well.' Kidanu faced front again.

Bishop drove. Minutes passed. Then he said, 'You sure got a way with kids.'

'You mean with Patrick? Yes, I like children. I find them easy to talk to.'

'That's a good character sign. Lots of people don't.'

Kidanu smiled. 'So by my actions, have I passed some kind of test?'

'I was just interested in watching you interact with Pat, that's all. So you got kids of your own?'

Kidanu lost the smile. 'Why? Is that relevant?'

'I don't know. I wasn't thinking that far ahead. But never mind. It's not important.'

Bishop carried on driving and let the silence fill the air. He wasn't bothered by Kidanu's reticence when it came to talking about himself. Bishop was the same. If the guy didn't want to talk, he didn't have to. Nothing wrong with silence. Truth be told, it was Bishop's favourite sound. He could go for weeks without speaking. And had done.

'You are not happy about leaving New York,' Kidanu said finally.

'You noticed that, huh?' Bishop said. 'No, I don't like the thought of being away from Amy for too long. Makes me itchy.'

'But if the answers are elsewhere, to stay would make no sense. And you have a permanent guard around her.'

'Right on both counts. I guess I'm just irrational.'

Kidanu tilted his head. 'No, not irrational. When family is involved, everything becomes . . . complicated.'

'Sounds like you're speaking from experience.'

Kidanu turned to the side window and asked, 'How long now?'

Bishop checked the dash clock. 14.26. 'About another half hour.'

In fact they didn't reach Janine Hernandez's address until 15.34. According to the street map Bishop had bought in the gas station, her house was located on North 6th Street between Curtin and Emerald. As he drove down the mostly empty thoroughfare, he could see straight away it wasn't one of the city's better neighbourhoods. The sidewalks were covered in litter and there were overflowing trash cans everywhere. Always a bad sign. And in between the numerous empty, overgrown plots of land were clapboard houses that had seen better days. Most of the stores they passed were boarded up. Even the bars.

Janine Hernandez's house was close to the Curtin Street intersection. It was a one-storey A-frame standing on its own, with empty plots on either side. The white paint at the front of the house was old and flaky, and there was a small crack in one of the windows. Bishop kept going past the intersection, then made a U-turn and went back. He pulled in to the kerb about twenty feet before the house and turned off the ignition.

They got out and walked over to the house. Bishop tried the buzzer, but it didn't work. He knocked instead. Nobody answered. He tried again, with the same result. Kidanu came back from looking in the window and said, 'I see some furniture inside. People live here.'

'But not at the moment,' Bishop said. 'We'll wait.'

FIFTY-ONE

Kidanu said, 'A woman and child are coming this way.'

Bishop opened his eyes and checked the dashboard clock. 16.44. The last time he'd looked it had been 16.11. He must have dozed off. If he'd been dreaming, he couldn't remember what about. But then, he never could. In fact, he wasn't entirely sure he dreamed at all. Even as far back as childhood. Just what did that say about him? He didn't know, but it was probably nothing good.

Yawning, he looked through the windshield. About forty feet away, a long-haired woman was walking hand in hand with a cute, dark-haired boy. She was a pretty, wide-hipped Caucasian woman in her thirties. The boy had darker skin and looked about six or seven. He was laughing at something his mother was saying. When they reached the house, the woman rummaged through her shoulder bag and pulled out a set of keys. She unlocked and opened the door and they both went in. The door closed behind them.

'Let's give her some time to settle first,' Bishop said.

Fifteen minutes later, they got out of the car. As they walked towards the front door, Bishop saw Kidanu was about an inch shorter than him, which would make him about six foot. And neither man was given to smiling much. In fact, they probably looked more like debt collectors than anything else. Bishop wasn't sure this was the image they should be projecting. Not if they were hoping to induce a single working mother to let them into her house.

Bishop took a moment to relax his facial muscles a little and look as non-threatening as possible. When he reached the door, he knocked twice and waited.

After a few moments, the door opened as wide as the security chain would allow. 'Yes?'

'Hello, Mrs Hernandez,' Bishop said. 'My name's Bishop. This is Teferi Kidanu, from the Konamban embassy in Washington, DC. We were hoping we might talk to you. I couldn't find a phone number for you.'

'Washington? I don't understand. What's this about?'

'It's in regard to your husband. Do you mind if we come in?'

'My husband? Cesar?' She was reaching for the chain when she stopped and pulled her hand back. 'Wait a minute. I think I'd like to see some identification first.'

'Very sensible,' Kidanu said, reaching into his inner jacket pocket. He pulled out his passport and handed it to her.

Janine Hernandez leafed through, then flipped to the back. 'I've never seen a diplomatic passport before. You say you work at the embassy?'

'As a security officer, yes.'

She handed the passport back to Kidanu and looked at Bishop. 'And you?'

Bishop smiled and said, 'I'm just a private citizen, Mrs Hernandez. But I can show you my New York driver's licence if you want. It's got a photo.'

She looked at him for a moment, then shrugged and took off the security chain and opened the door. 'Come on in, then.'

'Thanks,' Bishop said.

He and Kidanu entered the house and waited for Mrs Hernandez to close the door behind them. Then they followed her down a short hallway, though a doorway on the right and into a small living room. There was an old, threadbare couch and an equally ancient easy chair at one end. Set against one wall was a small table and two wooden chairs. A cheap, portable TV set stood in one corner of the room. Bishop noticed the carpet was spotlessly clean, as was the furniture. And there was a fresh jasmine smell throughout the house, too. Janine Hernandez was clearly someone who made the best of any given situation. Bishop warmed to her immediately. He liked that kind of attitude in a person.

'Sit where you like,' she said.

Bishop took the couch. Kidanu sat in one of the chairs at the table. Janine Hernandez perched on the easy chair with her elbows on her knees, hands clasped. She was wearing old jeans and a faded blue man's shirt. Her hair was pulled back into a ponytail.

'So you say this is about Cesar?' she asked. 'I don't understand. Do you have news for me, or something?'

Bishop said, 'No, nothing like that. Sorry if we gave that impression, Mrs Hernandez. We—'

'I prefer Janine,' she interrupted.

'Janine, then. We came to talk specifically about Cesar's problems with Artemis International.'

Janine's jaw visibly clenched at the last two words. She looked out the window and took a deep breath. Then she turned back and said, 'When you say Artemis, I assume you mean Roger Klyce.'

'That's right.'

She nodded. 'And your interest in all this is what exactly?'

'My sister works for them as a researcher,' Bishop said. 'Or she did. She's in hospital on life-support at the moment. On Tuesday evening, three men attacked and nearly killed her in a manner that was meant to look like a mugging. But I know it was planned. And I have reason to believe Roger Klyce might have had something to do with it.'

Janine's eyes had grown wider. 'What did they do to her?'

Bishop sighed. 'Imagine the worst and you wouldn't be far off. She's in a coma now, but she's breathing. But for how long, I don't know.'

'I'm so sorry,' she said. 'The poor woman. Have the police found the three men?'

'No. And they're not likely to.'

'You sound very sure.'

'Yeah, I guess I am.'

She looked ready to ask something else when the living room door opened. Janine's son wandered into the room and stared with wide eyes at the two newcomers.

Janine said, 'What is it, Joel?'

'Who are you?' Joel asked, staring at the intruders.

Bishop smiled. 'Hey, Joel. I'm Bishop and that guy at the table is Kidanu. We're just talking with your mom about a few things. That okay?'

Joel glanced at his mother and said, 'I guess. When's dinner, Mom? I'm starving.'

'Soon, sweetie,' she said. 'Now run along and finish yesterday's homework while I talk to these people, okay?'

Joel's shoulders slumped. 'But I want to stay in here with you guys. Why can't I?'

'But homework is very important, Joel,' Kidanu said. 'What is the subject?'

'Adding and subtracting,' the boy said. 'It's bo-o-oring. And it's hard, too.'

'Well, perhaps I can help you with it.' Kidanu raised an eyebrow at Janine. 'If your mother says it is all right.'

'*Bonus*,' Joel said, turning to his mother. 'Can he, Mom? Can he?'

Janine mulled it over for a few seconds, then finally shrugged and said, 'Well, if you don't mind, it's fine by me. But keep the doors open between us.'

'Of course.' Kidanu smiled as he rose from the chair.

'Come *on*,' Joel said, and grabbed Kidanu's hand and dragged him out of the room.

Once they'd gone, Janine tilted her head at Bishop. 'Well, *that* was weird. He usually clams right up around strangers. Your friend got kids of his own?'

'I don't know. He doesn't discuss his personal life much.'

'What about you?'

'Me? No. Although Joel there does remind me a little of Amy's boy, Patrick.'

'Amy? Is that your sister?'

'That's right. Amy Philmore. I was going to ask if you had—'

'I know that name,' Janine said, her eyes getting wide. 'Amanda Philmore, right? She sent me a letter – when was it? – last weekend, asking if it would be okay to drop by and talk to me about Cesar sometime. I was going to send a reply, but I just hadn't gotten round to it.'

'A letter? She didn't send you an email? Or call you?'

'It would have been a bit hard. I don't have a landline installed here and my cell phone's just a basic pay-as-you-go. And the last computer I ever used was Cesar's, and that's long gone. So no emails.'

'Oh. So do you still have the letter?'

'Sure. Wait here.' Janine got up and left the room. A few seconds later she came back with her shoulder bag. She sat down again and rooted around inside for a few moments. 'Here we are,' she said, and handed Bishop a folded envelope.

Bishop removed the letter and opened it. He immediately identified the handwriting as Amy's. It had last Thursday's date at the top.

Dear Mrs Hernandez, My name is Amanda Philmore and I work as a researcher for Artemis International in New York. I'm sure you recognize the name. I have only recently found out that your husband, Cesar, also worked here, and that he may have discovered certain things about the company that resulted in his being fired. I was wondering if I might come and see you on a day that's convenient for you so we might discuss this in more detail. Please send me a reply as soon as you can. Kind regards, Amanda Philmore.

Bishop looked up at Janine. 'And you were planning to meet her?'

'Sure,' Janine said. 'It's just finding the time, you know? My boss at the diner cuts me some slack 'cause she knows I have to take Joel to and from school on weekdays, but I have to make up the time in the evenings.' She pointedly looked at her watch. 'Speaking of which, I'll have to go in a couple of hours.'

'Don't worry, we'll be long gone before then. But going back to your husband, did Cesar discuss with you what he'd found out about Artemis?'

Janine shook her head. 'All he told me was he'd discovered the real reason for Artemis's existence, but he absolutely refused to give me any details beyond that. He said he didn't want to involve me or Joel in any way. But I knew whatever it was, it was eating him up. We were living in a small house in Queens and he'd just stay in his office in the garage and brood. And then one day he came home with the news that he'd been fired for sexual harassment against one of the female employees. Which if you knew Cesar at all, you'd know was bullshit. He said they must have found out about his research and wanted to totally discredit him so nobody else would take him seriously.'

'I take it he wasn't about to let it rest there.'

Janine snorted. 'Not Cesar. He spoke to one of his friends, who recommended this FBI agent he'd once met. Said he ought to talk to him, that he'd at least know what Cesar should do next.'

'Was the agent's name Arquette?'

'Right. I never met him, but I remember the name. Cesar came back from that first meeting with him sounding real pleased with himself. Like he'd finally found somebody who might actually be able to do something, you know? And despite his being out of work, the following week wasn't too bad. His spirits were up.' Janine's face fell. 'Then one evening Cesar left the house without telling me where he was going. And that was it. I never saw him again. I didn't know it at the time, but I was out a husband, and Joel a dad.'

'He gave no clue as to where he was going?'

'Not a thing,' Janine said. 'I reported him missing, of course, but all I got from the police was the usual runaround. They made it clear they thought he'd run off with somebody, and I got truly sick of trying to convince them otherwise. Let me tell you, a woman knows if her man's seeing somebody else, and Cesar wasn't. No way. And besides, he was absolutely devoted to Joel. He couldn't bear being away from him for more than a day.'

Bishop thought about what Arquette had told him in the limo, and said, 'You're right. I don't think Cesar was seeing anybody.'

'How do you know that?'

'I had a conversation with Arquette a few days ago. He told me Cesar believed Artemis were involved in illegal arms trafficking, and that he'd offered to break into their offices to try to get some evidence against them. Arquette said he wasn't happy about sanctioning a criminal act, but he wasn't about to stop him if that's what he wanted to do. But he thinks Klyce's people may have caught Cesar in the act and dealt with him themselves.'

Janine's jaw dropped. Bishop could tell this was news to her. She blinked and said, 'You mean murdered him.'

'Yes.'

She slowly sank back into the chair and pressed a palm against her eyes. 'I guess I always knew deep down something like that must have happened. I just didn't want to believe it. But it's been a year now with no word, and that can really only mean one thing, can't it?' Janine looked at Bishop with moist eyes. 'I really miss him. I have dreams where he just shows up on the front doorstep. He's full of apologies and then he explains he got lost coming home. I'm down for days afterwards. God*damn* it.' She turned and stared out the window.

Bishop said nothing to break the silence. What could he say? So he just waited.

After a while, Janine turned back to him and wiped her eyes with her hands. 'So that's what this was all about? Klyce was involved in arms trafficking?'

'He still is, but I think it's more than that. I just don't know what yet. We were hoping you might be able to help us figure it out.'

She sniffed. 'I would if I could. But I don't know what else I can tell you.'

'What about Arquette? Did he get in touch with you after Cesar disappeared?'

'Yes, he called a few times to check if I'd heard from him at all. When it became clear he'd really gone missing, Arquette said he'd do what he could. I didn't hear from him again, though, so I just assumed he hadn't found anything. Then what was left of my savings ran out and we had to move somewhere cheaper. And then he couldn't have called me even if he wanted to.'

'What about Cesar's belongings, like his computer? Didn't you bring them along?'

Janine shook her head. 'That would have been a little difficult, because not long after Cesar disappeared our place got burgled. His laptop was just one of the many victims.' She gave a sad smile and said, 'It never rains but it pours, right?'

FIFTY-TWO

To Bishop that sure sounded like Klyce tying up loose ends. Too coincidental otherwise. And Bishop didn't trust coincidence. Never had. 'What about notebooks or diaries?' he asked. 'Did Cesar ever have anything like that lying around?'

'You didn't know Cesar,' Janine said. 'He preferred keyboards to pens. A real technophile. If he ever needed to jot something down, he might use whatever what was at hand and then transfer it to his laptop or electronic organizer later. Like the back of an envelope or, if I was with him, my old pocket diary. But that was as far as it went.'

That got Bishop's attention. 'Did he often use your diary to make notes?'

'So often that I eventually told him to go and buy his own. He never did, though.'

'Do you still have it?'

Janine frowned. 'I don't know. A lot of things got left behind in the move out here. I could check, I guess. There's only a few places it could be.'

'It'd be great if you could,' Bishop said.

She glanced at her watch, then said, 'Okay,' and got up and left the room again.

Bishop stood, stretched and walked over to the window. They'd been here over an hour already. It would be getting dark soon. Another day almost gone with little to show for it. He still wasn't sure what he hoped to find here. At the moment, he was just fishing and seeing what he could pull from the water. But if this trip proved useless he might have to take a more direct approach with Klyce. Which meant finding him first, of course. But all things were possible when you had motivation. And he had that in spades. Because the longer they spent on this, the longer Amy was at risk.

He had Muro at the hospital, of course, and that was good. But his presence there only reduced the danger. It didn't get rid of it. If the people after Amy were determined enough, a single bodyguard wouldn't be able to stop them. Sometimes a whole team of them wasn't enough. He was reminded of the events of four years ago. Back on Long Island. The Brennan estate. He'd been in charge of a five-man team and it still hadn't helped. And they'd been the cream of the crop. Or they would have been if not for one rotten apple. It all felt like a lifetime ago now. Which, in effect, it was. He sure hadn't been the same man afterwards.

He turned when he heard Janine returning. She was holding a small book. 'Found it,' she said. 'Don't know what good it'll do, but you're welcome to look through.'

Bishop came over and took the book from her. It was a standard, faux-leather pocket diary that looked a little worn from age and hard usage. He sat down and flipped through it. Many pages were crinkled. Some had whole pieces torn out. The first three-quarters of the book was the diary. Here and there, Bishop saw a few notes written down, but not many. The last quarter was the address section. And this was filled with small writing.

Bishop went back to the beginning and went through it more carefully. Janine's handwriting was consistent throughout. It was neat and well spaced out, like Amy's, but Janine tended towards larger, rounded letters with smooth flourished strokes. The diary showed nothing out of the ordinary. Just basic reminders and appointments here and there. He leafed through the address section next. When he got to the Cs, he stopped at the second page. There was some blue text in the left-hand margin. The handwriting was different. It looked rushed and the letters were sharper and more crammed together. There was a name, Anthony Carter, followed by a number with a New Jersey area code.

Bishop showed Janine, his finger underlining the notation. 'This is Cesar's handwriting?'

Janine leaned forward, squinted at the page and nodded once. 'That's it. Tony Carter was a neighbour of ours in New York.'

'Uh huh.' Bishop continued looking through. He saw a few more names and numbers Cesar had scribbled down. Often they were crossed out, but they were still legible. Each time Bishop called out the name, Janine would identify the person as someone Cesar had either known or met in New York.

Bishop had reached the Fs when he stopped. Cesar's handwriting in the margin again. Except this one was an address. The entry read, *The Farm (Continental!!!), New Dub. Rd, Ottawa – DFTC!!* It had been underlined twice and then crossed out, presumably once Cesar had transferred the information to his organizer. There was no phone number. It looked like a possible connection to the Continental Surveying, Inc. mentioned on the CD. And an address in Ottawa, too.

Bishop especially liked the three exclamation marks after the Continental mention. Something about this entry had clearly excited Cesar, which in turn catalysed Bishop. This was something, all right. The way Cesar had written it, it almost looked like a eureka moment. He showed the page to Janine and said, 'Know anything about this one?'

Janine frowned at the entry and slowly shook her head. 'Never seen that address before. And we never went to Canada.'

'Any idea what DFTC stands for?'

She smiled. 'That was his shorthand for Don't Forget To Check.'

Bishop nodded. *Good advice, Cesar*, he thought. *Maybe I will at that.*

He proceeded to go through the rest of the book. But Janine had a good memory and was able to explain the reasoning behind every other name he called out.

Which just left 'The Farm'.

'Look, I really want to help you,' Janine said, 'but I'm still a working mom. It's already half past six and I need to feed Joel and get ready for my evening shift.'

Bishop handed back the diary and said, 'You've already helped a lot. Thanks. We'll get out of your way now.' He got up from the couch and paused as he looked around the tatty room, wondering how to phrase what he wanted to say next. 'Look, Janine, do you need any money? Like for a cab into town or anything? Or just for general expenses?'

Janine smiled with one side of her mouth as she led him to the doorway. 'Thanks, Bishop, but I never accept charity from strangers. No matter how tastefully it's phrased.'

'What about compensation then? How do you feel about that?'

She paused. 'You mean from Klyce?'

'Uh huh.'

Janine made a face. 'I don't see much chance of that happening, do you? At least not with the Klyce *I* remember. Besides, he's probably forgotten all about us by now.'

'Maybe I'll remind him the next time I see him,' Bishop said.

FIFTY-THREE

'That poor family,' Kidanu said, buckling his seatbelt. 'And I am being literal. They appear to be living just above the poverty line.'

'Yeah,' Bishop said. 'Just one more thing Klyce has to answer for. He sure loves spreading the misery around, doesn't he?' He turned the keys and the Infiniti's 3.5 litre engine immediately sprang into life. 'What happens to Joel when his mother goes to work?'

'There is an elderly woman a block away who looks after him. Joel told me she is very nice.' Kidanu turned to Bishop and said, 'So this new Continental Surveying lead of Cesar's. Do you think it is worth following up?'

'I've been thinking about it for a while now. Cesar sure seemed to think this farm was important, which means I do, too. Also, if I'm right and Klyce actually owns Continental Surveying, it's just possible he might be there right now. His receptionist said he'd be gone for a few days, and that when he said that it usually meant he'd be going out of the country.'

'And this farm is located in Canada,' Kidanu said.

'Exactly.'

Bishop leaned his head back and stared out at the darkening sky. But going to Canada would mean he'd be even further away from Amy. And for longer. But if there was a chance Klyce would be there, it was worth it. Especially as it was now the only lead he had. He tapped his fingers against the steering wheel for a few seconds, thinking, then pulled his cell from his pocket. He scrolled through his call log, found the number he wanted and called it.

'Hello again,' Muro said. 'No change here.'

'All right,' Bishop said. 'I'm mainly calling to see if you can do a little background checking for me without leaving that floor.'

'All I need is a phone and internet access and I can probably do it without leaving this chair. What's on your mind?'

'I'd like to know more about something called Continental Surveying, Inc. They've got an address on New Dublin Road in Ottawa, but that's about as much as I know. Also an EMC-Med Associates. And while you're at it, maybe you can see what you can dig up about an offshore company called Xerxes Holdings, Inc.' He spelt it and said, 'How long, do you think?'

'I should have something for you in an hour, hour and a half. But I'll call you, anyway. You realize I'll be charging you extra for this, right?'

'I wouldn't have it any other way,' Bishop said, and hung up. He turned to Kidanu. 'Now it's just a case of waiting for him to get back to me.'

'In that case, perhaps we should find somewhere to eat while we wait.'

'Good idea,' Bishop said, and put the gear stick into Drive.

FIFTY-FOUR

Bishop found an Australian steakhouse just out of town. Despite its fairly remote location, the large parking lot surrounding it on all sides was already close to full. Inside, a waitress led them to a booth and asked what they wanted to drink. Bishop ordered himself an iced tea. Kidanu ordered mineral water. The waitress left.

Kidanu scanned the busy restaurant. 'Many families come here, I see.'

'Yeah, we Americans love to eat out. Five times a week is the national average, I read somewhere.' He looked down at his menu. 'You haven't said much since leaving the house. Still thinking about Joel? Or is it that he reminds you of someone else?'

Kidanu turned back to him. 'Why do you say that?'

'Janine Hernandez asked me if you had kids yourself. I said I didn't know, but I think you do.' He turned a page. 'Or you did.'

Kidanu said nothing as he looked down at his own menu. He paged through it for a while and said, 'Parmesan pasta with steamed broccoli. I have not tried this before.'

Bishop shrugged. 'I get it. None of my business. Yeah, pasta's always good. Now let's see what we got here. Sirloin . . . Rib-eye . . . Yeah, I think I might go for a filet and baked potato. That sounds pretty good.'

After a few more beats of silence, Kidanu sighed and said, 'I had a son and a daughter.'

Bishop slowly closed his menu. 'Had?'

'Yes. A wife, also.'

'What happened?'

'Erasto Badat happened.'

'The Scythe. Yeah, I had an idea he might have been involved somehow.'

Kidanu nodded. 'I always give myself away when his name is mentioned. I cannot help myself. I live for the day that I . . .'

He stopped as the waitress returned with their drinks. Bishop and Kidanu gave their food orders and she went away again.

'You don't have to tell me if you don't want to,' Bishop said.

'It is fine. The words themselves can no longer harm me. And it all happened over fifteen years ago. That is a very long time.' He took a sip of his drink. 'I was twenty when I married Zainab. She was eighteen. A good woman. Two years later our daughter Gabra was born. Our son, Lebne, arrived a year later. A year after that all three were taken from me. Do you know Konamba's geography, Bishop?'

'You're a landlocked country, right? Eritrea to the north and Ethiopia on your south and east sides.'

Kidanu nodded. 'And the Sudan to the west. I come from a small town named Ksaneta, close to the Sudanese border. And totally unexceptional but for one small detail. Ambachu Kornma was also born there, thirty years before me. Do you know that name?'

Bishop frowned. 'It rings a bell. Isn't he an author or something?'

'Close. He is a filmmaker. And a highly respected one. He . . .'

Kidanu paused again when he spotted the waitress returning with their food. Once she'd placed their dishes on the table, she wished them a happy meal and left them.

For the next ten minutes they ate in silence. Bishop had almost finished his steak when Kidanu put down his fork, took another swallow of his drink and said, 'Ambachu had distant relatives in France and emigrated there with his family at an early age. Later, he entered the film business and began to make his reputation as a maker of important documentaries. Fifteen years ago, however, he gave some interviews saying he had just completed the project that meant the most to him, a ninety-minute film exposing the true horrors of Badat's reign since assuming power. It is unclear how exactly, but somehow a video copy of the film found its way to Badat before its release.'

'Not good.'

Kidanu drank some more water. Bishop saw his hands were steady. He seemed fully in control of himself, but somewhat detached. Bishop had seen this before with survivors of serious family trauma. How they'd trained themselves over time to look upon the horror as though it had happened to somebody else. To recall the events objectively, without breaking down.

'Not good,' Kidanu agreed. 'Badat then contacted Ambachu directly and said if he did not turn over the film negative and all copies, he would send an embassy courier to show *him* a documentary that he would direct himself. One showing Badat personally executing two hundred people from Ambachu's home town.'

'Don't tell me. Ambachu refused to turn his film over.'

Kidanu made a harsh nasal sound. 'Naturally. Later, he said he did not believe Badat would actually do it, but he must have known what he was capable of. After all, he had just made a documentary exposing the man's excesses. Not that he can be faulted for not giving in to that maniac, of course. What happened next was solely down to Badat.

'And so a convoy of eight trucks entered Ksaneta one morning, Bishop, just after dawn. The loud engine noises woke everybody up. Armed soldiers poured out of the trucks and began pulling us all out of our homes and into the main square. Zainab held Gabra while I cradled my infant son in my arms. A large overweight man whose face we had seen on posters was at the centre of everything, shouting orders. None of us could actually believe our president was here, in our village. But there he was, shouting and laughing as his men set up lights and cameras. None of us knew what was happening. We were all very scared.

'Once the whole town was present, Badat looked around and pointed at Yoseph, a good friend of mine. Four soldiers came over and dragged him and his two sons into the centre of the square. One of the boys was five years old, the other seven. His wife was screaming as soldiers held her back. The whole population was terrified at this point. I think we could all sense what was coming and that we were in the presence of true evil.'

Bishop's mouth felt dry. He picked up his tumbler and drank some of the iced tea.

'Badat did the work himself, as he promised. He used a machete and made it last a very long time, savouring every scream. Once Yoseph and his two children were dead, Badat calmly mutilated their bodies until they were no longer recognizable as human. It was like a bad dream, Bishop. None of us could believe our eyes. As Badat pulled his machete from one of the children's skulls I saw him ask the cameraman if the lighting was satisfactory. Insane.'

Kidanu gave a weary sigh. 'He took all day, not finishing until dusk. My children and my wife were taken just after noon, when the sun was at its hottest. I screamed to be allowed to join them, but Badat laughed and said it was my duty to bear witness. So that is what I did, Bishop. I watched Badat murder them, and then I watched him mutilate them. Along with the hundred and ninety seven others the soldiers left behind. I still see them all in my dreams.'

Bishop could find nothing to say.

'But there is a happy ending of sorts,' Kidanu said. 'Six months later, a large unified force made up of revolutionaries and army deserters finally seized control of the capital and gave the country back to the people. Government ministers and senior military personnel who hadn't already fled the country were arrested and subsequently executed. However, Badat and his senior ringleaders were not among them.'

'No surprise there. I take it you were personally involved in the coup?'

Kidanu shrugged. 'Naturally. And that is all thanks to The Scythe. I am one of his many sons. He created me. That is his legacy, but I live in hope that it will also be his obituary. You see, before I left Ksaneta I made a promise to my family's spirits that I would avenge them one day. And one thing I can guarantee is if it is left to me Badat will not face a trial. He will die anonymously by my hand, and it will not be a quick death. I will slowly tear him apart as he tore my family apart. And in the moment before I finally send him to hell in pieces, I want the last thing he sees on this earth to be my smiling face.'

Bishop took another sip of his drink. He wasn't sure how he would have handled it had he been in Kidanu's place. Actually, he had a good idea he would have lost it entirely and got himself killed along with his family.

He gave a single nod to Kidanu and said, 'All I'll say is watch out.

I know all about obsessions, and they'll eat you up from the inside out if you let them. Before you know it, you find yourself isolated from the human race and that's not a good place to be. Believe me, I know what I'm talking about.'

Kidanu shrugged. 'I appreciate the warning, but I will be fine.'

Bishop wasn't so sure about that, but it was Kidanu's life. He looked down at his watch and was surprised to see it was gone eight thirty. Muro should have called by now. He was about to check his cell phone when it chose that moment to ring.

'This could be Muro,' he said and pulled the phone from his pocket. Sure enough, he saw Muro's number on the display. Perfect timing.

He took the call and said, 'You find out anything?'

'That's for you to decide,' Muro said. 'As for Xerxes, you wouldn't believe how many shell corporations I had to wade through until I got to the real owners. And they were from all over the place, too. One company that was incorporated in the Caymans would lead me to another that was incorporated in Belize, and so on and so on.'

'So who owns it?'

'I finally narrowed it down to one guy. Roger Klyce.'

Surprise, surprise. 'What about the other two?'

'Well, EMC-Med Associates was a complete no-show. There's nothing listed under that name at all, so it's probably a letterhead rather than an actual registered business. But Continental Surveying, Inc. is also owned by Klyce, believe it or not. Their registered office address is 7512 New Dublin Road, Ottawa. All I know is it's a farm of some kind.'

'Wheels within wheels,' Bishop said. But it was what he'd been hoping to hear.

'You know it. So is that okay, or do you need anything more?'

'That's all for now, Muro. Thanks.' Bishop hung up, then updated Kidanu with what he'd just learned.

'So you were right about Klyce.' Kidanu frowned. 'But why would Continental Surveying bill Xerxes for their services if they are owned by the same person?'

'Possibly for tax purposes, to prove to the Canadian government they're a legit company with an income. But I like what I'm hearing.

It's looking more and more like Klyce is compartmentalizing his business affairs.'

Kidanu said, 'You mean he uses Artemis only for the legitimate side of his business?'

'Well, not entirely. If I'm right, he also uses it as a cover for a little arms trafficking on the side. But LCT must take a healthy slice of the profits from that. So maybe he set up another company, Xerxes, to handle his other not-so-legit sidelines.'

Kidanu nodded. 'Such as handling the payments for warning certain targets ahead of time.'

'Right. That statement we saw said there was already eighty mil in the company account, and that's all Klyce's. And then there's his Continental Surveying company, which must also exist for a reason, although I'm damned if I know what. For that matter, what's the significance of basing it north of the border? What's so special about Ottawa?'

Kidanu said nothing and sipped at his drink. Bishop drummed his fingers on the table, trying to come up with answers to his own questions. None came.

After a few moments, he said, 'Well, it looks as though my next stop's Canada.'

FIFTY-FIVE

'I assume you mean Ottawa,' Kidanu said, putting down his glass.

'Correct.'

'And you have your passport with you, or can Americans cross without one?'

'No, they changed that rule a while back. But as a New York resident I've got an enhanced driver's licence, and that doubles as a passport for land border crossings.'

'I see. And what do you expect to find in Canada?'

'I expect nothing. But I'm hoping I'll find Klyce there. Because the more I find out, the more I think he's behind Amy's attack. But I need to know for sure, and the only way I can do that is by confronting him directly.'

'And why should he admit anything to you?'

'I'll give him incentive.'

Kidanu stared at him for a few beats. Then, 'And if he admits it, what then?'

Bishop shrugged. 'Then I'll make sure he doesn't get to try a third time.'

'And what if he is not there?'

'Then I'll look the place over anyway and see what he's up to out there. Something's definitely not right about this set-up, so maybe I can use it as ammunition against him in some way. Look, you can do what you want, but I'm going.'

'Then I will go also. You plan to leave now?'

Bishop considered it. He wanted to keep moving, but he hadn't slept in thirty-six hours and even then it hadn't been for very long. And it was an eight or nine-hour drive to the border. He was shattered. Maybe having Kidanu along could solve that problem. 'Can you drive?' he asked.

'Yes, but not for some years. And I have also been awake for thirty hours now. I do not think it is safe for me to get behind the wheel of a vehicle for an extended period.'

Shit. So much for that idea. Bishop said, 'Okay, tomorrow's Sunday, so we'll grab a couple of rooms in a nearby motel and make a fresh start first thing in the morning.'

Back in the car, after making a quick stop at a convenience store where Kidanu picked up a few essentials, Bishop followed the waitress's directions to the Red Rail Motel. It was located on a cul-de-sac off the I-81, on the outskirts of town. Bishop pulled into the courtyard and saw a long two-storey structure with space for maybe fifty rooms. There were already about two dozen vehicles in the huge parking area out front.

At the front office, Bishop asked for two rooms. The guy slid a couple of registration forms across the desk for them to fill in. Bishop wrote a few things down on his, none of them true, and then the guy handed them each their key cards.

After agreeing on a six-thirty start, Bishop and Kidanu parted and went off to their first-floor rooms. Bishop had been on the go all day, so his first task was to take a long shower. Ten minutes later, feeling partially refreshed, he towelled himself off and slipped on a fresh pair of boxers. He lay on top of one of the twin beds and closed his eyes as he relived the day's events again.

First there was his capture at the Konamban embassy, which actually turned out better than he could have hoped. Okay, he'd been saddled with an initially unwanted partner in Kidanu, but the guy had proved useful today. And to be honest, Bishop preferred to have a man like Bekele for him than against him.

Then there was the discovery of Amy's CD and the files it contained, which was down to Kidanu, he had to admit. Of course, the information had ended up producing more questions than answers, but it also further implicated Klyce, assuming Muro's information on the various companies' ownership was correct. And there was no reason it shouldn't be. The CD had also led to Janine Hernandez, who had provided him with the Canada lead, so at least Bishop felt he was making some kind of progress.

And he thought about Kidanu's story, too. About how he'd been forced to watch the brutal slaughter and mutilation of his young family. That was something that would destroy most people. With Kidanu, it had just made him stronger. Or perhaps harder. There was a difference. Bishop knew from experience.

But it seemed their individual circumstances weren't so different from each other. They both had similar goals. Kidanu was intent on finding the man who'd destroyed his family fifteen years before, while Bishop was tracking those intent on destroying his right now. But where they differed was in their motives. Kidanu wanted revenge. Bishop just wanted Amy safe. That was a big difference right there.

Bishop brushed motivations aside for a moment and turned his mind back to the information they'd found on the CD, trying to see if he'd missed a connection somewhere.

He went through it all again and again, but at some point his mind just stopped working and he fell asleep.

FIFTY-SIX

The next morning, after a quick breakfast at a nearby diner, Bishop and Kidanu took the I-81 North out of Harrisburg. Kidanu had changed from his suit into a grey turtlenecked shirt and black jeans. Bishop was still wearing the black windbreaker, long-sleeved polo shirt and dark pants from yesterday.

Bishop stayed on the I-81 most of the way to Wellesley Island, where it morphed into the Thousand Islands Bridge. They reached the border crossing at 14.08. After the guard on the Canadian side waved them through without incident, Bishop continued along Highway 137 North for a couple of miles, then took a right when it joined up with the 401 Freeway.

'Canada is very spacious,' Kidanu said, looking out the window. It was a sunny day, with few clouds in the sky. 'Also very green.'

'More original forest here than any other country,' Bishop said. 'If you believe the tourist board. Which I'm inclined to do in this case.'

And hardly any traffic, either. Which made a nice change. Twenty-five miles and almost twenty-five minutes later, Bishop was driving northwest on Highway 29 outside Brockville. They hadn't seen another vehicle for almost a full minute when Kidanu spotted the turnoff for New Dublin Road on their right. Bishop slowed and made the turn.

The road was mostly farmland or forest on either side, with the occasional house or farm adding a little colour to the landscape. And all set well apart from each other. As Kidanu had said, space clearly wasn't an issue in this part of the world.

They passed more farms and houses, as well as a few business premises here and there, including a couple of buildings that looked like manufacturing plants of some kind. It was almost two miles later when Kidanu spotted the mailbox for 7512 on his side. Bishop slowed the vehicle to a crawl, at the same time looking past Kidanu at what lay beyond.

All he could see was a lot of flat farmland on that side. Evergreens concealed much of it from the road. Just past the mailbox was a long dirt driveway that ended in a gated entrance about a hundred feet further in. In the distance, he could just make out a large, one-storey farmhouse-type structure, with a barn on the left. Stretching off to the left and right of the gate was razor-wire-topped barbed wire fencing. Bishop thought he could see insulators on the permanent line posts, too. Which meant it was electrified. There was a ten-foot high steel post just past the gate, and affixed to the top was something that could have been a security camera. On either side of the gate was a small brick pillar. He thought he saw a tan box attached to the left-hand one, and then they were past.

He continued on for a few more yards until he was sure they were completely protected by the trees, and then pulled to the side of the road. About two hundred feet up ahead on the left, he spotted another dirt road entrance between some more trees. And a large sign outside that read *New Dublin Fire Station & Training Centre*.

'Well, it appears to be a farm,' Kidanu said. 'On the surface, at least.'

'I'd almost believe it myself except for the security camera above the gate. And the razor wire. That seems a little like overkill for a farm out in the middle of nowhere.' He turned to Kidanu. 'Have you got one of those smart phones with the large screen?'

'Yes. All embassy staff have them.' Kidanu reached into his jacket and pulled out a cell similar to Gerry's. 'Why?'

'Google Maps, that's why.'

Kidanu nodded, and played an index finger across the touch screen. A minute later he said, 'According to the street map, we are near the very end of this road. See?'

Bishop took the phone and saw a satellite view of this section of New Dublin Road, with an arrow pointing to their spot. Bishop used his thumb and index finger to enlarge the image until it was at full magnification. Beyond the trees lining the street, he could now make out the farmhouse he'd spotted in the distance. There were also two annexes – the smaller barn at the side and another building at the rear. The barn was probably a garage, but the one at the rear was only slightly smaller than the main house, with a covered walkway connecting the two.

And all around the land, roughly two acres according to the scale, was a fence. It was only really noticeable if you already knew it was there. Bishop doubted the electricity running through it would be strong enough to kill. Otherwise, why the razor wire at the top? More likely, it would be just enough to deter small animals. But it didn't matter. Bishop couldn't see how he was going to get in that way. Not without alerting those inside.

Bishop gave the phone back to Kidanu and leaned his head back against the headrest. He checked the dashboard clock and saw it was already 14.58.

'There are too many obvious deterrents to gain access via the gate or the fence,' Kidanu said.

'And possibly a whole lot more we don't even know about,' Bishop said. 'Which only leaves one real option.'

Kidanu nodded. 'They must come out some time, even if only to get fresh food.'

'But we'll need a place to watch from that's not too obvious.' Bishop jutted his chin at the training centre sign up ahead. 'And that might just be the answer.'

He drove on down the empty road until he reached the sign and turned left into the dirt driveway. It curved round to the right, but he couldn't see any kind of gate barring access. He followed the curve until he reached a large, empty parking area. At the end of it was a modern-looking, one-storey brick building with a blue roof. On the left-hand side was a double garage that looked big enough to hold a couple of fire engines.

'Perfect,' Bishop said, turning the car until they were facing the way they'd come. 'No training classes on a Sunday. I just hope we don't have to wait around too long, though. If anyone does turn up they'll wonder just what the hell we're doing here.'

He pulled to the side of the dirt driveway just before the curve, killed the engine and got out. It was still sunny, but the air was crisp. This far north, you could really feel the approaching winter. Kidanu also got out and stretched his arms.

'Okay.' Bishop pointed across the grass, towards the row of trees that concealed them from the road. 'I'll find a good vantage point over there and take first watch. You stay here by the car and be ready to move at a second's notice. I'll leave the keys in the ignition and wave if I see anybody coming.'

Kidanu nodded in response.

Bishop reached into the brown paper bag on the back seat and pulled out one of the gas station sandwiches they'd picked up on the way, along with a local road map. When in unfamiliar territory, it was always a good idea to familiarize yourself with the lie of the land. He walked across the grass towards the evergreens, found a space between two trees and crouched down. By leaning forward a little, he had a perfect view of the driveway entrance two hundred feet to his right. And with his dark clothes there was a good chance passing drivers wouldn't notice him.

Assuming anybody drove this route at all, that is. So far, he hadn't spotted a single vehicle.

Oh, well, nothing to do now but be patient and see what happens. With a mental shrug, Bishop opened the map and began memorizing the immediate area around New Dublin Road for alternative getaway routes. Once that was done, he began concentrating on the areas north and west of his location.

At 15.48, Bishop had just polished off the last of the sandwich when he heard the distant sound of an electronic gate in operation. It was coming from the right. And he'd been waiting less than an hour. Could he be that fortunate? It could be a false alarm, but he still needed to be ready. He stood up and looked behind him. The Infiniti's driver's side door was open. Kidanu was sitting in the driver's seat. Bishop waved his right arm back and forth in a big semicircle.

The driver's door immediately slammed shut and he heard the engine start up. He turned back to the road and peered right. Eight seconds later, he saw a silver Toyota Camry pause at the head of the driveway, ready to pull out. The left indicator light was flashing. He saw two figures in the front of the car.

Bishop turned and ran back towards the Infiniti.

FIFTY-SEVEN

'What are you hoping will happen?' Kidanu asked, watching the road ahead. They were on Highway 29, heading southeast at a leisurely forty miles per hour. There were just two vehicles separating them from the Toyota in front: a black Ford sedan and a red Izusu pick-up. A pleasant Sunday drive.

Bishop pulled the Zeiss spotting scope from his bag and said, 'That they'll go somewhere with a large parking lot. Then maybe I can hitch a ride without them knowing.'

'How?'

'Let's take one problem at a time.'

They'd driven for a mile when Bishop saw a crossroads up ahead. The black sedan signalled left and steered into the centre of the road. Kidanu drove on past it. Then it was just the red pick-up between them and the Toyota. Bishop knew if they carried on down this road it would take them into Brockville, a small city with a population of about twenty thousand.

At the next intersection, all three vehicles turned left into Centennial Road. It was a largely featureless thoroughfare, with trees and thick foliage lining both sides. They'd driven for about a mile and a half when Bishop saw a guard rail on the left. The trees thinned out and he saw the beginnings of a large lake going off into the distance. Just past that was a picnic area with a few tables and spaces for vehicles to park. As they passed, Bishop saw a large sign further in that read *Broone-Runciman Dam & Reservoir*.

They crossed over some train tracks. Soon, they all began to slow. The Toyota's left-hand indicator started flashing. At the side of the road up ahead, Bishop saw a large handmade sign advertising fresh vegetables. Then an entrance to a large circular driveway, leading to a white farmhouse with several large stalls out front, all overflowing with different-coloured vegetables. The Toyota angled across the road and turned into the driveway. The red pick-up kept on going. So it was a food run.

'Should I carry on?' Kidanu asked.

'Yeah,' Bishop said. 'But slowly.' As they were passing, he saw the Toyota make a U-turn until it was facing outwards and pointing a little to the right. The passenger side door began to open, and then the car was gone from sight.

Bishop faced front and saw some kind of storage place about a quarter-mile ahead. He pointed and said, 'Pull in when you get to that and turn us around. Then take us back to that rest area next to the reservoir. When they pass by, we'll follow.'

'*If* they pass by.'

'The driver left the car pointing in that direction. It's a gamble, but there's nowhere else to wait around here.'

At the storage place, Kidanu turned into the entrance, made a K-turn and headed back. As they passed the farmhouse, Bishop saw a man in the Toyota's driver's seat slowly combing his hair. Behind the food stalls, a girl in a sweater and jeans was filling a cardboard box. A woman in a raincoat moved down the line, pointing at selected vegetables.

Then they were past it again. As Kidanu turned into the dirt entrance next to the reservoir, Bishop looked the area over. It wasn't much. Just a small grassy rest area with some tree cover. Bushes and shrubs ran along much of the waterline. There was a wide gravel pathway leading directly to the lake, presumably so people could go and feed the fish.

When Kidanu was facing the road, he backed up a little until they were under the trees. They waited in silence. Bishop just hoped he was right about the Toyota coming back, otherwise they could be waiting a long time.

But the Toyota cruised past three minutes later, heading southwest. Hoping they had a few more errands to run before heading home, Bishop nodded to Kidanu, who pulled out and followed. When he closed the distance a little, Bishop raised the spotting scope and aimed it at the Toyota's rear window.

The passenger was in profile, saying something to the driver. It was clearly a woman. She had short hair and looked to be somewhere in her fifties. All he could see of the man was the back of his head. Then he turned to say something back and Bishop saw that he was a lot younger. Maybe late twenties. Bishop lowered the scope to the vehicle itself. The Camry looked like one of the mid-nineties models, which meant it wouldn't be equipped with the modern anti-theft systems most vehicles had nowadays. Those things were almost impossible to circumvent. Even for professional car thieves. And Bishop was hardly that.

The lights were green when they reached the end of Centennial Road. The Toyota turned left towards Brockville and Kidanu followed. Two miles later, they'd just passed under the 401 when Bishop saw a large, half-full parking lot coming up on the left. Further back was a large ValuMart with various satellite stores on either side. A tall sign next to the entrance welcomed drivers to the Brockville Shopping Centre. Bishop noticed it was already decorated with holly, although it was still only October. Christmas came earlier with each passing year.

'He is signalling left,' Kidanu said.

'Good.'

As soon as there was a gap in the traffic, the Toyota crossed and entered the parking lot. Kidanu waited for his turn while Bishop aimed the scope at the Toyota again. It was heading along one of the central aisles towards the ValuMart. It turned into another aisle and disappeared between two rows of parked cars. Bishop mentally marked the spot.

Kidanu finally pulled into the entrance and Bishop pointed towards the aisle where he'd last seen their quarry. Kidanu turned into it and slowed the car to a crawl. An empty silver Toyota Camry was parked about thirty feet away on the right, just next to one of the shopping cart corrals. There were plenty of free spaces nearby, including the bay on its immediate left. Bishop looked around and saw the backs of the woman and the driver as they walked towards the store.

Kidanu turned into the bay next to the Toyota and switched off the engine.

Bishop rolled down his window and took a good look at the other car's interior. He noted the placement of the inner door handle on the other side. It was in the locked position. He saw a cardboard box filled with vegetables on the rear seat, then focused his attention on the outer seal on the Camry's doorframe, picking out the best spot for what he had in mind. He placed the scope back in the knapsack and rooted around until he found the thin metal pry bar he'd used on the embassy window in DC.

'What is that for?' Kidanu asked.

'To make a gap between the seal and the doorframe. Then I simply insert a wire coat hanger in the space and open the door latch from the inside.'

'And do you have a wire coat hanger?'

'No, but ValuMart's bound to sell them.' Bishop opened the door and said, 'Wait here. I won't be long.'

Kidanu cleared his throat. 'Maybe the door is already unlocked.'

Bishop looked at Kidanu for a moment. Then he got out of the car and stared at the Toyota. The man had a point. Bishop already knew the passenger side door was locked, but that didn't automatically mean the other one was. This was Canada, after all.

He reached down with his free hand and grasped the driver's door handle. Then he gently pulled it upwards. The door clicked open.

'Well, how about that,' Bishop said softly. He turned and saw Kidanu watching him. 'I guess I'm just used to living in a country where everybody always locks their vehicles.'

Kidanu shrugged. 'I thought it might be worth checking.'

Bishop opened the door all the way and reached down for the trunk release lever on the floor. He pulled it upwards and heard the rear hatch unlatch itself. Closing the door again, he went back and opened the lid all the way. Inside, it was empty except for a tyre jack and a plastic tool bag in one corner. The spare tyre would be under the false floor. He calculated the available trunk space to be about fifteen cubic feet. Maybe less.

'That's a tight squeeze,' Bishop said.

Kidanu nodded. 'Better you than I.'

Bishop sighed and rubbed a palm across his scalp. 'God, I really hate small spaces.'

'I sympathize. You realize they will probably want to place their purchases in the trunk on their return?'

'Then I'll just have to persuade them to use the back seat instead.'

'And if they do not?'

'Then I'll be in real trouble.'

FIFTY-EIGHT

'They are returning,' Kidanu said. His deep voice sounded tinny through the hands-free earpiece. 'The woman is pushing a shopping cart with many bags inside.'

'Right,' Bishop said, and shifted position again.

He'd been waiting for over forty minutes and felt about as uncomfortable as a person could get. It wasn't claustrophobia exactly. Or maybe it was a mild form. No panic attacks, but he was finding it a constant struggle to keep his breathing level. The faint aromas of old engine oil and gasoline didn't help, either. But he needed to check out the 'farm', and this was the only way inside. He'd just have to bear it for a little longer, that's all. He'd put up with worse.

Kidanu said, 'The man is approaching the trunk.'

Bishop heard the man's footsteps getting louder and grabbed the lid latch with both hands. He was wearing the gloves he'd bought in New York. He heard the sound of a key being inserted into the lock, inches from his face, and pulled with everything he had as the latch turned one way and then the other. Then he felt the man attempt to manually lift the trunk lid. Bishop hung on for a few long seconds until the tension went away.

'God*damm*it,' a muffled male voice said. 'The stupid thing's stuck.'

'Try pulling down the rear seats.' A distant female voice.

'Yeah, yeah,' the man said. The key was removed. A few seconds later, Bishop heard the man unlock the Toyota's door.

He slowly turned his head and shone his Maglite at the rear seat-backs. In the middle of each was a security lever to prevent anybody from accessing the trunk that way. They were both still in their locked positions. He switched the light off again.

He felt the man grunting with the effort of trying to force the seats forward, but they didn't move a millimetre. Soon the man gave up and said, 'They're not budging either. Just stick everything in the back here. I'll fix the trunk once we get back to the farm.'

'It worked,' Bishop whispered into the mic. 'Keep me updated once we move off, okay?'

'Understood.'

Then came the sounds of bags being loaded into the back. A minute later, the Toyota's engine started up and the vehicle began to move. Bishop waited for the sound of voices, but the two up front clearly didn't have much to say to each other.

Eighty seconds later, Kidanu said, 'We are heading back the way we came.'

Bishop said nothing.

Then there was nothing to hear but the smooth running of the engine, combined with the soothing sound of tyres on asphalt. The smell of gasoline was a lot stronger when the car was moving, forcing Bishop to breathe through his mouth.

About five minutes later, Kidanu said, 'We are back on New Dublin Road. I overtook and got here first, as you suggested. I can see you in the distance behind me.'

Bishop remained silent. He knew Kidanu would park in the same place as before so he could act as Bishop's eyes.

It was just over a minute before Bishop felt the vehicle slow and make a turn. He heard the sound of tyres moving along a dirt road, and the ride became a lot bumpier. He pressed both hands against the chassis to steady himself. Then the Toyota came to a stop. One of the front doors opened and he heard footsteps moving away.

Kidanu said, 'You are parked just before the gate now. The man is approaching the stone pillar on the left. He is flipping open a tan-coloured box attached to the pillar and I see a black keypad inside. Wait . . .' There was a short pause, and then, 'Seven . . . nine . . . two . . . eight . . .' Another pause. 'His hand blocked the last number, but it was on the first row. So either one, two or three.'

Bishop smiled. First rule when infiltrating an enemy camp is always make sure you have a way out again. And now Bishop had one.

Assuming the exit code was the same as the entry one, of course. But in Bishop's experience, people generally preferred to keep things simple when it came to codes.

The next thing he heard was an electronic hum that could only mean the gate was opening, followed by the slamming of the car door. They began to move again.

'You are heading towards that barn-type structure to the left of the farmhouse,' Kidanu said. 'The double doors are open.'

Soon the vehicle came to a complete stop. Once the engine died, both front doors opened at the same time. They were slammed shut, one after the other, and then the rear doors were opened. He heard the rustle of grocery bags being lifted from the seat, followed by the crunching sounds of footsteps walking away from the vehicle. Bishop whispered into the mic, 'Who's carrying the bags inside?'

'Both are. And I see nobody else in the vicinity. You should be clear.'

'Understood,' he said, removing the earpiece.

There was no time to waste. Bishop switched the Maglite back on, shifted position so he was facing the driver's side, and pulled up part of the carpet he'd loosened earlier. Running along the steel chassis was a long, thin cable that led to the trunk release lever under the front seat. He grabbed it with both hands and pulled. There was a sharp, metallic *click* as the trunk's lock disengaged.

Bishop replaced the carpet over the cable and pushed the trunk lid all the way up. The car was facing into the barn. He saw daylight coming in through the wide open double doors in front of him and took a deep breath. Fresh air had never tasted so good.

He heard the sound of a house door being slammed open.

Bishop had three or four seconds at most. He didn't waste them. Jumping out, he checked he hadn't left anything inside, then gently closed the trunk lid until it clicked shut.

There were three other vehicles in the barn in addition to the Toyota. The rest was just empty space. Light was also coming in from two small windows on the upper level at the rear, which must once have been a hayloft. No bales of hay in evidence, just a lot of cardboard boxes lying around. And about thirty feet away to the left, in semi-darkness, Bishop saw a wooden staircase leading upwards. He ran for that and took the stairs three at a time.

He ducked down when he heard the crunch of footsteps and then the driver returned. He was looking at the trunk while tapping a couple of screwdrivers against his palm. With a melodramatic sigh, he pulled his keys from his pocket and inserted one into the lock. The lid opened immediately and the guy emitted a surprised bark of laughter.

The woman came back at that point and quietly took the last two bags from the back seat. She closed the door, said something to the driver and left. The driver, still shaking his head, closed the trunk and tried the key on it again. It opened just like before. Dropping the lid again, he pocketed the keys and walked out of the barn, closing the double doors behind him. Bishop didn't hear any sounds to suggest they were being locked. The only light now came from the windows in the hayloft.

Bishop moved over to the one overlooking the farmhouse. From this position, he could see most of the back of the house. There was a door at the near corner and another one at the other end. The driver walked over to the closest door, opened it and disappeared inside. The door slammed shut behind him. Probably one of those with self-closing hinges. He'd have to watch out for that.

The building at the other end of the walkway was also a one-storey job, but with no visible windows. The walkway itself was just a strip of concrete, with wooden posts every few yards to support the flat wooden roof running the length of the path. Still looking through the window, Bishop pulled out his cell phone and called Kidanu.

'I'm in the hayloft,' he said checking his watch. It was 17.32. 'Think I'll wait until 0200 hours before looking around.'

'Understood,' Kidanu said. 'I have good cover here, both from the road and from the house. I will watch through the scope for as long as there is daylight.'

'Right,' Bishop said, and ended the call.

He kept his face glued to the window. Waiting.

At 18.05, he saw a man wearing a dark hunting jacket and a baseball cap exit the nearside door, letting it slam behind him. It wasn't the driver. And it obviously wasn't Klyce. This guy was bigger in the shoulders, and tall. Bishop watched him walk slowly along the farmhouse wall towards the other building, arms at his sides. He crossed the space and continued walking along the wall of the annexe until he turned a corner and disappeared from view. Ninety-two seconds later, he appeared again and remained in Bishop's view until he reached the farmhouse. It looked as though it was a routine patrol. But how routine? And how regular?

When the man reached the back door again, Bishop checked his watch and saw it had taken him just under four minutes to complete his circuit of the buildings. Then the man passed by the door and continued along the same route for another go-round.

Bishop went over to the nearest cardboard box and slid it along the floor to the window. He sat down and watched the man walking away. It was going to be a long night.

FIFTY-NINE

When Bishop woke up, he immediately checked his watch. It was 01.56. Only four minutes out. Not bad.

He stretched and arched his back as he got up from his improvised seat. The evening had gone slowly. The perimeter guard had kept up his routine until 21.06 before going back inside. Nobody had come out to take his place. Before that, the only noteworthy event had been a third man exiting through the other rear door at 19.02. Again, it hadn't been Klyce. This man was short and stocky, and carried a large serving tray weighed down with covered dishes. He took it down the walkway, unlocked a door in the annexe and disappeared inside. Two minutes later he backed out empty-handed, locked the door and returned to the farmhouse.

So the second building was clearly home to somebody important enough to have his, or her, meals taken to them. But important in what way? Were they a prisoner, or were they here willingly? Was it Klyce in there? And if not, in what way was he involved? And how did this all link back to Amy? These were questions Bishop intended to answer before leaving this place.

At 21.45, when nothing further had happened, Bishop had decided to get some shuteye while he could. 'Sleep whenever possible,' was a mantra the instructors had drilled into him in basic training back in the Corps. Wise advice that Bishop had never forgotten.

Now he looked out the window again. There was a quarter moon in the sky and no cloud cover. All was still. About the only sound he could make out was a distant owl calling to its mate. Which reminded him. He picked up his cell and called Kidanu.

'What is the time?' Kidanu asked in a groggy voice.

'Almost two. I'm about to take a look around. Keep your eyes open in case I need you for any reason, okay?'

'Understood,' Kidanu said, and ended the call.

Bishop pocketed the phone and descended the staircase. He'd told Bekele he'd preferred working alone, but he couldn't deny it was good to have back-up in certain situations. That Kidanu didn't talk much was a bonus he hadn't counted on. He was actually starting to like the guy.

Bishop made his way over to the double doors. He'd checked the vehicles already and found them all unlocked, although he hadn't found any keys. In addition to the Toyota, there was a Ford Taurus, an Oldsmobile Alero, and a Chevy Lumina.

He placed a palm against the left-hand barn door and pushed a little. It gave. He pushed some more and the door opened a few inches. They clearly didn't believe in locks in this compound, which suggested they were putting all their faith in whatever external security systems they'd set up. Good when it came to keeping people out. Not so good if there was somebody already inside. But Bishop told himself to assume nothing, tread carefully and not get over-confident. No telling what was waiting for him in this place.

He slipped through the gap and looked in all directions. There was no movement anywhere. And no sounds. Even the distant owl had given up his cry for the time being.

Bishop worked his way along the front of the barn and peered round the corner. Seeing nothing, he crossed over to the side of the farmhouse and followed it to the end. When he reached the back door the driver had used, he noticed a window a few feet along and peered inside. In the faint moonlight, he could make out a sink against one wall, while further in he saw a large wooden table with a few chairs around it. So this was the kitchen.

He went back to the door and turned the handle. As he'd hoped, it wasn't locked. Wary of creaks, he took the strain off the hinges by lifting the door slightly as he pulled it open. But there were no sounds. The hinges were clearly well oiled. When he had a wide enough gap, he slipped into the kitchen and carefully closed the door behind him.

It didn't take long for his eyes to adjust to the darkness. His night vision was already at full capacity. It was a large kitchen area, and the table's presence in the centre of the room meant it probably doubled as a dining area, too. There was another window at the other end, overlooking the long driveway, and a key rack on the wall near the door he had come through.

He could hear sounds coming from an open doorway to the left, and see a very faint light source. It sounded like canned laughter. Possibly the night guard watching TV, but he needed to know for sure. Moving on the balls of his feet, Bishop walked across the hardwood floor towards the doorway. Peering round, he saw a wide hallway with two doors on the left and three on the right. At the end was another hallway running at right angles to this one. The third door on the right was partially open. That's where the light was coming from. Just a sliver, but enough to see by.

Breathing through his mouth, Bishop entered the corridor and slowly made for the light, pausing for a second after each step.

When he reached it, he moved to one side of the doorway and moved his eye to the two-inch gap. The sounds were coming from an unseen TV in the room. It sounded like an old episode of *Roseanne*. Through the gap he saw a long table against the opposite wall with eight monitors lined up in a row, all showing night-time images in various shades of black and green. Bishop recognized the first one as coming from the camera at the gate. It was a wide-angled shot of part of the driveway and a section of the main road. The other monitors showed parts of fields or woodlands beyond the fence, but none of them showed anything on this side. No shots of the farmhouse or barn. Nothing.

Bishop suddenly heard the harsh scraping sound of wood against wood and saw part of a chair as it was tipped back on its two hind legs. Sitting in the chair was the short, stocky man he'd seen earlier. He was wearing a shoulder holster over a short-sleeved shirt and dark pants, and chuckling at something coming from the TV.

At least Bishop didn't have to worry about hidden cameras on the grounds now. They only seemed to be concerned with possible dangers from outside, which suited him just fine. As long as he was quiet, he might be able to find the answers he wanted and get out again without anyone the wiser. Although getting past the gate without being seen was going to be a challenge. Still, he'd faced harder problems.

Bishop turned away and looked at the other four closed doors. Probably bedrooms for the three guards and the cook. But he still needed to check. He reached into a pocket and pulled out the wall microphone unit he'd used at the embassy. He'd brought the scope along as well, just in case.

After inserting both earbuds, Bishop switched on the unit and pressed the contact mic against the door directly opposite. From within, he heard faint breathing sounds interspersed with an occasional sigh, perhaps the result of a dream. To Bishop, the sighs sounded feminine. So possibly the cook. He tried the next door along and heard snoring. Male snoring. Without a doubt. Bishop carefully opened the door a few inches and peered inside. His night vision was back to full capacity again and he was able to see a man asleep on the single bed under the window. The driver.

Bishop carefully shut the door and tried the last room, the one next to the surveillance room. From inside this room he could hear nasal breathing. Steady and regular. He slowly opened the door and peered inside. It took a few seconds to make out anything, and then he saw it was the wide-shouldered guy he'd seen on patrol earlier. The guy's baseball cap was lying on the chair next to the bed. Bishop gently closed the door again, then slowly retreated towards the kitchen before letting himself out.

So that was the three guards and the cook accounted for. But no Klyce. Yet.

Bishop let himself out and looked over at the other building. Maybe he'd find the answers he wanted in there.

SIXTY

Bishop approached the door at the end of the walkway. It was made of steel. There was a steel handle, and underneath that a single keyhole. He crouched down. The lock looked simple enough. He straightened up and began walking around the annexe's perimeter.

It was a one-storey, timber-framed structure like the farmhouse. About two hundred feet by two hundred. The timber looked new, and not too weatherworn. Bishop guessed five years old at most. There were two air conditioning units at the rear, and he spotted small air vents in each of the four walls, but he didn't see a single window. Not one. And the only way in or out was through that steel door at the front.

He returned to the door, pulled his lockpick gun and tension wrench from another pocket and got to work on the lock. The night was totally silent. No barking dogs. No traffic noise. The only sounds were the ones he was making. It was a refreshing change from the city life he was used to. He couldn't remember the last time he'd heard nothing but silence. He liked it. That and the clean fresh air he took in with every breath. He could see how easy it would be to get used to country living. But not for him. At least not in this life.

Remember why you're here, he admonished himself. *Amy. And Klyce.*

Twelve seconds later he had the door unlocked. Pocketing his tools, he stood up, pushed the handle down and opened the door.

There was enough natural light to make out another hallway straight ahead. At the end of the hall, about sixty feet away, he saw what seemed to be a glass barrier. And beyond that, a number of tall plants, all lit by the faint moonlight coming in from a skylight above.

Bishop stepped inside and gently closed the door behind him. The muted light coming from up ahead allowed him to see two doors, one on either side of the hallway. The interior walls were made of cinder block and the floor was tiled. He walked to the end of the corridor. The glass partition at the end ran all the way up to the ceiling, and incorporated a glass door with an aluminium push handle.

Bishop opened the door and stepped into some kind of indoor garden, or recreation area. It all looked very tranquil. The skylight six feet above his head was only slightly smaller than the room itself, which was about fifty feet by fifty. In the centre of the space was a square stone table with four stone benches placed around it. Various potted plants and flowers were situated in all four corners and all around the borders. And surrounding it all were four concrete walls containing windows and doors. Entrances to the other rooms, presumably.

Bishop sniffed the air, but couldn't smell anything. He walked over to one of the tall plants and rubbed one of the leaves between his fingers. Plastic. They all looked real enough, though. Maybe the low maintenance upkeep was more important than authenticity.

He moved past the fake plants, stepped over to the wall to his immediate left and began checking the windows. The first showed a large, modern-looking living area beyond. Round the corner, the next window showed an office area that was about half the size of the living room. The next room along had a door but no window, so Bishop had no idea what its purpose was. It was clearly a big room, though, as it took up half of that wall and part of the adjacent one.

Bishop moved on to the window opposite the glass door he'd entered by. The drapes were drawn, but there was an inch gap in the centre. He peered through and saw a spacious bedroom with a king-sized bed set against the opposite wall. Bishop could just about make out an indistinct shape under the covers. Klyce? Or somebody else? Hoping whoever was under there continued to sleep peacefully for a while, Bishop moved round to the next window and tried to look inside, but the drapes were fully drawn. He couldn't see anything. The next one along was another bedroom, but the bed was empty. The last room was a small kitchen area, and then Bishop was back where he began.

He went back to the windowless room and tried the door handle.

It was locked. He had it open in seconds and saw only darkness within. The faint lightspill coming from behind didn't help much. He stepped inside, gently clicked the door shut behind him, and pulled out his Maglite. Switching it on, he saw he was in a large, empty, L-shaped space.

No, not empty.

At one end of the room were what looked like huge rolls of paper arranged on top of one another, reaching almost to the ceiling. In the corner, next to the rolls, Bishop saw numerous industrial-sized paint pots.

The rolls were all covered in protective brown paper. Each one was five feet high. Bishop walked over and found a slight tear at the top of one. He made the tear larger, saw white paper underneath, and managed to rip off a corner piece. It didn't tear easily. Shining the light on it, he held the scrap up close to his eye. Without proper daylight he couldn't be sure, but it seemed there was a very slight purple, or mauve, tint to the paper. He rubbed it between his fingers. The texture was almost rubbery. And running down one side of the sheet were identical watermarks of Ben Franklin.

Bishop knew he was holding 'rag' paper, that special kind of paper used to print currency. Normal paper was made from wood pulp, but rag paper was 75 per cent cotton and 25 per cent linen. Nobody knew the exact ingredients. The tint came from the red and blue fibres that got mixed into the paper at the manufacturing stage. He also knew real rag paper was supposedly harder to obtain than phoenix eggs. Yet there were reams of the stuff here.

And the pots over there with the steel strips around the lids? What were the chances they contained that special, colour-shifting, magnetic ink used in most countries' currencies? The stuff that, when printed, left a slight texture on the surface of the note?

Bishop felt the chances were better than even.

And all in a room large enough to contain a printing press. Possibly in parts, to be assembled on the premises. He knew a little about intaglio presses, though, and they weren't easy to come by. Not legitimately. Back in his close protection days, one of his earliest principals had been on the board of one of the big security printing companies in Philadelphia, and they'd used them there. Mainly for printing share certificates, driver's licences, passports, birth certificates, food stamps, things like that. But their main use was for printing currency. All kinds of currency.

As a result, sales of the presses around the world were closely monitored by the federal government. But Bishop knew how easy it was to arrange for certain merchandise to drop off the radar completely, as though it had never existed. It didn't matter how big it was. Or how closely monitored. With money in the right pocket, all things were possible.

Was that what was being planned here? Some kind of counterfeiting scheme? Maybe the guy in the bedroom could supply the answer to that one. Along with a few others.

Slipping the scrap of rag paper in his pocket, Bishop made his way back to the door and pulled it open.

And saw a man wearing shorts and a T-shirt staring right at back at him.

SIXTY-ONE

Bishop noticed a blur of movement to his left and ducked, but too late. The man's fist connected with Bishop's left temple, slamming his head hard against the door frame.

Dazed, Bishop dropped to one knee and immediately felt another punch just above his right eye. He fell back to the floor with one arm covering his face. A sneakered foot kicked him hard in the stomach. He doubled up, received another kick to his spine. He arched his back in pain. It was all happening too fast. Wham, wham, wham. The guy was all over him. Bishop hadn't even had time to catch his breath yet. He took another hard kick to the gut. Then another. Then he felt a hand grip his shirt and begin pulling him up.

And the guy had been doing so well up to that point.

First rule of unarmed combat: when a man's down, you keep him down. Any way you can. You don't drag him back to his feet again. Not for any reason.

Bishop showed him why not. As soon as he was upright again, he slammed his head forward and felt his forehead catch the bridge of the man's nose. The man released Bishop's shirt and staggered back into the garden area, one hand to his face. Bishop shook his own head, took a deep breath, and advanced on him with both hands raised. They were edging towards the stone furniture in the centre of the room. Bishop was aware of the butterfly knife in his back pocket, but didn't reach for it. He had no intention of killing the guy. At least not without knowing who he was.

'Look,' he said, breathlessly, 'we don't have to do this. Just tell me who—'

Bishop didn't get to finish the sentence. The man suddenly dashed forward, bending his right arm at the last moment and aiming the hard point of his elbow at Bishop's face. Bishop jerked his head to the left just before contact, and the elbow caught part of his chin instead. He shrugged it off, then ducked down out of the way and launched a left hook into the man's stomach, followed by a right to the jaw. The man grunted and stumbled back a few paces, shaking his head, one arm pressed to his stomach.

Bishop kept with him. He'd had enough of this. Time to grab himself some breathing space. While the man was still disorientated, Bishop ran forward, reached out with both hands and grabbed him by the front of his T-shirt. Then he swung him around in a 360-degree circle and let go, hurling him at the table and chairs five feet away.

The man hurtled towards the furniture like a sprinter reaching for the finish line. Just as he was about to make contact with one of the stone chairs, Bishop saw his foot slip on the tile and he lost his balance. As he fell, his head slammed against the chair seat with a sickening thud before ricocheting off. His body slumped to the ground in a messy heap and was still.

'Oh, shit,' Bishop said.

He went over and looked down at him. There was no blood, but his head was lying at an angle that wasn't natural for a living being. He looked about Bishop's age. Maybe a little older. His blond hair was cropped close to the skull. He had a Slavic face, with deep-set blue eyes, pronounced cheekbones, a long nose and a thin line for a mouth. Bishop knelt down and checked for a pulse. He stayed for a full minute before giving up. The guy wasn't getting up again. Bishop stood and rubbed a palm back and forth across his scalp.

He swore again.

It was stupid for the man to die like that. There was no need for it. Bishop had just wanted to talk to him. For all Bishop knew, he'd been kept here against his will. Unlikely, but even if he was here by choice, that didn't automatically earn him a death sentence. The man had simply woken up in the middle of the night to find an intruder on his patch and had decided to take care of things by himself. And Bishop had killed him for it.

Okay, accidentally. In self-defence. But the guy was still lying there, not breathing.

He sighed, then shook his head. Self-recrimination was a luxury he really couldn't afford. Not now, anyway. On the plus side, though, they hadn't made any noise during the fight. Which meant if somebody else was sleeping in the room with the closed drapes, he or she clearly hadn't heard anything. So maybe it wasn't a total disaster.

Time to find out one way or the other.

Bishop tried the curtained room first. He opened the door, found a light switch on the wall and pressed it. It was another spacious bedroom, laid out like a suite in one of the better hotels. Huge bed. Large TV. Desk and chairs. Two large cupboards. Connecting bathroom. The centrepiece was a double bed against the wall. An empty bed. There was also a musty smell in the air, which suggested nobody had been in there for a while. Bishop closed the door and moved on to investigate the next bedroom.

This one was all white and had the antiseptic feel of a hospital room. The bed, though large, had steel railings on each side. Bishop thought back to the information gleaned from the CD and thought this could be where the 'medical services' were performed. Whatever they might be. He checked the various cabinets and drawers, but found nothing that held any clues as to the room's specific use. The kitchen round the corner held a large supply of basic snacks and tinned goods, but not much else. And in the living area he found plenty of books, DVDs and CDs in various places, but nothing that might point to the purpose of this place.

And more important, there was no Klyce anywhere. Meaning the whole trip had been wasted. A whole day that Bishop could have spent doing something productive had just been flushed down the toilet with little to show for it. And Amy, whose welfare was still his number one priority, was still at risk and no better off than before.

Unless there was something of note in the office.

The door was unlocked. There was one large desk in the centre of the room which held nothing but a few legal pads and some pencils, and a smaller one set against the wall. The smaller desk's surface was taken up by a PC, a large monitor and all the usual trappings. There were two desk drawers. The top one held nothing but some standard stationery items. He closed the drawer and opened the second one.

Then closed it again. It was completely empty. He switched the PC on next. Once the monitor came to life, a prompt came up asking for a user name and password. Which pretty much put paid to that approach. Bishop wouldn't know where to begin. He turned it all off again.

Useless.

He checked the dead man's bedroom next. It had the same layout as the one next door. Bishop opened the cabinet and drawers and found various items of clothing inside. One black suit, some shirts, a sports jacket. In the drawers, he found fresh underwear and two tracksuits. There was a suitcase lodged at the back of the cabinet. It was empty. He carefully went through every item of clothing, but found nothing in any of the pockets.

In fact, there was no ID for the guy anywhere. No credit cards, no driver's licence. Nothing. It was as though the man had ceased to exist the moment he'd stepped through the steel door outside.

Bishop went back to the garden room and looked down at the body. The man's lifeless blue eyes were still staring up at the skylight above, but it was those Slavic cheekbones that caught Bishop's attention.

Back during his visit to the Artemis offices, Klyce had mentioned that Amy had recently been working on a case concerning the tracking down of some Serbian war criminals. And this guy sure looked like he came from that part of the world.

And Klyce had been correct when he said Amy was a good researcher. Bishop already knew she was one of the best. Always had been. Ever since school. In fact, it was she who'd taught him that the devil was often found in the details. He'd lived his life by that rule. Something else he owed Amy for.

So maybe she'd found out more than she should have, and a decision had been made to take her out of the picture for security's sake. And if that were the case, maybe this guy had had something to do with the decision-making. Or maybe not. Either way, the next step was to find out the guy's identity and see how he linked up with Klyce.

Bishop thought for a moment, then went back to the office and opened the drawer with the stationery items. He grabbed a small roll of Scotch tape, took a pencil and one of the legal pads from the larger desk, and returned to the dead man.

First, he rubbed the side of the pencil lead against the top sheet of the legal pad until there was a good large area of dark grey on the page. Then he lifted the guy's left hand and rubbed the pads of each finger and the thumb across the patch until they were smothered in graphite. Next, he tore off a strip of Scotch tape and pressed it against the index finger. Then he did the same with the other fingers. When he had all five, he tore off a blank sheet of paper and carefully stuck the strip of tape along it. He looked at the results. The prints looked clear enough. Maybe not CSI quality, but you could only work with what you had.

He couldn't leave the body here, though. That was clear. As soon as Klyce, wherever he might be, heard of a dead man on the premises it wouldn't take too much guesswork to figure out Bishop had something to do with it. Which would be totally counter-productive at this point. Or at any point, in fact. So, what, then? Even if he had the tools, burying the body would take too long. And if the night guard decided to do another patrol of the perimeter at any point, it would be all over.

Which left taking the body with him and disposing of it outside. And if he could make it look as though the man had left of his own accord and departed for destinations unknown, so much the better. Bishop took a few moments to think each step through, and decided it could be done. He even knew where to get rid of the body.

Bishop checked his watch. 03.14. Still a few hours left before sunrise. More than enough. But first things first.

He folded and pocketed the sheet with the prints. Then he reached down and hefted the body over his shoulder and took it into the bedroom and dropped it down on the bed. He removed every piece of clothing from the cupboard and laid them on the bed along with the empty suitcase. From the bathroom, he added the guy's toothbrush and razor. The rest he left. Then he squeezed everything into the suitcase except for one of the tracksuits. This he used to dress the body.

Once that was done, he pulled out his cell phone and took a photo of the guy's face. He stood up and checked the shot. The guy didn't actually look dead in the picture, more like he was drugged up to the eyeballs. That was good. It would actually help explain how Bishop was able to take the picture without the guy knowing.

Pocketing the phone, he took the suitcase to the hallway through which he'd entered, then opened the steel door and peered out. Still quiet, with no sign of movement anywhere. Suitcase in hand, he walked past the farmhouse towards the barn. He reached it without incident and went straight for the Toyota Camry, since he knew it had been used recently and would start without a problem. He opened the front door, disabled the interior light and placed the suitcase on the back seat.

Then it was back to the annexe for the body. After a final check to make sure he'd erased all traces of his presence, Bishop carried the dead man over his shoulder and out the front door, remembering to lock it behind him. Then back to the barn. Opening the rear door of the Toyota, he placed the body on the floor between the front and back seats, then ran back to the farmhouse kitchen. He carefully opened the rear door and listened. There were no noises from the TV any more. Bishop didn't know if that was good or bad. He stepped inside anyway. It wasn't as though he had a choice.

He crept over to the spot where he'd seen the key rack and got his Maglite out. Smothering most of the lens with two fingers, he clicked it on. Only three of the key ring fobs had logos on them. But one of the logos was the familiar oval badge with two more ovals set within. He lifted that set off the hook, switched off the light and returned to the barn.

Inside the car, he inserted the key in the ignition and turned it clockwise. The engine caught almost immediately and began purring like a cat. Excellent. He turned it off again and pulled his cell phone from his pocket.

Kidanu picked up immediately. 'Everything is all right?'

'Everything is not all right,' Bishop said. 'I'm gonna have to leave this place in a hurry, but don't follow me. For a number of reasons, I need them to think I'm alone. Give me a minute's head start, then meet me out by that rest area next to the reservoir.'

'Very well.'

Bishop ended the call and pocketed the phone. He was just about to step out of the car and open the barn doors when he heard a noise he recognized.

The sound of the kitchen door slamming.

SIXTY-TWO

Bishop very slowly pulled the driver's door until it clicked shut. The night guard making another patrol, or something else? Maybe he'd heard the engine start up. If he'd turned off the TV it was possible. Or maybe he'd gone to make a sandwich and seen three sets of keys on the wall rack where there should have been four. Either scenario was bad news.

Bishop looked in the rear-view mirror and grimaced when he saw a sliver of the night sky back there. He'd left the left-hand barn door partly ajar when he'd come back in. Only by a foot, but it might as well have been ten. Unless the guy was blind, he was bound to notice it. All Bishop could do was wait and see.

With his eyes glued to the rear-view, Bishop began to count the seconds. He'd reached sixteen when he saw the gap behind him start to widen. Then the barn door was pulled all the way open. A human-shaped silhouette appeared in the gap and a flashlight came on. Bishop lowered his head and turned a little to the right. The light was pointing towards the Oldsmobile two cars down. The light played over the vehicle for three or four seconds before moving to the Chevy next door. That told Bishop the guard hadn't checked the key rack. If he had, he wouldn't be bothering with the other vehicles.

It gave Bishop a little room, but not much. Another couple of seconds and he'd shine the light on the Toyota, and maybe see the body in the back. And Bishop couldn't afford that.

Time to leave. Now.

Bishop released the handbrake, took a deep breath and turned the ignition key clockwise. The engine caught. He sat up, shifted the gear stick into reverse and pressed down hard on the gas. The noise of the revs reverberated throughout the enclosed space and the rear tyres screeched against the dirt as the Toyota took off, its speed increasing with every second. Bishop steered using the rear-view only, making sure that gap stayed dead centre in the little rectangle. He saw the human shape grow larger in the mirror before jumping out of the way. He heard the side of the barn door scraping harshly against the vehicle's passenger side. Then he was out.

He kept his foot pressed to the floor as the barn receded. The moment the speedometer needle hit thirty-five, Bishop yanked the wheel left and hit the brakes. The rear tyres fought for traction in the dirt while the front end immediately started sliding round to the right. Bishop jammed the stick into Neutral and held the wheel steady as the vehicle went through its 180-degree spin. He was almost facing the front gate when he put the gearstick into Drive, released the brakes and stamped on the accelerator. The rear end began to fishtail to the right and he fought against the steering wheel to pull it back. Then he just went all out towards the gate a hundred yards away.

Good to know the tactical driving techniques he'd mastered back in his close protection days hadn't entirely gone to waste. He kept the pedal pressed to the floor and concentrated on the two stone pillars on either side of the gate.

Seconds later, he skidded to a stop six feet from the barrier. Leaving the engine running, he jumped out of the car and ran towards the left-hand pillar. There was a steel box attached to the post on this side. He flipped it open and saw the brother of the black keypad Kidanu had described. Recalling the numbers he'd given him, he pressed 7, 9, 2, 8, and 1.

Nothing happened.

He tried 7-9-2-8-2.

There was a whirring sound and the double gate began to open towards him. He ran back to the car and got in. As soon as there was a wide enough gap, he stepped on the gas and speeded through. He reached the end of the driveway and hung a left into New Dublin Road without stopping. Switching on the headlights, he increased the speed. Fifty. Sixty. Seventy.

He was alone in the world. The only lights on the road were his. When he reached the intersection for Highway 29, it was the same.

No traffic anywhere. He kept on, keeping his speed above sixty. He only met one other vehicle during the whole journey. A pick-up at the traffic lights for Centennial Road, heading the other way.

Then Bishop was passing the reservoir on Centennial. He spotted the turnoff for the picnic area just up ahead, reduced his speed and swung a left into the entrance. He turned off his lights, aimed the car towards the trees, and drove slowly along the gravel pathway that led directly to the lake. He stopped about fifteen feet before the water, set the handbrake and got out of the car.

He opened the rear door, lifted out the dead man and placed him in the driver's seat. Using the master switch on the driver's door, he lowered the passenger window and the two in the rear so there was a two-inch gap at the top of each. The driver's window he lowered all the way. After securing the man's safety belt, Bishop leaned in, placed a foot on the brake pedal and moved the gearstick into the Drive position. He pulled his foot off the pedal and the vehicle immediately began trying to inch forward, with only the handbrake holding it in check.

Bishop slammed the driver's door shut. The dead man stared straight ahead at the water. Bishop reached past him through the window and released the handbrake. He pulled himself back out of the way as the car suddenly sprang forward, picking up speed as it approached the lake. The front tyres splashed into the water, followed by the rest of the vehicle. The Toyota dipped at a thirty-degree angle and he watched it slowly sink. Soon the only signs of its existence were a few bubbles popping on the surface of the lake. Within seconds, they were gone, too.

Shame it had to end this way, pal, he thought. *But you won't be the first man I buried whose identity was a mystery to me.*

Although maybe that would change in this instance. He didn't know yet.

Bishop turned away and began walking back to the roadside. It was only a temporary solution anyway. Unless the reservoir was bottomless the vehicle would be discovered before too long. But just a couple more days would be enough for Bishop's purposes. Once Amy was out of danger it didn't matter who found him. But right now her continued safety overrode all other considerations.

He reached the empty road, rubbed a hand over his face and looked down at his watch. 04.09.

At 04.12, he saw headlights approaching from the southwest. He remained under the cover of some trees until he was sure it was the Infiniti. The vehicle came to a stop a few feet away. He saw Kidanu sitting behind the wheel, calmly watching him. Bishop walked round and got in the passenger side.

Kidanu turned to him as he shut the door and said, 'A car speeded out of the grounds approximately seventy seconds after you.'

'I never even saw him,' Bishop said. 'Okay, let's turn this thing round and get out of here.'

'Where to?'

'The border.'

SIXTY-THREE

Once they were through the checkpoint and back on US soil, Bishop breathed a small sigh of relief. He wasn't sure why. Maybe that sense of security of being back on home turf again. Purely psychological, of course. But he couldn't help how he felt.

He'd spent the short journey to the border filling Kidanu in on what he'd found in the annexe, leaving nothing out. Including the fight and its aftermath.

Kidanu, now driving them southwards on the I-81, said, 'The man's death was accidental. You did not plan it to end that way.'

'I know.'

'But something about it still bothers you?'

Bishop stared out the window and said nothing. There were lots of things still bothering him. As a soldier, Bishop had killed more than his fair share of nameless men, but that had been different. The uniform had made it different. But this death had just been stupid. Unnecessary. Or maybe he simply wasn't the man he used to be.

He shook his head. Back to the self-recrimination again. Futile and pointless.

Mainly, what was bugging him was that he'd come here for answers and he hadn't gotten them. Or Klyce. Of course, there had only been a slim chance of his being at the farm, but Bishop had still been hoping he'd find him there.

And Amy's continued safety was still in doubt. That's what bothered him most.

Kidanu cut into his thoughts. 'So that windowless room you saw seems to point towards some kind of counterfeiting operation, does it not?'

'Well, the beginnings of one, at least,' Bishop said. 'Except I don't know yet if it's connected with Amy at all. And if it's not, then I don't care.' He pulled out his cell phone and looked at the dead man's face once more, wondering again what he might have been doing at the farm.

Kidanu stayed silent and just drove. Bishop looked out the window at the scenery passing by. Not seeing it. Just thinking.

After a few moments, he said, 'The dead guy might have been a Serb.'

'A Serbian war criminal, you mean?'

'It's possible. Klyce let slip to me that Amy had recently been working on a case concerning Bosnian war criminals. So maybe this guy was one of them. I never heard him speak, but he had the right look. It could be that Klyce found him through Amy's research and then discovered he was a counterfeiting specialist too. So he simply made the guy an offer he couldn't refuse.'

'You mean Klyce simply saw this as another business opportunity?'

'Why not? We know he doesn't care how the money comes in, just as long as it keeps coming in. And counterfeiting can be extremely profitable if you've got the right equipment and the right people overseeing it. They already have the paper and ink for the job. Maybe this guy was just waiting for the delivery of the intaglio printer, which probably takes time. They're not easy to find. But once they get that, Klyce has got himself a brand new licence to print money. So maybe Amy found out about that part of it and Klyce somehow got wind of it and decided to take care of her.'

'By arranging the attack on her in the park?'

'Right.' And just the thought of it made Bishop angry all over again. Which was no good for rational thinking. He took a moment to breathe deeply and calm himself down.

Kidanu said, 'But what is the significance of that medical services invoice from last December?'

'I'm not sure. Plastic surgery for the dead guy, maybe? Assuming he *was* an international fugitive. That could also account for the room I saw, and that bill from EMC-Med Associates.'

'And the twenty-three names on the CD?'

Bishop exhaled loudly. 'That's where the theory kind of falls down. Maybe they're not even a part of this. Not everything we come across has to be connected.'

'You mean your Hollywood movies have been lying to us all this time?'

'Depends on the movie,' Bishop said. Then there was Gerry, whose recent behaviour still puzzled him. What did he have to do with it? He decided to try his cell phone again. They needed to arrange a time to meet and talk. Because Bishop was going to get some answers today, one way or another.

He tried the number and waited. And waited. But there was nobody answering.

Bishop hung up and sighed. *Brilliant. Either I can't get rid of the guy, or I can't get hold of him. No middle ground.*

But there was something else swirling around Bishop's brain that was still bothering him. Something to do with Gerry. What was it, though? He closed his eyes and thought back.

After about a minute, it came to him. Gerry's cell phone. That was it. Back at the apartment, Lisa had used her dad's phone to key in a number that turned out to be Klyce's office line. But when Bishop had taken the phone from her, instead of a number on the display there had been a name. Just a flash, not long enough to make it out clearly, but Bishop was sure it hadn't been Roger Klyce. He would have remembered seeing that. That meant not only did Gerry have Klyce's number in his regular contacts list, but he had it under an alias. Which indicated that, for whatever reason, Gerry was keeping his association with Amy's boss a secret from everybody.

Bishop very much wanted to know that reason. And sooner rather than later.

He tried Muro's number. It was picked up after only two rings.

'Good morning,' the private detective said.

'If you say so. How's Amy?'

'Well, she's still unresponsive, but she's no worse.'

'Well, that's something, I guess. Any sign of her husband since we last talked?'

'Yeah, I saw him yesterday.'

That got Bishop's attention. 'Really? At the hospital? When?'

'Mid-afternoon. About three, I guess. He just came in and whispered some stuff to Amy for a few minutes and left. He barely looked my way the whole time. I don't think he likes me.'

'Join the club. Look, if you see him again, call me immediately, okay? I really need to talk to him and he's not answering his phone.'

'Sure, no problem. Anything else?'

'Not right now, thanks,' he said, and ended the call.

So Gerry was purposely avoiding him for some reason. That was interesting. Once he got back to the city, he was going to make finding Gerry his number one priority. He'd had enough of being screwed around by that guy.

'No change with your sister?' Kidanu asked.

'Still the same.' Bishop checked the dash clock and saw it was just after five a.m. He closed his eyes and decided to try and get a couple of hours' shuteye.

SIXTY-FOUR

Bishop was woken by the vibration of the cell phone in his pocket. The dashboard clock said it was 07.22. He pulled out the phone and saw Arquette's number on the display. He pondered for a couple of seconds on whether to answer it.

Red or green? Red or green?

He finally pressed the green button, and said, 'I was asleep.'

'Sorry, but I've been on yet another all-nighter,' Arquette's voice said. 'Sometimes it's easy to lose track of other people's sleep habits. I was just curious to see if you've made any progress.'

Bishop paused and thought about what to say. Or more accurately, what not to. Was there any benefit in giving Arquette anything at all? What could Bishop get out of sharing information with him? His instinct was to tell him nothing, but those files on Amy's CD still held unanswered questions. Maybe Arquette could come up with some answers. Maybe find a connection that he and Kidanu had missed. Having an extra brain on board might speed things along. Anything that would aid him in his quest to find those responsible for Amy's assault was worth trying.

'I do have some stuff that will interest you,' he said. 'Let me think on a place to meet. I'll call you back in ten.'

He hung up and closed his eyes again. He thought about what he planned to give Arquette and what to hold back. For a moment, he briefly considered telling him about the mystery man in Canada. Arquette was a Fed, after all, and he was sure to have connections with other government departments with access to international criminal databases. But he quickly dismissed the idea. It was tactically unwise to give Arquette too much information about what he was up to. Fed or not, he was still law. But he would have to tell somebody if he was going to learn the guy's identity. And good as Muro was, this kind of thing was well beyond a private detective's remit.

Then it hit him. He *did* know somebody who might be able to get the information he wanted. Somebody from his distant past. Assuming he was still alive.

He thought back to a hot and humid summer in the Caribbean sixteen years before. Specifically, an air-conditioned seventh-floor hotel corridor, where a man had handed him a card with a number. Everything was blurry and indistinct, though. Bishop focused on that card and concentrated. Over the course of a minute, his memory worked on it until the phone number slowly came back into focus.

He smiled and opened his eyes. That little ability of his never ceased to amaze him. Just a shame he couldn't bottle it and sell it.

He keyed in the New Jersey number that had been on the card. Anything could have happened in sixteen years, but it was worth a shot. He counted nine rings before it was picked up. A harsh male voice said, 'Hello?' The man sounded a little out of breath.

'Is that Kelvin McIntyre?' Bishop asked.

'It is. Who's this?'

'My name's Bishop. You gave me this number a long time ago in a hotel in Haiti, shortly after that incident during the Secretary of State's visit. Do you remember?'

There was a long pause. Then McIntyre said, 'Corporal Bishop. Well, well. You made sergeant shortly after that, I recall.'

'That's right. I heard that was partly down to you.'

'I may have put in a letter of recommendation to your CO. So you held on to that number I gave you, after all?'

'In a way. And you're still in Trenton, then. I would have expected you to have a large corner office in that big building in DC by now.'

'Well, they keep trying, but over there I'd just be a small fish in a big pond. I like it here where people actually do what I tell them. More important, my family likes it here. Look, Bishop, I was just on my way out of the door before I picked up, so is there anything I can do for you or was this just a social call?'

'I don't do social calls,' Bishop said. 'But I would like to come out and see you today. I need your professional input on something.'

'You finally calling in that favour, huh?'

'If you like. I believe this'll be mutually beneficial, though.'

'In that case, feel free to come over to the office and say hello in person. You know where the courthouse is, right?'

'Yeah. It'll probably be early afternoon sometime.'

'Fine. I'll see you later.'

Bishop hung up and looked out at the traffic. A sign informed them there was a place called Clarks Green five miles ahead.

Kidanu turned to him. 'Who is this Kelvin McIntyre?'

'A face from the past. But he might be able to help identify the dead man. Can't hurt to ask.'

Bishop thought about the route into New Jersey and tried to recall the positions of the various rest areas along the interstates. Recalling one in particular, he began dialling Arquette's number and said to Kidanu, 'Turn off for the next town, okay? I need to find an internet café.'

SIXTY-FIVE

At 11.54, Bishop was leaning against the Infiniti in the large parking lot of the Secaucus service area, off the New Jersey Turnpike. It was one of those fully stacked rest areas with an on-site gas station and a small shopping plaza. Arquette was due at noon. Kidanu was getting himself a coffee from one of the stores in the plaza across the way. Bishop had advised him to stay there out of sight until Arquette was gone. As far as anybody was concerned it would be best if he was working solo today.

Playing things close to his chest, as usual. But then, some habits were hard to break. Especially when the law was involved.

At 12.04, Bishop spotted the same dark limo as before coming towards him. The thing looked as if it was gliding on air. The driver finally parked in a space twenty feet away from Bishop's car. Two other vehicles were between them. The rear door and the passenger side door opened at the same time and Arquette and Nowlan got out.

Bishop thought Arquette's thinning hair looked frail and wispy in the harsh daylight, and he noticed the Fed hadn't shaved in a while, either. There was at least a day's worth of stubble on his face and neck. But his black suit looked as crisp as ever. Arquette smoothed his jacket with a palm and walked towards Bishop, while Nowlan shut both doors and strolled off in the direction of the plaza entrance.

Bishop frowned as he watched Nowlan walk away. He kept his eyes on the man's back. When Arquette was close enough, he said, 'Where's he going?'

'To get me a very strong coffee,' Arquette said. 'I need something to keep me awake. So shall we talk here or in your car?'

'In the car.' With a final look at Nowlan, Bishop opened the driver's door and got in. Arquette came around and got in the passenger side.

He shut the door and said, 'So Kidanu's no longer with you?'

'I prefer to work alone when I can.'

Bishop reached over, opened the glove compartment and pulled out a CD in a generic paper wallet. Both had been provided earlier by a friendly internet café owner in Clarks Green. He handed it to Arquette and gave him a summary of what it contained. The EMC-Med and Continental Surveying bills. The bank letters and account details for Xerxes. It was missing the file containing Janine Hernandez's address, though. Amy had kept that one doubly hidden for a reason, and Bishop wasn't about to ignore her wishes. And also that list of names. Amy had worked hard to get that information. Bishop wasn't prepared to hand it all over to Arquette without good reason.

Once Bishop had finished his summary, Arquette looked down at the CD in his hand and said, 'So this is Amy's back-up of what she took from Artemis?'

'That's right.'

Arquette smiled. 'Good for her. This is better than I could have hoped for. I'll get on it as soon as we finish here. So is there something you want from me?'

Bishop looked out the windshield and saw Nowlan already on his way back, holding a tray with two disposable coffee cups. 'Just everything you find out,' he said.

'That's only fair,' Arquette said. 'I was planning to keep you in the loop, anyway.'

Nowlan come over to the Infiniti's passenger side and almost stumbled at the last moment. Arquette rolled down the window and took the cup Nowlan held out. 'You get me some sugar, too?' he asked.

'Sir.' Nowlan searched the tray, then looked at the ground and stooped down for something. He came back with the sugar packet he'd dropped and handed it over. 'Sorry.'

Arquette rolled the window back up as Nowlan walked back to the limo. Bishop had been watching carefully and hadn't seen any unspoken messages pass between them. It looked like Kidanu hadn't been seen. Arquette shook the little bag and turned to Bishop. 'So are you any closer to finding out who was behind your sister's attack?'

'I've got one or two ideas.'

'Care to share them with me?'

Bishop just looked at him and said nothing.

Arquette smiled, tore open the sugar packet and emptied its contents into the cup. He stirred his coffee and said, 'You still don't fully trust me, do you?'

'There any reason why I should?'

Arquette took a sip of his coffee. The strong aroma already filled the car interior. 'Well, I *am* a federal agent. I'd say that's a pretty good reason.'

'And I'm an ex-con. I'd say that's a pretty good reason why I shouldn't.'

'A *pardoned* ex-con. There's a difference.'

'Doesn't matter. Any time a cop checks my record, all he sees is I spent three years inside. The rest is irrelevant. To people like you, I've got the mark of Cain on me.'

'And that really bothers you, does it?'

Bishop smiled. 'Not really. The law goes its way, I go mine. And except for Amy, I've never cared what anybody thought of me.'

'Okay, I get the message.' Arquette blew on his coffee and took another sip. 'So have you discovered anything further about Artemis's illicit arms trade?'

Bishop shook his head. 'No, but then I wasn't really looking. Like I told you before, all I really care about is protecting Amy from further harm.'

Arquette nodded. 'Fair enough. Well, if you do discover something . . .'

'I'll let you know.' Bishop rattled the car keys and said, 'Well, I guess that's it.'

Arquette snorted at the dismissal, pocketed the CD and opened the door. 'It's been a real pleasure as always, Bishop. I'll be in touch.'

Arquette got out and Bishop watched him walk back to his limo, sipping from his coffee as he went. When he was in, the vehicle pulled out and slowly headed for the exit. The moment it joined the access road for the interstate, Bishop took out his cell and called Kidanu and told him to wait outside the front entrance. Then he turned the key in the ignition and the engine came to life.

Next stop: Trenton.

SIXTY-SIX

Bishop's soles squeaked faintly as he walked along the brown tile floor of the Trenton Federal Building & Courthouse, a six-storey art-deco building with Charles Wells murals affixed to the white marble-effect walls. Bishop felt as if he'd travelled back in time to the 1930s. The place smelled of floor polish, and the sounds of people walking and talking echoed in all directions.

He and Kidanu reached the main elevator bank and Bishop checked the directory attached to the wall. Soon the elevator arrived and they got in. Bishop pressed the 3 button. They exited on the third floor and turned left down the corridor.

Bishop stopped at a wooden door bearing the legend *Trenton Field Office* in small copper letters. Underneath was the suite number. There was no other identification. He pushed open the door and they entered a large waiting area.

Directly ahead was a long counter that doubled as a security barrier, covering the width of the room. The lower half was wood, probably with steel behind it. The upper half was thick glass. No doubt bullet-resistant. There was a door on the right with a keypad next to it. Behind the partition, Bishop saw a young, smartly dressed woman with neat brown hair down to her shoulders inputting something on her computer. She had a headset over one ear, but didn't seem to be conversing with anyone.

Bishop walked over to her and waited. The woman kept typing, even though she had to know he was there. Her long brown hair had a reddish tint to it. Bishop looked at her unlined face and guessed early twenties. He was counting the freckles on her forehead when she finally paused in her work and looked at him with raised eyebrows.

'I've come to see McIntyre,' he said through the gap. 'My name's Bishop. He's expecting me.'

The woman just looked at him, then at Kidanu. She picked up a phone, pressed two buttons and spoke quietly into it. After a few seconds, she replaced the phone with a frown.

'*Agent* McIntyre will be right out,' she said in a clipped voice. She pointed behind them. 'You can wait over there.'

Bishop turned and saw half a dozen empty chairs to the right of the entrance. He shrugged at Kidanu and they went over and took a seat.

'Friendly people,' Kidanu said.

'That's government employees for you. Kind of remind me of embassy staff.'

Kidanu just smiled and said nothing.

Two minutes later, there was an electronic beep and a medium-built man in a dark suit came through the door on the right and walked over to them. McIntyre had aged badly. He still had his hair, but it was cut close to the skull and was almost totally grey. He also had deep grooves running from nose to mouth that Bishop didn't remember seeing before, and the once youthful pale eyes now had heavy grey bags under them.

'Well, you look about the same as I remember, Bishop,' McIntyre said.

Bishop rose and shook the proffered hand. 'And you look like death, McIntyre. If this is what a career in the Secret Service does to you, I made the right choice.'

McIntyre snorted. 'Jesus, Bishop. Speak your mind, why don't you? It just so happens that it's the job that keeps me young. Blame the laugh lines on my four boys. Word of advice: you ever have kids, make sure you get daughters. Then it's the wife who gets all the headaches.' He raised an eyebrow at Kidanu.

Bishop introduced them to one another. As they shook hands, Bishop said, 'There someplace else around here we can talk? I get nervous around government offices.'

'Well, there are a couple of small conference rooms we sub-lease in the next hallway down. I know they're both free at the moment.'

McIntyre opened the outer door and let them exit first. They walked along the corridor until McIntyre halted before an unmarked door. He took out a set of keys from his pocket and unlocked and opened it.

Bishop went in first. It was a long, nondescript room. The wall opposite contained a shuttered window that looked out at more office buildings. Running down the length of the room was a wooden conference table, surrounded by around two dozen executive chairs. McIntyre closed the door, switched on the lights and sat at one end of the table. Kidanu took a seat near the centre. Bishop stood by the window.

'You called this meeting,' McIntyre said. 'So you get to go first.'

Bishop stepped over to McIntyre and handed him the scrap of rag paper he'd taken from the farm. 'I thought this might interest you.'

McIntyre took the scrap and studied it carefully. He rubbed it with his fingers and grunted softly. Then he reached into his inside jacket pocket and brought out something that looked like a jeweller's loupe. Holding the lens an inch away from his right eye, he held the piece of paper up to the light as he inspected it.

After a minute, he lowered the loupe and sat back in his chair. He looked at Kidanu. Then at Bishop. 'Where did you get this?'

'From a farm in Ontario,' Bishop said. 'How good is it?'

McIntyre brought his brows together. 'For a hundred dollar bill? I'd say this is the best I've ever seen. In fact, this could be the real stuff.' He held it up to the light again and said, 'It's practically all there already. The Ben Franklin watermarks, the colour particles embedded in the paper. All that's missing is the security ribbon and the colour-shifting ink. And the plates themselves, of course.'

Bishop nodded. 'Well, I don't know about the ribbon, but I saw plenty of large pots next to the paper rolls. I couldn't open one to check, but I wouldn't be at all surprised if they contained your special ink. And I also wouldn't be surprised if the plates themselves weren't being held in a safe somewhere. And all of it in a space large enough to hold an intaglio printer.'

'And did it hold one?'

'No, but I imagine it will soon.'

'Wonderful.' McIntyre sighed and rubbed his fingers across his forehead. 'Look, Bishop, maybe you'd better start at the beginning. What's your interest in all this? And where's this so-called farm you mentioned?'

Bishop took a seat and began to explain. He didn't cover everything, just the relevant details. Amy's assault. His vow to track down those responsible. The CD she sent to herself. The lead that took them to a farmhouse in Canada owned by Roger Klyce. What he'd found in that windowless room. And the man who was living on the premises. Bishop didn't mention he wasn't living any longer.

When Bishop had finished, McIntyre said, 'So no printing press means they're not actually in production yet. That's something, at least. But this guy living in the annexe. You've not got *any* idea who he is? Didn't you talk to him?'

'No,' Bishop lied. 'I don't know what junk he'd taken recently, but it must have been pretty strong shit. He thought I was a hallucination or something. But that's why I'm here. I've got his photo on my cell phone and I managed to take his prints once he'd passed out, but I'd really like a name. And when it comes to counterfeiting I know you guys keep files on all the major players around the world. I'm just hoping this guy's one of them.'

'Well, I'll admit it's possible I *could* identify him. But what's in it for me?'

'You still owe me that favour.'

McIntyre's eyes became hooded. 'Oh, yeah. But you know, what I'd really like is a more precise location for this farm of yours than "somewhere in Canada".'

'And I'll give to you. But later, not now. I can't risk word getting back to Klyce that we're onto that aspect of his operation yet.'

'We don't have leaks in the Secret Service, Bishop.'

Bishop smiled. 'And said with a straight face, too.'

'You think I'm kidding?' McIntyre turned to Kidanu. 'I'm also curious as to where you fit into all this.'

'It is no concern of your department, Mr McIntyre,' Kidanu said. 'All I will say is the Konamban government is interested in anything Bishop finds out about Roger Klyce.'

McIntyre turned back to Bishop and said, 'I can see why you two get on.' He gave a long sigh and held out his hand. 'Okay, Bishop, let's see what you got.'

SIXTY-SEVEN

Bishop pulled the folded sheet containing the fingerprints from his jacket pocket and passed it to McIntyre. He also took out his cell phone, found the shot of the dead man and placed the phone on the desk.

McIntyre was smiling at the sheet in his hand. 'Graphite and Scotch tape? Seriously?'

'I forgot to bring my fingerprint kit with me,' Bishop said. 'Are they good enough?'

'Well, I've seen worse. At least you didn't smudge them.' McIntyre put down the sheet and picked up the cell phone. He stared at the photo on the display and Bishop thought he saw a spark of something in McIntyre's eyes. Just a flash.

'You recognize him, don't you?'

McIntyre bit his lip. 'I might. I'm not sure.' He stared at the photo for a few more seconds. 'There's something not quite right with the face, but he does look very similar to somebody on our files.'

'And would this somebody be a Serb, by any chance?'

McIntyre tilted his head at Bishop. 'How did you know that?'

'I didn't. But Klyce has recently been involved in tracking down war criminals left over from the Bosnian conflict. I thought maybe this guy's one of them.'

'Well, I know we've got his prints on the database, so I'll check these against them later, but I'm pretty sure it's him. But he's had something done to his face. The cheekbones were never that pronounced before, and his nose is longer and wider. The hair's the wrong shade, too. In fact, everything's different. Only slightly, but enough to make you question your own powers of recall. Whoever the surgeon was who did this, he was good. The contours of the face

289

and the basic bone structure have been changed enough to mean he could probably pass through our facial recognition software without raising an alarm.'

'You gonna tell me his name?'

'Well, I don't know what it is now, but it used to be Janko Kordić.' McIntyre folded his arms and looked at both men. 'He's fairly high up on Interpol's Most Wanted charts. Neither of you ever heard of him before?'

Bishop shook his head, while Kidanu said, 'No.'

'Well, there's no reason you should, I guess. He was one of Milošević's boys, which gives you an idea of what kind of man he was. And probably still is. Interpol have been after him for years, but nobody's laid eyes on him since 1996.'

Bishop pulled out a seat and sat down. 'So who is he, exactly?'

'He held a senior position in Milošević's secret police. During the Balkan conflict, he was a key strategist in covert campaigns that terrorized and killed thousands of civilians. Witnesses say he got a little too zealous in seeking out spies and informants, too. They claim he personally rounded up and arrested untold numbers of civilians on trumped-up charges, then brought them back to the basement of the police building and tortured them for his own amusement. Sometimes for weeks. Men *and* women, that is. He even had his own incinerator down there to get rid of the bodies once he was done with them.'

Bishop's face showed nothing, but a definite weight had suddenly been lifted from his shoulders. Kordić's death had clearly been overdue for some time. Bishop had merely speeded up the process, that's all. The only shame was that he hadn't suffered as much as his victims had.

'This is nothing new,' Kidanu said, shifting in his seat. 'Certain officials in my country's recent past have been accused of doing exactly the same thing.'

'And summarily executed,' McIntyre said, 'from what I hear.'

'We are a new country, Mr McIntyre, but we are steeped in the old traditions. The eye for an eye rule is one of those traditions. The world will not miss scum such as they.'

'You sound like some senators I know.' McIntyre turned back to

Bishop. 'Anyway, Kordić and Milošević got together back in the eighties, but before that Kordić was already making a name for himself as one of the underworld's most talented counterfeiters. A real rising star in certain circles, apparently. That's probably how Milošević first heard of him. He began showing up on the Secret Service's radar as someone to watch, and then nothing. But it doesn't surprise me that he's back in the currency game again. I guess the small fortune he stole in bearer bonds before fleeing the homeland finally ran out.'

Bishop had his own theory on that. Things were finally starting to come together in his mind. Not everything. Not by a long shot. But in light of this new information, the few available facts were beginning to make a little more sense.

He picked up his cell phone and rose from his seat. 'Okay, thanks, McIntyre,' he said. 'It's been educational. You can consider the favour paid in full.'

'Not so fast, Bishop,' McIntyre said. 'Now I'd like that address.'

'And you'll get it. But not for a couple more days. Like I said.'

'That's unacceptable. If you're right, then Kordić's presence there is exactly the kind of bargaining chip I need to get the Canadians to chase this up. There are a lot of war criminals like him living in their country illegally, and they've been rabid in their efforts to hunt them down and bring them to trial. Especially after their parliament passed the War Crimes Act in 2000. Somebody like Kordić would be a big feather in their cap.'

'Like smashing Klyce's operation wide open would be a feather in yours?'

McIntyre stood up and exhaled loudly. 'Don't force me to get tough with you on this, Bishop.'

Bishop smiled. 'I'm not forcing you to do anything, McIntyre. And if you've read my history, which I'm sure you have, then you know there's nothing you can do to me that hasn't already been done. So go ahead, take off the gloves. See where it gets you.'

They just stood there eyeballing each other until Kidanu said, 'It was my understanding the two of you were on the same side once.'

'People change,' McIntyre said.

Bishop kept staring at him. 'Some more than others, apparently.'

'I don't apologize for placing national security before other considerations.'

'Spoken like a true patriot. All that's missing is the Star-Spangled Banner playing in the background.'

There was a long pause. Then McIntyre slowly sat down again. 'I'll expect that location within the next forty-eight hours, Bishop. It's in your very best interests not to make me wait any longer than that. You do get my meaning?'

Bishop smiled again. 'So long, McIntyre,' he said, and walked to the door.

SIXTY-EIGHT

They were heading north on the New Jersey Turnpike when Kidanu said, 'That meeting with McIntyre did not go the way you expected.'

Bishop shrugged as he changed lanes. 'McIntyre said it himself, people change. Especially over sixteen years. And we weren't exactly bosom buddies to begin with.'

'And that was because of this favour he owed you?'

'Kind of.'

Kidanu nodded. 'Intriguing. I would like to know more.'

Bishop just drove in silence for a while, trying to think of an excuse not to tell him. He really didn't like talking about the past, but Kidanu had shared an important part of his own history the other day. If not *the* most important. The guy deserved something in return, even if it was pretty insignificant in comparison.

Finally, he said, 'Back in the Corps, I was on the Security Guard Program. That's where they assign you to a US embassy somewhere and you get to wear your blue dress uniform. The first of my two fifteen-month tours was at the embassy in Haiti.

'One day my detachment commander told us the US Secretary of State would be arriving for talks with the newly elected Haitian president, and that due to my combat experience I'd been assigned to help the Secret Service keep a watch at his hotel. In civilian clothing, of course. McIntyre was one of the agents there. We got along okay.

'The second day, the Secretary was out at the National Palace with his protective detail. McIntyre and I were left behind at the hotel. The Secretary had been given the whole floor so we were spread pretty thin. When the three cleaners arrived at their usual time, I gave them a body search while McIntyre made a check of their carts, and then

293

we let them carry on with their work. But something was bugging me. I didn't know what. Just a feeling.'

'Yes,' Kidanu said. 'I have had such feelings before.'

'Well, I kept checking on the cleaners as they did the Secretary's suite, but didn't see anything out of the ordinary. But when they were finished my radar picked something up. I searched them again at the elevator. Nothing. Then I checked the carts and realized one of them was missing a box of detergent. When I questioned the cleaner, he said he didn't know what I was talking about. But he seemed nervous. I radioed McIntyre and that's when the guy suddenly pulled a pea shooter from the yarn of one of his mops, took a couple of shots at me and ran for the emergency stairs.

'I pulled my piece and winged him just before he reached the door. McIntyre sprinted past me and cuffed him. We found the detergent box inserted into a space in one of the bedroom wardrobes. Inside the box was enough plastique to take out the entire floor, and maybe the one above. And timed to go off at midnight, when the Secretary would be fast asleep.'

'And the cleaner?' Kidanu asked. 'Who was he?'

'Just another lone crackpot who didn't like the USA nosing into his country's business. The Haitian president had him executed the next day. Justice works fast over there.'

Kidanu nodded. 'But McIntyre missed the gun hidden in the mop.'

'Well, it was a little Kel-Tec P32, so it was fairly easy to miss, but, yeah, he should have spotted it. But since we both ended smelling of roses, neither of us ever mentioned it again. But McIntyre did say any time I needed a favour I should give him a call. He gave me his number and said I should also think about a career in the Secret Service when I got out.'

'And that held no interest for you?'

'Working for the Man? Not really my style. Besides, by the time I'd finished my eight years I'd realized I wanted a little more control over my own life. And I wasn't likely to get that working for the Secret Service, was I?'

Bishop glanced at the clock on the dash and saw it was just after three. His stomach was reminding him he hadn't eaten anything since yesterday. And they were running dangerously low on gas. The needle was already well into the red.

He got off at the next exit and took the US-1 into North Brunswick, hoping to find a gas station pretty soon. As he drove, something suddenly occurred to him and he said, 'Back at the embassy the other night.'

Kidanu turned to him. 'Yes?'

'How did you know I was on the premises?'

Kidanu smiled. 'Oh, that. I received a call from one of the police officers who patrol the street outside. He said he thought he might have seen some movement near the roof. I was preparing to check when I received that fake call about the pizza. I rewound the upstairs footage and spotted you walking towards the stairwell with a phone at your ear. After that, I simply searched every floor until I found you in the basement.'

'Oh, okay.' Bishop thought he'd kept himself well hidden from that patrol car. Obviously he'd been mistaken.

After a couple more miles, he spotted a small shopping centre just up ahead, and a gas station a little further on. He passed the shopping centre, pulled into the station and parked next to a vacant pump. He looked over and saw the place doubled as a convenience store, of which a large section was taken up by a burger joint containing several tables and chairs. There was also a coffee bar with a couple of high tables to rest against.

Perfect.

Handing the keys to Kidanu, Bishop said, 'I'll give the attendant enough for thirty bucks' worth, but you fill the tank, okay? I'm gonna order a burger or something inside. You need anything?'

Kidanu said a burger was fine and Bishop nodded and got out. He went in and handed the young male cashier three tens for the pump and then walked to the burger bar.

There was a young Indian guy in an apron behind the counter, and an elderly couple sat at one of the tables munching on their burgers and fries. The food didn't look all that great to Bishop. Probably reheated rather than made from scratch. Not that he particularly cared. A young couple were propped against one of the high tables in the coffee bar section twenty feet away, drinking from large disposable cups. A young, attractive black girl sat behind the counter beyond them, waiting for her next customer. That was all. It wasn't a busy place. He spotted a hallway close by, with signs for the restrooms and fire exit.

He went over to the counter and ordered two burgers and two fries. The Indian guy said he'd bring it over to the table in five minutes. Bishop paid and took a seat at one of the tables. A minute later, the guy brought over two tumblers of water.

Bishop picked up one of the tumblers and was taking a sip when Kidanu arrived.

'Got you a burger,' Bishop said.

Kidanu said, 'Thank you, but first I must report to Colonel Bekele and my battery is down to almost nothing. I saw a cell phone store in that shopping centre we passed, so I will go and get a replacement now.'

'You can always use my phone.'

Kidanu smiled. 'The colonel insists on face to face reports. He is peculiar that way. We use video conferencing and I know your cell phone lacks that capability. I will get a new battery.'

Bishop shrugged and watched as Kidanu walked back the way he had come. Then the Indian guy brought over the food he'd ordered and Bishop began to eat. It was edible, but only just. He took a sip of his water and watched two businessmen in suits come in and sit at the coffee counter. They looked like salesmen. The black girl laughed at something one of them said and then went to prepare their drinks.

Bishop went back to his meal and played over what he'd learned so far.

Thanks to McIntyre, he now had the answer to a minor piece of the puzzle. Janko Kordić. But that wasn't the most interesting thing McIntyre had said.

He'd also mentioned something that reminded Bishop of a piece he'd read in *Time* magazine a while back, about the Crimes Against Humanity and War Crimes Act the Canadians had passed over ten years before. And then there were those extra bedrooms at that annexe.

That was important. And it also went some of the way towards explaining a few things on Amy's CD.

And then there was the other thing. That one extra item that possibly gave everything a whole new slant.

Bishop went through it all again. He noted where the problem areas were – like all those generic names, and those three letters, N, C and L – and tried to come up with plausible, or logical, explanations based on what he'd learned today. He was munching a soggy French fry when the answer came to him. One that explained the significance of the names. And the three letters. He'd been right. Once you knew what those three letters stood for, everything else fell into place.

Almost. There was still the problem of those fake phone numbers. But he even had an idea about those, too. And that extra name, S. Bainbridge, might also hold the answer. Bishop had no doubt Muro could check it out easily enough.

I'm not far from the finish line now, Amy, he thought. *And then you'll be safe again. I promise.*

He absently reached down for another fry and discovered the plate was empty. He looked up and saw the elderly couple had already left. So had the young couple drinking coffee. Bishop hadn't even noticed. The two salesmen were still there though, quietly drinking their coffee at one of the high tables. Bishop looked at his watch and saw over fifteen minutes had passed since Kidanu left.

He pulled out his cell and tried his number. It went straight to voicemail. Perfectly reasonable, of course, since Kidanu's battery was almost dead. But he was getting that old feeling in his gut. The one that warned him whenever something was out of kilter. Maybe he should visit that phone store and see what Kidanu was up to.

Bishop wiped his hands with a napkin, then got up and walked down the hallway towards the restrooms. The men's room was on the left. He went inside. It was empty.

A minute later, Bishop was washing his hands when he heard the door open behind him. He was turning his head when there was a sudden, sharp pain at the base of his neck. Every muscle in his body immediately tightened up as his nervous system went haywire. He fell to the floor and for the next several seconds it felt as though someone was reaching in and ripping his muscles apart with a fork.

Then everything went black, and he felt nothing at all.

SIXTY-NINE

Bishop's first thought upon waking was that he'd been tasered, and then given an extra something to put him out. Chloroform, maybe. Whatever it was, he still felt groggy from the effects.

His second thought was that he'd screwed up, big time. Whatever this was, it hadn't just happened to him. Bishop had *allowed* it to happen. He was to blame.

He'd known something was off-kilter, but he'd let his guard down when he should have been paying more attention to his immediate surroundings. Like those two 'salesmen' arriving at the coffee bar and then spending fifteen minutes nursing their drinks at a table. *That* was what had been wrong. Most business types would simply order drinks to go and get back on the road to wherever they were going. Those two had gone against the norm, but Bishop hadn't given their behaviour enough weight. And now he was going to pay for it.

And Amy? If he didn't make it out of this situation, what would become of her? That weighed on his mind more than his own life.

His chin was against his chest. He opened his eyes part of the way and saw a sturdy wooden chair under him. His shoes were resting on a grimy concrete floor. So probably a warehouse. Possibly still in New Jersey. Depended how long he'd been out. His arms were behind the back of the seat. Something held his wrists together. It felt like flex cuffs. Or maybe zip ties. He hoped the latter. He flexed his arm muscles a little. Just enough to realize his wrists weren't attached to the chair, just to each other.

Which meant he was being watched right this second. And watched closely. So that if he tried to get up they'd immediately slam him down again. But his captors definitely knew how to keep quiet, which proved they weren't amateurs. Bishop heard no sounds. Not from in here. Not from outside.

Without moving his head, Bishop looked left. He saw four more chair legs a few feet away. Nothing to his right. So he was the only captive. Unless that extra chair meant they were expecting someone else to join him. Maybe Kidanu.

He heard sounds of movement to his right. Saw a shadow on the floor.

A fist suddenly smashed into his right cheek, just below the eye. Bishop's head snapped to the left while his bound arms held his body in place. The chair remained totally stationary. It didn't move an inch. Obviously attached to the floor.

Bishop spat a large globule of blood and saliva. It landed on the floor, close to the hitter's black shoes. 'I'm awake,' he said.

'Sure about that?' a harsh, nasal voice asked. 'Cos I got plenty more if you want it.'

Bishop spat a second time, then raised his head. The room was maybe thirty feet by thirty. Illumination came from a row of halogen lights in the high ceiling. No windows. There were two doors that he could see. One in the left wall and one straight ahead. Both were shut. Other than the two chairs, the only piece of furniture was an old, long wooden desk pushed against the right-hand wall. As he'd guessed, the room's other occupants were the two guys in suits from the gas station.

One of them was perched on the desk with an unlit cigarette in his mouth, watching Bishop. He was of medium build, had a full head of prematurely greying hair and wore tinted spectacles. The other man was standing two feet to Bishop's right. He was about twenty pounds overweight with a prominent pot belly. His dark hair was cropped close to his skull, like Bishop's. He also had eyes like pool balls, with plenty of white space around the dark brown pupils.

Crazy eyes.

Grey Hair swung his legs and said, 'Okay, so you've had your nice rest. Now it's time for a few answers. Like where's Kordić?'

'I don't know,' Bishop said. 'What's a Kordić?'

The fat one lashed out again, his fist smashing Bishop in the jaw. Bishop's head swivelled round ninety degrees and he tasted blood. He spat on the floor again. More red.

'One more time,' Grey Hair said mildly. His voice was fairly deep. Bishop noticed a hint of Boston in there. 'Janko Kordić. Where is he?'

'Look, would it help if I told you I don't know what the hell you're talking about?'

Fatboy pulled his arm back for another shot.

'Hold off for a second,' Grey Hair said with a raised hand, and Fatboy relaxed. 'Let's cut the shit, okay, Bishop? We know you drove back from the Canadian border early this morning. Once we got the make of car and the licence plate from the rental agency, it was easy. There are only a few routes you could have taken, and we had them all covered. We finally caught up with you just before you stopped off at that rest area for your meeting with that Fed. So let's not waste any more time. Janko Kordić was the man at the farm. Now what did you do with him?'

Bishop thought fast. If they'd seen him at the rest area, they must know Kidanu was with him. Did they grab him, as well? Or was he already dead? Maybe they'd purposely waited until they were separated so he could snatch Bishop alone. A smart man like Klyce would probably want to avoid having a group of very angry Konambans after his blood if he could help it. Or was Bishop overestimating him? Only one way to know for sure.

'I don't talk to the hired help,' he said. 'Get me Klyce.'

'Who?' Fatboy said.

Bishop looked at him and shook his head. Clearly not the brains of the operation. Grey Hair seemed to have a glimmer of intelligence, at least. He glared at Bishop for a moment, then he removed the unlit cigarette from his mouth, reached into his inner pocket and pulled out a smart phone. He wiped his index finger across it a few times and brought it to his ear. He began talking, but all Bishop heard was an indistinct muttering. After about thirty seconds, Grey Hair came over and stopped five feet in front of Bishop. He held out the phone and said, 'Talk.'

'Who's on the other end?'

'Who do you think?' Klyce's voice said through the speaker. 'You and your sister have been causing me a lot of problems recently, Bishop. I'm getting truly sick of you and your whole goddamn family.'

'They told me you were out of the country,' Bishop said, 'or I would have come to see you in person. When did you get back?'

'What difference does it make to you? No more screwing around, Bishop. I want to know what you've done with Kordić, and I want to know now.'

'He's safely hidden.'

'Where?'

'Forget it, Klyce,' Bishop said. 'I thought you might try something, so I took him as my bargaining chip. Get your goons here to untie me and I'll tell you where I stashed him.'

A soft chuckle came through the speaker. 'That was smart, Bishop. Except what if I told you I'd also decided to take out a little insurance of my own? Would that surprise you?'

Bishop said nothing and kept his face a mask. He had a feeling he'd just been outmanoeuvred. And that he probably wasn't going to like what came next.

'No response?' Klyce asked. 'In that case, we better force one out of you. Mickey, do the honours.'

The fatboy, Mickey, snickered and walked towards the door on the left. So it looked like they'd grabbed Kidanu after all.

Mickey opened the door and disappeared into the adjoining room. Then he came out again, gripping his bound captive by the arm.

It wasn't Kidanu.

Staring back at Bishop with wide, frightened eyes was his thirteen-year-old niece, Lisa.

SEVENTY

Bishop felt his skin go cold. He tried to swallow, but found there was a large cotton ball stuck in his throat. *Lisa. God, not her.*

She was wearing a brown suede jacket over a black T-shirt, blue jeans and white sneakers. Her shirt was crumpled as though Mickey had simply yanked her from the other room like a toy doll.

Bishop could already feel the rage threatening to take over. Lisa's eyes were moist and she was sniffling. She had her hands cuffed behind her and duct tape across her mouth. Her blond hair was in disarray and falling across her face. Bishop tried to calm himself and keep his expression neutral. It was difficult, but he didn't want to frighten her even more.

All he could think was they must have snatched her when she came out of her school building on 182nd Street. Which meant Bishop had more than just these two to worry about. Her kidnappers would also be around somewhere. Maybe keeping a lookout.

From bad to worse.

He made a silent oath that whoever grabbed her would pay for abducting her and bringing her here, but it was an empty promise, given the circumstances.

'How's our guest taking this new development, Jeff?' Klyce's tinny voice asked.

'Well, he's a lot paler than he was,' Grey Hair said, smiling.

Klyce chuckled. 'Wish I could have seen his reaction for myself. I find a young family member works so much better in these kinds of situations, don't you agree, Bishop?'

Bishop didn't trust himself to speak. He'd probably only make things worse. If that were possible. He and Lisa already knew too much to be allowed to leave here alive.

'Mickey,' Klyce said, 'have you offered the little lady a seat yet?'

'On it, Mr K.' Mickey grinned as he dragged Lisa across the room and threw her at the chair at Bishop's left. She lost her balance and fell to the floor. Bishop breathed heavily through his nose, getting angrier with each second. He forced himself to keep it in check as Mickey grabbed Lisa by her shirt and pulled her to her feet. Still grinning, he positioned her in front of the chair, placed a palm against her left breast and pushed. Lisa fell back onto the chair. She didn't cry. She must have known that would only exacerbate matters.

Smart girl. Her mother's daughter.

She turned to Bishop, sniffled, and shook her head once.

'I know, Lisa,' Bishop said. 'Just hang in there. I'll get us out of this.'

'That's the stuff,' Klyce said. 'And you can start right now with Kordić's location.'

Bishop felt doubly glad that he'd memorized the relevant parts of that street map while waiting outside the farm. Now he brought to mind one of the westerly routes, quickly calculating the distances. Anything over an hour's drive would strain belief, so it would have to be somewhere within sixty miles of the farm. What was that weird-sounding street he'd seen off the 41? Frazzle Road? No, Frizzell Road. That was it.

'I'm waiting,' Klyce said.

'What guarantee have I got that you'll let Lisa go if I tell you?'

'None. But I *can* guarantee she'll regret it if you don't. Now where's Kordić?'

Bishop took a deep breath. 'I gave him enough Propofol to put him out for twenty-four hours, then tied him up and stashed him in an old abandoned farmhouse I found. It's about sixty miles east of your place.'

'He better still be there, Bishop. That's all I can say. Now give me the precise directions. And just so you know, I've got a street map on the screen in front of me.'

'Okay. You need to follow the 401 east for about fifty miles until you reach Napanee. Then you take the Highway 41 North exit and keep on that for another ten or twelve miles. Somewhere around there on the right, there's a street called Frizzell Road. About half a mile along that road, you'll see an overgrown driveway on the left that leads to this decrepit-looking farmhouse. You'll find your guy in a windowless room at the back.'

There was silence on the line that stretched out for twenty seconds. Then Klyce said, 'Okay, that all jibes with the map. Jeff, you and Mickey keep our guests on ice while I get Jed to check this out. You should hear from me again in an hour.'

'You got it, Mr K.' Jeff hung up and placed the cell in his jacket pocket.

'Goons, huh?' Mickey said, raising a fist. 'That's not nice.'

Bishop tried to turn his head in time, but Mickey was too fast. The sledgehammer connected with his jaw and spun his head around to the left. That one was definitely going to leave a mark. Bishop probed his lower teeth with his tongue, but none felt loose.

'I'd be careful around Mickey here,' Jeff said. 'He's got a fairly short fuse.'

'Yeah, I noticed,' Bishop said.

Jeff smiled, then went over and perched on the desk again, pulling the unlit cigarette from his pocket and placing it in his mouth.

One hour, Bishop thought. *Just one hour to come up with something.*

This Jed would surely find Frizzell Road without a problem, but everything after that was pure fantasy. But even if he had hidden Kordić there, they'd still have to kill him and Lisa. All he'd done was buy some time, so he'd better start making use of it. Because there had to be a way out of this. There *had* to be.

Mickey was sauntering back to the room where they'd held Lisa. He came back out with an old office chair and placed it beside the girl. He sat down and whispered something in her ear, then reached into his pocket and pulled out Bishop's *balisong*.

And Bishop had thought the situation couldn't get any worse.

Mickey tried flipping it open one-handed and failed. He turned to Bishop and said, 'This is some piece you got, Bishop. How do the gangbangers flip it open like they do?'

'Don't ask me.'

'Well, I got an hour to get the hang of it. This sweet little thing here can watch me as I practise. You'd like that, wouldn't you, honey?'

Lisa clamped her eyes shut. Bishop tried to avert his gaze, but it was difficult. The poor girl was being brave, but she was also terrified. And Bishop wasn't doing too well himself. By grabbing Lisa, Klyce had gone straight for his weakest point. But Bishop had to find a way to keep himself distanced and focus on the job at hand if he was going to find a way out of this. He had to. Because they didn't have much time left.

Something vibrated against his leg. His cell phone. So these two hadn't removed all his possessions. If he still had his cell, what else did he have? He turned to his left and looked down at Lisa's hands. Her restraints looked like zip ties rather than flex cuffs. Which meant his restraints were probably the same. That was good. They were still no walk in the park, though. It depended on what else they'd left him.

Bishop moved his fingers until he could feel the back of the chair. He went lower and his fingers touched the back of his pants. He shifted in the chair and felt something hard dig into his butt. Good. He inserted the fingers of his right hand into the slit of his back pocket. When they touched metal, he almost smiled. They'd left him his house keys. He felt along each one until he reached his miniature multi-tool key fob. With thumb and index finger, he pulled back the slide device and detached it from the keychain. Then he very carefully pulled the tool from his pocket.

He just wished he'd gone for the full multi-tool, rather than the flightsafe version. But he could only use what he had. And what he had was a combo bottle cap opener and wire stripper, a nail file with a flat-head screwdriver at the end, and a blunt, inch-long saw containing a half-dozen widely spaced teeth.

Not much, but they'd have to do.

Bishop carefully extracted the saw tool, then tried to adjust his hands and get it into position. It was difficult. The zip ties were high up on his wrists, which meant he had to bend his left wrist all the way back before the saw made contact with them. But once it did, Bishop raised his head to keep Mickey and Jeff in sight, then began to slowly move the miniature saw back and forth across the hard plastic. Back and forth. Back and forth . . .

Fifty-seven minutes later, Klyce still hadn't called back. Bishop was making decent progress. Or he believed he was. He checked again with his free hand. Almost through the plastic now. Just a little more to go.

Mickey was still playing with the knife and trying to open it with one hand. And still failing dismally.

Lisa was keeping her eyes on the floor as much as possible, probably wondering when she was going to wake up from this nightmare. Bishop wished he could give her an answer.

Jeff was still perched on the desk, playing with his phone.

That was the good news. If you could call it that.

The bad news was Bishop still hadn't figured out a way of disarming and immobilizing his two watchdogs once he got free. They hadn't shown him their firearms, but he knew they were packing as surely as he knew night follows day. And all Bishop had was a miniature version of a very blunt saw. And that wasn't taking into account the guy who'd snatched Lisa. Maybe a fourth guy, as well.

And if that weren't bad enough, the muscles in his arms felt numb from having been in such an awkward position for so long. Once he was through the cuffs, he'd have to get the circulation going again somehow.

The first few bars of an old Nirvana track suddenly echoed through the room. Mickey stopped playing with the knife. Lisa's head snapped upright. She quickly glanced at Bishop, but his attention was on Jeff, who pressed something on the cell phone in his hand. The music immediately stopped and he brought the phone to his ear.

That's it, Bishop thought. *Time's up.*

SEVENTY-ONE

Jeff just listened for a while. Then he got off the desk and walked over to Bishop. He looked vaguely disappointed as he held the phone out again. 'Go ahead, Mr K.'

'Bishop, you've just made a very bad mistake,' Klyce's amplified voice said. 'One your pretty little niece is now going to pay for. Then you, right after.'

Bishop heard a sharp intake of breath at his left. He didn't dare look at Lisa. He just kept rubbing the saw along the plastic at his wrists. 'What are you talking about?' he said. 'I gave you the right address.'

'Frizzell Road? The street exists all right, but my man found no abandoned farmhouse anywhere along it. What did you do with Kordić? Kill him and dump the body in a forest somewhere?'

'Why would I kill him? I didn't even know his name until Jeff here mentioned it.'

There was an audible sigh on the line. 'You're a half-decent actor, Bishop. I'll give you that. But you've had your chance and my patience is at an end. Jeff, I know we usually keep them breathing until they're at the yard, but I can't get away right now, so do it at the warehouse and make sure you clean up after. We might need to use that place again. Then call me back when it's done. And Mickey, I know what you're like, so don't spend too long on the girl. If I don't hear back from you within half an hour, I'll be angry.'

'I'll be done before then, Mr K,' Mickey said happily.

'Fine,' Klyce said. 'Goodbye, Bishop, you stupid son of a bitch.'

The line went dead.

Mickey gave a loud whoop. He jumped to his feet and flipped open the *balisong* again. 'I think I'll do you first, baby,' he said to

Lisa. He turned to Bishop and smiled. 'And you get to watch, smartass.' He closed the knife, then opened it again. He was having fun.

Jeff shook his head at Bishop and said, 'He's right, you know. You really are stupid.'

Lisa was sobbing faintly in the next seat. Bishop just kept working on the zip ties. He was almost there.

A loud, electronic buzzing sound filled the air. Muffled, as if it was coming from another room. Then again.

Mickey suddenly had a revolver in his right hand. A .357 Magnum with a four-inch barrel. 'Who the hell's that?' he said.

'Quiet,' Jeff hissed, pulling a Glock from under his jacket. He pointed it at Bishop's head. 'Use your knife on this guy. Now.'

'No way. He gets to watch. It's part of my plan.'

Jeff sighed. 'Okay, get over here then, but put the gun away. No noise. If he shouts, cut his throat. Whoever's at the door, Mal will let us know once they've gone.'

Bishop felt the saw cut through the last strand of plastic. He quickly grabbed hold of the zip tie before it could fall on the floor, and palmed it. Mickey had holstered his piece and came over to stand at Bishop's side. He pressed the edge of the blade against Bishop's neck. Bishop just hoped he didn't look down at his hands.

'Shout and you bleed,' Mickey said. 'Understand?'

'I won't shout,' Bishop said.

The buzzing sound erupted again. For much longer this time. Bishop silently thanked whoever it was. Maybe a courier. Or the landlord, if they were renting this place. But now he knew he had three of them to deal with. He just didn't know how. Still keeping his wrists together, Bishop used his right hand to carefully place the zip tie in his back pocket. He gripped the multi-tool in his left so the little saw protruded out from between his index and middle fingers. Not much of a weapon, but better than nothing.

Jeff was walking over to the other door. He stood to one side of the doorframe, trying to listen. Mickey held the knife firm against Bishop's neck, but kept his eyes on Jeff.

Bishop slowly turned his head. Lisa's bloodshot eyes stared back at him.

He mouthed the words *bang bang bang* and looked pointedly at the floor behind her chair. Trying to get the message across that she should get out of the way once the shit hit the fan. He went through the mime a second time and raised his eyebrows. Lisa nodded once. He forced a smile and hoped she really had understood. The thought of her being killed or seriously wounded because of him was unimaginable.

All he could do now was wait. The moment was coming.

Bishop knew Mickey was right-handed, so his gun would be under his left shoulder. He also knew this Mal would come by and let them know when the coast was clear. That minor distraction would have to be enough. Bishop controlled his breathing and calmed his mind. He flexed and unflexed his hands to get the blood circulating again. He also felt his heartbeat begin to slow the way it always did just before a major skirmish. He'd never understood why that happened, but he was always grateful when it did.

Seconds passed in silence. The seconds turned into a minute.

There was a knock at the door. The blade at Bishop's neck dug in a little more. Bishop felt a rivulet of blood tickle his skin as it ran down his neck.

Jeff said, 'Yeah?'

'It's me,' a muffled voice said. 'Mal. Okay to come in?'

'Sure, come on in,' Jeff said.

The handle turned. As the door began to open, Bishop moved.

He lowered his left shoulder, pulling his head away from the blade. At the same time he swung his left hand upwards towards Mickey's face. Mickey had time to shout 'Hey' and then the blunt saw entered his left cheek, just below the eye. Bishop held on and yanked downwards, tearing the skin apart.

Mickey screamed and brought his free hand to his ruined face. Blood was pouring onto the floor. Bishop dived out of the way as Mickey jabbed at him with the knife. He rolled and got to his feet in a single movement. A barrage of shots was coming from the other side of the room. Bishop didn't turn to look. He shouted, '*Down, Lisa,*' and saw she was already on the floor.

He ran forward, knocked Mickey's knife hand out of the way and reached for his holster. He grabbed the handle of the revolver and pulled it out, waiting for the bullets to hit him. There was a sudden stinging sensation in his left side. He ignored it, stuck the barrel under Mickey's chin and pulled the trigger. There was a sound of thunder and the back of Fatboy's head exploded. Blood and brain matter shot into the air and the body went limp.

Bishop let the corpse drop to the floor and turned with the .357, wondering why the gunfire had stopped.

He saw Jeff leaning against the wall twenty feet away. He'd already pulled a spare magazine from his jacket pocket and was about to insert it into the grip of the Glock. A big man was lying on the floor half in and half out of the doorway. His chest was a blood-soaked mess. And underneath him was another man. A black man. Bishop's eyes widened when he recognized Kidanu. There was a gun lying on the floor, inches from his hand. Bishop couldn't tell if he was dead or alive.

Jeff rammed the magazine home and pointed his Glock at Kidanu's head.

Bishop aimed the .357 and shouted, '*Jeff, look out.*' The man turned his head at the sound of his name and Bishop pulled the trigger. The blast echoed through the room and a red rose appeared above Jeff's collarbone. As he fell back against the wall from the impact, he aimed his own gun in Bishop's general direction and got two shots off. Bishop didn't even bother ducking. The guy's aim was way off. Bishop fired again and got Jeff in the left cheek. Blood erupted from the man's face and Bishop fired another shot into the same area. Then what was left of Jeff just slowly slid to the floor, his life's blood smearing the wall behind him.

Bishop ran over to Lisa. She was lying on her side, facing away from the rest of the room. Bishop's heart sank as he knelt down beside her. Her eyes were shut and she wasn't moving. He quickly checked her body for wounds, but saw none. Then he placed his fingers against her carotid artery, and breathed a sigh of relief when he felt a pulse. A beautiful, healthy pulse. The kid had passed out, that was all. Bishop could only hope she'd missed seeing her favourite uncle blow Mickey's brains out.

He got up and ran over to the doorway. Kidanu was still alive, too. He was using one hand to push the dead man off his chest. Bishop reached down and helped. Kidanu's other arm was bleeding from a wound just below the shoulder.

'That man is heavy,' Kidanu said.

'How bad is it?'

'Just a flesh wound. The bullet went straight through.' Kidanu carefully raised himself to a sitting position and said, 'Was that Lisa I saw before?'

'Yeah. The bastards snatched her in order to get me to talk. She passed out while all this happened, but she's unharmed.'

'That is good. Somebody of her age should not see this.' Kidanu frowned at Bishop's mid-section and said, 'You are bleeding, also.'

Bishop looked down at himself. Kidanu was right. The left side of his black shirt was wet with blood and he felt a dull throbbing in that side. The pain would come soon. He placed his hand against the wound and could tell it hadn't been caused by a stray bullet. Mickey must have got a good one in with the knife before he died. It didn't feel as though it had gone too deep, but he still needed to plug the leak.

'Let's see what kind of supplies they got around here,' he said.

SEVENTY-TWO

Bishop winced and placed another strip of tape over the wound. He'd found some duct tape in the very basic kitchen area located at the rear of the warehouse. The blood had entered the clotting stage and he was hoping the tape would keep the wound from opening again.

He and Kidanu were in one of the other rooms. There were six in total, including the kitchen. Kidanu had told him the warehouse was in a small industrial park in an out-of-the-way section of Hillside, New Jersey, not far from the Garden State Parkway and I-78 interchange. And that most of the neighbouring buildings were vacant.

And there had been four goons, not three. Kidanu had spotted a man sitting in a car by the side of the warehouse when he'd driven by. Kidanu had used him to get inside, clubbed him unconscious, then used Mal as a shield to access the room where they were holding Bishop. Once inside, Jeff had emptied a whole magazine into Mal's chest as Kidanu returned fire. Kidanu hadn't been successful, and the dead man had eventually fallen back on top of him, trapping him with his weight. Bishop, busy with Mickey, had missed that part of it, although he'd brought it to a satisfactory conclusion.

The fourth man was in the front reception room now, unconscious, his feet and hands bound with spare zip ties. Lisa was lying a few feet away from Bishop. She was still unconscious, too. For which he was extremely grateful. The less she saw and remembered of this place, the better. He'd already removed the cuffs and the tape from her mouth, and was happy just to study her peaceful, sleeping form for a few moments.

'She should be fine,' Kidanu said. He was calmly tying a handkerchief around his injured arm. 'Children adapt better than most adults in these kinds of situations.'

313

'I sure hope so.' Bishop looked up at Kidanu and said, 'You still haven't told me how you found me in the first place.'

Kidanu shrugged. 'We placed a tracking device in your phone at the embassy. Very discreet, but it only has a fifteen-mile radius so it took me a while to pinpoint your exact location on my phone.'

'That's something else I owe you for, isn't it? Thanks, Kidanu. I mean that. Did you manage to talk to Bekele?'

Kidanu nodded. 'Just before I returned to the gas station. It sounded like he was at the airport. Possibly waiting for a visiting official. Anyway, he said he would have preferred more progress, but he is also a patient man. Sometimes.'

'So he's happy for you to stay the course?'

'He left it to my own judgement.'

'And?'

'I can be patient also. So what do we do with the three bodies in the next room?'

'Do? Nothing. Let them rot.'

'But do you not think . . .'

Bishop held up a hand. He could hear that Nirvana track again, coming through the wall. He stood up and went next door. He walked over to Jeff's body, reached into his jacket and pulled out the phone. The caller was *Mr K*. It had only been twenty minutes. Klyce must have simply got tired of waiting.

Bishop thought back to Jeff's speech patterns, and said a few random words until he felt he had the pitch right. He also practised using a few broad A's until he judged he had the slight Bostonian accent down. Then he took the call.

'Where have you been?' Klyce said. 'It's been half an hour.'

'Tidying up,' Bishop said in his altered voice. Best to keep his responses short.

'Good. Any problems?'

'None.'

'Fine. You know what to do next. Harry will be locking up the yard at six, so make sure you go there after then. I don't want any of the employees seeing you. Mickey should have the keys. I'd tell you to wait for me – you know I like to operate that crusher myself – but

I need to stick around for an important meeting later I hadn't counted on. And all because of this shit.' He sighed. 'Plus it's always better with live specimens, anyway. Right, Jeff?'

'Right, Mr K.'

'Now when you're finished, grab yourselves something to eat. But no alcohol. Not even beer. And I want you all back at the office no later than eleven, is that clear?'

'Right,' Bishop said, but the line was dead. Klyce had already hung up.

Bishop switched off the phone, wiped his prints from it and put it back in Jeff's pocket. That mention of 'the yard' again. What the hell was that? A dumping ground for anybody who displeased Klyce? The crusher seemed to suggest an auto junkyard. But if so, which one? And that meeting later. Bishop very much needed to be a fly on the wall for that one.

He checked Jeff's pockets and found his wallet. He flicked through the business cards, but saw nothing of any use. He replaced the wallet, removed a spare magazine from another pocket, then picked up his Glock and went over to Mickey. In the guy's billfold he found two dog-eared business cards. The first was from a brothel in Storey County, Nevada. He hit paydirt with the other one. The card had the words *First Choice Auto Salvage* at the top in large capitals. It was located at Leesville Avenue in Rahway, New Jersey. Which was about seven or eight miles south of Hillside. Bishop memorized the address and replaced the card in the billfold, and put the billfold back in Mickey's pocket. He patted the guy's pants pockets, felt some keys in the left side and pulled them out.

Back in the other room, Bishop picked up the weapons Kidanu had taken from the other two on top. Another Glock 17, a Smith & Wesson M&P .45 Compact, and two spare magazines. He carried his haul into the reception room, past the unconscious man on the floor, and opened the front door.

It was almost six and starting to get dark outside. The road out front was empty of traffic. He could see the three warehouses directly opposite all had large For Rent signs on the gates. No vehicles in any of the parking bays. Nothing moved. All Bishop could hear was the distant sounds of traffic from the interstate. Perfect. No witnesses.

Bishop stepped outside, turned right and kept going until he reached the end of the building. The Infiniti was parked along the side, just behind the fourth guy's Chevy. In front of that was the Subaru sedan Jeff and Mickey must have used to transport him here. He felt certain both vehicles would find themselves under new ownership before too long. Especially as Bishop had left them unlocked with the keys inside. He placed the weapons in the Infiniti's trunk and closed it. Back inside, Kidanu was already putting on his suit jacket again. The bullet hole wasn't too obvious.

'Let's get going,' Bishop said. He carefully picked Lisa up in his arms and carried her out. He was placing her in the back seat of the car when she opened her eyes and looked around in all directions. Then she focused on him.

'Hey, kiddo,' he said. 'How you doing?'

She smiled and said, ''Kay, I guess.' Then she saw Kidanu come around the corner. 'He's here, too? Where are we?'

'Jersey. We'll be heading back to the city soon.'

'Jersey?' Lisa hugged herself. Bishop thought she shivered a little. 'Oh, yeah. I remember now. I thought I dreamed it.'

'Don't think about it any more, okay?' Bishop said. 'You're safe now.'

'What about . . . you know, the others?' She stared at the floor. 'Especially that one called Mickey.'

Bishop relaxed. That question meant she hadn't actually witnessed Mickey's death. No kid should have that kind of image in her consciousness.

'He's gone,' he said. 'They're all gone.'

Lisa raised her head and looked at him for a moment. He could see the question in her eyes. But instead, she said, 'Good. Can we go too, please?'

'You bet.' Bishop kissed her cheek again, then stood up and faced Kidanu. He handed him the keys and said, 'You want to get the car pointed in the right direction? I just need to do something.'

Kidanu looked down at the keys, then stared at Bishop. 'Are you sure?'

'I don't like loose ends. I'll just be a minute.'

Bishop left them and went back inside, shutting the door behind him. With the shutters drawn across the windows, nobody could see in. Bishop crouched down and checked the fourth man's pockets. He felt a wallet in one, but left it there. He wouldn't need to know this one's name. In another pocket he found a small, spiral-bound notebook. He opened it and flipped through the pages. On the most recent page Bishop could just about decipher a list of groceries. Underneath that was the name of Lisa's school and the 182nd Street address.

Like he'd thought. This guy had either grabbed Lisa himself, or he'd helped. It didn't matter which. He would have also been aware of Lisa's ultimate fate. Might even have helped get rid of the body once Mickey was done with her. And Bishop too, of course. But that was irrelevant. Bishop was old enough to take care of himself.

And he always kept his promises.

Bishop replaced the notebook and cut the zip ties from the man's hands and feet. The man gave no sign of regaining consciousness, which was good. Better if he wasn't awake for the next part. Bishop didn't particularly want the guy to suffer. He just wanted him gone.

A quick twisting motion combined with a few pounds of pressure was all it took.

Bishop left the building and saw Kidanu already had the car pointing towards the exit gate with the engine idling. He wiped the handles on both sides of the door and then used his jacket tail to pull it closed. From his pocket, he took the padlock he'd found in the kitchen, looped it through the steel hasp and snapped it shut. He wiped his prints from that too, then walked to the Infiniti and got in the passenger side.

Kidanu gave him a questioning look.

'Let's go,' Bishop said.

Kidanu nodded and released the handbrake. 'Where to now? Back to the city?'

Bishop was thinking of that auto salvage place a few miles from here. It would just be a brief detour. 'Not just yet,' he said.

SEVENTY-THREE

At 18.33, they were parked off Leesville Avenue, in a recess that served as the entrance to First Choice Auto Salvage. Next to the run-down front office directly ahead was a wide, padlocked steel gate. A ten-foot-high corrugated steel fence stretched off to left and right. Bishop assumed this whole area was Jersey's version of the Iron Triangle in Queens. They were surrounded on all sides by numerous auto-based businesses, including a few auto wreckers and even more car junkyards.

The last of the daylight was almost gone. A few businesses were still operating, but most had either finished for the day or were in the process of doing so. First Choice was already closed. At least Bishop hoped so. He couldn't see any lights inside.

'Why are we here, exactly?' Kidanu asked.

'Klyce mentioned this place on the phone. He intimated he came out here fairly often, and I need to see why.'

'There may be security guards.'

'I doubt it.' Bishop held up the keys. 'Besides, I won't be breaking in this time.'

The cell phone in his pocket started vibrating. He'd forgotten to check the missed calls. He pulled it out, saw the display and turned to Lisa in the back. 'It's your grandfather.'

She looked crestfallen. 'Not Dad?'

'No. I've been trying to reach him, but he's not answering his phone.'

Bishop took the call. Before he could speak, Arnie said, 'Lisa's gone missing, Bishop. She left school and nobody's heard from her. Tell me she called you, because I . . .'

Bishop broke in. 'Are you alone?'

'What?'

'I said are you alone?'

'Janice is here with me. Why? What difference does that make?'

'It makes a big difference. Lisa's okay. She's with me right now.'

'Oh, Jesus. Are you serious? She's okay? Really?'

'Really. Hold on.' He covered the mouthpiece. 'No details, Lisa. I'll do that. Just tell him you're okay and that everything's cool, then hand the phone back to me.'

Lisa nodded and took the phone. She told her grandfather she was fine, apologized for not calling and listened for a while. Then she said she was helping Bishop out with something, and quickly handed the phone back.

'It's me again,' Bishop said. 'Look, Arnie, I need you to listen for a moment.'

'Sure. I'm just relieved she's okay. I'll have to call the police back and tell them.'

'It'd be better if you didn't,' Bishop said.

'But I reported Lisa missing an hour ago. They need to know she's okay.'

'Listen, I can't go into the reasons now, but it would really help me out if you held off for a while. Don't worry about the police. They get hundreds of missing person reports every day. One more won't make much difference.'

'Well . . . I don't know, Bishop. This all sounds a little weird. Where are you taking her now?'

'To some friends of mine. I'll have her call you once she's settled. All I'm asking is that you pretend this phone call never happened. Can you do that for me?'

'I guess. Will you tell me why later?'

'Yes,' Bishop lied. 'Does Gerry know about this at all?'

There was a brief pause. Then, 'No. He's not here and I haven't been able to contact him for a while.'

Bishop thought about that pause. It seemed neither of them was being entirely open with the other. Arnie definitely knew something about Gerry's whereabouts. Bishop didn't want to get into it over the phone, though. Not with Lisa listening in. But he'd definitely need to have a talk with Arnie very soon.

'Okay, Arnie. I have to go now.' He hung up.

'What friends?' Lisa asked from the back.

'I'll tell you later. You both stay here while I look this place over. I won't be long.'

Bishop pressed the trunk release lever on the instrument panel, and got out before either of them could ask him anything else.

He went back to the trunk and armed himself with the Glock and the .45 Compact. Then he shut the lid and walked over to the gate. He pulled out the keys, found the largest and tried it on the padlock. It opened first time. Bishop slid it through the hasp, then pushed the gate open and entered.

Fourteen minutes later, Bishop came out again, his curiosity sated. It certainly hadn't been a wasted journey. After locking the gate behind him, he got back into the Infiniti's front passenger seat.

Kidanu spoke first. 'What did you find in there?'

'Lots of dead cars stacked on top of each other. Also a very large crusher that Janine Hernandez's husband probably had a good look at from the inside. And from what I gather, not just him. Okay, let's head back now.'

As Kidanu started the engine, Bishop pulled out his phone and dialled a number. After seven rings, Seth Willard's voice said, 'I didn't expect to hear from you so soon.'

'So much for your fortune-telling skills. So have things improved with you and your girlfriend?'

'Kind of. Ellie's stopped yelling at me, but she ain't saying a whole lot either. Why?'

'My young niece, Lisa, needs a safe place to stay tonight. I was hoping you two might be able to accommodate her.'

'Hey, you got it. Having a guest around might even thaw Ellie out. You remember my address, right?'

'Yeah. And can you call Doubleday and see if he can join us there? I think I might need his help. Maybe yours, too. We can talk about it.'

'Okay, whatever you say. See ya soon.'

They both hung up at the same time.

From the back seat, Lisa said, 'Where are you taking me now?'

'To a little house in Jamaica,' he said.

SEVENTY-FOUR

Willard's home was located in 171st Place in Jamaica, Queens. It was a railroad apartment that took up the ground floor of a narrow two-storey brick house. As the name suggested, the interior was laid out like the inside of a railway car, with a single hallway running down the right side of the building from which all the rooms could be accessed. Kidanu and Willard were currently talking in the front room while Ellie, a pretty brunette in her late twenties, showed Lisa the rest of the apartment. Doubleday hadn't arrived yet. He'd told Willard he wouldn't be able to get there until 20.30 at the earliest. It was now 20.15.

Out on the front porch, Bishop was talking on the phone 'So I'd be grateful if you could get back to me ASAP on this,' he said.

'Well, it shouldn't be too difficult with this Bainbridge,' Muro replied, 'especially now you've given me a jumping-off point. I know somebody who knows somebody, et cetera. The other two things, I don't know. I can't promise anything, but I'll try.'

'That's all I ask. But you'll earn yourself a fat bonus if you can get me everything within the hour.'

'Now *that's* the kind of incentive I live for. I'm gone.' The private detective hung up.

Bishop put the phone away. If Muro didn't come back to him in time, it was no big deal. All he'd be doing was confirming what Bishop already knew anyway. But there was nothing like being sure. He went back inside and saw Ellie and Lisa walking down the hallway towards him. They were both smiling about something, which was promising.

'Everything okay, Lisa?' he asked.

'Yeah. Ellie's gonna let me watch her finish some dress designs later.

321

She only works at one of the big fashion design houses in town, which is like, *exactly* where I want to be when I finish college.'

Bishop smiled at both of them. 'No kidding.'

She'd had him worried on the drive back. Sometimes it took a long time for a victim to get over a particularly traumatic incident. Sometimes they never did. Lisa had started exhibiting the signs he'd seen before in others. The grim silence for one. The empty stare for another. Which wasn't exactly surprising. First her mother's attack, then her own kidnapping and threatened murder. Most adults wouldn't be able to handle what she'd been through. But she seemed to be doing okay now, thank God. It seemed Ellie had managed to return some much-needed normality to her life. If only temporarily.

'I really appreciate you letting Lisa stay the night, Ellie,' he said.

'Hey, no problem. She's already paid her way by pulling me out of my funk. If you or your friend need anything, just come and ask, okay? Or tell that idiot boyfriend of mine to get off his ass and get it for you.'

'I will. Thanks.'

Lisa and Ellie disappeared into the next room along, while Bishop returned to the living room. Kidanu was sitting on one of the two easy chairs while Willard was on the couch. Bishop took the other easy chair and said to Kidanu, 'How much have you told him?'

'Everything I have witnessed so far,' Kidanu said. 'Well, almost everything.'

Willard sipped at his bottled mineral water and said, 'Man, you two sure been busy since DC. We'd just got to the part where Kidanu came and saved your ass at the warehouse. Impressive stuff. So are those four goons safely tucked away now, or am I better off not knowing?'

'The second one.'

'O-o-kay. So I guess the big question now is what's your next step?'

'Well, Klyce said he's got an important meeting later. Sometime around eleven thirty would be my guess. And I definitely want to be there for that.'

Willard scratched his beard. 'Why?'

'Klyce said the meeting was called "because of all this shit", by which he must have meant me. So I've a strong hunch some, if not all, of the major players will be present tonight and I'll get my questions answered. And once I've got those I'll be free to act.'

'Eleven thirty,' Willard said, looking at his watch. 'That's only three hours away.'

'Which is why I hope Doubleday shows up soon.'

'And what about this other black guy at the park? The one you thought might have been Kidanu's boss? Still no news on his identity?'

'Nothing concrete, but I've a strong feeling he'll also be at Klyce's offices tonight.'

Kidanu furrowed his brow at Bishop.

The sound of a doorbell interrupted them. Willard got up and left the room. A few seconds later, Hector Doubleday entered, wearing a leather jacket and jeans. He'd finally gotten rid of the designer stubble, but the short, spiky hair was still present and correct. He looked at Bishop and said, 'Willard said you needed some help, so here I am.'

'Appreciate it,' Bishop said, and introduced Kidanu and Doubleday to each other.

Doubleday sat on the other end of the couch and said, 'So what have I missed?'

It took about ten minutes for Bishop to cover the main details. Once he'd finished, Doubleday whistled and said, 'Man, trouble seems to follow you around, don't it? But I got two younger sisters. If the same thing happened to one of them that happened to yours, I'd probably be doing the same thing. And now your niece, too? *Madre de Dios.* Screwing with a man's family is a place you don't wanna go to.'

Kidanu nodded slowly and said nothing.

Willard said, 'So I got another question. Amy found out all this info about Klyce's schemes and put it onto a flash drive, right? So who had she arranged to hand it over to?'

'That's a very good question,' Bishop said. 'I've got a guy named Muro on it at the moment. Along with a few other things.'

Willard puffed out his cheeks. 'So you any closer to figuring out what this is all about, Bishop? It's gotta be more than just counterfeiting or arms trafficking. Amy found out something else about Klyce, didn't she? Some other scheme of his that fits in with all the facts you and Kidanu picked up. So what is it?'

'It's actually really simple,' Bishop said. 'Amy found out her boss was bringing the dead back to life again.'

SEVENTY-FIVE

'Huh?' Willard said.

'Uh, yeah,' Doubleday said, nodding. 'What he said. And if I hear the word "zombies" at any point, I'm walking.'

'No zombies,' Bishop said, 'but there *are* some real-life monsters in all this. I met one of them already.'

'Janko Kordić,' Kidanu said.

'Correct. I gave this a lot of thought earlier, Kidanu. You remember McIntyre mentioning the Canadian Crimes Against Humanity and War Crimes Act?'

'I remember.'

'That's what turned my head around. See, for a long time now, the Canadians have been pissed that so many war criminals end up on their territory. Not too surprising when you consider the population to land ratio, though. Once you're out of the major cities, you can pretty much lose yourself there. But that's why they passed this statute, so they could prosecute any fugitive found in their country without the need for an international tribunal.'

Willard shrugged. 'So?'

'So where others saw a troubling trend, Klyce spotted another a business opportunity. What if he was able to track these fugitives down and instead of turning them in give them whole new faces and identities? And most important of all, offer them legitimate US citizenship with all the benefits that come with it? Like a US passport, for example, which is about the strongest travel document in existence. With that in your pocket, you can go almost anywhere you want. Except Cuba, I guess. But it means these wanted murderers are able to live out the rest of their lives without having to look over their shoulders the whole time.'

Kidanu was watching Bishop with an expression of total concentration.

'I don't see how,' Doubleday said. 'From what I hear, the new biometric passports have just about killed off the fake passport market.'

Bishop nodded. 'Right. These days the best way to become an American citizen under the table is to use an existing identity that's already on all the databases. All the hard work's already been done.'

'Identity theft, you mean,' Willard said.

'They call it "ghosting" when the victims are no longer living,' Bishop said. 'But it's the same thing.'

'The list of names on the CD,' Kidanu said.

'Right,' Bishop said, nodding. 'Klyce simply brings the dead back to life, with his new clients assuming the roles. And with new faces, thanks to a plastic surgeon he calls on. That's why they pick loner types with no living relatives. Too much chance of one showing up on the new Mr X's doorstep and ruining everything. But if anybody *does* show up, the client's got a common enough name to be able to say, "Sorry, mister, you got the wrong guy. Try the Mr X on the next street." Just an added level of security to help the client fade into the background. Klyce has probably got people constantly scouring local obituaries to find recently deceased people that fit the criteria.'

'Those letters next to the names,' Kidanu said. 'N, C and L. Do you know what they stand for now?'

'Well, it finally occurred to me that there was only one name with an L next to it. Martin Garcia. And Garcia's the most common Hispanic surname in the US. So if that L stands for Latino, it's a good bet the other two stand for Negro and Caucasian. Not exactly official racial categories, I know, but they get the job done. Because, obviously, for this to work the deceased and the client need to at least share the same ethnicity.'

Kidanu scratched his chin. 'And those fake phone numbers . . .'

'. . . are Social Security numbers,' Bishop said. 'With an extra digit at the beginning to make it read like an area code. Muro actually checked one of the names out while we were on the phone. Pretty simple when you think about it, but it had me stumped for a long

time. I'm not sure why Klyce bothered to disguise them, thou,
Maybe he's just naturally paranoid.'

'That can't be right,' Doubleday said. 'I'm pretty sure once you die,
your Social Security number dies with you.'

'It does,' Bishop said. 'Which means Klyce must have somebody
inside the Social Security Administration who can delete certain death
certificates from the Master Death Index and elevate the numbers to
active status again. Then all the client needs to do is move to a whole
new city where nobody knows him, open up a new bank account and
keep everything going as normal. Then he can get himself a new
driver's licence and all the rest.'

Kidanu sat back in his seat. 'So Klyce uses Artemis as a legitimate
way of tracking down these people and informs the people who hired
him when he has been successful. Then, as they prepare to send in a
seize and capture team, Klyce approaches the target and offers to
provide him with a way to escape them, and his past. For a hefty fee,
of course.'

'Right,' Bishop said. 'Probably through a third party, though. If
the target turns down the offer, Klyce won't want any record of his
approaching him directly. And I think those who do turn him down,
or those who don't have enough money to pay, he allows to be captured,
thus improving Artemis's reputation. Either way, it's a win-win for
him.'

Doubleday placed his bottle of water on a side table. 'Klyce could
charge millions for an all-in service like that.'

Bishop nodded. 'I get the impression that most of the major war
criminals still at large siphoned off large amounts from their countries'
coffers before making a dash for the border. Most of it now probably
salted away in offshore numbered accounts. Right, Kidanu?'

'Yes, that is so. At least in my experience. Many of these people
plan ahead.'

'And this farm in Ontario,' Willard said. 'What's that? Some kind
of safe house?'

'Yeah,' Bishop said. 'It's the perfect place for a client to rest up
while his new life's being arranged for him. And to heal after his
plastic surgery, away from prying eyes. All his meals are taken in by

...ards, but I expect the only person to ever get to see him is the ...urgeon. And Klyce himself, of course. I saw two bedrooms there in case of an overlap, but I imagine Klyce tries to make sure there's only one client in residence at any one time.'

'Also,' Kidanu said, 'it is very close to the American border.'

'That's right,' Bishop said. 'As soon as everything's ready, Klyce hands the client his new passport and then they cross the border and go their separate ways. Another satisfied customer, free to begin his new life wherever he wants.'

Kidanu's eyes were boring into Bishop's like iron spikes. 'Nine months ago in Peru,' he said, 'Erasto Badat fled two days before he was due to be extracted by my team. If he also used this specialized service, then Klyce surely knows the new name he lives under, as well as his new location. Quite possibly right here in the United States.'

'More than likely,' Bishop said.

'Then I am closer than ever,' Kidanu said, and slowly smiled. It was a smile totally devoid of humour. Bishop imagined it was the same one he was saving for Badat.

'I'm missing something,' Doubleday asked. 'Who's this Erasto Badat?'

Bishop's cell phone began to vibrate. As Kidanu explained The Scythe's history to them, Bishop got up and left the room. In the hallway, he pulled out his cell and looked down at the display. He immediately recognized the number. He took the call.

'I didn't think you'd get back to me so soon,' he said. 'Or at all, for that matter.'

Arquette said, 'Not a very trusting soul, are you, Bishop? I said I'd keep you in the loop, although it's still early days, you understand. For instance, I didn't get very far with the FPT Bank in the Caymans, although one official did let slip that the balance of that Xerxes account is currently in the low nine-figure range.'

'Impressive.'

'That's one word for it. And there *is* a company called EMC-Med Associates. It was registered in Bermuda seven years ago. Other than the fact it's a one-man operation, I don't have any other details as yet, but I will in a few hours.'

'Good. Let me know what you find out.' The phone vibrated aga
in his hand. He looked at the screen, then said, 'I got another calle.
waiting.'

'Okay,' Arquette said. 'Talk to you later.'

Bishop hung up and took the other call. 'Got something for me?'

'I have,' Muro said. 'And well within the deadline, too. I hope you
noticed that.'

'I did.'

'Okay, then. First off, Steven Bainbridge *is* an employee at the
Social Security Administration offices. He's a senior supervisor and
has been there for almost seventeen years. According to my contact
over there, he's a good solid worker, if unimaginative.'

You might be surprised, thought Bishop. 'Okay, what about the rest?
Anything?'

'Plenty. Okay, let's see now . . .'

Bishop leaned against the wall and for the next three minutes
listened without interruption. Once Muro was done, Bishop said,
'That's good work. You've just earned yourself a bonus.'

'Thanks. That'll keep my landlord happy, at least. Anything else
you need?'

'Just notification if Amy's condition changes at all.'

'You got it,' Muro said, and hung up.

Bishop pocketed the phone and stood with his back to the wall,
staring at nothing. Muro hadn't told him anything he didn't already
know, but it was always sensible to double check your facts. And now
he had. He spent a few more quiet moments thinking about what
he'd learned today and what he still needed to do.

He turned, entered the living room and took his place on the couch
again. Then he explained to Kidanu, Doubleday and Willard what he
wanted from each of them tonight.

SEVENTY-SIX

Two hours later, Bishop was crouched on the roof of a two-storey commercial building on 33rd Street in Queens. The first floor held the office headquarters of an amusement supply company, while the second floor was broken up into a dozen individual business units. Bishop had managed to break in through one of the first-floor windows along the narrow passageway that separated the building from its next-door neighbour and disable the alarm system. He'd then ascended two flights of stairs, made his way through the roof access hatch and climbed outside.

He was at the rear of the building, aiming his pocket scope at the small stair access bulkhead on the roof opposite. Artemis International's roof. Foot-high coils of razor wire surrounded the perimeter as security. The two buildings were almost the same height, with a gap of about ten or twelve feet separating them. In the centre of the stair penthouse was a weather-worn steel door with a keyhole and a handle. If it had been the type with a push-bar lock he'd have had to find another way inside. But a tumbler lock he could cope with.

He pocketed the scope, stood, and backed up about twenty feet. He took a deep breath and slowly let it out. And again. Then he simply launched himself towards the Artemis building at a straight sprint. Two feet before the roof edge, Bishop leapt into the air with his arms outstretched. He sailed over the rear yard below, missed the razor wire by an inch or two, and touched down on Artemis's roof. The moment his foot made contact, he rolled his body into a ball and let the momentum carry him along for a few more feet. Then he got up, brushed the dirt from his dark clothes and walked over to the bulkhead.

He gave the lock a brief inspection, then lowered himself until he was lying on his stomach. He'd already noticed a faint light coming from under the door. Reaching into his pants pocket, he pulled out the fibre-optic scope, inserted the tiny tube into the space between the door and the frame and looked through the eyepiece.

He saw a simple narrow stairway that ended in another door at the bottom. A single bare bulb provided a dim light. He wiggled the insertion tube around until it was pointing back on itself and saw a matching handle on the other side of the bulkhead door. He played the scope around the frame, but saw no wires. And no obvious alarm. Which didn't have to mean anything.

Was it worth the risk? Bishop breathed in and out slowly, considering. The sound of sirens a few blocks away filled the night air. The sirens got louder and louder until he began to think they were coming his way. Then they began to get fainter again. Pursing his lips, he pulled the insertion tube back through the gap and stood up. He brought out his pick gun and torque wrench and went to work on the keyhole. He had it unlocked in less than ten seconds. He pocketed his equipment and gripped the handle in his left hand.

The moment of truth.

Bishop quickly yanked the door all way open and just stood there, waiting. But there was no alarm. No sounds other than the fading sirens and late night traffic in the distance. He breathed out again and entered the stairwell. Carefully closing the door behind him, he descended the short flight of stairs and placed an ear against the other door. He heard nothing. He tried the door handle. It was unlocked. He pushed it down all the way and pulled the door open an inch. Looked through the gap. The lit hallway beyond was empty. He pulled the door open a little more and peered right. Also empty. Not only that, but it was a dead end.

Bishop pulled Jeff's Glock from his waistband, checked the safety, then put it back. He stepped into the hallway and gently closed the door. The corridor went on for another twenty feet before a sharp turn left. He tried to visualize where he was in the building, but he'd only seen a little of it when he'd visited before. He knew from the placement of the stairs that he was on the south side and close to the rear, but it was all guesswork after that.

331

He approached the turn and peered round the corner. The next hallway ended in another left turn about fifty feet away. There were windows along the right side of the corridor, but no doors. And two doors along the left side, with a darkened window next to each. He went over to the closest window on the right and saw the building from which he'd just jumped. Now he knew where he was. And he knew the turn up ahead would lead to the hallway containing Klyce's office.

Bishop walked towards the end, ears attuned to every sound. As he got closer to the turn, he began to hear muffled voices. Or maybe just one. It was hard to tell. It was coming from one of the rooms in the next corridor. A little voice in his head told him to use the fibre-optic scope to check this time. He stopped just before the turn and pulled the instrument from his pocket. He aimed the tube around the corner and looked into the eyepiece.

Good thing he'd listened to that voice. A shaven-headed man in a suit stood fifty feet away. He was leaning against the wall and sipping from a paper cup. Beyond him was the open-plan bullpen area Bishop had seen before. The lights were all on, but he couldn't see anybody else down there. On the right of the passageway were the three doors he remembered. The nearest one was Klyce's office. The one furthest away was a conference room. Either one would serve as a perfect location for the meeting later. Which meant Bishop needed to get into the middle room, whatever it was.

He checked his watch. 23.02. He couldn't do anything while that guy was standing there. The muffled voice was still talking. It sounded angry. Bishop was fairly sure it was coming from Klyce's office. He stepped back and leaned against the wall, thinking. He couldn't stay right out in the open like this. Maybe one of the two darkened offices he'd just passed. They were better than nothing, and it would only be temporary.

A door suddenly opened very close by. Bishop heard Klyce say, 'Lars, what the hell are you doing up here?'

'Just getting a coffee from the machine, sir.'

'Well, you've got it now, so get your ass downstairs where it belongs. I need you to let me know as soon as they arrive. And I still can't get hold of the others, so keep your eyes open for anything that looks wrong, understand?'

'Yes, sir.'

'And I want you by the stairs, Eddie. Go on. Move your ass. I'm not in the best of moods right now, so don't make me tell you again.'

Then the door slammed shut and Bishop heard receding footsteps. He peered round and saw two suited men walking into the bullpen area. They reached the stairwell area at the end, and the shaven-headed one, Lars, said something to his dark-haired partner before descending the stairs. The other one laughed at something, then turned a corner and disappeared from view.

Bishop stood completely still. Watching. Listening. A minute later, he heard Klyce's muffled voice again. Sounded as though he was bawling somebody out on the phone this time.

Bishop was so close, with Klyce only inches away from him. It was tempting to just walk in and deal with him right now, but that would be counterproductive. After all, it wasn't just Klyce he wanted. Best to stick with the plan. He stepped into the passageway and approached the second door along. He tried the handle and found it locked. Naturally.

Breathing slowly, Bishop pulled out his tools and went to work as silently as possible. He had it unlocked on the second try. He opened the door, slipped inside, then clicked the door shut after him.

It was pitch black inside, which meant no windows. A store room, maybe. Standing perfectly still, Bishop pulled out his Maglite and clicked it on.

The room was long and narrow. Six-foot-high steel filing cabinets ran the length of the wall on the conference room side. Set against the opposite wall were two smaller wooden cabinets filled with stationery, legal pads, files and so on. There was also a long desk bearing various items of computer equipment and leads. Then a large photocopier and a couple of heavy-duty laser printers.

Bishop went over and sat on the desk next to the wall. He pulled the contact microphone and amplifier from his pocket. After switching the unit on, he put the earbuds in place and pressed the stethoscope part against Klyce's office wall.

The walls had to be pretty thick as the voice was still muffled a little, but Bishop could hear what Klyce was saying well enough.

'. . . worry about it, didn't I? I told you I'm taking care of it at this end. Now I don't want to be bothered again tonight. Anything else can wait till tomorrow.'

There was the sound of a phone being slammed onto the desk, followed by a sigh.

Bishop didn't know what that had been about, but it was a sure bet it had something to do with him. Sounded like he was really getting to the guy.

Just wait, he thought. *It gets worse.*

Then came the sounds of fingers tapping on a keyboard. Bishop got himself comfortable and turned off the flashlight. He pulled out his cell phone and dialled a number.

When the phone was picked up, he whispered, 'I'm inside. Just waiting for the others now. How about you?'

'We are almost ready,' Kidanu said.

'Good. I'll be in touch.' Bishop hung up and deleted the number from the call log. He sat back and listened to the sounds of Klyce working next door, and waited.

SEVENTY-SEVEN

Bishop opened his eyes at the faint sound of classical music coming from the next room. Sounded like the opening bars of a Mozart symphony. He didn't recognize which one. After a few seconds the music stopped. There was silence, then Klyce's muffled voice said, 'Good. How many? . . . Okay, once you've made sure it's them, you and Eddie bring them up to my office . . . No, don't search them ; . . Right.'

Sounded like the gang was all here at last. Bishop removed the earbuds, went over to the door and pressed his ear against it. He counted one hundred and eighteen seconds before he heard a single cough in the distance, followed by the sounds of low conversation. The voices got a little louder as they approached, and then stopped.

Bishop went back to the desk and put in the earbuds again. He pressed the mic against the wall and waited. There was a knock on Klyce's door.

'Come in,' Klyce said. The sound of the door opening. Then, 'And on time, too. I expected you to make me wait.'

Bishop checked his watch. 23.32.

'I'm not into power games,' the visitor said. The voice came out as muffled as Klyce's, but Bishop recognized it well enough.

'The traffic was also with us,' a third male voice said. It had a strange lilt to it. Almost English sounding.

'Sit down, then,' Klyce said. 'You others can wait outside. Fair enough?'

'Fair enough,' the second man said.

There were sounds of people moving about and then the door was closed. Bishop heard people walking past outside.

'Have you brought the money?' the visitor asked.

'It's here. Don't worry about that.'

'So what about this other problem of ours? Any closer to a solution on that?'

'You mean Bishop?' A sigh. 'A little closer, yeah. You know, I think the bastard might have cost me four of my men earlier.'

'*Four*? You serious?'

'I am. But the day isn't over yet. Anything could still happen. Am I right?'

'I guess so,' the visitor said slowly. 'Why ask me?'

'I'm not. I'm asking our friend.'

'Friend? What are you talking about, Klyce? Is this some kind of set-up?'

'No set-up,' Klyce said. 'At least, not concerning you. I'm just talking to our other friend out there. You hearing me okay, Bishop?'

Bishop closed his eyes and sighed. *Loud and clear*, he thought. He didn't know how, but he'd been made. Not only that, but Klyce had clearly been expecting him. And Bishop had fallen right into his hands.

'What is this, Klyce?' the visitor said. 'I thought we were alone.'

'Relax. This'll be interesting. Bishop? I know you can hear me. I also know you're somewhere on this floor. I don't know which room exactly, but there aren't really a whole lot of options. And I've got a hunch you're *very* close by. Maybe only a few feet away. Am I getting warm?'

Bishop shook his head, and wondered if the guy had pulled the wings off flies when he was a kid. *Come on, Klyce, stop playing games. Get it over with*.

Klyce continued, 'Now, let's try doing this the easy way, shall we, Bishop? Right now my men are directly outside the room you're hiding in, with their guns aimed at the door. One word from me and they'll start firing. Now neither of us wants that, so what I want you to do is very slowly open the door and come out with your hands behind your head. You've got ten seconds, starting now.'

Bishop also had a hunch. And it was telling him Klyce wasn't bluffing. That he knew exactly which room Bishop had chosen. Bishop removed the earbuds and pocketed his gear. He carefully made his way to the door and grasped the handle. He pulled it down and opened the door a crack. Interlocking his fingers behind his head, he used his left foot to slowly open it the rest of the way.

The two men he'd seen before were standing against the wall opposite, at his ten and two. Both had guns pointing at his head.

'You've got a piece somewhere,' the one called Lars said. 'Where is it?'

'There's a Glock in the back of my waistband,' Bishop said.

'What else?'

'Nothing else.'

'Turn around and back out of the room slowly.'

Bishop did as he was told. On his third step, he felt his gun being removed. Then he was shoved against the wall. Something cold pressed against the back of his neck, and hands moved up and down his body. He felt his pockets being emptied.

A hand grabbed the neck of Bishop's shirt and shoved him towards Klyce's door. Bishop reached down for the handle and paused when another man in a suit appeared around the corner, gripping a Sig-Sauer in his right hand. He was a large black man. Maybe a couple of inches taller than Bishop, and much wider in the shoulders. He could have been a linebacker.

'I know you, don't I?' Bishop said.

'Only from a distance,' the man said, smiling.

Each word was clearly pronounced. Bishop knew it was the same voice he'd heard a few minutes ago. The one with the mid-Atlantic accent.

'But you saw my sister close up, didn't you? At the park last Tuesday? Then again in her hospital room, when you tried to kill her.'

Still smiling, the man said, 'Why don't you just open the door and go inside like a good boy?'

'We'll talk later,' Bishop said, and opened the door. A hand shoved him forward and he came to a stop a few feet inside the room. Klyce sat smiling behind his desk, his fingers interlaced across his stomach, looking like the cat who ate the canary.

The visitor sat in the chair opposite, with one elbow on the desk as he half turned towards Bishop.

'Hello, there,' Dermot Arquette said. 'I was wondering when you'd show up.'

SEVENTY-EIGHT

'I was thinking the same thing about you,' Bishop said.

The FBI agent lost the smile. 'How long have you known?'

Bishop took a look behind him. Lars had his back against the closed door, watching him. His gun was pointing at the floor. Bishop wasn't fooled. He knew one wrong move and he'd get one in the back. Probably more than one. He turned back to Klyce and said, 'So. My two least favourite people in the world, together in the same room. Where's a frag grenade when you need one?'

'Things not going the way you planned?' Klyce asked. 'I feel for you, Bishop. Really I do.'

'You expected me.'

'Of course I expected you,' Klyce snorted. 'You think I'm an idiot? I tried calling Jeff a few hours ago about something else, except he wasn't answering his cell. And when none of the others answered theirs, it didn't take a genius to realize who I'd been talking to on Jeff's phone. How did you get the jump on four armed men, by the way?'

'Magic beans.'

Klyce smiled. 'Very good. So anyway, I knew you'd be coming straight for me, and that you'd want to see what this meeting I mentioned was all about. So I spent a couple of hours preparing for your arrival. Even left a light on in the roof access stairway so you could find your way in. As soon as you unlocked the door it triggered a silent alarm in here. Then the boys and I put on a little show, giving you a chance to find the perfect hiding place. You were my rat in a maze, Bishop. You went exactly where I wanted you to go.'

'I'm starting to see that.'

'And you didn't answer my question,' Arquette said. 'When did you first suspect?'

Bishop turned to him. 'That it was you who enlisted Amy's help in the first place? That it was you she was supposed to meet on Tuesday night? I guess the first seeds were planted when I saw Nowlan get a coffee refill in the hospital cafeteria. That casual gait of his reminded me a little of the fake janitor I saw in the surveillance footage. But plenty of people walk like that, so I didn't think anything more of it at the time. I take it he's here, too?'

'He's around. Go on.'

'Then at the service station, when he dropped the sugar after handing you your coffee, I thought he was passing you a message, but he was actually placing a tracker under the car. That's the only way Klyce's boys could have known I was at the diner later. The one called Jeff handed me some crap about how they had all the roads covered back from the border, but I don't see how. Not unless Klyce here had an army of men, which he doesn't. Besides, I confirmed it later when I found the device under the passenger side door.'

'I thought he worked that gag pretty smoothly, myself,' Arquette said.

'Plus I never got to see your driver, Wescott. Once I began to suspect you, I had a hunch you were keeping him away from me for a reason. And one possible reason is he was the fourth man present at the park that night. That's something else I've just confirmed.'

Arquette turned to Klyce. 'Didn't I warn you not to underestimate this guy?'

'So where did you find your two playmates?' Bishop asked. 'I assume they're not real federal agents.'

Arquette tilted his head. 'What makes you say that?'

'You said it yourself. The FBI's vetting process generally weeds out those with questionable characters. Nothing's perfect, of course, since you somehow slipped through the net. But I'd say the chances of there being two more equally corruptible sleazebags in the agency, and you just happening to know both of them, are pretty slim.'

'Watch your mouth,' Arquette said. 'You're in a very precarious position here.'

'Precarious?' Bishop said with a sneer. 'I'm a dead man walking, which means I can say whatever the hell I like. If you don't like it put one in my forehead right now. Or get somebody else to do it, since that's more your style.'

Arquette smiled. 'Go ahead, Bishop. Keep talking. Where else did I slip up?'

'By calling the Konamban embassy and warning them of an intruder on their grounds. Kidanu said a cop made the call, but I only saw one patrol car pass by and I know he couldn't have spotted me. And since your two pals were no doubt busy planning that second attempt on Amy's life in the hospital, that just leaves you. I just can't figure out how you knew I was there that particular morning.'

'So you *don't* know everything, then? You never hear of a Stingray device? With one of those, the FBI can track any cell phone as long as it's switched on. Once it told me you were on the embassy grounds, I decided to give them a friendly call. That all?'

'Not quite. An associate did a little checking and discovered Larry Ratner *was* a federal agent, but he never partnered with you. Also, he retired with a full pension and lives in a condo in South Florida. But why let facts get in the way of a good story, right?'

'Exactly.'

'That's what I don't get. All that effort to set me on the Konambans' trail. It must have occurred to you that Bekele would have an alibi for the time I thought I saw him.'

Arquette shrugged. 'To be honest, I didn't expect it to get that far. Once I realized you weren't about to give up, I just wanted you out of the way permanently. And I figured sending you after Bekele was a perfect way to do it. He's got a reputation for acting before thinking when it comes to dealing with insurgents, and I honestly thought he'd cut your throat as soon as he set eyes on you. I guess the bastard must have mellowed in his old age.'

'Or maybe he just got smarter,' Bishop said. 'Unlike some people in this room. I heard money being mentioned before. Is that why you recruited Amy? You planned on her gathering enough evidence on Klyce so that he'd be forced to go into partnership with you?'

Arquette said nothing. Bishop turned to Klyce. 'That piss you off much?'

Klyce shrugged. 'Arquette here knows how to play a winning hand. If I have to have a partner, that's the kind I want. Plus he's got an enviable amount of law enforcement contacts across this great nation. For somebody in my business, that's worth its weight in gold. Speaking of the Konambans, Arquette mentioned Kidanu was partnering with you earlier. Where is he?'

'I cast him adrift a while back,' Bishop said, thankful he'd deleted their last conversation from his cell's call log. 'He's kind of preoccupied with you and I didn't want him screwing up my plans.'

Klyce smiled and shook his head. 'Still obsessing about Erasto Badat, is he? Dumb bastard should let the past stay in the past where it belongs.'

'That's good coming from you,' Bishop said. 'Aren't you the one who goes around erasing people's pasts altogether?'

'Only for those who can afford it. So you figured that part out too?'

'It wasn't hard once you ruled out all the other possibilities. I assume a now unrecognizable Badat is now living freely under one of those names on the list?'

'Ah, Mr Foster, you mean?' Klyce grinned. 'You know, other than a wish to settle down someplace tropical, that maniac was desperate to erase all the trappings of his old life and start afresh as an American taxpayer. He actually told me I was the answer to his prayers when I approached him. Which I guess isn't all that surprising when you think about it. That's a man with a whole lot of baggage.'

'That's one way of putting it,' Bishop said. 'You're a real class act, Klyce, dealing with these animals on a regular basis. But I guess like attracts like, huh?'

Faint red splotches began to appear on Klyce's cheeks. 'And how is your little niece?' he said. 'Lisa, isn't it? According to Mickey, she's a real looker. I think I'll have the boys pay her another visit once you're gone and give her a real coming-out party. Or even better, I can just finish the whole family in one go. You took out four of my people, so why shouldn't I take four of yours? Sound fair to you, Bishop? Because the symmetry really appeals to me.'

Bishop glared at him and said nothing.

'And I haven't forgotten the matter of Kordić, either. I invested a lot of time and money on that man, and then you came along and ruined everything. If anything, I'm more angry about that. Why did you have to kill him?'

'It seemed the appropriate course of action at the time.'

'And the worst. Because killing him suddenly made it personal between us.'

'Not suddenly. It always was.'

'If we can just get back to the reason for this meeting for a moment,' Arquette said. 'I believe we were talking about a sum of money, Klyce. You said you have it here?'

Klyce's face relaxed. He reached down into a desk drawer and pulled out a small manila envelope and placed it in front of Arquette. 'Count it.'

'Make sure you check the watermarks,' Bishop said.

Klyce glared back at him, but said nothing. Arquette picked up the envelope, unrolled the top and reached in. Frowning, he pulled out two wads of hundred dollar bills and began carefully flicking through the first one. Once he was finished counting, he slammed the thick wad down on the desk. 'Fifty thousand,' he said. 'And two stacks makes a hundred.'

'Correct,' Klyce said.

'So what are you trying to pull? We agreed my first payment would be five times this.'

'And it will be.' Klyce reached into the same drawer and pulled out another manila envelope. This one was bulging at the seams. 'There are eight more identical stacks in here. Once Bishop's out of the way, you'll get this and our partnership officially begins.' He placed the envelope back in the drawer, locked it and put the key in his jacket pocket.

Arquette pulled his brows together. He tapped his fingers against the two thick stacks, then slowly put them back in the envelope. 'So what aren't you telling me?'

'Be patient,' Klyce said and made an odd twirling motion with his index finger. Bishop heard a single step on the carpet behind him, then a thunderbolt struck him at the base of his neck.

He was out by the time he hit the floor.

SEVENTY-NINE

Bishop awoke to the sound of tyres moving at speed along smooth asphalt. He had one bitch of a headache. And his hands were tied behind his back again. His arms were already aching, which told him he'd been out for a while. The question was, how long?

He raised his head from his shoulder and winced at a sharp stinging sensation at the back of his neck. Lars must have struck him with the Glock. He opened his eyes and saw Arquette smiling back at him.

They were in the back of that damned limo again, with Bishop facing the rear like before. Arquette was holding a glass of clear liquid and smiling his cheesy, smug grin. There were travelling along a three-lane highway. Bishop couldn't tell in which direction they were going. He looked for road signs, but couldn't make out any. The tinted windows didn't help.

'Welcome back,' Arquette said. 'Still seeing stars?'

Bishop moved his wrists. There was no play at all. It felt as though they were glued together. And he couldn't get his fingers up far enough to tell what his binds were made of.

'Standard departmental-issue flex cuffs, in case you're wondering,' Arquette said, sipping his drink. 'Almost unbreakable. A sharp knife'll do the job, but you don't have a knife. Or anything else. Believe me, you were very thoroughly searched.' He motioned with the glass. 'I'd offer you something from the mini fridge again, but what would be the point?'

'Not thirsty, anyway,' Bishop said, though he was. 'Where are we going?'

'To a place you won't be coming back from. Does it matter where?'

Bishop said nothing. Kidanu. And Doubleday. Where were they right this second? Were they close, or totally beyond his reach? With

344

an effort, Bishop forced himself not to think about it. He was on his own for the time being. Deal with it. 'What time is it?'

'Late. Again, what difference does it make?'

'None, I guess. So clue me in on Amy's involvement, Arquette. She's the reason I'm here, after all. What made you choose her for your little scheme in the first place?'

Arquette smiled. '*Little* scheme?'

'I'd say it's little. You've seen how much Klyce has got stashed away in the Caymans. Half a million's chump change to him.'

'Oh, that,' Arquette said, glancing over at the mini fridge. 'That payment's more a gesture of intent than anything. After tonight Klyce and I will be equal partners. Everything down the middle. It'll soon add up, believe me. As for Amy, I simply used my resources to delve into Artemis's employee histories. You'd be surprised at how many researchers there are only interested in a regular paycheck. Amy was different. I discovered she was a respectable working mother with a long history of involvement in humanitarian causes. She took the job to make a difference. Which made her perfect for my needs.'

'You hand her the same bullshit story you gave me?'

'More or less. Besides, most of it was true, and truth usually hits the spot with somebody like that. For example, the illegal arms shipments. True. LCT being behind Artemis. True. Ex-Artemis employee Hernandez approaching me after being fired. Also true. And of course, I am a bonafide federal agent. Why would I have to lie to get what I want?'

'You must have already known it was about more than illegal arms shipments at that point, though.'

'Naturally. Hernandez had already figured out that much himself. He would have figured out the rest had he not got himself killed at the final stretch. That was annoying. He'd given me some interesting documentation, but only enough to raise questions, not much more. I needed a few more pieces of corroboration, that's all. Just enough to force Klyce into a choice of going into business with me or facing serious jail time. And Amy came through with flying colours. Once I added that bank correspondence and the other documents to the stuff I already had, I was able to get my point across very effectively.'

rquette smiled. 'And you placed it right back in my hands. I'm actually really grateful.'

'What are you talking about? The CD I gave you was just a straight
copy of the flash drive Wescott took from Amy's bag on Tuesday
night.'

'You only *assumed* it was, Bishop. Thing is, she'd already told me
over the phone what she'd found, but when I came to inspect the
drive only about half of the files she mentioned were on it. All I can
think is the damn woman must have been in a rush and ejected the
thing before it finished copying everything over.'

Bishop thought about that for a moment. He glanced out the
windows and saw they were finally exiting the freeway. He looked for
signs to tell him which freeway, but he was facing the back of the car.
Not an ideal position for navigating. Slowly, a thin smile spread across
his lips. 'That's not the reason,' he said.

'No? What is, then?'

'She didn't trust you, Arquette. Not fully. That's something that's
been bothering me since I discovered you were behind all this. That
she fell so easily for your act. It's not like her. Amy's instincts are even
better than mine. Always have been. With what I know of her character, at some point she would have started having serious doubts
about you. Did you give her that story you gave me about Klyce and
your imaginary partner?'

Arquette gave a single nod.

'That's it, then. She must have done a little digging, found out
what I found out, and realized her new friend from the FBI wasn't
all he seemed to be. She probably decided to hold some stuff back
until she knew for sure.'

It also explained why she hid that file containing Janine Hernandez's
address, and why she'd been preoccupied at home. Not because of
what she'd discovered about Artemis, but because of the misgivings
she had about her FBI contact.

Arquette shrugged. 'You could be right. It's all academic now,
though.'

'So then what?' Bishop asked. 'You arranged the handover for
Tuesday night and sent Wescott there in your place, along with the

three thugs he hired. Any particular reason you wanted Amy dead, or was it just a simple case of unfinished business?'

'You already know the answer to that.'

'Explain it to me anyway,' Bishop said. He was still looking out the windows, trying to figure out their location. And from there, their possible destination. The buildings they were passing were mostly industrial, many of them separated by vast empty plots of land. So probably not New York State. More likely, he was back in Jersey again, which suggested they'd come off the turnpike just now. But which exit?

'Come on, Bishop,' Arquette said, 'once she realized I wasn't doing anything with the information she'd given me, she would have started making a noise. You know it. I know it. A headstrong type like that would have taken it to my superiors at the agency, as sure as dawn. I couldn't afford to risk that happening. Far easier to take her out of the equation entirely.' Arquette sighed and emptied his glass. 'Unfortunately, Wescott ended up hiring the three stooges for the job. I was not best pleased when I discovered they couldn't follow a few simple instructions. Idiots. Some people really are just too stupid to live.'

'Well, you solved that little problem.'

Arquette smiled. 'You mean *we*, don't you? Or am I supposed to believe it wasn't you who filled Vasilyev with holes?'

'I was present,' Bishop said, not really caring what he believed.

'Sure you were,' Arquette said. 'But your getting to him before Wescott got there kind of forced my hand. Since I had to assume he'd told you what little he knew, I knew I had to make contact with you first and see how far you'd got, then persuade you to look in another direction. The Konambans fit the bill perfectly. Until Bekele let me down, that is.'

'That still doesn't explain the second attempt on Amy's life. She only gave you partial information on the flash drive. Didn't you want the rest?'

Arquette snorted. 'Oh, more than you can imagine. But do you honestly think she'd turn it over to me if she woke up? Not really likely, is it? My name would probably be the first words out of her

347

mouth. And not in a good way. Not that she'd be able to prove anything, of course, but I didn't want my name attached to her in any way. Since I'd already played my hand, I had to see it to the end. And I will. Once you're out of the way I'll arrange another accident. And this time there won't be any last minute reprieves.'

'Got it all planned out, haven't you, Arquette? You take care of Amy while Klyce goes after her husband and kids. I still can't figure out who's worse out of the pair of you.'

Arquette pulled his earlobe and smiled. 'If you're trying to antagonize me, it won't work. I'm in far too good a mood. My advice is just relax and enjoy the ride.'

Bishop looked out the window and saw a sign on the other side of the road with US-1 on it. So, New Jersey, then. Wescott slowed and took a left turn. More rundown industrial buildings passed by on either side. Then another left turn.

'So who gets to pull the trigger on me?' Bishop asked, still looking out. 'Wescott or Nowlan? Or are you actually gonna do the dirty work yourself this time?'

'I believe Klyce has reserved that pleasure for himself.'

'There's a surprise. So where is he?'

'Not too far away. I think we're almost there now.'

Bishop didn't need to wonder about their destination any more. He recognized some of the buildings they were passing. He'd seen them only a few hours ago, when Kidanu had driven him and Lisa down Leesville Avenue. They were headed back to First Choice Auto Salvage.

And if Klyce was with them, it meant Bishop was likely to be on very intimate terms with that large crusher very soon.

EIGHTY

The limo turned into the recessed entrance and came to a stop next to a shiny black Mercedes. Also with tinted windows. Bishop shuffled along the seat, looked out and saw the one called Eddie at the entrance gate. He'd placed the open padlock on the hasp and was pushing the gate all the way back. He gestured with an open hand and the Mercedes eased forward and drove through the gap. The limo slowly followed it.

Bishop looked back at the street they were leaving and saw no other traffic. It was completely deserted. Not even any vehicles parked against the kerb. This clearly wasn't a popular area after dark. Through the rear window, he saw Eddie close the gate and latch it from this side. As the limo came to a stop right behind the parked Merc, Eddie unlocked the side door to the small front office and disappeared inside.

'Well, here we are,' Arquette said, and opened the limo door. 'You can get out yourself or I'll get Wescott to help you.'

'I'll manage.'

Bishop rolled his shoulders to get rid of the stiffness, then got out. As soon as his feet touched dirt, he straightened up and looked around the yard. There were tall lampposts positioned at intervals, but none of them was switched on. Only the headlights from the cars provided illumination. It was very quiet. He could just about make out traffic noise in the distance. A dog barked incessantly a few blocks away. That was all.

The engine died and he heard Arquette shut the limo door. The other two, Wescott and Nowlan, also got out and stood there, looking the area over. Lars and Klyce exited the Merc. Doors slammed shut.

The yard lamps suddenly came on one at a time, gradually bathing the whole area with muted light.

I don't know if that's better or worse,' Arquette said and Wescott chuckled.

'Hey, I think I recognize my first car,' Nowlan said, pointing. 'That old Plymouth convertible over there. See it?'

Bishop tuned them out, glad he'd taken time to give the place an extensive once-over before. He knew they were currently in the main aisle that ran like a major artery through the centre of the scrapyard. Lined up on either side of them were stacks and stacks of vehicle husks, some rising as high as twenty feet. Further down, there were two vehicle-sized gaps on the left and one on the right. Each one led to another aisle of scrapped cars. Bishop had checked them already. The aisles on the left were just smaller versions of this one. The one on the right was filled with bundles of already flattened vehicles, all ready to be taken to the shredder mill.

Right at the end of this one, about a hundred yards away, was the unmistakable shape of the compactor. He'd already seen it up close. And it wasn't one of the newer, portable crushers that come on wheels either. It was one of the old-style static jobs. Old and rusty. A real monster. Bishop shivered involuntarily at the sight of it.

Klyce made his way back to them. He was smiling. 'How d'you like my little piece of heaven, Arquette? Isn't this place great?'

'That's probably not the word I'd use,' Arquette said. 'But I can see how it would come in useful.'

'That it does.' Klyce turned to Bishop. 'And how about you? I'm always interested in my special guests' first impressions. Be honest.'

'Decaying,' Bishop said, looking around. 'Colourless. Past its prime. I'd say you and this place were made for each other, Klyce.'

'Ah, you're just a poor loser,' Klyce said, waving a dismissive hand. He grabbed hold of Bishop's arm. 'Come on, we'll walk from here. I'll introduce you to my favourite piece of equipment. Only thirty-five years old and already an antique, but it's in full working order. They built things to last in those days. Cost me a small fortune, I don't mind telling you. But it was worth it.'

'Supplied you with hours of fun, I bet,' Bishop said.

'Klyce,' Arquette said, 'do I really need to be present for any of this? Your idea of a good time isn't exactly mine.'

Klyce let go of Bishop's arm and turned to him. 'You're here for very good reason, Arquette. You've no doubt noticed that while you've got a strong hold over me, I don't have a thing on you. That's not exactly a good start for an equal partnership, is it? So your presence here tonight will even things out some. I'll press the switch, but you'll be an accomplice just by your presence. Then after tonight, we'll each have something on the other. A full partner in everything, Arquette. That's the way you wanted it, right?'

Arquette just looked at him and said nothing.

'Or we can call it quits right now. You go your way. I'll go mine. Your choice.'

Arquette snorted. 'You're bluffing. We call it quits and you'll spend the rest of your life in prison. I guarantee it.'

'I don't bluff, Arquette. If you know anything about me, you know that. Besides, you'll have to catch me first. And the world's a big place. Now, you can stick around and everything's rosy. Or you can go now, and that hundred thousand's as much of my money as you'll ever see. You'd better make up your mind now before we go any further.'

Arquette stared into the night sky for a few beats, then sighed and took a step forward. 'Okay, Klyce,' he said. 'Let's just get this thing done. The sooner we get started, the sooner we finish.'

EIGHTY-ONE

Klyce led the way with Bishop a few feet behind, flanked by Lars and Wescott. Arquette and the other two were bringing up the rear. There was no conversation. The only sounds were their footsteps on the hard, uneven earth, and the same dog barking in the distance. At least it sounded like the same one.

The dim lamps on either side made Bishop feel like a death row prisoner being led to the chair. What did they call it? The Last Mile? Good name for it. That's what it felt like.

And that massive crusher just sat there at the end, thirty yards away. And getting closer with each step. Which was probably how Klyce planned it. No fun if the victim didn't get to anticipate his final fate in full. But Bishop was too buy taking in his surroundings for the second time. Everything was still the same. A little to the right of the crusher was a four-wheel-drive loader with a forklift at the front end. It was beaten up and weather-worn, but Bishop didn't doubt it was in full working order. To his left, he could see the top part of a large hydraulic crane peeking over from the next aisle along.

The compactor itself was a large, rusted, hardened steel box about fifteen feet high and thirty feet across. Bishop had seen one in action before, although it had been about half the size. The crushing area was the open mouth at the front, with one thick steel plate for a roof and another serving as the bed. On each side of the compactor were large hydraulic pumps that controlled the top plate. There was also a control panel on the right-hand side, just in front of the diesel engine that powered the whole thing. Once a button was pressed, the upper plate descended, flattening everything underneath until it was almost two-dimensional.

'Isn't she a beaut?' Klyce said when they were still about ten yards away.

'Are we looking at the same thing?' Bishop said.

Klyce turned and smiled at him. 'It'll grow on you.'

Bishop stared at the ground ahead. To the left of the crusher, about ten feet away, was the heavily dented and rusted remains of an old aluminium bumper. And something else under it, almost hidden from view. Bishop knew if he was going to make a move, it had to be now. He altered his direction, picked up his pace and aimed for the bumper.

'Where do you think you're going?' Wescott said from his left. He placed a hand against Bishop's arm to push him back on course. But Bishop moved out of reach and quickly turned side on to the large man. With lightning speed, he dropped his left shoulder and with his right leg delivered a sliding side-kick towards the man's groin area.

Fast, but not fast enough. His foot hit air. Wescott had already moved his body back out of range. As though he'd been expecting it. The bastard was even smiling. He straightened up and darted forward with both fists clenched. Bishop ducked as he feinted to the left before changing direction, coming at Bishop's right side. He was fast. Bishop never saw the fist that hit him, just felt a sharp blow at his right temple. His head rocked back with the impact. Losing his balance, he staggered back like a drunk, tripping on the bumper and falling on his back. Something sharp dug into his waist and he groaned in pain. Meanwhile he moved his bound hands up and down his back, his fingers frantically searching the ground under the bumper for what he wanted. *There.*

The large black man looked down at him and slowly shook his head. 'What are you trying to achieve?'

Bishop didn't answer. He could hear the others laughing, but he didn't care. He had other things on his mind. His hands were also working overtime back there, out of sight.

Wescott grabbed Bishop by his jacket lapels and yanked him to his feet. He spun Bishop round, said, 'Hello,' and then punched Bishop hard in the base of his spine. Bishop arched his back in pain and immediately lost his grip on the item he'd been holding. He fell to his knees and watched Wescott reach down for it.

'What was he going for, Wescott?' Arquette asked. He had a Glock in his right hand. The others were also crowding around, some of them similarly armed.

'Just this.' Wescott showed them all the long, jagged shard of mirror glass. Then he checked Bishop's flex cuffs. Bishop knew he'd find no tears in the thick nylon. He hadn't had time.

Klyce came over and took the shard from Wescott. 'Have to give you points for trying, Bishop. I like to see perseverance in an opponent.'

Bishop sighed. 'Makes things more interesting for you, I suppose.'

'Oh, yeah. Some beg. Some try to make pathetic deals for their lives. But you just look for an opening and act. I like that.'

'And what about Hernandez last year? How did he go?'

Klyce frowned for a beat, then smiled. 'Of course, you would have known about him. Well, he wasn't very different from you, believe it or not. Mostly silent. He screamed at the end, though. As you will.' He turned and said, 'Let's get started, Eddie. The loader.'

'Right, Mr K,' Eddie said, and retreated from view.

'Any particular preference in regards to your final resting place, Bishop? We've got almost every make here, from a Yugo to a top-of-the-range Lexus. Go on, take your pick.'

Bishop looked at the stack of three vehicles to the immediate right of the crusher, partly hidden by the loader. At the bottom was an old, brown Ford Thunderbird with both its front doors missing. Then a Chevy something in even worse shape. Then a Caddy shell. 'That Seville at the top there,' Bishop said. 'I always had a thing for Cadillacs.'

'Good choice,' Klyce said, and went to talk to Eddie at the loader.

Wescott pulled Bishop to his feet, placed him in front of the crusher and moved out of kicking range. Klyce came back, inserted a key in the compactor's control panel and pressed a button. The diesel engine coughed a couple of times, then roared into life and began chugging away. He pressed another button and the hydraulic pumps began to activate. The top plate began to slowly descend. Klyce rotated a switch anticlockwise and it slowed down to a snail's pace. Anything to prolong the suffering. Klyce really was a sick bastard.

Arquette appeared beside Bishop. 'Not exactly my scene,' he said, 'but I guess Klyce has his reasons.'

Bishop turned to him and leaned in a little, as though he didn't want anybody else to hear. 'We all have reasons,' he said quietly. 'You know, Arquette, my gut tells me Klyce is already thinking up ways to get rid of you. Probably right this very second. In case you haven't noticed, he's not the kind of man who works well with partners.'

'Gee, you don't say. Well, maybe I've got a few ideas of my own on that score.'

Bishop smiled. 'Excellent. Maybe you'll wipe each other out. Do the world a favour.'

'Maybe, maybe not. Whatever happens, you won't be around to see it.'

'Possibly. But I think in your case, the end's coming quicker than you might think.'

'What are you talking about?' Arquette said.

Bishop watched Klyce turn from his beloved crusher to see what effect it was having on his latest victim. He frowned when he saw the two of them talking.

'Just wait and see,' Bishop said. 'Because it's coming.'

'What is? Is this more of your bullshit? Because if it is . . .'

'Look out,' Bishop said, suddenly pulling his head away. 'Klyce is coming over. Just act normal.'

'Huh?' Arquette turned to look at Klyce walking towards them, then back at Bishop. 'Are you finally losing it, Bishop? Is that what this is about?'

'And what are you two talking about?' Klyce said, pulling up to them.

Bishop remained silent and watched the crusher.

'I think Bishop's nerves are finally getting to him,' Arquette said.

Klyce looked at them both for a moment, then said, 'It happens to the best of us.' He turned to their right. 'Here comes your casket now, Bishop.'

They all watched as Eddie steered the loader towards the crusher, the Cadillac shell balanced on the front forks. He placed the wreck in the open mouth, then gently lowered the forks until the tyreless wheels made contact with the steel bed. Eddie backed up, leaving the Caddy where it was, parked the loader in the same spot as before and jumped down.

'It's time,' Klyce said, and motioned to Wescott.

Bishop felt a hand shove him hard in the back. He turned and saw Wescott with a revolver in his hand, grinning at him.

'Do that again,' Bishop said, 'and I'll make you use that gun.'

'Come on, come on,' Klyce said. 'Walk by yourself and he won't have to.'

Bishop walked slowly over to the crusher, stopping a couple of feet from the Caddy. Klyce wrestled with the front passenger door until it burst open with a metallic screech.

'Get in,' he said.

'Or?'

'Or I'll get Lars to kneecap you in both legs and put you in there himself. One way or another you're going in. It's up to you as to the method.'

Bishop looked inside. There was no windshield, no side windows, no dashboard, no gearstick. Nothing. Everything of worth had been salvaged long ago. The seats were battered and torn. Chunks of safety glass were scattered everywhere. Bishop turned and glanced meaning-fully at Arquette. Then he crouched down and got in the passenger seat.

'Let's get you tucked in.' Klyce reached in, pulled down the seatbelt and ran it across Bishop's chest, and clicked it into the housing at the side. Bishop was surprised the belt hadn't been removed for parts. Or maybe there was just no market for second-hand safety equipment.

Klyce tested the belt, then backed out of the car. 'No residences for a half mile in every direction,' he said, 'so feel free to scream when the time comes. Nobody'll hear you.'

'Just get on with it, asshole. I'm sick of hearing your voice.'

Klyce smiled and slammed the door shut. The vehicle rocked with the impact. Bishop turned and saw the others gathered around, waiting for the show to begin. Eddie was leaning against the loader, smoking.

Wescott and Arquette were standing next to each other. Nowlan and Lars stood a few feet apart. Wescott was the only one with his gun still out.

Bishop faced front and saw Klyce press something on the control panel. The sound of the hydraulic pumps suddenly filled the night and Bishop knew the top plate was starting to descend. If it was on the slowest speed, Bishop estimated he had about a minute. Possibly a little more. More likely a little less.

Aware all eyes were on him, he shifted position and moved his hands down to his back pocket. He reached in and carefully pulled out the other item he'd palmed from under the bumper, along with the mirror shard.

His butterfly knife.

Knowing Klyce's special interest in this place, and the crusher in particular, Bishop had placed the two items there earlier. Just in case. Bishop had learned long ago that success or failure often depended on the amount of preparation you were willing to undertake. He also knew people generally see what they want to see and ignore the bigger picture. As expected, once Wescott spotted the shard in Bishop's hands, he hadn't bothered checking him for anything else. Good old human nature.

But he could pat himself on the back later, assuming he was still alive. First, he needed to free his hands.

Working by feel alone, Bishop moved his fingers over the steel knife until he found the safety catch. He flicked it with his thumb and carefully opened the handles to reveal the blade. Grabbing both handles with one hand, he rested the sharp end of the blade against the part of the flex cuffs furthest away from his wrist and began moving it up and down.

He cut through the cuffs seventeen seconds later.

Keeping his hands behind his back, Bishop leaned forward as far as the seatbelt would allow and saw the upper plate slowly descending. And only about five feet away from the roof of the Caddy. Which meant it was moving a lot faster than he'd anticipated. Not good. About twenty seconds to go. Maybe.

He gripped the knife by the blade with his left hand. Aware most of his body was hidden by the door panel, he sat back and used more precious seconds to carefully bring his right hand to his front. He grabbed hold of the door handle and grasped it firmly. He didn't need to lean forward to mark the upper plate's progress now. He could see it was less than two feet away.

Bishop didn't waste another second. He turned to the observers twenty feet away and yelled, '*Arquette, what are you waiting for? Give your back-up team the go signal. NOW.*'

And at that precise moment, all the lamps along the main aisle went out.

EIGHTY-TWO

Immediately, Bishop pulled the handle, shouldered the door all the way open and dived out of the car into the darkness. He hit the ground, rolled with the impact and rose to a crouch, left arm pulled back. Knife ready.

He could hear Klyce yelling, '*It's a goddamn set-up. Get me out of here.*' Shapes were ducking and moving in different directions. Then more panicked voices, interspersed by the sound of a single gunshot. And another. Probably aimed at Bishop. They both missed.

They were followed by automatic gunfire. And plenty of it. The air was full of the sounds of bullets pinging off metal. And more shouting. He also heard a heavy crunching sound behind him as the crusher reached the Caddy's roof.

Noise. Chaos. Confusion. Exactly how Bishop wanted it.

He was scanning the people in front of him, trying to decide on a target. He couldn't tell who was who in the darkness. The new moon didn't help.

Then he noticed one of them was crouched down. Bishop saw a flash and heard a round strike the crusher behind him. The guy was shooting at him. Bishop didn't hesitate. He aimed for the centre of the man's body, swung his arm forward and at the last moment let go of the knife.

He didn't see it connect. The gunman simply collapsed to the ground like a marionette with its strings cut. One down, five to go. Except Bishop was now right out in the open and weaponless. That needed to change. He got up and sprinted to his left, towards the loader. He didn't see any sign of Eddie. He closed the distance in less than two seconds, dived between the loader's front and rear wheels and crawled under the machine. He kept crawling until he emerged

359

on the other side. Then he made for the old Thunderbird at the bottom of the stack. The one with the missing front doors.

He reached the vehicle and leaned in. Inserting his hand in the space under the front passenger seat, he pulled out the Smith & Wesson M&P .45 Compact he'd hidden there earlier. And the spare mag. The Glock 17 was hidden in an old Mustang across the way.

Just went to show: a little forethought and planning often did half the work for you. Although extra manpower helped too, of course.

Kidanu had been the one responsible for turning the lamps out at the designated moment. He would have been already hiding somewhere in the front office, as they'd planned, and must have destroyed the fuse box as soon as he received the signal from Doubleday, who was currently hiding in the back of a nearby wreck. One with a good view of the crusher. Right now the special effects guy was working his remote detonator to activate the hundreds of explosive squibs he'd previously positioned on vehicles around the scrapyard. Making it seem as though an army was laying siege to the place.

Bishop checked the .45's magazine, rammed it home and flipped the safety off. He raised himself up and scanned the immediate area, using the loader as cover. The sounds of gunfire still filled the air. He saw flashes as more squibs exploded on random wrecks.

Beautiful. No wonder the studios paid Doubleday the big bucks.

The area in front of the crusher was empty now, except for the man he'd gotten with the knife. But Bishop knew they'd still be on site. They couldn't leave by car, since Kidanu had locked the gate with the new padlock he'd brought along. And the only other way out was through the locked front office itself. Which Kidanu was now guarding from inside, armed with Mickey's .357 Magnum.

But so far it was all working out as Bishop had planned. If Klyce hadn't already known he was in that supply room in the Artemis offices, he would have had to make his presence known some other way. He'd needed answers, and he knew the only way he'd get the truth was by placing himself directly into the enemy's hands. People became a lot more candid when they felt they held the winning hand. And so it proved. Bishop still didn't know every detail, but he had enough to satisfy him.

He'd also gambled that once Klyce had him, he'd bring him to the place where he'd disposed of Hernandez. The scrapyard. He'd made that clear during the phone call at the warehouse. And he'd want Bishop alive and breathing, as well. It was a big risk, but one Bishop was willing to take. Then once he was brought here, it was just a case of setting Klyce and Arquette at each other's throats, then picking off whoever was left.

That was the theory, anyway.

Bishop paused when he saw movement next to one of the vehicle stacks across the way. A man was kneeling with one hand on the ground for support. From his posture, he didn't look too healthy. Not Lars. This guy had hair. So one of the other four.

Bishop moved out from behind the loader, gun first. He walked across the open area, his eyes moving in every direction. He slowed when he reached the guy he'd nailed. He could see it was Wescott. His eyes were glassy orbs and there was a mass of blood in the centre of his chest. The butterfly knife was in his left hand. Bishop couldn't see the revolver anywhere. He reached down and used the knife to slit the man's throat, just to be sure, then closed it again. He got up and kept going. The kneeling man still hadn't noticed him, and the sporadic gunfire was concealing any noise Bishop's footsteps made.

Ten feet away now. Eight. Six. Now Bishop could see it was Eddie. He had an automatic in his free hand. He must have sensed something, because he raised his head. Then he saw Bishop and began to raise the gun.

Bishop shot him twice in the head.

Eddie fell back and lay still. Bishop went over and saw two large holes in his forehead. There were also large black stains on his left thigh and his left shoulder. All Bishop had done was put him out of his misery. Practically a mercy killing, if you looked at it that way.

He reached down and plucked the gun from the man's grip. It was a black, short-barrelled 9mm semi-auto. A Ruger P95PR from the looks of it. He checked the magazine and saw it was half full. He searched the man's pockets, grabbed a spare magazine from one and put it in his own, along with the gun. The knife he held on to.

Two down, four left. Arquette, Klyce, Nowlan and Lars. With any luck they were still busy trying to kill each other. If they hadn't already succeeded. As long as they were dead, Bishop didn't care who pulled the trigger.

The sound of squibs going off had stopped. Doubleday must have exhausted his supply. But Bishop could still hear small arms fire coming from the next aisle. The one with the crane peeking over the top. It was likely Eddie had come from there.

Bishop walked close to the stacks for another forty feet until he reached the gap that led to that aisle. He looked around and saw more junked vehicles, and another turning on the right. Bishop advanced slowly and peered round an old Nissan on the corner. He saw the crane in the next aisle. It was about forty feet away and towering over everything. It was one of the crawler types, with tracks instead of wheels. Then Bishop saw flashes come from behind the crane, accompanied by the sound of two shots. He rested his arm against the Nissan body and kept the .45 aimed at that general area.

More gunshots. But coming from behind him this time. Far behind him. Possibly from the front office. Sounded like Kidanu was holding his own over there, making sure all the players stayed on the field.

Movement in front of him caught Bishop's attention. He blinked and gradually made out a human silhouette walking this way from the direction of the crane. Already thirty feet away and closing. He looked healthy enough, so maybe he was the cause of the flashes. Sounded like he'd finished off one of the others. Bishop carefully aimed his gun at a point midway between his stomach and chest. He waited until the man was a little closer, then squeezed the trigger five times. The shots came so fast they sounded like one continuous explosion. The man's body jerked with each hit, then he dropped to the ground like a rock.

Three down. Possibly four. Bishop kept the gun aimed in the same general area. Waiting for more movement.

Then from behind him, Arquette's voice said, 'That wasn't nice, Bishop. What did Nowlan ever do to you? Now throw the piece and turn around slow.'

EIGHTY-THREE

Bishop slowly relaxed his shoulders and began lowering his gun. He had no choice. He still had the *balisong* in his right hand, but it was closed, the blade hidden within the handles.

'Throw it where?' he said.

'Just as far away as possible. Do it now.'

Bishop pulled his left arm back and lobbed the .45 towards the stacks of cars straight ahead. He heard it clatter against one of them and then it was quiet again. Even that dog had stopped barking. He and Arquette could have been the last two people in the world.

'Now turn around, real slow,' Arquette said.

Bishop turned without making any sudden movements. He kept his right hand out of view. If nothing else, he might be able to throw the closed knife at Arquette. Maybe distract the Fed for a second and allow him to move in. A long shot maybe, but it was all he had.

He completed the about-face and saw the figure of Arquette standing about ten feet away, his gun aimed at Bishop's chest.

The rogue agent said, 'So it turns out *you're* the one who had it all planned out.'

'All except this part,' Bishop said.

'Glad to know I'm not as predictable as the others.'

'You'll still end up the same way. Who did Nowlan get at the crane?'

'That idiot with the shaved head. I forget his name. So just you, me and Klyce left. And in a few seconds, just me and Klyce.'

'You plan on wasting him, too?'

'What for? We're partners. If he hasn't already figured out this was your doing, he will once I've explained it. Then it'll be business as usual. For a while, at least. I assume all that gunfire was created from squibs? Very nice. Where's the man pushing the buttons?'

'Outside somewhere. Probably miles away by now, if he followed my orders.'

Bishop was actually hoping Doubleday was watching them right now. Arquette could pull the trigger any second. *Just throw something against a car, Doubleday*, he thought. *Anything that makes a noise. A brief distraction's all I need.*

'Maybe I'll check the yard anyway once you're gone,' Arquette said. He raised the gun. 'Not that it'll matter to you. So long, Bishop.'

There was a ricochet flash on a vehicle at Bishop's right, accompanied by the sharp crack of a gunshot.

Arquette's gun hand wavered and Bishop immediately dived left, into the next aisle. He heard gunshots hit the Nissan behind him, but he was already on his feet and sprinting for the crane directly ahead. He ran past Nowlan's body and began zig-zagging when he heard more shots at his back. Unlike the first one, he knew these were real. It seemed Doubleday hadn't entirely exhausted his supply of squibs, after all. He'd have to thank him properly, assuming he ever got out of this.

He reached the crane in one piece, ran round it and leaned against the main cabin. He couldn't see Lars's body anywhere. Behind the crane was an open area with about a dozen automotive hulks lying around, waiting to be stacked. Then more stacks behind them, forming an impenetrable wall. Which meant no way out except back the way he'd come.

Bishop pulled the Ruger from his pocket and turned and peered through the crane cabin window. He saw Arquette moving this way at a fast clip. He was playing it smart by keeping close to the stacks of cars on the right side. Bishop saw movement, but no defined human shape. If he shot from here he'd miss. No question. And then Arquette would know he had a gun.

Bishop silently pulled back the slide on the automatic and backed away from the crane. He carefully moved around one of the wrecks, gripped the gun in both hands and aimed it at his previous position, using the roof of the car as support.

'All you've done is postpone the inevitable,' Arquette called out from behind the crane. 'There's no way out of there. Force me to come in after you and I'll do you a piece at a time, and neither of us wants that. So come out now, and it'll be quick. I guarantee it.'

You're right about that, Bishop thought. *Show yourself and you'll see just how fast.* He stayed silent and continued to wait.

There was a metallic sound to the right of the crane. Like somebody had brushed against a vehicle and jarred something loose. Bishop wasn't about to fall for that one. He aimed the gun at the left side of the crane. It wouldn't be long now.

It took another three seconds before a shape slowly materialized around the front of the crane, gun in the low ready position. He was still side on to Bishop, who bided his time. Then Arquette brought his gun up, turned the corner in one swift movement and aimed the gun at the spot Bishop had just vacated.

Bishop aimed for his middle and fired the Ruger once. And again.

Arquette slammed against the cabin and Bishop heard his gun fall to the ground. Still aiming the Ruger, Bishop came around the car and walked towards the fallen man. Arquette was half perched on the crane's tracks, breathing heavily, with one hand pressed against his stomach. Bishop scanned the ground until he found the man's Glock and kicked it away. Then he looked down at Arquette and said, 'So this is how it ends. With you bleeding out in a junkyard, surrounded by shit. Very fitting.'

Arquette coughed once and looked up at him, his face a picture of pain. 'You gutshot me.' He winced. 'God*damn*, I never realized it could hurt so much.'

'Now you know how my sister felt once your thugs were finished with her.'

Arquette hugged himself and coughed again. He began to rock back and forth, holding himself in, then looked up and saw the gun Bishop was aiming at his head. 'Look, you don't have to . . . don't have to kill me, Bishop. We can work . . . something out.'

'I already have,' Bishop said, and pulled the trigger.

A hole appeared just above Arquette's left eye and his head slammed back against the cabin door. Bishop watched as his body slowly slid off the tracks and crumpled to the ground. Bishop let out a long breath. So did Arquette. His last. Finally, it was done. Amy was safe.

Or almost safe. Only Klyce to take care of now. Assuming Kidanu hadn't done that already.

He was ejecting the almost empty magazine from the Ruger when he heard a brief flurry of shots in the distance. Coming from the same direction as before.

Bishop rammed home the spare magazine, chambered a round, then began running for the front office.

EIGHTY-FOUR

When he reached it, he saw the office door was wide open. One of the two windows running along the rear of the small building was completely shattered. The other had a long crack at the bottom. The interior was in darkness. There were no sounds.

He moved to the side of the doorway and said, 'Kidanu? You in there?'

He strained to hear something from inside. Anything. After a while, he thought he might have heard a faint shuffling sound. Like someone moving slowly along the floor. Kidanu or Klyce? One way or the other, he had to know. Without further thought, he dashed through the doorway and dived to the floor with his gun raised.

Nobody shot at him. There was only silence.

He looked around. The muted light coming through the windows allowed him to make out a few faint shapes. A filing cabinet here, a desk there. Not much else. Then from his left, at floor level, a familiar low voice said, 'Bishop?' It was almost a whisper.

'Yeah,' Bishop whispered back. He moved along the grimy floor in the direction of the voice. He brushed against a chair and a wastepaper basket, then his hand touched a leg. Some of the cotton material surrounding it was damp. And then there was that recognizable metallic smell. 'You hit bad?' he asked.

'One in . . . the thigh,' Kidanu said. 'Another . . . in my side.' He grunted. 'I will . . . live.'

'And Klyce?'

'Held him off . . . but he must have . . . entered another way. Shot me . . . from behind. I dropped gun . . . somewhere. Hallway . . . to our right. Saw him leave . . . through door at the end. Maybe . . . thirty seconds ago.'

'Okay.'

Bishop got to his haunches and searched Kidanu's pockets until he felt a cell phone. He pulled it out and pressed a button. The display lit up and he shone it on Kidanu's two wounds. There was some blood, but not as much as he'd thought. Based on past experience, the injuries didn't look life threatening. No major arteries had been hit, although he'd need medical attention pretty soon. If not sooner. But it was strange. Klyce clearly had the opportunity to finish Kidanu off, but had decided not to. Why?

'Go,' Kidanu said, pressing a hand against his side, 'before he . . . disappears.'

'You sure?'

'Go.'

Bishop paused for a moment, then got to his feet. Kidanu was right. He needed to find Klyce now, while the odds were still on his side. He looked to his right and saw a thin sliver of faint light. Looked like a partially open door at the end of a hallway. Bishop began walking in that direction. The sliver got bigger. When he felt he was only a few feet away, he reached out with his hand.

Then he felt a displacement in the air just behind his left shoulder. Barely noticeable, but there. He was in the process of turning when a truck smashed into his back. Or something that felt like one. The pain was sharp and intense. He slammed face-first into the corridor wall. As he slid to the floor, he could feel the Ruger being plucked from his grip.

He collapsed onto his back and groaned in pain. He heard something big land on the floor a few feet away. A chair, maybe. Then a beam of light shone right in his face, blinding him.

'And you thought you were so smart,' Klyce's voice said. 'Did you actually think I'd leave without settling accounts first? If you think I'm looking over my shoulder for the rest of my life, you've got another think coming.'

Now Bishop understood why Kidanu had been left alive. So he could unintentionally lead Bishop right into Klyce's hands. Easiest trick in the world to pretend to leave when you haven't. Especially in the dark. And Bishop had fallen for it. What a smart guy he was.

Keeping his face averted from the flashlight, Bishop slowly moved his right hand towards his right pants pocket. The *balisong* was his only chance now.

'Arquette's toast,' he said in an effort to keep Klyce talking. 'Back in the car, he told me he left the evidence on you with someone he trusted. That it would get mailed to the papers if anything happened to him. You're screwed, Klyce.'

'Nice try, Bishop. But why would Arquette tell you of all people? He—'

Without warning, a heel suddenly stamped into Bishop's right wrist just before it got to the pocket, crushing it. Bishop grunted in pain and tried pulling it away, but it was held fast. After a few moments the weight was lifted and he yanked his hand back and held it to his chest. He felt a shoe tap the knife in his pants pocket.

'What have you got in there, Bishop?' Klyce said. 'Another little surprise? You really don't give up, do you?' He chuckled. 'But all good things come to an end.'

Bishop said nothing. And he'd been so close to the finish line. So close. The best he could hope for now was that Klyce would be satisfied with his death and maybe leave Amy and her family to live in peace.

He heard a hammer being cocked above him. He took a single breath. Held it.

The single shot was deafening in the enclosed space.

Bishop waited for the darkness to become total. But he could still see. And he still breathed. The flashlight fell to the floor. Bishop reached over and grabbed it, at the same time pulling the butterfly knife from his pocket with his left hand. He flipped it open and shone the light around until it landed on Klyce. The older man was on his knees, his body wavering like a drunk's, a look of confusion on his face. One hand was pressed against his neck. The other hand still held the gun. It was still pointing in Bishop's direction.

Bishop aimed the light directly into the man's eyes and swung his left arm around towards Klyce's head like he was delivering a round-house punch. The *balisong* blade entered Klyce's temple almost all the way to the hilt. The dying man made a short 'ugh' sound and his body fell sideways from the impact. The gun clattered to the floor. Bishop held on to the knife and quickly twisted it one way, then the other. He pulled it out and shone the light on Klyce's eyes again. There was no life behind them. He was history.

Bishop looked around, picked up the gun and aimed the light down the hallway.

Kidanu was about ten feet away. He was on his knees and leaning against the wall, his gun still pointing at the spot where Klyce had been. Bishop got up and went over to him.

'Thanks,' he said. 'That's two I owe you.'

Kidanu said nothing as he slid down to a sitting position. Bishop took his cell phone and called Doubleday and told him to get over to the front office. A minute later, he heard footsteps in the other room.

Doubleday called out, 'Bishop? Where are you?'

'In the corridor,' Bishop said. 'Just follow the light.'

The younger man jogged down the hallway and stopped when he saw Kidanu. 'Oh, Jesus. He's hurt bad.'

'I will . . . be fine,' Kidanu said, and smiled. It didn't look very convincing.

Bishop said, 'Doubleday, where'd you park the rental?'

'In the next street down. Not far away. But what about the shooter?'

'That's him behind me. Now listen, earlier I remember passing a hospital a couple of miles northwest of here on Madison. So what I want you to do is bring the car round to the front, help Kidanu into it, then get him over to their emergency room ASAP.'

'And what'll you be doing during all this?'

'Cleaning up here,' Bishop said. 'I got a lot to do before daylight.'

Which was something of an understatement. Bishop needed to erase as much evidence of tonight's events as possible before he left here. He couldn't do much about the shattered office windows, but the rest was manageable. He'd have to clean up the blood in here first, then find and collect all the weapons outside. Then he'd need to gather all the bodies together and place them in the two vehicles that had brought them here. After that, the crusher could get busy doing what it did so well.

'Oh,' Doubleday said, frowning. 'Okay. But the hospital are bound to call the cops when they see gunshot wounds. What'll I say?'

'Say you found him by the side of the road and you don't know him from Adam. Kidanu, you've still got your passport on you, right?'

Kidanu nodded.

'Fine. Just say you were a victim of a drive-by shooting a few blocks from here, okay? You heard some racist taunts and then they started shooting. You don't remember too much. Just keep it simple and use your diplomatic credentials on any cop who tries to make you talk. I'll fill Bekele in on some of this and tell him where you are.' He turned to Doubleday and said, 'You'd better go get the car now.'

'Right.' Doubleday trod carefully around the corpse on the floor, then he pushed the door open and was gone.

Bishop sat down next to Kidanu. The clean-up could wait for a few more minutes. He looked down and noticed the wound in Kidanu's side was leaking again. He took off his jacket, rolled it up and handed it to him. 'Use this as a compress,' he said.

Kidanu took it and pressed the material against his side. 'I was . . . close, Bishop. To finding . . . The Scythe . . . And now . . . with Klyce's death . . . he is out of my reach.'

Bishop thought about that as he sat back against the wall. He was remembering back to the conference in Klyce's office earlier tonight. And that reference to a Mr Foster. If it was the same James Foster as the one on Amy's CD, and he suspected it was, then he also had the man's social security number. And once you had that, all things were possible.

Bishop smiled to himself and said, 'Not necessarily.'

EPILOGUE

Sitting on the couch in the dark living room, she kneaded her feet and tried to work the aches out. Seemed like every day they got worse. She sure wasn't looking forward to tonight's shift. Still, the steady pay cheque was all that counted. At least she could sleep in tomorrow morning. In the last year, she'd learned to take life's little pleasures where she could get them. And these days a few extra hours in bed was something to look forward to.

Life had to change for the better soon, though, she told herself again. It just had to. An opportunity would come her way and she'd grab it like she was supposed to, and things would start to improve. For both of them.

It was a mantra she told herself every day. Part of her even believed it.

There was a knock at the front door. She looked at the wall clock and saw it was just gone seven. Maybe Meg come to tell her she wouldn't be able to babysit tonight. God, she hoped not. That was all she needed. She got up off the couch, trudged down the hallway and unlatched and opened the front door.

A young man in a FedEx uniform stood there. He was holding a power pad and a brown cardboard box covered in masking tape. 'Mrs Janine Hernandez?' he asked.

'Yes?'

'Package here for you. Sign at the bottom, please.' He handed her the power pad and one of those electronic pens. Janine signed her name in the space and handed it back. The courier handed her the box, wished her a nice evening, and left.

Janine frowned at the box in her hand as she absently closed and latched the door. It was about twelve inches by fifteen and three inches deep. And quite heavy. It felt like a large book, maybe. Except she hadn't ordered one recently. And there was no return address listed. She walked back down the hallway and carried the box into the kitchen.

Joel was sitting at the main table with one of his Mickey Mouse colouring books open in front of him, carefully filling in spaces with a look of deep concentration on his face. He probably hadn't even heard the knock. Janine smiled and went over and pulled out a knife from a kitchen drawer. She laid the box on the counter, carefully made a slit down the middle and opened the flaps.

And just stared at the contents with her mouth open.

Inside the box were ten stacks of hundred-dollar bills, each one wrapped in a thick rubber band. She pulled one stack from the box and slowly flipped through it. It was a very thick wad. All non-sequential bills. Maybe four or five hundred of them. She shook her head and pulled out another pile. It was the same size. Which meant there could very well be half a million dollars lying there on her kitchen counter. *Jesus H. Christ.*

Janine swallowed and checked the rest of the box, but it was empty. No note. Nothing. But she already knew who'd sent it. And she knew where he'd gotten it from. She just didn't know how. Janine decided right then that maybe she was better off not knowing.

Opportunities are there to be grabbed.

She smiled and shook her head again, wondering which was the closest airport to Anaheim, California. She'd have to find out. She was also pondering on whether they should go first class or not. It was a nice conundrum to face. 'Joel, honey?' she called out.

Her son paused and looked up from his book. 'Yeah, Mom?'

'How would you feel about meeting Mickey Mouse in person?'

It was almost one thirty in the morning. The night was extremely humid. Almost tropical. It reminded him of nights in his home village all those years ago. Which was appropriate.

Kidanu entered the large second-storey bedroom and quietly locked the door behind him. Not that he really needed to. Nobody would disturb him. The two bodyguards he'd encountered downstairs had been complacent and slow. It had been reasonably easy to immobilize them and then put them out for a few hours before locking them in the cellar. Hardly any effort at all, in fact. Which was fortunate, as he still wasn't fully fit.

After three weeks, two of them spent recuperating in hospital, the wound in his side was mostly just a memory now. But he still walked with a slight limp. He should have waited until he was completely healed, but the need for vengeance burned inside him like a fever. Had done ever since Bishop told him about 'James Foster', and the luxury house he'd bought in West Palm Beach, Florida, only eight months before. With cash, apparently. The fever burned even brighter when Bishop had shown him photos of the man. He looked different now, of course, but no amount of cosmetic surgery could change those black eyes. Kidanu would never forget those eyes. Never.

Kidanu noticed the windows were open and went over and shut them. Then he walked over to the king-sized bed and placed his knapsack on the floor.

The hunter looked down at his prey.

He'd waited a lifetime for this. Whatever debts Bishop felt he owed him, he'd paid off tenfold. Now Kidanu could finally honour the oath he'd made to his family's spirits.

The faint moonlight coming through the windows allowed him to see Erasto Badat was a little fatter than before, but not overly so. His hair was greying, and receding at the temples. He was also alone for once. Usually he had female company brought in. He had the last three nights. But not tonight. Kidanu watched him for a few more moments. He was in no rush. Just the opposite. Badat's face looked very peaceful. He almost seemed to be smiling. Kidanu briefly wondered what he was dreaming about.

He opened the bag and pulled out a cotton handkerchief and a small bottle of chloroform. He removed the stopper, placed a tiny amount of the liquid on the handkerchief and held the material against Badat's nose and mouth for five seconds. When he took it away, the only difference was Badat's breathing was a little deeper. He'd be out for several minutes at most. That would be more than enough.

Kidanu got to work.

Two minutes later, he backhanded the man's right cheek. Hard.

Erasto Badat's eyes snapped open and he looked up at Kidanu, uncomprehending. Kidanu had drawn the drapes and turned on the lights and now he could see Badat's eyes were exactly as he remembered. Badat was breathing deeply through his nose. He couldn't breathe through his mouth because of the duct tape Kidanu had pressed over it. He couldn't move his arms, as his wrists were handcuffed to the headboard, while rope bound his feet to the foot of the bed. He was wearing nothing but a pair of boxer shorts. It wasn't a pleasant sight.

Kidanu was wearing a thin, disposable polyethylene coverall over his own clothes. He'd brought it along specially. The next few hours were going to get very messy.

'*Dehaando amsikee, presidente,*' he said, wishing Badat a good evening in Tigrinya, the language of Ksaneta. In English, he added, 'Also your last, I might add.'

Badat was breathing very rapidly and making muffled sounds under the tape. Kidanu reached down for his knapsack, slowly pulled out a long machete, and laid it on the bed. At the sight of it Badat began struggling frantically against his bonds. Kidanu let him. He reached into the bag again and began pulling out various other metallic implements and laying them out in a row. They were all very sharp. Badat's black eyes followed Kidanu's every movement and his own struggles got wilder. Globules of sweat were already trickling down his face.

As Kidanu pulled out more items, he spoke the words he'd wanted to say for so long.

'Fifteen years ago, *presidente*. A small town called Ksaneta, near the border. You have not forgotten, I hope? I would be offended if you had. You spent the whole day there enjoying yourself, butchering my people one after the other with a machete just like this one. And at noon you slaughtered my two children and my wife, then cut them into small pieces, simply because it amused you to do so. But you made one very big mistake. You left me alive.'

Pulling the last of the knives from his bag, Kidanu tested its point on his thumb. A tiny pinprick of blood appeared. He sucked at it and nodded in satisfaction. 'And now I have found you,' he said, 'and it is my turn to be amused.'

Badat's eyes were almost popping out of his head now. Kidanu gave the mass murderer the smile he'd been practising for years, and played the knife point lightly down Badat's large stomach until it rested between his legs.

'Now,' Kidanu said, 'let us begin.'

Bishop was smiling.

He'd been smiling a lot in the past couple of hours. Basically, ever since he got the phone call from Lisa that morning, telling him breathlessly that Mom had woken from her coma and to get over to the hospital as soon as possible.

Bishop had arrived half an hour before and was now sitting in the waiting room, reading a copy of *USA Today*. Waiting for the kids to finish with Amy. And her husband too, of course. He didn't want to intrude on an intimate family moment. He could be patient.

But he was also smiling at the two-column story he'd been re-reading in the paper. The one that said the West Palm Beach PD in Florida still hadn't found any clues or motive for the savage killing and dismemberment of a James Foster at his luxury home three days before. Apparently, it had been a real mess, with body parts and blood everywhere.

What goes around comes around, Bishop thought. He was just glad he'd stayed on Kidanu's good side through all this. That was one guy you did *not* want to piss off.

He looked up and saw Lisa, Pat and Gerry come through the doors. They looked happy. Bishop dropped the paper on the chair and stood up. They saw him and came over.

'What are you doing out here, James?' Lisa asked. 'Mom's been asking for you. You should have come in with us. I mean, we're family, aren't we?'

'We sure are, kiddo,' Bishop said, and ruffled Pat's hair. 'I just figured you all deserved to be with her first. It's okay, I'll go in now.'

Gerry was watching Bishop and gave him an amiable nod.

Bishop nodded back. These days they were merely polite with each other, and that was enough for Bishop. It seemed Gerry had learned something through all this, at least.

His brother-in-law had reappeared the day after the junkyard incident and finally explained why he'd been acting the way he had. He'd told Bishop his previous night watchman job had been for a Russian-owned import business and that one night he'd overheard a conversation he shouldn't have. It seemed the company had a nice little sideline of smuggling in premium vodka direct from the homeland and then selling it on to reputable wholesalers at cost. Unfortunately, Gerry made the mistake of mentioning this to a colleague, who took it upstairs to the boss, who immediately fired Gerry and warned him that if he ever mentioned his suspicions to anybody else he'd regret it. Gerry had taken the warning seriously.

Then a few weeks later came the assault on Amy. When Gerry learned one of the perpetrators was Russian he freaked out, thinking he might have been partially responsible for Amy's condition, despite not telling anybody about the black market vodka scam. Consumed with guilt, Gerry had killed Yuri partly out of revenge and partly in the hope that Bishop would never learn of his involvement in Amy's attack, even though he hadn't been involved at all. That's also why he'd steered clear of Bishop as much as possible in the following days, little realizing that he was making Bishop's job even harder.

Bishop couldn't really blame him, though. After all, hadn't he felt exactly the same way upon learning Amy might have tried to ask him for help beforehand?

As for the Artemis connection, the reason was very simple: Gerry had simply been looking for work. Before the assault he'd been in regular contact with Graham, the office manager at Artemis, using his relationship with Amy as leverage to get some temporary work. He'd even tried contacting Klyce himself, which is why he had the man's office number on his cell. He'd listed him under an alias simply because he didn't know how Amy would react to the possibility of the two of them living *and* working together. But when it became obvious they weren't interested in hiring him, he soon gave up and tried elsewhere.

After the assault, Gerry spent even more time contacting old associates in order to find employment. With Amy in hospital, he still had to pay the mortgage and bills somehow. Fortunately, an old colleague of his had come to the rescue and found him an assistant accounts manager position at a paper manufacturers on Lexington. The pay wasn't great, but they liked his work and said a full managerial position wouldn't be too long in coming.

Bishop was glad things had worked out for him. And Amy, too, of course. With Artemis no longer an option for her, at least the family had a regular income again.

He gave Lisa a final smile, then turned away and walked through the doors into the next hallway. When he reached the door to room 32, he looked through the glass panel and saw his sister sitting up in bed, her back resting against two pillows. She was staring sadly out the window. She looked tired and pale and thin. Her blond hair was still damp and lifeless. But the bruises had gone.

To Bishop, she looked as beautiful as ever.

He opened the door and stepped inside. Amy turned and saw him. The big grin she gave him immediately lit up her whole face. 'Hey, Bish,' she said.

'Hey, yourself,' Bishop said. And as he went over to his sister, he found he was grinning as broadly as she was.